BOOKS BY PAUL BISHOP

The Fey Croaker Novels

Twice Dead

Kill Me Again

Tequila Mockingbird

Other Mysteries

Chapel of the Ravens

Sand Against the Tide

Citadel Run

Shroud of Vengeance

CHALK WHISPERS

A Fey Croaker LAPD Crime Novel

PAUL BISHOP

S C R I B N E R

New York   London   Toronto   Sydney   Singapore

SCRIBNER
1230 Avenue of the Americas
New York, NY 10020

Text set in Electra
Manufactured in the United States of America

1 3 5 7 9 10 8 6 4 2

Library of Congress Cataloging-in-Publication Data
Bishop, Paul.
Chalk whispers: a Fey Croaker LAPD crime novel/Paul Bishop.
p. cm.
1. Croaker, Fey (Fictitious character)—Fiction. 2. Police—California—Los Angeles—Fiction. 3. Los Angeles (Calif.)—Fiction. I. Title.
PS3552.I7723 C42 2000
813'.54—dc21
99–049408

ISBN 0-684-83010-8

For Dell and Greg,
without whose support
there would be no reward

Homicide Detectives

No greater honor will ever be bestowed
on detectives or a more profound duty imposed
on them than when they are entrusted with
the investigation of the death of a
human being.

It is their duty to find the facts regardless
of color or creed, without prejudice,
and to let no power on earth deter them
from presenting these facts to the court
without regard to personality.

Acknowledgments

Without cohorts in crime,
a writer's life would be an empty shell.
My thanks to my coconspirators
Lee Goldberg, Bob Crais, Kevin Staker, and Jay Hansen,
who are always there with
a helping hand, a barbed comment, or a gentle push.

Prologue

Ellis Kavanaugh's grubby raincoat smelled of ripe body odor and cheap wine. Strands of unwashed black hair fell into his eyes as he skittered through Hollywood Park racetrack in a daze. He weaved awkwardly through the crowd, repeatedly looking over his shoulder. The man with the sunglasses and crew cut was still there, still moving toward him.

The crowd of spectators for the running of the $750,000 Breckenridge Handicap cleared a natural path as Ellis stumbled forward, bumping hard into a man wearing a yellow-and-black-plaid sport coat. Ellis almost pulled himself and the man to the ground.

"The train," Ellis said. "We gotta save the railroad."

"What are you talking about?" The man pulled his arm free and pushed Ellis away.

Ellis staggered and almost fell again. "The secret is in the Gamewell. The Gamewell can save the railroad."

"Get away from me," the man said.

Ellis looked quickly over his shoulder. The man with the sunglasses and crew cut was still there, along with another threat.

Frank Bannon, a plainclothes security officer, had noticed the commotion.

Ellis watched Bannon walk past the man in the sunglasses and crew cut, talking into a small radio. Ellis knew Bannon from previous painful encounters.

"The train," Ellis said loudly. "They know about the train." With jerky movements, he slid away.

The man in the loud plaid checked his race card. Chattanooga was the number-four horse in the Breckenridge. What the hell, he thought. Maybe it's a sign. He turned toward the betting windows.

The voice of the track announcer came to life over the PA system. Bettors, clutching tickets, surged toward viewing stands and closed-circuit television sets.

Pushing through the crowd, Bannon saw the tail of Ellis's overcoat disappear around the corner leading to the men's bathroom. Bannon followed, and the man with the sunglasses and crew cut slowed to watch.

The stinking old man had been told to stay away from the track. He was a nuisance. The employees at the entrance gates all had a photo of the old man, along with photos of other persona non grata citizens who had caused problems in the past. Somehow, though, Ellis always seemed to slip in. Bannon would love to discover how he did it.

The hallway past the men's bathroom was empty. Bannon entered the bathroom, his sense of anticipation heightened. This time he was going to give the old man a thrashing to remember.

The track announcer's voice boomed out, "Annnnnd they're off!"

The concrete floor under Bannon's leather shoes was covered with wet powdered soap. There was no sign of Ellis, but Bannon knew he was in there.

Suddenly, the door on the nearest stall flew open. Ellis charged out, brandishing a toilet seat.

"The train," he yelled. "Must save the train!"

Bannon grinned. He loved a fighter. He stepped in toward Ellis. As he did, his shoes slid on the soapy concrete. Grabbing for a sink, he missed and crashed to the floor.

"Get the Gamewell! Get the Gamewell!" Ellis screamed. He swung the toilet seat as hard as he could. Its edge struck the security man on the top of the head. Bannon grunted and slumped.

Ellis knew he had to escape. Charging through the bathroom door, he saw the man with the sunglasses and crew cut moving down the empty corridor toward him.

The horses were rounding the bend leading into the home stretch when Ellis burst onto the track. The jockeys in their colorful silks had no chance to avoid him. For ten steps, Ellis ran ahead of the horses before the first of the closely bunched leaders slammed into him. As his body lost momentum, he was hit again and driven into the hard-packed dirt of the track.

Riding atop race favorite Afterburner, Gil de Leon cursed and yanked the horse's head roughly to the left in an effort to dodge Ellis's cartwheeling arms and legs. Afterburner responded but had nowhere to go, his flank crashing into Frequent Flyer, racing next to him.

Unable to avoid the human obstacle, Afterburner's right foreleg came down on the uneven surface of Ellis's back. The leg buckled and the huge horse fell to his knees in a tumbling mass of speeding disaster. Afterburner's hind legs slid between Frequent Flyer's and brought the filly plunging to the ground nose first.

Both jockeys flew from the saddle. Gil de Leon's arm twisted under him with an audible snap as he hit the dirt. He was luckier than Sammy Tinto, who hit the inside railing, driving splinters of ribs into his lungs.

Behind the falling horses, jockey Alisha Cromwell, on Chattanooga, gave her horse the whip and charged straight into the disaster. The blinkered Chattanooga ran over the body of Ellis Kavanaugh, veered to the outside, sprinted past the chaos along the rail, and breezed toward the finish line.

Four other horses running behind Chattanooga were not as fortunate, crashing to the ground in a withering mass of screaming horseflesh and shattered bones.

The horses at the rear of the pack either pulled up or swung wide to avoid the catastrophe. Every jockey still in the saddle knew the freak collision was going to be one of the worst on record. Win, place, and show were insignificant in relation to the tragedy.

Ambulances and track security raced onto the track. Spectators held their breath in fascinated horror, the cries of injured horses piercing the shocked silence.

Ellis Kavanaugh lay trampled in the dirt. He was face-down when the first paramedic reached him.

"Don't move," the paramedic said.

Defiantly, Ellis turned his head to the side, spitting out dirt and blood. His lips moved slowly, giving voice to his last, semicoherent thought.

"Train the Gamewell," he said, loud enough for the paramedic to hear, and then he died.

1

CHANGE WAS coming. Fey could sense it in the mood of the squad room.

Tall and angular, dressed in his traditional black, Arch Hammersmith paused in the process of typing a follow-up report and swiveled his head to make eye contact with Fey. She shrugged.

The West Los Angeles area detective squad room was full of the normal late-afternoon activity. The CRASH unit was holding a briefing by the robbery unit's desks, and the juvenile unit had three handcuffed delinquents sitting on a low bench in front of the detective lockers.

Devoid of partitions, the squad room was filled with individual clusters of desks. Each defined an investigative unit—Homicide, Major Assault Crimes, Robbery, Juvenile, Burglary, Autos, and the CRASH unit—and appeared to be separate crime-fighting amoebas, a gathering of fanciful antibodies poised to fight the diseases of the human condition.

Rhonda Lawless also raised her head, responding instinctively to Fey and Hammer. Known affectionately as Hammer and Nails, Hammersmith and Lawless were the homicide unit's point guards, partners in marriage as well as the job. She was only slightly shorter than Hammer, her build a twin of his slender, wiry muscularity. Her high cheekbones let her get away with the spiky punk cut of her hair.

"What's up?" she asked.

Hammer shrugged. "I'm not sure."

"Beats me," Fey said. "But there's something going on."

The unit had gone four weeks without a homicide in its jurisdiction. For the moment, West L.A. was a haven of tranquillity.

Brindle Jones and her partner, Abraham Benjamin Cohen—referred to as Alphabet by anyone who knew him for more than thirty seconds—were bent over a desk going through a case file from a two-year-old unsolved murder of a local transient.

Their pairing was a study in contrasts. Brindle's skin was a dark mahogany, her movements spare and pantherlike. By comparison, Alphabet was a dump truck on legs. Balding and round, he displayed all the grace of an unmade bed. The scut work the pair were doing was driving them, and everyone else, crazy.

"You think we've got a cold one?" Brindle asked.

Fey had a reputation for almost psychic instincts when it came to anticipating imminent change.

"Maybe, but I don't think so," Fey said. "It doesn't have that feel."

Before the discussion could go further, the Detective Division's commanding officer, Captain Mike Cahill, stuck his head out of his office and beckoned Fey.

"Here we go," Fey said. She grabbed a coffee mug from her desktop and gulped the contents.

Inside Cahill's office, the captain waved Fey to one of the

chairs around a large circular table. "What have you been doing that I don't know about?" he asked.

"Heck of an interrogatory technique, Mike, but you forgot to read me my rights."

"Quit fooling around, Fey," Cahill said. "I just received a call from the chief's office. The man himself wants to see you."

"You're kidding."

"You know I don't kid. What have you done?"

"Nothing." Fey raised her palms. "I've been behaving. There's been nothing new on the books since the new chief took over a month ago."

Cahill looked frustrated. "Come on, Fey. Homicide supervisors don't get called to a private audience with the chief of police without cause. I'm trying to make commander here, and I can't afford to have any screwups."

"It is all about you, isn't it, Mike?"

"That's not what I mean and you know it. I've always backed you."

"If you say so."

Cahill knew better than to push the issue. "What about Hammer and Nails? Could they be into anything?"

"Always, but since their baby was born, they've been pretty calm."

Hammersmith and Lawless had been partners for most of their careers, but their off-duty relationship had been kept as private as possible until eighteen months earlier, when Nails became pregnant. Since then, they had married in a small civil ceremony and Nails had given birth to Penny Hammersmith—or Sledge, as the detectives called her.

Married detectives working the same assignment were unique in the department, but Hammer and Nails had more friends than enemies in high places, and they had enough evidence on their enemies to keep them quiet.

"If it's not something you or those two Rottweilers have done, what do you think the chief wants?"

"How do I know? Maybe he wants to give me a medal, or kick my butt. Maybe he wants a date for Saturday night." Fey shifted in her seat. "When does he want to see me?"

"Now."

"Then I better get down to Parker Center."

Cahill looked concerned. "If you take a fall, promise you won't drag me down with you."

Fey grinned. "Hell is supposed to be a lonely place, Mike, but somehow I'm sure I'll see you there."

CHIEF OF POLICE Gordon O. Drummond was built like a bucket of gnarled fists. His cynical eyes took in the world from under unruly, rust-colored brows. His smile, however, transformed his hard features into a promise of shared secrets.

His appointment to head the LAPD had shocked everyone. The choice of a redheaded Irishman was not exactly politically correct in Los Angeles. But the bloodletting at Parker Center following the prior chief's departure for a presidential appointment had left few candidates unscathed, and Drummond's name ended up on top of a short list.

Not wanting to again make the mistake of appointing a chief from outside the department, the police commission, the mayor, and the city council had been forced to accept Gordon O'Malley Drummond as the best qualified candidate from within the hierarchy. When the other candidates, each representing a different political agenda, had fought themselves to a draw, Drummond emerged as a compromise. The king was dead. Long live the king.

GOD, as he was referred to behind his back, had been a popular choice with the department rank-and-file, and had already shown signs of being the leader needed to rejuvenate the LAPD.

Sitting across from Drummond, Fey was impressed with the man's command presence. In a stark white shirt with the tie lowered and the sleeves rolled up, he looked more like central casting's idea of a rural newspaper editor than a big-city chief of police. Fey didn't know if this was a cultivated image, but she was willing to give him the benefit of a doubt.

The first thing Drummond had done as chief was to reduce the size of his personal office. The prior chief had expanded his inner sanctum to the point where the civilian secretaries and the chief's adjutant in the outer office had developed acute claustrophobia from the overcrowded conditions.

Giving the worker bees back their space had endeared Drummond to them as nothing else could have done. He'd immediately earned their trust and loyalty—something his predecessor had demanded but never received.

Drummond also scored other easy brownie points. When appearing in uniform, he eschewed the fancy trappings of office. Gone was the hat with the brim full of braid. A standard uniform cap was more Drummond's style, as was the standard uniform shirt, the pips on his collar being the only concession to his office.

Deputy chiefs, commanders, and captains who had coveted and now enjoyed the pomp and circumstance of their positions suddenly looked as if they were dressed for a canceled costume ball. Drummond was amused. He was determined to wipe the smugness out of command-level staff and bring back accountability.

"How are you, Fey?" Drummond asked. The two knew each other but had never worked together.

"Other than wondering what this command performance is about, I'm fine."

Drummond smiled. "Relax. I haven't asked you here for a wood-shedding. Quite the contrary."

"Somehow, I think I'm going to end up wishing for the wood-shedding."

Drummond grunted and gave a slight nod of his head. He stood up, stretched, and walked to the corner of his office where two picture windows met to reveal the city beyond. "You've been through an interesting few years in West L.A."

"I could have done without the headlines," Fey said.

"Maybe so, but you've solved a number of high-profile cases, investigations that might have ended up in another unit's cold file."

"Solving those cases made waves. Sometimes I wonder if it would have been better not to solve them."

"You don't really believe that, do you?" Drummond turned to face Fey, his eyebrows rising.

Fey shrugged. "The price was pretty high."

"Are you talking personally or professionally?"

"Perhaps both."

Drummond nodded. "I understand your personal concerns, but I don't think you care about offended sensibilities."

Fey was blunt. "Solving crimes and putting villains in jail is my job. I don't have the time or energy to worry about putting noses out of joint."

Drummond's smile appeared slowly. "You should know something about me, Fey. I place nothing above the truth. Not my job, not my position, not my reputation, and I expect nothing less from those who work for me. I admire you. I admire your integrity. You're my kind of cop."

"Are you trying to say I'm a tough broad?"

Drummond laughed. "I was trying to be more subtle, but it's another way of putting it. You're tough, tenacious, and honest."

"Where is all this leading?"

Drummond leaned back against the window, his face filling with backlit shadows emphasizing his crooked nose. "I'll get to the point. Do you have any idea where you placed on the lieutenant's test?"

Fey felt a lump rise in her throat. "The list hasn't been released yet."

Fey had taken the written part of the civil service promotion exam without preparation. Passing had surprised her, but it hadn't made her study any harder for the oral interview, which comprised the second half of the testing process. Promotion didn't hold any allure for her.

The last of the promotional orals had been given three months earlier, and there were a lot of people waiting anxiously for the official ranking list to be announced. Fey hadn't counted herself among them—until now.

"The list will be released this afternoon," Drummond said.

"You've had an advance look?" Fey's voice sounded much more casual than she felt.

"Mmmmm." Drummond made the noise a positive affirmation. He pushed away from the window and sat in the chair next to Fey. "You're in the top band of candidates."

Fey was glad she was sitting down. She couldn't feel her feet. She hated when she wasn't in control of a situation affecting her life. "I'm surprised," she said. This time her voice quavered slightly.

"Don't be. Cream has a way of rising to the top."

Fey wondered where this was heading. Did she give a far more brilliant oral than she had thought? Or were political strings being pulled? Civil service procedures were supposed to be sacrosanct, but she was cynical enough to know anything could be manipulated.

"And why are you personally telling me this?"

"Because you've more than proven yourself in area homicide units, and it's time for you to move on. I need you. I'm expanding Robbery-Homicide Division by a full team. I want you to take charge of it as a lieutenant."

Fey was stunned. She'd spent half her career at odds with Robbery-Homicide, the department's elite corps of detectives. They were assigned high-profile murder investigations and other long-term cases where geographic homicide units could not provide the necessary manpower. They could also snatch up any other case they deemed to fit their jurisdiction.

"Don't thank me. It's my pleasure," Drummond said, holding up a hand when Fey did not immediately respond. He seemed to be enjoying himself.

"I'll remind you of that the first time you come howling for my blood," she said.

Drummond laughed. "I'm sure we'll have our moments. Until then, let's enjoy the honeymoon."

Fey smiled weakly.

"You don't seem pleased," Drummond said.

"I'm too shocked. This was the last thing I expected."

"I assume you're worried about your people."

"We've been through a lot together. Leaving them behind isn't going to be easy."

"You're not leaving them behind."

"What?"

"I told you, I'm adding a full team to Robbery-Homicide. Your people are coming with you. You're the only one changing civil service ranks, but the others will all be given pay-grade promotions. Monk Lawson will be made a detective three. Hammersmith, Lawless, Cohen, and Jones will all be put up to detective two. What do you think?"

"All of those individuals whose sensibilities I've offended are going to have quite a reaction."

It was Drummond's turn to shrug. "If it doesn't worry me, it shouldn't worry you. However, there is a kicker."

"There always is," Fey said.

Drummond's smile became predatory. "Your first case is already waiting for you, and it's a real bitch."

3

OUTSIDE THE chief's office, Fey's first feeling was of disorienta-
tion. Her life had suddenly been drastically altered. She walked
toward the elevators, unaware of her surroundings.

In a way, the news hit her almost like a death. Her comfortable environment, where she knew the rules and the players, was
suddenly gone. There was no going back, no changing what was
done.

It didn't matter that the move was an affirmation of her worth
as a detective. Nor did it matter that in six months or a year, she
might be delighted with her new situation. Right here, right now,
Fey felt adrift.

In the elevator, she hesitated before pushing the button for
the third floor. She wasn't a coward and she knew at some point
she had to walk into Robbery-Homicide Division's lair. If this was
going to be her new home, she should get the initial encounter
over fast.

Several heads turned as she entered RHD's overcrowded

squad room, but Fey realized people wouldn't be aware yet that she was the new kid on their block. The heads turned away again, ignoring the incomer.

"Hey," a gently mocking voice said behind her. "What are you doing down here? Slumming?"

Fey turned to see Frank Hale. He was an RHD veteran whom she'd worked with in the past.

"I was getting bored in West L.A., so I thought I'd come and see the varsity play."

"Still into sarcasm, huh?"

"You have to go with what works."

Hale chuckled. "What's up?"

"I need to talk to Captain Whitman."

"Whitman?" Hale was clearly curious. "He should be in his office." He pointed toward the back of the squad room. Whip Whitman ran RHD. Everyone had a chance to prove themselves under his gentle guidance, but screw up enough and Whitman would grind a detective into dust without further thought.

"Thanks," she said. "I'll catch up with you later, okay?"

Moving toward Whitman's office, Fey realized there were no female supervisors in Robbery-Homicide. Never had been. She closed her eyes for a second. Damn the chief. The last thing she needed was to be dumped into the middle of another battle of the sexes.

Whitman saw Fey coming. He was an average-size guy with a full head of crinkly white hair, and a potbelly from too many fast-food dinners. He'd been involved in over eighteen hundred homicides during his twenty-eight years on the job, but had never lost his enthusiasm for the hunt.

"Hello, Fey," he said, ushering her into his office and closing the door behind her.

"How are you, Whip?" Fey asked. They had bumped around each other for years.

"More to the point would be how you are."

"Shocked at the moment," Fey said. The chief had told Fey Whitman was already aware she was headed his way.

"I can imagine," Whitman said.

"I didn't ask for this," Fey said. She felt awkward.

Whitman smiled. "I know."

"I have no clue why the chief made this decision."

"I think I do," Whitman said. "Robbery-Homicide needs shaking up. We need fresh blood, but change is hard for everyone. The chief and I think you and your team are the best people for the job."

"You both think?"

Whitman nodded. "Yeah. Believe it or not, I was the bright boy who asked for you. I know coming into RHD won't be easy. It's a very closed world, but you won't be without allies. You do the same type of work for me as you've done in West L.A., and I'll see you're okay."

"I don't mean to sound ungrateful, but I've heard that before."

"Not from me, you haven't. I'm not Mike Cahill. He's got his head so far up his ass, I'm surprised he doesn't have to have a window installed in his stomach to see where he's going."

Fey laughed. "I may like it here after all."

"Well, you aren't going to have much of a chance to get settled. The deployment period doesn't end for another week and a half, but I want you and your people prepared for a nine o'clock briefing tomorrow morning."

"Okay," Fey said, nodding. "We'll be here. Has anybody told Cahill yet?"

"The chief is probably breaking the bad news to him as we speak. I'll tell the people here. When the deployment period changes, West L.A. will be brought back up to strength with new detectives. Until then, your esteemed boss will just have to suck it up."

"You want to give me a hint about this big case?"

Whitman shook his head. "Another twenty hours won't make a difference. Get yourself and your team moved. Tomorrow will be soon enough to ruin your life."

THE PARTY WAS spontaneous. Once the initial shock of the announcement had worn off, the West Los Angeles detectives had insisted on an immediate going-away party. It was tradition.

The Blue Cat was the natural venue for the festivities. A small jazz club in Brentwood, it offered refuge from trendier watering holes and a secure environment for the detectives to let down their hair. The regulars knew who the detectives were and left them alone.

The drinking started around four-thirty in the afternoon when the first shift of detectives finished work. Things really started flowing when Fey and the rest of the homicide crew arrived at six after moving their gear from West L.A. to their new quarters at Parker Center.

Everyone in the unit was happy with the unexpected promotions and pay raises, but not with the thought of working downtown out of the glass house, as Parker Center was called.

Fey slid into her regular booth next to Monk Lawson. He ran a hand over his bald, black skull and reached out to take a beer glass from Booker, the Blue Cat's bartender and owner.

"I hear a celebration is in order," Booker said.

"You have good ears," Fey told him.

Hammer and Nails joined the group. Nails was on her cell phone talking with her mother, who took care of baby Penny while she and Hammer were at work.

"I hope this doesn't mean you'll be deserting our humble juke joint now you gonna be fancy Robbery-Homicide dicks."

"Not a chance," Fey told Booker. "You know this is home. And that's the last crack I want to hear out of you about Robbery-Homicide."

Booker chuckled and moved off to get more drinks as Alphabet and Brindle joined the group. Other West L.A. detectives came over to offer congratulations.

"Robbery-Homicide," Alphabet said. He took a long swallow of beer. "How did we end up assigned there? I thought we agreed those guys were all assholes."

"You've always done a pretty good sphincter impression," Brindle teased him.

"I appreciate your input," Alphabet said.

During the past year the partners' work product had improved, and they seemed to bring out the best in each other. They weren't romantically involved, but there was a certain sexual tension between them.

"You had no clue about what was going on?" Hammer asked Fey.

Fey shook her head. "I was floored."

"The old boys' club at RHD isn't going to like it," Nails said. She put her phone back in her purse. "Having us turn up en masse is going to put them all on the rag."

"They're certainly not going to know what to do with three women detectives," Monk said.

"Especially when one is a lieutenant," Brindle added.

"Screw 'em," Fey said. "We don't have anything to prove. We're not asking to join anybody. If they want to join us, fine. If not, then we don't need 'em. You report to me. I report to Whitman."

"We're going to have to look out for sabotage," Hammer said. "Professional jealousy can get ugly."

"Perhaps," Fey agreed. "But Whitman appears to be on our side. He's spent most of his time in South Bureau homicide. He only took over RHD after everything that went down with Vaughn Harrison last year. He wants to shake up the old guard, and he's using us to do it. He needs us to succeed if he's going to succeed."

"It sounds good, but what do you think they're going to dump on us tomorrow? Why the rush to get us down there?" Hammer asked.

Fey shrugged. "A homicide is a homicide. We've solved our share of high-profile cases. Whatever they give us tomorrow, we can handle."

Booker came over to the booth with another round of drinks. Up on the small stage, the Tab Nelson Trio was getting ready for a set later in the evening.

Booker and Fey had met through Fey's lover Ash, an FBI agent who had often sat in on the Blue Cat's piano. His death had been devastating to both Booker and Fey, albeit in different ways, but the pain had forged a solid bond between them.

Booker returned quietly to the table. "Hey, Lieutenant—" the bartender said softly to Fey.

"Cut it out, Booker," Fey warned.

Booker grinned. "There's a man asking about you." Discretion had stopped him from pointing Fey out to a stranger.

None of the detectives looked around, experience overriding curiosity.

"What does he want?" Fey asked.

Booker shrugged. "He's a suit. Don't think he's one of yours, though. Lawyer, maybe."

"Have we done anything lately to get sued over?" Fey asked the table in general.

"Not so you'd notice," Monk told her.

As Booker moved away, Fey turned her head to look at the end of the bar near the entrance door.

An older man stood there looking uncomfortable. He was wearing a well-cut gray suit with a starched white shirt and a bow tie with blue polka dots. Wire-rimmed glasses sat high on his nose. His salt-and-pepper hair looked as if it was cut and styled at least once a week.

Fey didn't recognize him, but he didn't appear threatening. "I'd better go and see what he wants," she said. "If somebody sent him down here from the station, it may be important."

Monk slid from the booth to let Fey out, and then glided along behind her as backup.

Fey walked up to the man and introduced herself.

"What can I do for you?" she asked.

"Actually," the man said in plummy tones, "it's what I can do for you." He reached into an inside pocket and produced a business card. She took it and glanced at the typeface. *Martin Freeman, Attorney at Law*, with a prestigious address on Wilshire Boulevard in Beverly Hills.

"Okay, Freeman. I'll bite. What's going on?"

Freeman lifted a battered briefcase and placed it flat on the bar. "I am here to execute a will codicil for the estate of Ellis Kavanaugh. He was unfortunately killed in an accident last week. I have been directed to give you this."

"I don't know any Ellis Kavanaugh."

"Well, he obviously knew you. He left a locked briefcase with our firm over thirty years ago for safekeeping. Recently, he returned to establish a codicil to his will—which was held by another firm, naming you as the recipient of the briefcase in the event of his death."

Fey looked at the briefcase. "Do you know what's inside?"

"No," Freeman said. "When Mr. Kavanaugh lodged the brief-case with our firm, it was locked, and I'm afraid we do not have a key."

"No problem," Fey said, reaching over the bar and picking up the knife Booker used for paring limes. She stuck the tip under the right briefcase lock and gave the knife a sharp twist. The lock was cheap and popped open easily. She repeated the performance on the left lock.

As the second lock gave way, the briefcase lid sprang upward and hundred-dollar bills spilled across the bar.

5

Fey lay in bed trying to remember who had said, "The past is always with you." She pulled a pillow tight around her head and attempted to regulate her breathing, but sleep still refused to come.

The shock of receiving the briefcase full of money—two hundred and fifty thousand dollars—had seriously startled her. Not knowing where it came from, or why, only added to her confusion. She had put the money back in the briefcase and secured the case with duct tape provided by Booker. It was now on the recessed top of her bedroom wardrobe.

The name Ellis Kavanaugh had not immediately meant anything to Fey. Freeman, however, had offered further information that Kavanaugh had been best known by his middle name, Jack.

Jack Kavanaugh, Jack Kavanaugh—the name echoed through Fey's head, bringing with it unwanted memories. Memories of Garth Croaker, her abusive policeman father, the threats, the pain, the sexual depravity of a man who couldn't keep his hands off his daughter, couldn't keep his fists off his wife, and who used menace toward his young son to keep Fey compliant to his whims.

Jack Kavanaugh had been her father's last partner on the job. Fey remembered him as a slim man who always seemed to be afraid of her larger, hulking father. On duty, the two men seemed like a standard Laurel paired with a muscular, demented Hardy.

Another fine mess, Fey thought absently as she turned over in bed, disturbing Marvella and Brentwood, the two cats who slept on her feet. Marvella was a disgruntled ball of electrified orange fur. She opened one eye and for no reason swatted at the sleek whiteness of Brentwood before settling down again.

Fey's mind continued to turn over the situation. Why would her father's ex-partner leave her two hundred and fifty thousand dollars in his will?

The lawyer said Kavanaugh died impoverished, almost a street person, yet this briefcase full of money had reposed in Freeman's law offices for thirty years. Where had the money come from? And why had Kavanaugh not spent it, or at least put it in the bank to earn interest? Why not leave it to his own family, if he had any, instead of the daughter of his former police partner? And why did Kavanaugh recently name Fey as the recipient? Somewhere there had to be answers, but Fey wasn't sure she wanted to find them.

When Freeman told Fey how Kavanaugh died, she vaguely remembered seeing a photo in the sports pages. An intrepid photographer had immortalized Kavanaugh as he ran ahead of the horses in the seconds before he was trampled. She hadn't recognized the name or the face at the time, and the photo had only been a passing image in her mind.

The other cops at the Blue Cat controlled their curiosity. Monk had covered Fey's back while she'd talked to Freeman and had overheard the conversation. He'd scrambled to help pick up the spilled cash and return it to the briefcase before too many eyes could catch what was happening. Fey knew she could rely on his discretion, but she'd still given an abbreviated explanation to the rest of the crew before using Booker's back room to count the money.

She tried questioning Freeman further about his firm's relationship with Kavanaugh, but was unable to pin down anything concrete.

"I'm sorry," Freeman had told her. "All I know is Mr. Kavanaugh walked into our offices thirty years ago and asked for assistance in storing this briefcase. Our office contacted him several times over the years to ask for instructions. He updated his fees on those occasions and asked us to continue storing the case. Two months ago, Mr. Kavanaugh came to our offices personally and had us create the codicil regarding the property in our possession."

"How did you find out Kavanaugh was dead?" Fey asked.

"We were notified by another law firm, Alexander and Kelly, with whom Mr. Kavanaugh had lodged his complete will. In that will there was reference to our codicil, and we were contacted to execute it."

Fey knew Alexander and Kelly as an all-purpose law firm whose advertisements appeared in *The Blue Line*, the monthly publication of the LAPD's Police Protective League. The firm's primary customer base was law-enforcement personnel and their families.

Now, in the darkness of her bedroom, Fey sought to find an explanation for the strange course of events. She swallowed. She tried to breathe evenly but failed. Shallow, ragged breaths didn't give her enough air to clear the pressure building in her chest as she fought against the tears that threatened to erupt.

She was so damn alone. Her mother was dead, her father was dead, her brother was dead, and good riddance to them all.

Three ex-husbands could testify her marriages were dead. Ash, a man who had meant more to her than any other, had been dying when she met him, and now he was gone too—physically if not spiritually.

Over forty-five years on this side of the grass, over twenty-five years on the job, and her personal life was a disaster. She constantly fought to put the past behind her, battled to keep the Pandora's box chained and locked, but there was always something that came along to release her demons.

Normally, a windfall of two hundred and fifty thousand dollars would be cause for celebration. The course of events in Fey's life, however, had never been normal, and she could feel the metaphoric storm clouds gathering.

Finally able to force a deep, cleansing breath into her lungs, she worked to blank her mind again. The answers to Jack Kavanaugh's legacy would have to wait. There were more pressing issues.

In a few hours, she and her crew would be taking on their first assignment for Robbery-Homicide. She needed to be sharp. She was being pushed beyond her comfort zone by forces she couldn't control, and that scared her almost to inaction. Even though she had little in her private life besides her animals, she did have *the job*, and *the job* meant everything.

6

GOD WAS IN his heaven, but all was not right with the world. Gordon O'Malley Drummond paced behind the gathered detectives, listening to the briefing being overseen by Whip Whitman.

The RHD offices at Parker Center were overcrowded and full of activity. Briefings were therefore often held in a commandeered lunchroom on the mezzanine level.

"Yesterday we confirmed the victim's identity as Bianca Flynn, a prominent local lawyer specializing in children's rights. Her body was found three days ago in an abandoned warehouse near Gower and Sunset." The speaker was Thad Jacobs, the taciturn D-III from the Hollywood Area homicide unit.

Fey knew him and didn't like him. He had a holier-than-thou attitude and thought working Hollywood added inches to his penis.

"The body was naked and tied to a chair next to a workbench," Jacobs continued. "The victim's right hand was clamped in a vise and there was clear evidence of a serrated blade being used to slice open the flesh."

"Torture?" Monk asked from his chair next to Fey. The rest of Fey's crew were also present, scattered around the briefing room.

"Obviously," Jacobs said. "Aside from the damage to the right hand, the victim had been shot numerous times with an industrial stapler. Half-inch staples had been fired into her thighs, elbows, and breasts. Also, her mouth had been smashed—her teeth were a mess."

"A fist or some other blunt instrument?" Hammersmith asked. He was looking at a series of close-up photos of the victim's face taken by the coroner.

"Too much damage to be done by a fist. The coroner says the injuries to the mouth were probably caused by being hit with the butt of the staple gun, or something similar."

"Before or after the injuries to the hand?" Fey asked.

"What difference does it make?" Jacobs asked.

"If the blows to the mouth occurred before the hand injuries, the suspect may have been trying to break the victim down quickly, before more serious torture. If the blows to the mouth occurred after the other damage, it could mean the suspect was growing frustrated with the victim's refusal to give up whatever information the suspect was after."

Jacobs grunted. "And that would get you further along in the investigation? The cause of death was still heart failure."

Fey stood up. "Let's get this straight. You had this body for three days before you identified the victim, and you've done crap-all to figure out who done it. Now, we find out the victim isn't some black street whore who picked up a bad john and whose murder the public would ignore, but the lawyer sister of a police commissioner and the daughter of a judge. You now get to dump this whole screwed-up mess in our laps, and you're giving us attitude?"

Jacobs leaned forward. "You've only been in Robbery-Homicide five minutes, Croaker, and already you've picked up their elitist demeanor. We didn't screw up anything. This started out as a run-of-the-mill murder, just like the forty other run-of-the-mill murders my unit is working. We don't get to pick and choose our cases. Hollywood isn't West L.A., where your entire unit handles ten homicides a year. Each one of my detectives handles ten homicides a year—minimum. Your people in West L.A. can't even spell homicide."

As all the other detectives in the room had been working West L.A. until that morning, Jacobs's remarks were not well received. There was a definite rumbling of trouble.

"This is ridiculous!" said a stocky black woman sitting next to Whip Whitman. "You are squabbling among yourselves while whoever did this to my sister is still walking around free." Cecily Flynn-Rogers had recently been appointed to the L.A. Police Commission. It was far from usual to have a family member of a victim present during a homicide briefing, but Flynn-Rogers had exercised her powers as a police commission member and insisted.

"I told you, Bianca's husband did this. If he didn't do it himself, he had it done. Why aren't you out investigating instead of playing these silly games? If this is the service you offer, it's no wonder women—especially black women—are not safe in this city." Everything with Flynn-Rogers came back to race and gender. The current political mystery was what leverage her father, appellate court judge Luther Flynn, had over the mayor that was damning or profitable enough to get Cecily appointed to the police commission.

Unlike other major cities, such as New York or San Francisco, which had only one police commissioner, Los Angeles had a board of appointed commissioners—each with his or her own varied political agenda.

"Calm down, Cecily," the chief said. "Let the detectives do their job. Everybody needs to blow off a little steam. We'll find out who did this to your sister. I guarantee it. If your brother-in-law is involved, we'll get him."

"Don't give me that 'everything will be okay' crap, Drummond. I know what the murder clearance rate is, so don't give me guarantees." Flynn-Rogers was standing now. She turned toward Fey. "When you're done fighting over turf, I want to see you in my office this afternoon. Two o'clock sharp. Be there." She turned and stalked toward the lunchroom door.

"Ms. Flynn-Rogers," Fey said, stopping the commissioner, "I don't answer to you. I answer to Captain Whitman, who answers to the chief, who has to deal with you. I'll be in your office at two o'clock, but it will be my interview, not yours. I expect you to cooperate to help us find who killed your sister."

Flynn-Rogers glanced at the chief, but found only a stone-faced expression. She opened her mouth to speak, then clamped her lips closed. She turned and left the room.

"Don't push her too far," Drummond said to Fey. "She has friends in high places."

"If you're talking about her father the judge, he's going to be your worry, not mine," Fey told him. "My worry is catching a murderer who already has a three-day lead."

7

"THIS SUCKS," Alphabet Cohen said, voicing the agitation felt by the entire unit. Everyone knew he wasn't talking about the case. All the detectives were feeling unsettled and out of their element. The change from their area unit to RHD had been too abrupt. There had been no time to accept the reorganization, to settle into their new quarters, or to deal with being looked upon as intruders into a closed world. They might be assigned to RHD, but they were a long way from being accepted.

Alone now in the commandeered lunchroom, they felt oppressed and without clear direction. The murder book—a blue, two-inch, three-ringed binder containing all of the information gathered on the investigation to date—had been left behind by the Hollywood homicide detective. It sat in the middle of a long lunch table as if it were a witch's book of spells.

Both Chief Drummond and Captain Whitman had departed after giving out assurances of trust and backing. Nobody believed the platitudes. Trust and backing were not concepts understood or applied by management in any organization. Results were the only thing that counted, and one *oops, sorry* outweighed a career's worth of *attaboys*.

"Okay, people," Fey spoke up. She was experiencing the same depression as her team, but it was up to her to lead them through it. "This is nothing new to us. We've handled high-profile cases before. The only thing different is we've got some catching up to do, but we'll get there—procedure doesn't change."

Monk Lawson scooted his chair closer to the table and reached for the murder book. Hammersmith and Lawless exchanged their ritual glance of communication and nodded slightly at each other. Alphabet pushed away from the wall he was leaning against and moved closer to Brindle. For her part, Brindle stood up, running a hand through her hair, and began looking over Monk's shoulder as he turned pages.

"Nails," Fey spoke to Rhonda Lawless, "you and Hammer take the crime scene. I don't care what Hollywood did when they were there. I want it done again—fingerprints, criminalists, the whole shebang. Door-knock the neighborhood. Track down who owns the building where the body was discovered, as well as who found the body. Go over the interviews in the murder book and then redo them."

"Got it," Rhonda said. Hammer nodded.

"Alphabet, I want you and Brindle to start doing background on the victim," Fey continued. "Find out how she was identified, if she was reported missing and by whom. It appears she was fairly prominent in her field, so do a workup on her history—look for any grudges or motives for murder. You know the drill."

The oddly matched pair nodded their heads in assent.

"Monk and I will start with the body at the coroner's office," Fey said. "Then we'll be back here to deal with the delightful Ms. Flynn-Rogers."

"What about Judge Flynn, the victim's father?" Brindle asked.

"Good question," Fey said. "I wonder why he hasn't already been on the phone to the chief. While you're doing your workup on the victim, get us a rundown on the judge and the sister. We'll put off dealing with the judge until we have the basics covered. Okay?"

Everyone nodded.

"Anything else?"

"Yeah," Alphabet said. "When's lunch?"

8

THE CHILLED air circulating through the coroner's office had its usual macabre effect on Fey, piercing its way deep inside her. It took her forever to get warm again after a visit.

She and Monk sat in a small office waiting for Deputy Coroner Rex Powers.

"I still can't believe they have a gift shop in this place," Fey said. They had passed the Skeleton in the Closet gift shop on the way to Powers's office. "Anything to make a buck."

"Actually," Monk said, "all the proceeds go to a charity program."

"It's still weird. One of those only-in-L.A. things. You come down here to identify a corpse, then stop by the gift store to pick up a souvenir of the trip."

Monk chuckled. "Give it a break. They have a lot of tours come through here—interns, writers, civic groups, dignitaries. You know the drill."

"Maybe, but the next thing they'll be selling is kids' clothing with *My Dad Was Autopsied, and All I Got Was This Dumb T-Shirt* printed on them."

"Sounds like a hot seller," Rex Powers said as he came through the door. His tall, thin build was emphasized by the drape of an extralong white lab coat. "Anyway, what's wrong with beach towels imprinted with chalk outlines of dead bodies?"

"Yuck," Fey said. "Don't people realize how sordid murder is? Chalk outlines are whispers left behind by the dead."

"That's a bit fanciful, isn't it?" Powers shook his head, bouncing the long hair that curled over his collar. "What about cops? They're the first ones to start making jokes at a murder scene."

"Cops are entitled. They've earned the right to joke. John Q. Public hasn't."

Powers gave Fey a thoughtful look. "I wouldn't have thought you were so sensitive after all the cases you've handled."

"I have professional calluses, but I'm still offended by murder and murderers," Fey said. "Making light of homicide is depraved. It's how we become desensitized as a society."

"From what I've seen over the years," Powers said, "I'd say it was a little too late to start worrying. Anyway, are you here to discuss the state of the world or the state of your case?"

"The case," Monk told him. "Definitely the case."

Powers removed his glasses and pinched the bridge of his nose before settling the glasses again. He sniffed. "By the way, congratulations on the promotions. Well deserved."

"Thanks," Fey said. "But it only means our private parts can now be twisted harder in the wringer."

"Interesting image," Powers said. "But you do seem to get a lot of tough cases."

"I take it this time is no exception?"

"I've seen worse," Powers said. "But I hear the victim is suddenly high profile—sister of a police commissioner, daughter of a judge. Makes things tricky."

"Another minefield without a map," Fey agreed. "So, what can you tell us that you didn't tell Hollywood?"

"I wish there was something," Powers said, unbuttoning his lab coat to reveal a sweatshirt and jeans underneath. He moved behind his desk to where a coffeepot rested in a small brewing machine. Gathering up three semiclean glass beakers, he poured coffee into each and handed them around.

"You know the cause of death was heart failure?" he asked, plopping down in the executive chair behind his desk.

The two detectives nodded.

"The victim was a heavy smoker. Her heart was already in pretty bad shape, but I don't think she knew it—at least not the extent."

"Why?" Monk asked.

"Because if she'd seen a doctor for any related problems, she would have been in an operating room in a heartbeat—no pun intended."

"That bad?"

"I'd say so. The heart was diseased and enlarged—probably an inherited trait—and the left anterior descending artery was almost completely blocked. The condition was unusual for a woman, and she was young enough not to have been experiencing any physical symptoms, but she was a prime candidate to have the big one at any time."

"And the stress of being tortured caused the heart attack?" Fey asked.

"Hell of an added factor," Powers agreed.

"What about the torture itself?" Monk asked.

Powers bounced up with energy that belied his years. "Come on. I'll show you." He moved quickly out of his office to lead the detectives down a maze of echoing corridors.

Fey had worked with Powers for a long time. He was by inclination a teacher and never passed up an opportunity to dispense knowledge.

After insisting the detectives don hospital greens, gloves, booties, and masks, Powers guided them to the solid meat freezer–like door that opened into the mortuary. The change in temperature as they entered the large, stark room seemed more than just a change from cold to colder.

Bodies were everywhere. Wrapped in clear plastic and stacked on metal shelves or stainless-steel gurneys, they appeared like so much cordwood.

Powers moved to a gurney holding the overflow from the shelves. With Monk's help, he lifted one of the bodies off the gurney and stacked it on top of another body on a shelf. He then checked the tag on the body that remained.

"This is our girl," he said, unwrapping the clear plastic sheeting.

Fey had seen enough corpses to view them as little more than lumps of cold clay, but the empty shell deserved vindication.

Homicide cops viewed themselves as superior to all other detectives because only they could bring justice for the dead. It never mattered how many murders a homicide detective solved; it was always the ones they didn't solve that haunted them. Unsolved murders were what drove homicide detectives to drink, to haphazard copulations, and to consider eating their guns in the cold hours of the morning.

Powers pointed out the punctures in the victim's armpits, legs, and breasts.

"Industrial-size staples," he said.

"How many altogether?" Fey asked.

"Thirteen," Powers replied.

"Then the questioning must have gone on for an extended period."

"I'd say so," Powers agreed. "The killer certainly took his time over mutilating the hand." He held up the right wrist to facilitate inspection. "I'd guess a small jigsaw. The cuts are pretty precise — done a little at a time."

"Any sexual mutilation?"

"Nothing other than several staples in the breasts, but I think that was simply a conveniently painful place to shoot them, as opposed to an action designed for sexual arousal."

"So you don't think the torture was related to sadomasochistic fantasies?"

Powers shrugged. "There was no indication of rape or sodomy. No foreign objects inserted into the vagina or rectum. No semen in the mouth or anywhere else on the body. My best guess is this was strictly torture for information. The fact the victim was naked was more for intimidation than sexual purposes."

That put a more interesting spin on the situation for Fey.

"What about the trauma to the mouth?" she asked.

"Ah, there's a possible clue for you."

"How so?"

"The damage was postmortem. There was a lack of bleeding, indicating the heart had stopped pumping."

"The conclusion being that the victim died before giving up the information," Fey said.

"And in a fit of anger," Powers finished the thought, "the suspect strikes the victim in the mouth, causing the postmortem trauma. Rather ugly, but it fits."

"Anything else like this come through recently?" Monk asked.

Powers shook his head. "This MO is a first for us, but I've sent out a request to other jurisdictions for similars. We'll have to wait and see what turns up. If you want Sherlock Holmes—the killer is a five-foot-four-inch-tall, left-handed mason who is blind in one ear—you'll have to ring Scotland Yard."

"So your big clue," Fey said, "is that we should be checking anger-management courses for Tim the Tool Man?"

"I thought you said you didn't joke about murder."

9

"FEY SAYS the mouth trauma was postmortem, indicating the victim didn't talk before dying," Rhonda Lawless told her partner as she turned off her mobile phone. Even though she was now married to Arch Hammersmith, she retained her maiden name for professional purposes. Being married and working together was something that would count against them sooner or later. No sense in pushing their luck.

Hammersmith scratched his head and looked around. "The victim must have been a tough lady. I'd be shooting my mouth off the second someone started shooting staples into my armpits and whittling on my fingers."

"Somehow, I don't think so."

Hammer shrugged. "Well, I'd certainly be making a hell of a lot of noise."

"Which explains the suspect's choice of location," Rhonda said.

They were standing in the soundproofed back room of an abandoned warehouse. It was the property of a B-movie production company specializing in direct-to-video horrorfests—all gore, screams, and bare breasts.

The inside of the warehouse had been split into several different soundstages, all neglected now, with leaning walls and odd cables hanging here and there. Hammer and Nails were in the smallest of the rooms at the back of the warehouse.

There was a heavy wooden table along the back wall of the soundstage with a new vise bolted to one end. The metal jaws of the vise were painted blue under the dried blood. Next to the table, on the end near the vise, was the metal folding chair where Bianca Flynn had been tied. The chair was battered and bent. Like the table, it appeared to have been in the warehouse long before the crime went down.

Rhonda ran her fingertips along the front edge of the scarred table. She touched half a dozen slightly protruding staples shot into the wood. "Warm-up threats," she said.

Hammersmith grunted agreement as he watched Rhonda wander around the torture room, unaware of his scrutiny. The sight of her never failed to stir him.

They had known each other a long time. They had been partners a long time, and lovers a long time. Ever since their initial contact during an ambush shooting, there had been a voltage that was clear to everyone who came in contact with them. Since the baby, however, Hammer had sensed a misfiring somewhere. On the surface everything appeared normal, but deeper down there was a short in the relationship. Hammer didn't know what to do about it yet, but he knew they would handle it together. Always had, always would.

Thinking to amuse, Hammer slipped into a bad impersonation of a game show host. "Today's *Jeopardy!* categories are Scene of the Crime, Motive, Method of Operation, Clues and

Leads, Case Breakers, and Hodgepodge. We'll start with you, Rhonda."

Rhonda turned around with a smile. "I'll take Motive for fifty dollars."

"Fine. Please remember your answers must be in the form of a question. The game board reveals the word *information.*"

"*Errrrrrrr!*" Rhonda made a noise like a buzzer. "What did the suspect want from the victim?"

"Correct. Sexual torture looks very different from this setup. There are no signs of ritualistic behavior, and the method of torture was not designed to lead to death. Let's move on."

"I'll take Method of Operation for a hundred."

"*Scopolamine.*"

"*Errrrrrrr!* What is the most common drug used by pros to get information?"

"Exactly right. Which means our suspect is not a pro. Trying to get information from somebody in this manner is stupid and sloppy."

"Let's try Hodgepodge for two hundred."

"There is nothing in the Hodgepodge category," Hammer said. "So, I think this bit of nonsense has run its course."

"I don't get to go on to the bonus round?"

"Sorry. You don't even get the home game."

"What a gyp."

"Maybe so, but at least we know we're on the same track. The victim was naked and tied up, but that speaks more to intimidation than sexual abuse. There was no indication of rape or sodomy, and the criminalists found no semen or other fluids that could be tied to the suspect to indicate sexual arousal. The victim's death was not a planned part of the scenario—the heart attack was a surprise."

"So, our suspect isn't a serial killer or a sexual pervert," Rhonda agreed, "but neither is he a professional torturer. Where do you think he got the staple gun?"

"Brought it with him."

"Obviously, but did he just buy it or did he bring it from a personal toolbox?"

Hammer thought for a moment. "I'd say he bought the stapler and whatever he used to cut up the victim's hand prior to coming here. Maybe the vise as well. Everybody has watched enough television to know you have to dispose of the weapon. If he had a stapler and a saw of his own, he wouldn't want to use them and then throw them away. Are there any hardware stores nearby?"

"We'll have to check." Rhonda scribbled on the clipboard she was carrying.

"The tip about the body was anonymously called in, right?"

"Yeah. The 911 call was traced back to a local pay phone. No fingerprints."

"I don't see the killer giving the tip-off, so it must have been somebody else."

"Maybe a homeless person or a junkie who broke in to use the warehouse as a crash pad."

Hammer nodded. "We'll have to get in touch with the Hollywood transient detail and get a list of any locals who frequent this area—see if we can find who discovered the body."

Rhonda made another note on the clipboard.

The duo had already called in the forensics circus from Scientific Investigation Division for a second go-round. The criminalist, photographer, and fingerprint personnel had grumbled about doing the same crime scene twice, but they had come and gone competently before leaving the two detectives alone at the scene.

"The guys at Hollywood aren't completely incompetent," Rhonda said.

"Maybe not," Hammer said, "but I've heard Thad Jacobs is looking for a synchronized-idiocy partner for the next police Olympics."

"Okay, he's an exception. Still, I'm sure his team searched this area as thoroughly as we have, so how about we expand the crime scene—go over the area outside the warehouse?"

"You think this guy dumped his equipment nearby?"

"It's possible," Rhonda said. "The staple gun is over the top— movie stuff. If the killer is making those kind of decisions, maybe he's making other mistakes."

"It's worth a try," Hammer agreed. "The guy doesn't appear to be a mastermind. Probably can't even phrase his answers in the form of a question."

"Who knows?" Rhonda said. "Maybe he'll turn out to be the perfect synchronized-idiocy partner Jacobs needs."

10

"Where are Hammer and Nails hiding?" Fey asked as she and Monk joined Alphabet and Brindle in the RHD office.

"They're still at the crime scene," Brindle reported. "They called in and said they didn't have anything substantial, but they're working on it."

"Let's hope they come up with it because clues were scarce at the coroner's. How about you guys? You have any ammunition I can use with Cecily Flynn-Rogers?"

"I hate double-barreled names," Alphabet said. "It's like naming your dog Rover-Spot or Fido-Prince."

"Is this a distraction to save yourself from telling me you didn't come up with anything?" Fey asked.

"Actually," Brindle said, pulling out a sheaf of notes, "we came up with quite a bit. Bianca Flynn was a real piece of work. We're going to have more suspects than we want or need."

"Okay, give," Fey said, sitting down in the chair she had

brought with her from West L.A. She opened the middle drawer of her desk and shut it again. The movement was smooth and unhurried. With a face wiped clear of expression, she reached for the pile of copied newspaper articles Brindle placed on the desk blotter.

Brindle had been close enough to see the inside of Fey's desk drawer. She forced herself to copy Fey's nonchalance.

The bustling of the RHD detectives in the room had stopped, as if they were actors in an E. F. Hutton commercial. Then they started to move again with something like a collective release of breath. The moment of suspended animation had passed.

"These . . ." Brindle started, stopped, and then started again. "These came from a Nexis computer search we did at the library. Bianca gets herself in the news quite a bit regarding child custody cases."

"She specializes in children's rights," Alphabet said. He knew something was going on concerning Fey's desk, but he was sharp enough not to ask.

"She's litigated a number of high-profile appeals where allegations of sexual or physical abuse were leveled against a parent— usually the father—in the original case," Brindle continued, "but the courts, not satisfied by the evidence presented and gave non-supervised visitation rights to the accused parent. In some cases, the accused parent was even given sole custody, with the courts determining that the allegations were unfounded and the other parent was an obsessive liability."

"All of which means the accused parent continues to have access to the child to continue the abuse, which may or may not have been going on in the first place." Fey had heard the story before. "I take it Bianca always represented the underdog?"

"Goes without saying, doesn't it?" Alphabet agreed. "A Goody Two-shoes."

"Not if you're the accused parent and the accusations are unfounded."

"Where there's smoke, there's fire."

"Come on, Alphabet. You know better," Fey said, slightly exasperated. "I'm first in line to champion the cause of molested children."

The sexual abuses of Fey's past were not a secret to those who worked with her. Fey's childhood horrors had been splashed across the newspapers a couple of years earlier when tapes from her psychiatric sessions had been leaked to the press during a major murder investigation involving JoJo Cullen.

Cullen had been an NBA Rookie of the Year basketball star arrested for murdering a series of young males. It had been Fey's crew who'd handled the investigation. After Cullen's arrest, however, the case had been transferred to RHD because of the notoriety. It was then that Fey began to have doubts about Cullen's guilt, but trying to convince RHD proved impossible. They had their suspect and their glory; the case was closed.

Fey and her team refused to let the issue go. Aided by Fey's lover, the FBI agent known only as Ash, they overturned the case and captured the real villain—but not before the personal cost to Fey took its toll.

"You know the first mud to be slung in any child custody dispute involves allegations of sexual or physical abuse." Fey continued to direct her tirade at Alphabet. "And most of it remains unprovable."

"Bianca Flynn didn't think so," Alphabet said. "She fought and won new judgments in most of the cases she took on."

"It was the cases she *didn't* win, though, that caused the biggest controversy," Brindle added.

"Tell me," Fey said.

"It seems whenever Bianca didn't win a case, the children and the nonaccused parent would disappear on the Underground Railroad."

"Disappear?"

"As in vanish," Alphabet said.

"The synonym training is great," Fey said. "But what I really need is an explanation of how they disappeared."

Brindle found a clipping and held it out to Fey. "This is an article on something called the Underground Railroad. It's a loose-knit coalition of rogue social workers, civil rights lawyers, children's rights activists, churches, sanctuaries, and otherwise law-abiding citizens who harbor fugitive parents and their kids. These parents believe their kids have been sexually molested and are ready to do anything—including defying the courts and fleeing—to make sure it doesn't happen again."

"I always thought the Underground Railroad was something to do with slaves," Fey said.

"The original was," Alphabet said. "During the mid–nineteenth century it was established to help slaves escape to freedom. This new version, however, is for parents and kids trying to escape abusers. It's like a renegade Federal Witness Protection Program, except many of the families involved are actually being chased by the FBI."

Fey took the article from Brindle. As she did so, Frank Hale walked by and dropped a folded square of paper on her desk. Fey scooped it up quickly.

"How big is this Underground Railroad?"

Brindle pointed to a paragraph in the article. "Supposedly about five to six hundred families are involved, with over two thousand–plus safe houses nationwide."

"And Bianca Flynn was part of this movement?"

"So it appears," Brindle said. "Which means somebody could have been trying to get information from her regarding the whereabouts of their kids."

"Good grief."

"It gets even more complicated," Alphabet said.

"Of course it does," Fey said.

"Bianca Flynn had two children, a five-year-old girl and an

eight-year-old boy. She was also estranged from her husband, Mark Ritter—"

"Don't tell me," Fey said, holding up a hand. "I can see this coming. She'd made allegations of sexual abuse against Ritter and was hiding her children."

"Got it in one," Alphabet said.

"Hey, Croaker," a voice yelled from the front of the squad room.

Fey and the others turned to see Vic Rappaport, a slovenly practical joker who was part of the old guard at RHD. Rappaport came across with a self-satisfied grin. "You got a customer at the counter. Some guy named Mark Ritter. And he's got a bunch of lawyers with him."

11

"TIMING IS everything," Fey said quietly. "I'll be right there," she told Rappaport. She pushed the fingers of both hands through her hair and blew out a heavy breath. "This day is getting longer by the minute."

"At least we don't have to spend time tracking down the main suspect," Alphabet said.

"We don't know he's the main suspect yet," Brindle said.

"Give me a break. First rule of homicide investigation: the spouse is always the main suspect."

"The *first* suspect, maybe, but we don't know if he's the *main* suspect."

"Semantics."

"Stop bickering," Fey said, "or I'll have to put you both down for a nap."

She turned her attention back to the papers in her hand. Behind the cover of the article, she opened the note dropped on her desk by Hale. It had a single name written on it—*Rappaport.*

"Is he the bastard who put that thing in your desk?" Brindle asked, looking at the note over Fey's shoulder.

"I'd say so," Fey told her. "Maybe we do have some allies down here."

"Don't bank on it," Alphabet said. He tapped the desktop lightly with the tips of his fingers. "What's in the drawer?"

"Wait and see," Fey told him. "All will become clear."

In the small Robbery-Homicide Division lobby, Mark Ritter was surrounded by five interchangeable men in dark suits, pristine white shirts, nondescript ties, and flashy cuff links. Lawyers.

Ritter stood out because of his height. He was at least six-five with a lean build and a sculpted face. His hair was tar black and razor cut, his suit a perfect light gray pinstripe set off with a sharp maroon silk tie. His most outstanding feature, however, was that he was white.

Ritter caught Fey's look. "You seem surprised, Detective."

"I am," Fey said. "I didn't know you were white." She figured she might as well be candid.

"Do you have a problem with interracial marriage?"

"Not so you'd notice," Fey said. "Do you think it has something to do with your wife's death?"

"I don't know," Ritter said. "I don't know anything about my ex-wife's death. All I'm concerned about are my children. Do you know where they are?"

"Until a minute ago, I didn't even know there were children. My team was only assigned the case this morning, and we're still doing a lot of preliminary work. Perhaps you'd like to step into an interview room and discuss the situation with me."

All five of the lawyers moved forward. Fey held up a hand. "I'm sorry, gentlemen. Our interview rooms are very small. I'm sure Mr. Ritter won't need more than one of you."

"Pembroke," Ritter said, and one of the clones joined him.

"Arthur Pembroke," the man said, extending his hand toward Fey. He was roundish and had a prissy little mustache that reminded Fey of Hercule Poirot. His face gleamed with a sheen of perspiration. "I'm Mr. Ritter's personal lawyer."

Fey wondered if that meant the other men were Ritter's impersonal lawyers. She shook Pembroke's hand and ushered the two men into a small interview room to the left of the main squad bay. She directed them toward chairs on the far side of a battered wooden desk. Both the desk and chairs would have been more at home in an impoverished inner-city school.

"You have my condolences, Mr. Ritter," Fey said. "This must be a very hard time for you."

"You have no idea, Detective Croaker. But it's because my children are missing, not because my ex-wife is dead."

Fey wondered if Ritter always sounded so pompous. "I was unaware you were divorced. I thought you were simply estranged."

Pembroke leaned forward. "My client was in the final stages of divorce proceedings. Papers had been filed, but the battle for custody was ongoing."

Fey smiled at the lawyer. "Mr. Pembroke, I don't mean to be rude," which meant she did mean to be rude, "but your client is not being interrogated. This is an interview only. No Miranda warning, no accusatory questions, simply a quest for information. I would appreciate it if you would let Mr. Ritter answer for himself, or you will be asked to leave."

"You can't do that," Ritter said.

"Yes, I can," Fey told him. "And if you expect to get any help from me, you'd better see if we can work together."

Fey knew if Ritter was arrested later, this interview could be used as evidence. However, Ritter wasn't under arrest, so Miranda didn't apply. Fey was sure Pembroke knew this as well, but it was a fencing match.

Ritter looked at Pembroke, who settled back in his chair with a fastidious nod. "My apologies, Detective Croaker," Pembroke said. "Simply trying to earn my fee."

"No problem, counselor." Fey switched her attention back to Ritter. "Tell me, what do you do for a living?"

"I'm a partner in a corporate law firm."

"Which one?" Fey was surprised she needed to ask. Usually lawyers blurted out the name of their firm as if you should already know it.

"Flynn, Barrington and Simmons."

"Flynn?" Fey asked. "As in Judge Luther Flynn, your wife's father?"

"Yes. He is, of course, a figurehead while he sits on the bench."

"Of course," Fey replied. Why hadn't Ritter wanted her to know he was in the family firm? she wondered. "How long have you been with them?"

"A little over two years."

"And already a partner?"

"I brought an established clientele with me."

"I see," Fey said, not sure that she did. "How long have you been estranged from your wife?"

"Two years."

Interesting, Fey thought. "And she had current custody of your children?"

Ritter made an impatient movement with a sweep of his hand. "The court originally ordered joint custody, but Bianca fought the decision by making absurd allegations of sexual abuse against me regarding our daughter, Sarah."

"Was there an investigation?"

"Of course."

"And the results?"

"The district attorney's office refused to bring charges on the basis that there was no corroborating evidence."

"So, there was a disclosure made by your daughter?" Fey knew the drill with child abuse cases and easily read between the lines of Ritter's statement.

Ritter grunted. "My daughter was four when she was interviewed by a district attorney and an LAPD child abuse investigator. It was determined she was not qualified to testify in court
because of her age, and the statements she made were the result
of coaching on the part of Bianca. It was all nonsense. I would
never hurt my children."

Fey knew it was not unusual in child custody cases for one
parent to coach a child, to the point of brainwashing, to say things
against the other parent. She would have to pull the file from
Child Abuse to get the full story. "What about your son?"

"Mark Junior is now eight. He told the district attorney that
Bianca had made Sarah repeat things over and over."

"Is there any reason other than her desire for sole custody that
your wife would do something like that?"

"Bianca was a fanatic, Detective Croaker. She was obsessed
with child sexual abuse. When she was a child, she made the
same unfounded allegations against her own father that she had
Sarah make against me."

"Was she upset when you joined her father's law firm?"

"The silly bitch wouldn't see sense. It meant financial security, a place in the community. It gave us everything we could
want."

Everything *you* could want, perhaps, Fey thought, seeing
where this primrose path was really leading.

"This nonsense about sexual abuse was all in her mind. She
fed on it. She was like a raging alcoholic desperately searching for
the next drink."

"Was she like this when you married her?"

"Nowhere near as bad," Ritter said. "I knew she had a cause
and strong beliefs, but I never knew she would go over the edge
like she did. If you know anything about her, you know there
were charges pending against her for harboring parental fugitives
and their children from rightful custody parents. And now she's
done the same thing with Sarah and Mark Junior."

"How so?"

"It's clear your department's left hand doesn't know what its right hand is doing."

"Not an unusual occurrence in any big organization," Fey agreed. She was not bad at dancing the old soft-shoe. "Why don't you fill me in."

"A month ago, family court reconfirmed my rights to joint custody," Ritter explained. "Bianca refused to comply and hid the children. She was heavily involved in this Underground Railroad. She supported it and used the people involved for her own means. My children are now adrift in an illegal program that could be run by pedophiles and other perverts for all we know."

Fey took the last statement for what it was worth. "You reported all of this, of course, when it happened?"

"Detective Sloan in Wilshire Division is currently handling a child concealment case in which Bianca is named as the suspect. The district attorney's office is, well . . . was considering bringing charges against her."

Fey nodded. "I can certainly understand your concern for your children, and I can assure you that we will make every effort to locate them. To do so, however, I'm going to have to continue investigating your wife's murder. Can you tell me who would want information from your wife bad enough to be willing to torture it out of her?"

"Besides myself?" Ritter asked.

Fey smiled in acceptance of the statement she had left unsaid.

"Am I a suspect?" Ritter asked boldly.

"At this point even I'm a suspect," Fey said. "So, besides yourself, can you think of anyone who would want information from your wife?"

"Certainly," Ritter said, sounding pompous and plummy. "Anyone, like me, whose children she was helping to hide."

•   •   •

FEY RETURNED to the RHD squad room after seeing Mark Ritter and his entourage out of the office. She would need to interview Ritter again, but she needed much more information before doing so. He had provided her with several names of other disgruntled parents whose children Bianca Flynn had spirited underground.

Fey's head was full of powerful images—child custody and nonprovable sexual abuse allegations—nightmare ingredients for any detective. All she needed now were satanic rituals.

She found Alphabet and Brindle at their new desks drinking coffee and going through Hollywood's original murder book.

"That must have been fun," Brindle said.

"You ready to book him yet or what?" Alphabet asked.

"Can't book a man simply because you don't like his manners," Fey said.

Alphabet twitched his head. "That's the trouble with progress."

The squad room was still busy, but the activity seemed more genuine this time. Nobody was watching Fey or her team.

"Speaking of fun . . ." Fey said, noticing the momentary lack of attention being paid to them. Vic Rappaport was standing by himself next to a file cabinet, engrossed in a case package. "How about we strike back before the point is lost?"

"What do you have in mind?" Brindle asked.

"Can you distract Rappaport?"

"Does the pope sleep in a single bed?" Brindle moved away from the desk, straightening her skirt as she went.

"What do you want me to do?" Alphabet asked. He'd taken a surreptitious look in Fey's desk drawer and did not want to be left out.

"Sorry," Fey told him. "This one is strictly girls' night out." She casually opened her desk drawer and removed the offending item. Holding it down beside her leg, she waited for Brindle to go into action.

Passing by Rappaport, Brindle bumped hard into the edge of a desk. "Damn!" She swore loud enough to attract the attention of anyone in the room who hadn't heard the collision.

Acting as if she weren't the center of attention, Brindle slid the hem of her skirt up her thigh to check her nylons. "Crap, I've got a run."

Rappaport was riveted by the display of skin and wouldn't have noticed Fey moving up behind him if she'd been driving a tank. His colleagues, however, saw what was about to happen and let Fey's revenge run its course.

As Fey reached Rappaport, she chose her moment perfectly.

"I think this belongs to you," she said sweetly, grasping the rear band of Rappaport's Sans-a-Belt polyester slacks and sliding the black, ten-inch, hand cream–dripping rubber dildo down the gap.

12

WHILE VIC Rappaport was swearing and twisting about trying to grab the gross object tangled up in his shorts, Fey quickly left the RHD squad room and walked down the stairs. Waiting for the elevator might have spoiled her exit.

Over the years she had become accustomed to sexist jokes. If a woman complained, she was a spoilsport or a whiner. If she became angry, she was a bitch with no sense of humor. If she laughed and played along, she must be easy, and lurid attempts to get into her shorts escalated.

The only way to handle the juvenile debasement was to return the harassment. Metaphorically, if you were cut, you shot back. If you were shot, you blasted with a cannon. You let everyone know you never brought a knife to a gunfight. It didn't take long for the lesson to be learned, but it was boring having to teach it over and over.

Exiting on the first floor of Parker Center, Fey turned left and covered the short distance to the police commission offices. She pushed through the glass-fronted doors and headed for Cecily Flynn-Rogers's office.

The door was open, and Fey stepped inside, rapping lightly with her knuckles. The office was more functional than plush, but the furniture was several steps up from anything found in a squad room.

Flynn-Rogers was sitting behind her desk in a studded leather executive chair the color of eggplant. She was smiling and talking to a solidly built older black man with a large head sporting close-shaved hair. He had a salt-and-pepper mustache and a deeply dimpled chin. His suit was midnight blue with a red and white polka-dot handkerchief spilling out of the breast pocket. The smooth curve of a white scar ran from the left corner of his mouth and disappeared under his chin.

Flynn-Rogers and her companion looked up as Fey entered.

"Detective Croaker," Flynn-Rogers said, standing up and coming around the desk to offer her hand. "Let me apologize for my inexcusable behavior at the briefing this morning."

Yeah, right, Fey thought. However, she said, "Don't worry about it. This whole situation must have put you under a lot of stress."

Still holding Fey's hand, Flynn-Rogers turned to her other visitor. "This is my father, Luther Flynn."

"A pleasure, Detective Croaker. I hear very good things about you." The big man's voice was deep, matching his size.

"You must be talking to the wrong people," Fey said lightly. "I'm sorry we have to meet under these circumstances."

"We live in a violent society," Flynn said. "It touches all of us."

So much for familial sorrow, Fey thought.

"Have you made any progress since this morning's briefing?" Cecily Flynn-Rogers asked.

"Inquiries are proceeding as rapidly as possible," Fey said, meaning *not much*. "I've just come from interviewing your sister's estranged husband. He told me about Bianca violating the court order to share jurisdiction of their children. He also seems to think somebody tortured her to get information about other children Bianca was helping to hide."

"A smoke screen to remove himself from the top of the suspect list," Cecily said, some of her earlier fury reemerging.

"Possibly," Fey agreed.

"Now, Cecily." Luther Flynn stepped in. "I think you're being totally unrealistic. There's no evidence against Mark."

"I heard what Sarah told Bianca."

"You heard what Bianca force-fed Sarah. We've had professionals testify Bianca was acting out, completing a cycle. She was obsessed."

Fey didn't want to referee an episode of *Family Feud* between the Flynns. Interjecting herself, she asked Cecily, "What did you hear Sarah tell Bianca?"

Fey watched as Cecily fought not to look toward her father. "Sarah told us what that pervert she is forced to call a father did. There is no doubt in my mind Mark Ritter was molesting his children."

"Both of them?"

"Yes."

"I didn't think Mark Junior made any disclosures of abuse."

"Boys don't," Cecily said. "It's much harder for them."

Fey didn't buy into that theory, but she kept her own counsel. "What exactly did Sarah allege?"

A look of vast distaste crossed over Cecily's features. "It was disgusting. She said her father was rubbing her private parts and sticking his finger in her anus."

"By private parts, I assume you mean her vagina?"

"Yes." Cecily spat the word out as if she'd bitten into a chocolate with a soft center she didn't like.

"Was there any medical evidence?"

"The doctor noted fissures and redness in Sarah's anus."

Fey nodded. "But Sarah was four, and the doctor wasn't able to state unequivocally that the fissures weren't caused by other factors, such as constipation, which is common in children of that age." It was a familiar story in child abuse cases.

Cecily grunted. "When the courts refused to block Mark's access to the children, Bianca had no choice but to do what she did."

"Do you know where Sarah and Mark Junior are?" Fey asked.

"No." Cecily was emphatic. "Bianca wouldn't tell me. She was petrified of Mark. She wouldn't tell anyone where the children were in case he found out. A secret is no longer a secret when another person knows."

Fey turned her head toward Luther Flynn. "Mark Ritter also told me Bianca made allegations against you when she was a child."

Luther sighed. "My daughter Bianca and I were never close. I have tried to support her over the years, but she always made it difficult. I'm sure you're aware Mark Ritter is a partner in my law firm. He was struggling in his own practice, and I thought bringing him into the fold would help both him and Bianca. Don't get me wrong—Mark is a good lawyer with a good future. I'm sure he told you about Bianca's delusions, knowing you would find out anyway and you would be suspicious of why you weren't told up front." Luther shifted his weight to rest a haunch on a corner of Cecily's desk.

"In 1969, my wife, Mavis, was murdered by her cousin, Eldon Dodge." Luther's voice had taken on a storytelling tone. "We were estranged after she found out about an affair I was having. She went to live with Dodge as he was the only family she had in the area. Mavis was a spiteful woman, however, and claiming sexual abuse of children in order to keep custody is nothing new, as I'm sure you know. Mavis fabricated stories of abuse, but Bianca never made any disclosures because there was nothing to disclose." He sighed again as if the telling was a burden.

"The whole situation ended tragically. Dodge was a radical, a Black Panther whom the FBI was investigating for committing an armored-car robbery in which two security officers were killed. When the police went to get my children back from Mavis, in compliance with my court-ordered rights, Eldon thought they were coming for him. He tried using my Mavis as a human shield, but when he started shooting he hit her in the back of the head."

"A smoking gun case," Fey said without irony.

"Yes." Luther Flynn nodded. "The only good things to Come out of the situation were that Eldon Dodge was sent to death row—where he is still awaiting execution—and my children were returned to me." He reached out a hand and stroked Cecily's hair as if she were suddenly five years old again. Cecily turned into his semi-embrace and kissed her father's hand.

"It was an ugly and tragic time for me, but it is all in the past," Flynn said. "It has no bearing on anything except as it speaks to Bianca's frame of mind. Mavis could have had no idea of the damage she was doing to Bianca by instilling in her the images of abuse she wanted Bianca to spout against me. It unfortunately formed the background of my daughter's whole life—it became her cause célèbre and has led to nothing but further tragedy."

To Fey, the speech seemed well prepared. Was it Luther throwing up a smoke screen to hide something, or was he truly reflecting on a tragedy with no bearing on the present except as it affected Bianca Flynn's state of mind? Fey mentally shook off the thought.

Mavis Flynn was murdered thirty years ago. Bianca had been eight, Cecily five; Fey herself had been a teen. How could there possibly be any tangible connection to the present?

"Tell me, Detective Croaker," Luther Flynn continued, "was your father on the job?"

Fey frowned. "Yes. Why do you ask?"

"How odd. If I remember correctly, Croaker was the name of the policeman who arrested Eldon Dodge for my wife's murder."

13

FEY STRUGGLED to avoid all expression. She knew about the children of silence, and the lack of attention authorities and parents had paid to allegations of incest thirty years earlier. She knew because of her father.

Bringing Garth Croaker's name into the interview immediately turned Fey against Luther Flynn. She was ready to believe anything about him that was even rumored to be true. At least Mavis Flynn had made an effort to save her daughters from abuse. Fey's mother hadn't even tried. It just wasn't done.

Fey fought to remain professional. She had to handle this like any other case—she must be objective. Yeah, right, she thought again.

She was back in the muck. All murders were sordid, but how was it she always ended up with the battered and the molested?

Fey mentally replayed Luther Flynn's mention of her father. Had Flynn been watching for a reaction? Had he been probing to see if she knew something? And if there was something to know, what was it?

Fey answered Flynn's statement as evenly as she could manage. "Really? Well, that would be a coincidence." But she didn't believe in coincidence. Fate, kismet, double-damned-crap-awful luck, maybe—but not coincidence.

Life had symmetry. All things were connected. Fey knew she couldn't escape her past no matter how far, or how hard, she ran. She had become a cop to confront her past, but even then she had spent the best part of her career avoiding it.

Now it appeared to have caught her.

Fey directed her attention to Cecily. "I'd like to get access to your sister's residence. I can obtain a search warrant, of course, but if you or your father now have dominion over the location, it would be easiest if you would give us permission."

Cecily puckered her lips. "I'm afraid neither my father nor I can grant you such permission."

"Excuse me?"

Luther Flynn waved a hand. "We're not being obstructive, Detective. We wish to cooperate in any way we can. We simply can't give you permission to search because Bianca was living with another woman, Ferris Jackson. The residence belongs to Jackson."

Fey sighed. A warrant would be necessary if Jackson would not cooperate.

FEY LEFT Cecily's office and called Monk on her cell phone. "Something doesn't ring true in all of this," she said after filling him in on the interview. "They're all blowing smoke up my ass."

"Kinky," Monk said.

"Shut up," Fey said with a chuckle. "Any word from the dynamic duo?"

Monk knew Fey was referring to Hammer and Nails. "Not yet. Do you want me to leash them in?"

"You ask that like it was a possibility. No, better to let them run. What's on your agenda?"

"I'm working with Alphabet and Brindle on the names of the disgruntled parents you got from Mark Ritter."

"Let them keep digging, but you switch to Ferris Jackson, Bianca's roommate. Get a warrant for Bianca's phone records. To be safe, let's also get a warrant for the residence she shared with Jackson."

"When do you want to see her?"

"Tomorrow morning. We'll serve the search warrant at the same time."

"Where can I reach you?"

"I'll be on the mobile. I have to follow my nose on something."

"Don't get it slapped with a newspaper."

"Now *that's* kinky," Fey said and hung up.

With the major parts of the investigation in hand for the moment, she felt easier about following another direction.

If her father had arrested Eldon Dodge for Mavis Flynn's murder in 1969, Jack Kavanaugh would have been his partner at the time. Surely Kavanaugh's odd death was not connected with Bianca Flynn's murder, but there the two deaths were, teasing Fey to prove they were related.

Thirty years ago Mavis Flynn, mother of Bianca Flynn, was murdered by Eldon Dodge. Thirty years ago, Jack Kavanaugh, partner of the man who arrested Dodge, had stashed two hundred and fifty thousand dollars in a lawyer's office. Where did coincidence stop and inevitability begin?

In the new Chevy Cavalier detective sedan she'd been issued through RHD, Fey drove the few short blocks to the law firm of Alexander and Kelly. On the way, she took out her cell phone again and dialed a number from memory.

"Is that you, Tucker?" she asked when a male voice answered

the ringing at the other end. "Still playing mix-and-match with the primary colors in your fashion wardrobe?"

"Hey, Frog Lady," Zelman Tucker crackled back at Fey. "I figured you were too important now you're a big-time Robbery-Homicide dick to be talking to the likes of me, a humble journalist toiling tirelessly in the pursuit of truth."

"Give it a rest, Tucker. You don't even know how to spell *humble*, and the only thing you're in pursuit of is your next headline."

"You wound me."

"Not possible. How'd you hear about the RHD switch already?"

"Now, that really does hurt. I always have my sources. The least you could have done was call to tell me the good news."

"How do you know I'm not doing so now?"

"Because you never call me unless you want something."

"Okay, I give up. But you can't say it's never to your advantage."

Zelman Tucker was born to be a scandalmonger. He'd parlayed his natural talents as a digger of the dirtiest dirt into a career with *The American Inquirer*, a tabloid trash magazine where Tucker had broken more real stories than *The Washington Post*.

Fey had met Tucker through Ash. Tucker had written several true-crime books based on Ash's cases, and had gone on to write a bestseller about the case Ash and Fey had worked together.

Tucker was now an established literary icon, but in his heart he was still a scandalmonger. He loved the sleaze and had more contacts in odd places than the intelligence apparatus of a small country.

Tucker chuckled. "You have something new for me?"

"Not yet," Fey told him. "Maybe later. Right now I need you to punch into sleaze mode and dig out everything you can on Luther Flynn." She knew she was grinding a personal ax, but she didn't care.

"Judge Luther Flynn?"

"As ever was."

"Oooh, I can smell this one coming." Tucker sounded excited.

"I want everything, Tucker—the dirtier the better."

"Gloves off?"

"Gloves off," Fey agreed. "No rules."

"Could run into money."

"You're rich."

"I get the full story later?"

"Have I ever let you down?"

"Good enough. When do you want this?"

"Yesterday," Fey said and hung up as she pulled into Alexander and Kelly's parking lot.

The original figurehead, Robbie Alexander, was long since retired, and the original Kelly had passed on. His son, Scott Kelly, however, welcomed Fey into his office with genuine interest.

"We keep things simple around here," Kelly said, indicating the plain but comfortable office decor by a circular gesture of his hand. "My father always drilled into the staff that the work was important, not the surroundings." He smiled. "Since most cops don't like lawyers, we don't want them to feel we're inaccessible—not all high-and-mighty."

Fey wondered if the frankness was another fabricated technique to put cops at their ease. "I've seen your ads in *The Blue Line*."

"Ninety-five percent of our business is law enforcement related. Both my father and Robbie Alexander, the firm's other original founder, were on the job before passing the bar. Their original goal of working within the law-enforcement community is a tradition we obviously still follow."

The guy's got a nice smile, Fey thought, but he's a lawyer—always has to lecture instead of converse.

"I understand you recently executed the will of a retired officer by the name of Ellis Jack Kavanaugh."

"Yes," Kelly said. "I didn't handle it personally, but I saw the paperwork. Fortunately, it was all very simple and straightforward."

Legalese for *easy money.*

"If I can, I'd like to view a copy of the will and also know if there was any next of kin," Fey said.

"I don't see a problem. As far as I know, the will has been fully discharged. Let me get the file."

Kelly left Fey in his office for the few minutes it took him to get the appropriate paperwork. While he was gone, she looked around at the plaques on the wall—Kiwanis, Rotary, Chamber of Commerce. There were appreciations from the Police Protective League and other law-enforcement–related organizations. The guy was a regular Conan the Rotarian.

Fey knew all of it would drive her crazy. Glad-handing, rubber chicken dinners, chasing business, fighting with other lawyers, talking lawyerspeak, fancy suits, politics—all for what?

As far as she was concerned, putting villains in jail was what her job was about. If she couldn't do that, her life wouldn't mean much to her. All of this other law-enforcement–related crap was just so much garbage. Half the kids wearing a badge today were nothing more than glorified security guards—wouldn't know an observation arrest if it came up and hopped into the back of their police car. If you ran around the fringes of the job and weren't even wearing a badge, then you were the worst kind of wanna-be. You were either on the job or you weren't. It was that easy. *Them versus us.*

Fey mentally smirked at herself. She was becoming a curmudgeon.

Kelly came back into the room carrying a buff-colored folder. He wore reading glasses and was studiously turning pages as he walked.

"There doesn't seem to be much here. I understand Mr. Kavanaugh had sunk into a state of mental confusion before dying—very unfortunate. The estate wasn't very large. There were the contents of a small apartment left to a son and daughter, and that was about it, except for a codicil fulfilled by another firm."

"I'm familiar with the codicil," Fey said. "It's part of the reason I'm here. There was nothing else beyond the apartment contents? No other assets that were left to his children?"

"Not that I can see. Do you want an address for his son, Brink Kavanaugh? He was the coexecutor of the will."

"That would be great."

Kelly gave Fey a speculative look. "Are you familiar with Brink Kavanaugh?"

"Should I be?"

"Not necessarily, but I think you'll find him quite a character."

14

HAMMER AND NAILS sat watching the exterior of the murder scene warehouse. They were in Hammer's personal black van eating Taco Bell and drinking cold coffee. The van was parked in an alley, its flat nose barely visible from the street in the deepening twilight.

Through the van's windows, they could observe the warehouse, the street in front of it, and the alley on the south side. They had chosen their position carefully, wanting to be able to see the warehouse Dumpsters.

There were other warehouses nearby, along with a row of grungy shop fronts. The shops were a blend of periphery businesses—a liquor store, a small market with Persian hieroglyphics marking the windows, a movie poster and memorabilia store, a foreign-language video rental and music outlet, a head shop, and an adult arcade. The fronts of several of the warehouses had been opened to display goods that had most likely fallen off the back of a truck sometime the night before.

The rest of the neighborhood was a mishmash of decaying apartments housing prostitutes, WAMs (waiter/actor/models), and aspiring screenwriters. The run-down glamour of Hollywood Boulevard was only a block or two away, but nobody in this community was ever going to get a star on the Walk of Fame.

All of this was mildly interesting and provided for a certain amount of foot traffic, but after four hours there was nothing that promised to provide a clue to Bianca Flynn's murder.

Aside from the occasional customer for the stores, there were a number of winos sitting on the curb and around a small wooden table outside of the market. None of them appeared interested in the warehouse.

Flipping through a book of I-cards, Rhonda tried to match up the physical descriptions and the bad Polaroid photos stapled to the investigator cards with the homeless/semihomeless population roaming the street. The book had been supplied by the Hollywood Area Transient Detail, threatening the death penalty if Hammer and Nails did not return it.

"Here's a winner," she said, holding a card for Hammer to see. "I think it's the guy over near the lamp standard."

Hammer glanced at the description. "It says he has AIDS, hepatitis, and herpes. If we have to arrest him, you're doing the search."

Rhonda turned the card back toward herself. "It also says he has a ring through his penis, and two others through his nipples."

"Ouch!"

"Personally, I think body piercing is a good idea. It gives the rest of us fair warning that somebody is seriously deranged."

"And how many holes do you have in your earlobes now?"

Rhonda threw a tortilla chip at her partner. "Shut up."

Hammer sat up quickly in the van's driver's seat. "This might be something," he said. Rhonda followed his gaze.

The duo were used to long stakeouts—part of their reputation came from their patience—but it was nice when the effort paid off. As they watched a woman approaching the Dumpster across the street, Hammer felt his energy level kick in.

The woman was one of the many homeless or transient types who followed the same rounds day after day, checking the same Dumpsters and alleys for the substance of bare survival. Aluminum cans, bottles, and anything recyclable often provided a thin protection from starvation. Rotting food, newspapers, short-dogs, and stubbies were luxuries.

Scavaging, fighting street predators, making troubled brains function just enough to get through one day to the next was damned hard work. Maybe the hardest work there was.

Hammer and Nails watched as the woman, wrapped in numerous layers of deteriorating clothing and wearing a silver Dolly Parton wig, pushed a two-wheeled cart along to the Dumpster beside the crime scene warehouse. She went up on tiptoe to look over the edge of the metal receptacle.

"Got her," Rhonda said, sliding an I-card out of the transient book. "Willetta Rendell. She usually stays in a women's shelter a few blocks north of here on Gower. She's listed as bipolar/manic-depressive. The notation says she's friendly enough if she's taken her meds."

"We couldn't be that lucky," Hammer said. He opened the van door and slid casually to the ground. Rhonda followed him out as her door was too close to the alley wall.

They had already talked to a half dozen street people who had cruised close to the crime scene warehouse. None of the contacts had proved of any value, and they were starting to get discouraged. They were tired and bored. Perseverance was a virtue, but there was a limit.

Willetta didn't see them crossing the street, but as soon as they entered the mouth of the alley, she turned as if scalded.

"Get away from me!" she yelled. "I got AIDS and I'll bite you!"

Hammer stopped his approach with Nails behind him. He

flexed his knees and crouched down, his back straight. "It's okay, Willetta," he said calmly. "We're not going to hurt you. We just want to talk." He had crouched to make himself smaller, less of a threat.

"I don't want to talk. I'll bite you!"

"Do you know Officer Heising?" Heising was one of the Transient Detail officers. "I work with him." Hammer held out his badge. "I'm Detective Hammersmith, and this is my partner, Detective Lawless." Hammer kept his voice even, almost singsong. Rhonda had always been impressed by Hammer's ability to almost hypnotize suspects and witnesses simply by using voice inflection. It was a tool developed through years of experience, and it often saved wear and tear on bodies and clothing. It was far better to talk somebody to jail than fight them into a cell.

In this instance, however, it didn't appear to be working.

"I'll bite you!" Willetta said again and pushed her cart behind her.

Rhonda wondered how many times this woman had been a victim, how many times had she used this empty threat. The woman was in no shape to ward off an attack from any kind of determined aggressor.

"Do you know Miss Susie at the shelter?" Rhonda asked. She had stepped past Hammer to make herself the focus.

"What if I do?"

"I know her, too," Rhonda said. "She's a friend of ours. She'll tell you we don't want to hurt you."

Willetta appeared to consider. "What do you want?"

"Just to talk."

"Are you going to take me to jail?"

"No. I promise you, we just want to talk."

"Do you have any cigarettes?"

"We'll get you some from the liquor store," Rhonda said, continuing to take the lead in the interview.

Hammer slowly came up from his crouch. He casually side-stepped out of Willetta's direct line of sight, leaving Nails in the spotlight.

"Why don't you go down to the liquor store and get Willetta some cigarettes?" Rhonda said to her partner.

"And a bottle of Jack," Willetta said, pushing her luck. "Big bottle."

"Be right back," Hammer told the pair. "You two go on getting acquainted."

As he moved away, he heard Willetta calling after him. "Get Camels. Don't you be bringing back no filtered crap."

Hammer was only gone a short while, but in that time Rhonda had established a tentative rapport with Willetta. The two were now sitting on the ground by Hammer's van, talking. Willetta was going through the contents of her two-wheeled cart. Scraps of blankets and newspaper were scattered around her, along with crushed cans and various unidentified bits and pieces.

Willetta looked up when Hammer came back, withdrawing defensively.

"It's okay," Hammer told her, crouching down again. "I've brought your cigarettes." He held out a pack of Camels.

Willetta reached out and grabbed the pack, hiding it in the folds of her clothing. "What about the Jack?"

Hammer displayed a quart bottle of Jack Daniel's. "If you can help us, it's yours."

Willetta looked at the bottle and licked her lips. "I don't got much, but what I got is worth a lot. Isn't it?"

"We don't know," Rhonda told her. "It depends on what you have."

"I got a hubcap." Willetta pulled a battered round of metal from the interior of her cart. "Give me the Jack." She held out her hand.

"We don't want the hubcap," Hammer said.

Willetta appealed to Rhonda. "You said I could have the Jack if I gave you what I got."

Rhonda shook her head. "I said you could have it if you gave us what we wanted—tools, any kind of tools you may have found on your rounds."

"This is a tool," Willetta said. She thrust the hubcap out toward them.

"No. That's a hubcap," Hammer said.

"It's a tool," Willetta said angrily. "I'll bite you!"

"Easy, Willetta," Rhonda said. "It might be a tool, but it's not the type of tool we want."

"What kind do you want?"

"We're looking for a staple gun or a small saw."

"Don't got no gun. Give me the Jack."

"Not a gun, Willetta. We're looking for a big stapler."

Willetta looked back and forth between the two detectives. "You going to take me to jail?"

"No, Willetta. We just want to help you. You can go back to the shelter anytime you want. Miss Susie will keep you safe."

"Yeah, she's good at that, Miss Susie. Don't let nobody mess with you or take your stuff while you're asleep." Willetta agreed vigorously. A sly look then came over her face. "You got any money?"

"Willetta . . ."

"You want something, you got to pay for it. They always tell me that at the store."

"Okay," Rhonda said. "What have you got?" It was clear this was the road Willetta had been taking them down from the beginning.

"Twenty bucks," Willetta said.

"Ten," Hammer said.

"Twenty! And the Jack! I'll bite you!" She bared decaying incisors and made a gnashing sound in the back of her throat.

Rhonda put her hand out to touch Hammer. "Twenty," she said. If there was something here, it was worth twenty. And the Jack.

Rummaging around in her clothing, Willetta pulled out a rectangular, three-quarter-inch-thick metal object with a hole for fingers and a lever on the top. "Stapler gun," she said. "Give me the Jack. I'll bite you!"

15

"WHAT THE HELL are you doing here? You're early. You know I'm still working. Why didn't you use your key?"

Fey was surprised by the words, as they didn't make much sense. The metal door she'd knocked on was set into a larger warehouse roll-up door. It had been flung open by a giant of a man. He was over six-foot-four and wore nothing but a pair of nylon running shorts almost hidden by a leather tool belt. He had meaty shoulders and a barrel chest covered with broad pectorals and matted hair. He looked like an angry bear disturbed from hibernation. He rudely turned to walk away from the door, leaving it open.

"Excuse me," Fey said, still not understanding his reaction. "Are you Brink Kavanaugh?"

The giant whirled around in surprise at her voice, his eyes taking Fey in as if for the first time. He was about her age. The crow's-feet surrounding his eyes spoke of independent character and too much time spent in the sun. The scent of fresh sweat and musk came off him in waves of animal heat. In one hand he held a short-handled mallet, in the other, a large, razor-sharp steel chisel.

He wiped a forearm across his grit-powdered brow, the muscles in his shoulder and biceps rippling. "I'll be damned," he said, and then appeared to catch himself and come back to planet Earth. "I'm sorry. I thought you were somebody else." His voice was deep and raspy, and the wide, reckless grin of a born rogue dimpled his cheeks and tightened the cleft in his chin.

"Come in if you want, but you'll have to wait," he said. "The rock is ready." He gestured wildly with the chisel, as if that were explanation enough, and stomped away.

Curiouser and curiouser, Fey thought. This guy might not be the White Rabbit, but I'm beginning to feel a lot like Alice.

The address Fey had been given for Brink Kavanaugh was centered in a strip of renovated buildings in the heart of Santa Monica. Commercial premises fronted the buildings at street level, with living quarters or offices above.

Unlike the dismal and dilapidated area surrounding the warehouse where Bianca Flynn had been murdered, the properties in Santa Monica were referred to in real estate brochures as bohemian or eclectic. The artists and craftspeople who made a home for themselves in the area were impoverished, but they weren't starving. There was hope here, along with the promise of prosperity—a stop on the way up, not on the way down.

Entering Brink Kavanaugh's domain, Fey was unprepared for the sight that presented itself to her. The small warehouse was filled with the light and shadows created by a bank of high windows running across the rear brick wall. In the middle of the floor, a large sandpit was contained within a framework of railroad ties. In the middle of the sand stood a monstrous chunk of granite.

Wide at the base and tapering up, the rock was ten feet tall, almost reaching to the high ceiling that marked the start of the warehouse's second floor. The granite was so large in circumference, a small car could have been hidden behind it. It was a mountain growing in the middle of the building.

Kavanaugh stood before the monolith in worship, arms extended, mallet and chisel held in either hand. Natural sunlight tempered the scene. Dust motes moved languidly within the streams of light, and shadows thrown by the rock made eerie pockets of nothingness.

Kavanaugh was no longer aware of her presence, no longer aware of anything except the rock. His long hair was pulled back with a leather thong, the resulting ponytail cascading down between his shoulder blades. He brought his hands together in front of him, the muscles in his back glistening with sweat, fighting one another for prominent definition.

"Magnificent," Fey exclaimed involuntarily. With breath caught in her throat, she had no idea if she was referring to the rock or Kavanaugh—or perhaps they were inseparable.

Keeping his tools grasped in the crooks of his thumbs, Kavanaugh reached out and ran his fingers along the granite. He was humming gently, communing with the stone.

With abrupt decisiveness, he climbed up a short pile of railway ties at the base of the rock. He ran the fingertips of his left hand across a crease near the top of the rock, steadied the cutting edge of the chisel where his fingers had touched, and smashed the mallet down onto the chisel, a prehistoric roar escaping from inside him.

For a second nothing happened, then there was a cracking and scraping noise, and a large chunk of the rock slipped away and crashed to the floor. In its passing, it left a smooth curve that somehow looked almost human.

Kavanaugh was suddenly a man possessed. With incredible

speed, he wielded the mallet and chisel to pare away more stone. Two more huge chunks dropped away, diminishing the rock in size but enlarging it in grandeur. Other smaller bits were splintered and knocked away in the cloud of stone dust raised by Kavanaugh's activity.

When he finally stepped back from the stone with a sigh, there was still no immediately identifiable shape to the stone, but there was something there, something emerging from the rock womb.

"Ah, well," Kavanaugh said, his voice even raspier than before, dry and filled with satisfaction and granite dust. "There's a start for you. The first cut is always the hardest. Once it's struck it defines the entire piece. Hit it wrong and you can lose the whole rock."

Fey had been awed by the performance. She scrambled for something—anything—to say. "Do you lose many rocks?"

Kavanaugh turned toward her and shrugged. He resurrected his piratical grin. "One or two. One or two. Can't afford to do it often. Never be able to earn a crust that way."

Fey stared at Brink, trying to see the thin, anemic-looking man she remembered as Jack Kavanaugh in the giant of a man who was the son. It was difficult, if not impossible.

"That was amazing," she said eventually. "The first time I've ever seen anything like it."

"I know what you mean," Kavanaugh said. "The first time I saw somebody strike a stone, I was dumbfounded. It was my father. He worked on a much smaller scale as a hobby, but he was very good. He made me a stone frog, not detailed, you understand, more of an Impressionist version of a frog. He took a stone the size of two fists and with his tools he cut away everything that wasn't a frog. What was left was still a rock, but it was also a frog. I was amazed and enthralled, and I loved that frog more than any stuffed toy. Since then, I've wanted to do nothing else, and now I don't."

Fey stared at the rock. "You do this for a living?" For some reason she felt as if she had observed a once-in-a-lifetime experience.

Kavanaugh's laugh was rich and fruity, echoing in the warehouse. "Every day. No different than a carpenter or a bricklayer."

"Jeez." The inarticulate comment seemed inadequate, but Fey didn't know what to say to capture her feelings. "What is it going to be?"

Kavanaugh ran a hand over an emerging curve in the rock. "What does it look like?"

His question was casual, but Fey sensed she was being tested.

She reflected, taking a few steps to view the rock from another angle.

"Don't think about it," Kavanaugh said abruptly. "Tell me what it makes you feel."

"Confused," Fey replied instantly. Then, "Three figures! I see three figures." The shapes had suddenly coalesced in her mind's eye.

"Good," Kavanaugh told her with a smile.

"I'm right?" Fey smiled back, delighted.

"No." Kavanaugh laughed as Fey's expression fell. "But it doesn't matter. The rock reaches everyone differently. If you were a sculptor, you would sing differently to the stone."

Fey looked back at the rock. "Are you sure there aren't three figures?"

Kavanaugh shook his head. "Only two. Lovers. One is leaving the other. This is their final embrace."

Fey scowled. "How do you know?"

"I feel it here," Kavanaugh said, pointing to the middle of his chest. "And I know it here." He pointed to his head.

They both stared at the rock in silence.

Finally, Kavanaugh asked Fey why she was there. The question caught her off guard. Kavanaugh's initial off-the-wall reaction to her, the emotions stirred in her while watching him work the rock, and talking about the transforming stone had almost made her forget her purpose.

"I don't quite know where to start anymore," she said. "My name is Fey Croaker. I'm a lieutenant with the LAPD." She still wasn't comfortable describing herself by that rank. "My father, Garth Croaker, used to be your father's partner."

Kavanaugh's face clouded over. "My father is dead."

Fey shook her head. "Yes." She almost stammered. "Yes. I know. I'm . . . I'm sorry. Look, I don't know exactly why I'm here or what I want, but if you can give me a few minutes of your time, I'll try and untie my tongue long enough to explain."

Kavanaugh appeared to accept her rambling and put a smile back on his face. "Come upstairs," he said. "Let me shower this damnable dust off, and we can have a real drink."

"Great," Fey said and began to follow Kavanaugh toward a wooden stairway leading up to a second floor. She swallowed. The strong scent of the man was deep in her nostrils. What she had really wanted to say was "To hell with showering off the dust! Take me right here, right now, and take me hard."

"I WAS never close to my father," Kavanaugh said, rubbing his hair dry with a fluffy white towel. He had given Fey coffee laced with a heavy dollop of Irish whiskey to occupy her while he showered. Now, wearing a pressed white T-shirt and old jeans resting loosely on his hips, he tossed the towel over the back of a chair and used the leather thong to tie his hair back again.

"He was always a secretive person," Kavanaugh continued. "In the past year, he'd become worse. I only saw him twice in the last couple of months—when he needed money—and on both occasions it was clear he was slipping into dementia."

Fey let Kavanaugh fill her coffee cup again. "There was nothing you could do for him?"

Kavanaugh shook his head and grimaced. "Not for *my* father. Don't think I didn't try. But he wouldn't have any of it."

"What about your mother?"

"She's in a retirement home. Still has most of her marbles, thankfully, but she needs someone to look after her. I'm afraid I'm not that responsible—never grew up." He gestured vaguely to his hair and to his surroundings.

Fey smiled. "Men will be boys?"

"At least I admit it—forty-five going on twenty-five. Younger women, older whiskey, faster cars."

Fey laughed this time. "Bullshit," she said.

Kavanaugh mugged with his eyebrows. "Hey, I can dream."

"Are those what you really want?"

Kavanaugh appeared to think. "Older whiskey and faster cars maybe, but I like being able to talk to a woman after making love—something the young ones don't know anything about."

I do! I do! Fey wanted to shout, her hormones raging. Instead she said, "Were your parents still married?"

Kavanaugh refreshed Fey's Irish coffee and cracked an icy beer open for himself. "Good grief, no. Mother divorced him when I was thirteen and Jenna, my sister, was eight. Mother couldn't take the police work any longer. My father was obsessed with it—like your father."

"You remember my father?"

"Sure. When he was partners with Dad, he'd pick Dad up every day. He'd play with me and Jenna—nothing much. Toss a ball around, roughhouse wrestling. He was an okay guy. He treated Mom okay. Looking back, I get the feeling he was maybe treating her a little too nice, but I was just a kid then and didn't know any better."

Fey tried to swallow the lump blocking her throat. Her father had never played with her or her brother, Tommy. The thought that he played with somebody else's kids while beating the crap out of his own made her feel dizzy. What had she and Tommy ever done to him to make him hate them so much?

Kavanaugh was watching Fey's eyes and saw his statements were having an unexpected impact. He sought firmer ground. "Why do you want to know about my father?"

The second floor comprised Kavanaugh's living quarters along with a small bathroom and a sectioned-off kitchen area big enough for one person to turn around in. The main part of the floor was a large, open space containing two comfortable chairs and a sofa gathered around an entertainment center, a double bed pushed into one corner, a heavy oak table, and a scattered collection of abstract sculptures.

Each of the sculptures was made from a different type of rock. All were about waist height and looked, in their scattered, arbitrary placing, like a ragged line of misshapen chess pawns. The effect was not unsettling, however, as the feeling they gave off was of powerful solidity. It did occur to Fey, though, that getting to the bathroom in the dark was probably hazardous.

"Were you aware your father left me something in his will?"

"I knew there was an odd codicil that was to be carried out by another law firm, but I didn't concern myself with it. I knew my father had nothing of value, and even if he did, I didn't want it. I let the other executor handle the details. Did the codicil pertain to you?"

Fey nodded. "You could say so. Your father left me something he'd lodged with the other law firm thirty years ago."

Kavanaugh shrugged. "So, what was it and why do you feel so guilty about it?"

Fey felt herself flush at Kavanaugh's obvious reading of her feelings.

"It was two hundred and fifty thousand dollars, and I have no idea why he left it to me."

Kavanaugh looked shocked. "Holy crow!"

"Exactly."

"My father never had that kind of money. He was always pushing to make ends meet."

"Then there had to be an awfully powerful reason why he never touched this money in all those years. I hoped you'd know something about it."

Kavanaugh shrugged again. "Beats me. But I'd never contest the money, if that's what you're worried about. I don't want it or need it."

"Must be nice—but, no, that's not what I was worried about. Are you sure you have no idea where the money came from or why your father would leave it to me?"

"Not a clue."

Drinking her coffee while Kavanaugh drained his first beer and started a second, Fey tried changing her approach. "Who did you think I was when you answered the door?"

Kavanaugh gave her a funny look. "I'm sorry about that. I really did think you were someone else at first."

"Who?"

As serendipity would have it, the pair heard the metal door downstairs opening. A woman's voice called out, "Hey, Brink!"

"Upstairs," Kavanaugh responded. "Come on up." His eyes stayed on Fey's face, making her uncomfortable.

"The rock looks marvelous," the woman's voice said, coming up the stairs.

As the physical presence materialized at the top of the stairs, Fey saw why Kavanaugh had thought she was someone else. Though the woman was a few years younger, her hair and facial structure was close to Fey's in appearance.

"Oh," the woman said, spotting Fey.

Kavanaugh looked over at her, his piratical grin in place. "My sister, Jenna," he said.

16

WILLETTA grabbed the bottle of Jack Daniel's, but Hammer made her wait for the twenty-dollar bill until she showed them where she'd found the staple gun. It was a Dumpster three blocks away from the crime scene warehouse. Flies buzzed over it, and putrid odors reeked from its crowded innards. It hadn't been emptied in several weeks.

Hammer made a face. "You wouldn't be putting us on, would you, Willetta? Are you sure this is the place?" He couldn't imagine anyone, not even a desperate homeless person, picking through the Dumpster's contents.

"This is the one," Willetta said. She'd been chain-smoking cigarettes since Hammer had bought them for her. Ash was scattered heavily across her clothing. "I check it every day. It's good for food."

Hammer stared at her in disbelief.

"Fish," Willetta said when she saw Hammer's look. She pointed down the street.

Several doors away, Hammer could see a Cap'n Bob's fish restaurant, a low-rent, fast-food franchise—ptomaine catfish being a specialty.

"They dump the overflow here. Stops their store smellin' when trash ain't been picked up and the fish rots. If you get it as soon as it's dumped, it ain't too bad. Found the nail gun in a bag on top."

Hammer looked at Nails and then back at the Dumpster.

"In a bag? Are you sure?" he asked again.

"I'll bite," Willetta said aggressively.

"Okay, okay." Hammer held up his hands. "I believe you."

"How do you want to play this?" Nails asked.

"Only one way to play it," Hammer told her, already feeling green. "We're going to have to go bin diving."

BOTH IN smell and texture, the viscous contents of the Dumpster were a match for the viscera left over after an autopsy. Even protected by disposable nylon coveralls, complete with face mask, booties, and shower cap, Hammer felt he was being contaminated beyond redemption. He wouldn't get the smell out of his nostrils for days.

The protective clothing had come from the crime scene kit in the back of Hammer's van. When blood was present at a murder location, the suits were worn against the threat of AIDS and other diseases. They were standard equipment in the modern age.

Wearing a similar rig, Rhonda stood outside of the Dumpster. She was using a long stick to stir through the contents Hammer tossed or poured over the side.

Several Hollywood-area uniformed patrol officers had closed off the area around the Dumpster and were keeping the looky-loos away while Hammer and Nails worked. Uniforms usually felt they got stuck with the dirty or menial jobs while detectives got the glory. However, none of the uniforms present wanted any part of the glory of this investigation.

Perched on a wooden crate near the Dumpster, Willetta alternately smoked, drank from the bourbon bottle, and looked like a self-satisfied queen. This was the best entertainment she'd had in ages.

"I'm going to reek of fish forever," Hammer said with disgust. He dumped a plastic bucket of rotting fillets over the side of the Dumpster. "Every stray cat in town is going to think I'm its new best friend."

"Quit whining," Rhonda told him as she stirred through the muck. "You're worse than an old woman."

"I suppose *eau de cod* is your favorite perfume."

"It kinda turns me on," Rhonda said.

"You're sick." Hammer dumped another bucket over the side.

"I thought you liked the smell of anchovies."

Hammer straightened up in the Dumpster. "How come you can make sexist jokes but I can't?"

"Because mine are funny."

"Do you want to climb in here and finish the job?"

"Not on your life," Rhonda said. "One of us has to be able to hold the baby when we go home."

Hammer grunted and returned to his labors.

The wet cardboard boxes, which had contained frozen fish fillets, rotting zucchini, and brown, chip-cut potatoes, had been easy enough, if messy, to remove from the Dumpster. So, too, the collection of other rubbish: broken plywood, various chunks of cement, black plastic bags of refuse from the fish shop and several other surrounding stores, and even two kitchen chairs and a smashed VCR. Once that had all been removed, what remained was a three-foot-deep glutinous mess of stinking, wet, almost unidentifiable debris—half-rotten food, a mishmash of disintegrating papers, and other putrefying items of garbage.

Hammer poured another bucket of slush over the side. Rhonda stuck her wooden stick in it and stirred it around.

"This is a waste of time," Hammer said, repeating the process.

"I think Willetta is putting us on, or maybe there's nothing else to find."

"Hold on," Rhonda said. She pulled something toward her with her stick. Using a gloved hand, she reached into the sludge and picked up a fine-tooth handsaw. "Bingo," she said.

Hammer was watching her over the rim of the Dumpster, excitement rising inside him. "What's that?" he asked, pointing.

"Where?"

"Near your foot—the bag with the red markings. I think I recognize the logo."

Rhonda bent down again and rescued an opaque plastic bag from the muck. She held it at arm's length. "Is this what you mean?"

"Yep." Hammer hoisted himself over the side of the Dumpster. He took the bag from Rhonda, shook it, and then smoothed it flat against the side of a wall. He showed it to Rhonda again.

She read the logo. "Dollar Hardware Emporium."

"Get your dollar's worth," Hammer said, reciting the well-known commercial jingle for the chain of Dollar Hardware Emporiums. Humming the annoying tune from the jingle, he opened the apparently empty bag and rummaged inside.

"Yes!" He pulled out a small rectangular piece of paper. "We are cooking with gas now."

Hammer's excitement was infectious. Rhonda snatched the paper from him and looked at it herself.

The computerized receipt was for the cash purchase of a handsaw, a vise, and a staple gun. It was dated the day of the murder.

THE NEAREST Dollar Hardware Emporium was ten blocks away. The manager, whose name tag read *Mr. Taylor*, confirmed the receipt was from his store.

Dollar Hardware Emporiums were the latest entry in the do-it-yourself superstore sweepstakes. The cavernous interior of the business was filled with everything a general contractor or a weekend handyman might need, priced to put traditional mom-and-pop hardware stores out of existence.

"Can you tell from the receipt what register the items were purchased through?"

Taylor nodded. "Sure. I can even tell you the clerk who handled the transaction."

Customers walking past the two detectives at the front of the store sniffed and turned to look around. Hammer and Nails tried to look innocent, but Taylor was blowing their cover by standing a pace or two back from them as if they might be contagious. He was trying to be polite, but he didn't even want to touch the receipt Hammer was proffering.

The duo had ditched the coveralls, deeming them as beyond reclamation. They had washed at a nearby service station, but the smell of rotting fish persisted.

Taylor adjusted a pair of thick glasses and took a step closer to look at the receipt. Hammer saw he was holding his breath.

"You'd never be able to handle a week-old stinker on the hottest day of the summer," Hammer said.

"What?" Taylor looked confused.

"Nothing. What about the clerk?"

Taylor squinted at the receipt before turning to punch numbers into a computer on the customer-service counter. A readout of the transaction, identified by the receipt number, jumped onto the screen.

Taylor put a finger on the screen and ran it across. He picked out an employee ID number, cleared the screen, brought up another format, and entered the new information. The screen flashed again, producing further data.

"Chandra Wellington. She handled the transaction."

"Is she here today?" Rhonda asked.

"Yeah. She's on register three."

"Can we talk to her?"

Taylor sent another clerk to relieve Chandra, who came over wearing a big, natural smile until she ran into the smell of rotting fish.

She made a face and waved a hand in front of her face. "Ewwwww. What's that smell?"

"You'll have to excuse my partner," Hammer said quickly before Rhonda could get in. "Clinical flatulence. It's a chronic personal problem."

"Gee, I'm sorry," Chandra said, looking at Rhonda as if she were terminally ill. "Must make it tough getting dates."

Hammer had to bite the inside of his cheeks, especially as the comment seemed to be made in all concerned seriousness.

"It's something I've learned to live with," Rhonda said. She elbowed Hammer hard, took the receipt from him, and held it out to Chandra. "I know you have a lot of customers, but do you remember the person who bought these items?"

Chandra looked at the receipt. She nodded her head. "Yeah. This was the last day I worked, and the guy bought this stuff just before I ended my shift. He was real cool-looking—buffed out with a crew cut and sunglasses." She took the receipt from Rhonda and looked at it more closely. "I asked him if he was in the movies—just kind of flirting, you know—and he said, yeah, he was a stuntman." She snorted. "I told him he was full of crap, but he said no way. I asked him what films he'd been in, and he reeled off a bunch of titles I never heard of before."

"Would you recognize him again?"

Chandra shrugged. "Maybe. What did he do?"

Rhonda was intense. They were on the edge of a break-through. She shook off Chandra's question and asked, "Would you help us try to put together a composite—a drawing—of the guy?"

Chandra looked riveted. "Sure. I'll try. Hey, this is just like in the movies, isn't it?"

"Yeah," Hammer told her, trying to contain his own excitement. "Brought to you in wide-screen Smell-O-Rama."

17

BRINK WAS the first to voice what moments before had been unthinkable for Fey or Jenna Kavanaugh to contemplate. Brink had an advantage. He knew his original response to Fey had been because of her resemblance to his sister. He'd had time to consider the implications of the intense physical similarities between the two women, time to see the significance.

"Looks as if somebody's momma wasn't exactly faithful to their daddy," he said, amused as the two women looked at each other.

"What are you talking about?" Jenna asked, obviously confused.

Kavanaugh made introductions. "Jenna, this is Fey Croaker. She's an LAPD detective. Her father was Dad's partner during his last years on the job. You probably remember him. He used to come by and play with us before driving Dad to work."

"So?"

"So?" Kavanaugh laughed. "So, look at the two of you!"

It was hard for the two women not to look at each other. Jenna

Kavanaugh was a few years younger, a few pounds lighter, had smoother skin, and a more prominent, sharper nose. Beyond those points, the women were remarkably similar—same hair color and wave, same body shape and size, hands and fingers the same, same high cheekbones and piercing eyes. Even the wry twist to their mouths was the same.

"This is too much," Jenna Kavanaugh said. "Who are you?"

Brink laughed.

"Fey. Fey Croaker. My father was Garth Croaker. I think he was also in the police academy with your dad in the late forties." Fey held out her hand. Jenna Kavanaugh took it and held it. The women continued to examine each other.

Jenna Kavanaugh finally broke the contact and turned to her brother. "Are you trying to tell me my father isn't my father?"

Kavanaugh shrugged. "Either that or her father isn't her father. The resemblance is too strong."

"No way," Jenna said, and turned to look at Fey again.

Fey felt the ground shifting beneath her. This wasn't possible. How could it be possible? Her only brother was dead. Her parents were dead. Ash was dead. She was an orphan. She didn't have anyone.

Didn't want anyone.

"Can I sit down?" Fey asked.

Brink took Fey's arm and led her to an armchair. She lowered herself into it.

"Don't let him screw with your mind," Jenna spoke up. "He's done that to me ever since we were kids."

Kavanaugh shrugged and sat down opposite Fey. "If you say so, sister dear. Just because you don't want to accept something doesn't mean it isn't true." He steepled his fingers and asked Fey, "Do you have any brothers or sisters?"

"A younger brother—Tommy. He's dead."

Kavanaugh raised his eyebrows.

Fey caught herself looking at the expression, looking at Kavanaugh's size from a different perspective. There was something there, or was there?

Kavanaugh seemed to read her mind. "Who knows?" he said. "Maybe we're also related."

"Don't even go there," Fey said. She thought about the erotic impulses she'd had watching Kavanaugh carve the stone. She couldn't feel that way about a half brother, could she?

"What did your brother look like?" Kavanaugh asked.

"Small, wiry," Fey said without thinking the statement through. Then she caught the insinuation. "Like your father."

Kavanaugh laughed again. "Well, what a little den of wife swapping we're conjuring up."

"Bullshit," Fey said. "This is ridiculous. So your sister and I look a little bit alike. What's the big deal?"

"A little bit alike?" Kavanaugh was incredulous. "That's the same as saying country music songs are only a little bit alike."

"They're not."

"Yeah, right. If you play any of them backward, you get your wife back, your dog back, your pickup truck back, and you get out of jail."

"I'm still confused," Jenna said. "Why did you come to see Brink?"

Fey explained about the codicil in Ellis Kavanaugh's will leaving her two hundred and fifty thousand dollars. "I didn't understand why," Fey said. "I want to know where the money came from and why it had been sitting in a lawyer's office for thirty years."

Kavanaugh and his sister looked at each other. "Any ideas?" he asked her.

"Daddy didn't have that kind of money," Jenna said. "If he did, he would have gambled it away."

"Where did Ellis live?" Fey asked.

Kavanaugh twitched his head, indicating a direction. "He had a crash pad in the Oakwood projects."

"You're kidding?" Oakwood was a notorious gang zone in LAPD's Pacific area. Fey knew there were a number of retired folks who also lived there, but not by choice. "Have you been there since Ellis died?"

Kavanaugh and Jenna shook their heads. "There's no reason to go there. It's a dive. A dump. He had nothing of value, couldn't have in that area. He lived on his pension—forty percent of his salary from thirty years ago after Mother gets half. I learned the hard way I couldn't give him money. He'd only gamble it away. It was an addiction. He couldn't stay away from the horses. He survived, nothing else."

"He'd become a nutcase," Jenna chimed in. "Our old man was over the edge. A conspiracy fanatic, part of the tinfoil-helmet brigade, thought there were X rays from outer space invading his brain."

"Shut up, Jenna." Kavanaugh showed his first flash of temper. "He wasn't that bad." It was an obvious sore point. Guilt got to everyone. So did the fear you would end up like your parents.

"Would you mind if I went and looked around?" Fey asked.

Kavanaugh and Jenna exchanged glances. "I think you're wasting your time, but sure, why not?" Kavanaugh said. "We'll come with you. I'd also like to know what Dad was doing with a spare two hundred and fifty grand lying around."

ELLIS KAVANAUGH'S apartment wasn't as bad as Fey had imagined, given the area and what Fey had been led to believe about the man.

In reality, Ellis was reasonably tidy. The cheap studio apartment in the run-down complex of stucco buildings was dank and nasty. Inside, Ellis's few clothes were folded, and everything was stored with almost military precision. Fey had seen the same kind of habits kept by ex-cons. It came from having so little in life that what you had became ornamental.

There were several bent but clean pots and pans on a counter near a hot plate. In the small bathroom there was a chipped sink containing a knife, a fork, and a spoon. The toilet next to the sink was clean but rust stained. A pile of racing pages sat on the floor.

The character of the main room came from the books. They were stacked everywhere, mostly paperbacks with lurid science fiction covers. The few hardbacks had no dustcovers and were scattered around without apparent pattern.

The room was dominated by a double bed and a battered armchair. A small black-and-white television sat on the floor next to a portable radio and a cheap VCR. All the comforts, Fey thought.

Driving with Jenna and Brink to the apartment, there had been no further speculation regarding parentage. Their talk had been general, a time period when strangers who have a token bond begin to explore the edges of their new relationship.

Parking in a battered asphalt lot outside the complex, Brink produced a key to Ellis's apartment and led the way inside. While Fey looked through the books and paltry possessions, Brink and Jenna appeared to be in a trance. Their father was only recently dead, and it was clear his passing had affected them in ways they were still discovering.

Fey walked slowly around the room. A row of framed photographs along a built-in counter showed Brink and Jenna in various stages of growing up. Propped against the wall was a shadow box. Mounted inside were Ellis Kavanaugh's service revolver, police whistle, hat badge, service pins, and other memorabilia. Fey stared at the box. She had seen enough of them over the years, but there was something missing from this one. What was it?

There was no badge, but that was normal. Until recently, the department insisted badges were the property of the city and were to be returned at the end of employment. Many officers "lost" their badges shortly before retirement, but they still didn't show up in shadow boxes, as you couldn't display what was either lost or—if found and not returned—stolen.

If not the badge, then what? Fey stared at the box, not knowing why she felt it was important.

Jenna moved to sit on the bed, picking up her father's pillow and hugging it to her chest. She let out a sigh that was not quite a sob, no tears but an exhalation of grief. Fey turned to look at her.

"That's it," she said, snapping her fingers.

Brink and Jenna looked at Fey to see what she was talking about.

"There," Fey said, pointing to where Ellis's pillow had been. She reached over and snagged what appeared to be a slender piece of old-fashioned brass about four inches long. "It's a call box key." She held it out. "It should have been in his shadow box."

"A call box key?" Jenna asked, surprised.

"For a police telephone call box," Fey told her. "Years ago, when I first came on the job, before communications became computerized, there was a call box system throughout the city. They were all painted blue with a logo of a phone and a lightning bolt on the front."

"Yeah," Brink said. "I remember the key hanging from Dad's uniform belt."

"They issued the keys in the academy," Fey said. "But the phones have long since been done away with. The call boxes have become collector's items. They were notorious hiding places for bottles of booze, throw-down guns, and other illicit property. The keys were generic. They fit all the boxes." Fey tossed the key up and down in her hand. "The call box system was almost out of use when I came on the job. I don't think there's any around anymore, certainly none in working order. I wonder what made him treat this as special?"

"You can't think it's special because it was under his pillow," Brink said. "I hate to admit it, but Jenna's right. Dad wasn't together mentally. There was probably no logical reason for him to put the key there. It must have been something that only made sense in his mind. He was obsessive about inconsequential things."

"I don't know," Fey said skeptically. "Everything in this room except for the books is in its proper place. Maybe the key was as well."

A title of a book on the edge of the armchair caught Fey's eye. *Sexual Abuse of Children.* It was a standard tome used by sex-crimes detectives. Fey picked it up and saw Ellis had highlighted passages throughout the text.

She rummaged around in the pile of books next to the arm-chair and found they were almost all books on child abuse, sexual molestation, and dissertations on the effects of child pornography. Two in particular had been extensively highlighted: *Children of the Silence* and *Hidden Rage.*

The former was an exposé of organized trips to Thailand for those interested in sex with children. The latter was a small-press publication instructing parents what to do when they believed their children were being molested and the traditional courts of resort wouldn't, or couldn't, do anything.

Fey flipped through the first book and found a surprise. Inserted between the pages were two photographs. The first was a police academy class graduation photo from 1948. Fey picked out her father and Ellis with help from the second photo, a shot of newly minted officers Ellis Kavanaugh and Garth Croaker with their arms around each other's shoulders.

Fey took a shallow breath.

Not wanting to go where her memories were taking her, Fey began to leaf through the second book and found an even bigger surprise. In the text, Bianca Flynn had been quoted liberally, and each time her name appeared, Ellis had not only highlighted it in yellow, but circled it in red.

18

Fourteen-year-old Judy Brenner was working in Fey's back-yard when Fey arrived home. Wearing a man's plaid shirt over jeans and battered cowboy boots, Judy had stepped in to help take care of Fey's horses, Thieftaker and Constable, when her sister Lori had gone off to college. She was smoking a cigarette as she mucked out the stalls.

Fey was glad to see her. Judy was a change from the people, the stresses, and the situations Fey dealt with all day. She needed space and time away from the job to put things into perspective—something Judy and the horses could provide.

Fey didn't know where any of the information she was gathering was leading, but the more she uncovered, the more there appeared to be an unlikely link between Ellis Kavanaugh and Bianca Flynn.

"Your mother will kill you if she catches you smoking," Fey said to her young friend.

"Not a chance," Judy told her. "If she smells it on me, I tell her it was you smoking and the smell got on me."

"Thanks a lot. It's bad enough being a reformed smoker without being blamed for continuing to smoke."

"You gonna tell on me?"

Fey shook her head. "Not a chance, kid. I need you around. Can't afford for you to be grounded."

"You won't be able to afford my bill if you don't pay me sometime soon."

Fey laughed and took her checkbook out of her shoulder bag. Did I have a mouth on me like that when I was her age? she wondered. Where do these kids get their confidence?

Fey handed over a check. "How about saddling up and we'll take a trail ride? I need to get away from things for a while."

"Sure," Judy said, going for the saddles as Fey went inside to change.

Fey wanted to chastise Judy for smoking around the barn— chastise her for smoking to begin with—but she couldn't bring herself to do it. Every kid needed a mother, but they only needed *one* mother.

Fey changed into a sweatshirt and jodhpurs under Wrangler jeans. Real cowboys didn't wear Levi's because the seams on the inside of the pant legs rubbed thighs raw.

She hummed to herself, purposely not letting her conscious mind form troubling thoughts. There were no worthwhile conclusions to be reached with the limited information she possessed. Better to let the subconscious sift through the detritus of clues, half connections, emotions, guilt, anger, and impossibilities.

Experience had taught her to trust her subconscious to nudge her toward the missing links the conscious mind would recognize as solid evidence. Sometimes, of course, the subconscious let the conscious mind take a long time before grudgingly putting the pieces together, but life was just that way.

Fey poured a fifty-fifty concoction of vodka and 7 UP into a plastic drinking bottle and went outside to help finish preparing the horses. She didn't want to think about the possibilities of infidelity leading to half sisters and maybe half brothers. She was getting used to being alone. She didn't want to start feeling again.

She really didn't want to be related to Brink Kavanaugh. What she wanted was to have him jump her bones.

He couldn't be her half brother.

Nah—no way.

RHONDA FINISHED breast-feeding Penny and laid her gently down in her crib. She then pumped her breasts so her mother, who took care of Penny during the day, could feed her later. It was exhausting, but there was also something satisfying in the process.

The day had also been satisfying in many respects. They had located Willetta and the staple gun. A willingness to look foolish, along with hard slog and attention to detail, had turned up the saw and the receipt in the Dumpster. And amazingly, Chandra, the clerk from the Dollar Hardware Emporium, had come up with a serviceable composite of the man who had bought the staple gun and other items.

Hammer was a whiz with the computerized Smith & Wesson composite program installed on his laptop, but producing a good composite was a team effort between the operator and the witness. If the witness had a hazy recollection or an inability to articulate the differences in a suspect's features, any resulting composite was worthless.

Luckily, Chandra had been starstruck by her customer's good looks and his supposed Hollywood connections. But luck was part of the game, and you made your own by pushing hard and never giving up. For most detectives, finding the receipt in the first place would have been impossible, but not for Hammer and Nails. It was why they were who they were.

Hammer translated Chandra's memories of the suspect into

the beginnings of a composite by using the examples provided as part of the computer program. Chandra chose from different hairstyles, face shapes, noses, lips, chins, and eyes to form a basic picture. It was then Hammer's job to use various shape-changing options, shading, and free drawing to fine-tune the composite and individualize it.

The process took two hours, but when Hammer was done, Chandra was convinced the face staring back at her from the computer screen was the same as the man who'd bought a few innocent hardware items from her. She still didn't know what all the fuss was about, but she'd been happy to be the center of attention. It gave her something to talk about during her next lunch hour.

Chandra also gave them another lead. Although she'd never heard of any of the suspect's movies, she did remember a title, *Bad Blood*.

It didn't mean anything to Hammer or Nails, but if the suspect had been telling the truth and not just bragging, it was probably a straight-to-video B flick. As a lead, it was tenuous but it could have potential.

Rhonda watched as Penny smiled up at her. She felt choked as she looked at the baby's slightly oversize head and flat features. Rhonda had believed she and Hammer were the perfect couple, perfectly matched, perfectly in sync. Down's syndrome hadn't even occurred to her as a possibility for their baby.

The baby had changed everything. Before Penny, she and Hammer would still have been on the case, still pushing the composite, the movie title lead, anything they had. Now, workdays came to an end.

Penny needed to be picked up from Nanna's, needed her own mother, needed her father. The change didn't appear to bother Hammer, but Rhonda felt claustrophobic. Hammer relied on her, but he could also take care of himself. Penny couldn't. There was no end in sight. Ever.

Hammer came up behind Rhonda and wrapped his arms around her waist, resting his chin on her shoulder.

"She's beautiful," he said, looking down at Penny. He felt Rhonda tense within his grasp. "Hey, what's the matter?" He stood up, allowing her to turn around and push him gently back.

"Nothing's the matter."

"Of course something's the matter. You just don't want to talk about it. I know you. I love you. What's wrong? Is it me?"

"Why do you think it's you?" Rhonda raised her voice. "Does the world revolve around you?" She moved off toward the door of the room.

Hammer exercised his right to remain silent, moving to lean over the crib. He put a finger into the palm of Penny's right hand, marveling as the baby's fingers grasped his. He sensed Rhonda lingering, but didn't turn to face her.

"Doesn't it bother you?" Rhonda asked.

"What?" Hammer asked, still keeping his back to her.

"Don't play dumb. Doesn't it bother you she's retarded?"

Hammer felt himself tense this time. He straightened, but still did not turn around. "Now who's being dumb? You know she isn't retarded. Penny has Down's syndrome. She's going to be challenged. She's going to be a lot of work for us. But Down's syndrome children are very special lights." He did turn around now, to face the woman whom he cherished above all else in his life along with his daughter. "The Down's syndrome isn't your fault. It isn't my fault. It just is. Penny just is. Get your mind straight. Whatever challenges Penny has, we will face as a family."

"I can't believe you," Rhonda said. She started to cry. "I want to believe you, but I can't. I want to love her, but I can't."

"Why? Because you don't think she's perfect?"

With her back pressed against the wall, Rhonda slowly slid to a sitting position with her knees pulled up to her chest. "Yes!" It was a wail of anguish.

Hammer came over and crouched in front of her, wrapping his arms around her knees. "Rhonda—Penny *is* perfect."

Rhonda was crying in a jag, gasping for breath. "How can you say that? I let you down. Don't tell me you wouldn't trade her for a normal child in a heartbeat!"

"I certainly wouldn't." There was sharp anger in Hammer's voice. He shook Rhonda's legs roughly. "And don't you ever ever say that again."

"What?" The shock of Hammer's statement was enough to interrupt Rhonda's crying. She gulped and sniffed. "What?"

Hammer more gently rocked Rhonda's legs back and forth. "Penny is our child. Whatever challenges she has, she is still our child, our creation. She will love us, and we will love her as we love each other, with every fiber of our being."

"But—"

"There is no *but*. I'm not much for organized religion, but you know I believe in something we conveniently label God. You do too. Penny hasn't been sent to punish us; she's been sent to bless us. She's special. We have to believe she's special. If we give her everything we give to each other, she will give back to us tenfold."

Rhonda reached out and grabbed Hammer's shirtfront with both hands. "How do you know? How can you know?"

Hammer smiled softly. "Because she came from you and me, and we're perfect together, so she must be perfect, whatever the disguise she's wearing."

Rhonda gave a small, gulping laugh. She swallowed hard, released Hammer's shirt with one hand, and wiped her nose on her sleeve.

Hammer laughed at her.

She laughed back, still crying a little, and scooted forward to throw her arms around him.

19

DAY TWO AT Robbery-Homicide was slightly more relaxed than day one. Fey and company were still incomers, but major cases had broken for two of the other teams, and everyone was busy with their own work. The noise level in the squad room was high, with detectives either on the phone or talking to one another in the staccato shorthand that passes for communication in the cop shop.

Fey's crew had all turned up early. Coffee in hand, they sat around their grouping of desks. Hammer and Nails passed out bulletins containing a copy of the computerized composite along with the physical description of the possible suspect.

"Outstanding work, you guys," Fey said, impressed with the effort. "I don't know how you do it."

She had spent a lot of the previous night lying in bed thinking about the investigation. About two o'clock in the morning, she had swung her legs out of bed, turned on a lamp, and opened up the suitcase with the money from Ellis Kavanaugh's legacy.

There was no way Ellis could have come by the money legally. There was far too much for a cop to lay his hands on in the normal course of things. The manner in which Ellis had handled it, leaving it with a strange lawyer to dispose of as part of a codicil, also pointed to something irregular. Kavanaugh was guilty of something. The question, however, was what?

The bills were thirty years old, but were still in crisp, virtually perfect condition. The money was unbanded, but it must have been almost new when Ellis came into possession of it.

She spent an hour checking serial numbers and determined several different sequential progressions. She made a list of her findings before putting the money back in the suitcase. There was no doubt the money was hot—well, maybe only tepid by this time, but it still must have been stolen.

Fey's decision was easy. She didn't want the money. Even if it wasn't stolen, it was still tainted by the connection to her father. If she wanted to be rich, she could have taken the money left to her from Ash's estate. Instead she had put it in trust for the charities Ash had initiated. She was already comfortable. She didn't need the responsibility of being rich.

In the morning, she brought the money and the list of serial numbers to the station with her.

"How close do you think this composite is to the suspect?" Alphabet asked. Composites were notoriously hit-and-miss.

Hammer shrugged. "It felt good. The witness got a reasonable look at the guy. He even took his sunglasses off when she was talking to him."

"How sure is she of the crew cut?" Brindle asked. "It's not exactly a current fashion statement."

"The wit was adamant," Rhonda answered. "She specifically stated it was a crew cut, not spiked or styled. A standard buzz."

Alphabet had been thinking over the new information. "I know we're supposed to be bracing Ferris Jackson this morning, but if you can spare us, I'd like to take the composite and make a run at the movie company that owns the crime scene warehouse. Maybe this film *Bad Blood* was something they produced, and the suspect worked for them. We can also check with the Stunt-men's Association, see if they recognize the composite."

Fey nodded. "Okay, go with it. If you get a hit, don't chase it without us."

Alphabet touched Brindle on the shoulder, and the pair started gathering their stuff.

Hammer and Nails were quiet. The composite was their lead. They should have been given the assignment to chase down the alleys where it led.

Fey winked at them. "Take it easy," she said softly. "There's more than enough work to go around. You guys did a great job, now let it go." She needed to maintain Alphabet's and Brindle's enthusiasm. If they wanted a shot at following up on the composite, she would let them have it. Hammer and Nails were more than capable of accepting the redirection. "Monk and I have another lead to follow up," she told them. This was news to Monk, who managed to keep a straight face. "You guys handle Ferris Jackson. I know we're spreading ourselves thin, but the leads are too hot to ignore."

Hammer picked up the search warrant for Ferris Jackson's residence. "How do you want us to play this?"

"Use a light hand and let's see what we can get. We need more information on this Underground Railroad situation, but finding where Bianca hid her own kids is a top priority. There may be something they can tell us."

When both pairs of detectives left, Fey turned to Monk.

"So, what's this other lead?" he asked, smiling gently.

Fey sighed and filled him in on her thoughts regarding Ellis Kavanaugh and the money he left her, not mentioning the possible family ties between herself and Kavanaugh's offspring. She didn't see the link as germane to the investigation. If her perception changed, she would deal with it then.

"You want to try tracing the money?"

"It may give us a start."

Monk shook his head. "These ties between Ellis Kavanaugh and Bianca Flynn are tenuous. Are you sure they're not coincidence?"

"No, I'm not. But I can't ignore the implications. The setup stinks. Why would Kavanaugh leave me this money? What did he expect me to do with it?"

"Spend it?"

"Har-har. I have a feeling if I deposited or spent this money, alarm bells would start going off."

"Maybe it's what he wanted."

"Maybe," Fey agreed. "Perhaps raising the alarm was Ellis's way of revealing something that happened all those years ago."

"Like what?"

"Hell if I know."

Monk shrugged. "Okay, so where do you want to start?"

"I want to book the money into Property Division as evidence and go from there."

THE LOS ANGELES field office of the Federal Bureau of Investigation occupied several floors of the federal building located opposite a large veterans' cemetery in Westwood. Fey and Monk waited in the lobby of the seventeenth floor while visitors' passes were processed. A secretary handed them clip-on badges and led them through a maze of hallways to a corner office inhabited by Freddie Mackerbee, special agent in charge of the L.A. field office.

"Fey!" Mackerbee exclaimed in delight. "It's been a long time." He was a short man, built like a throw pillow. His hair receded into a widow's peak, but was still thick and dark.

"Hello, Freddie," Fey said, grasping his outstretched hand. "How are you?"

Pleasantries exchanged, Fey introduced Monk, and several minutes were spent catching up. Mackerbee had been Ash's boss during the time Ash and Fey worked together. He was aware of their romantic entanglement and shared in Fey's loss. Ash had been a good friend to Freddie as well as a colleague respected for his work as an agent. His death had left a hole in the lives of many people. Fey knew she could rely on Mackerbee's help even more from their mutual connection to Ash than because of any professional courtesy.

There was little love lost between the FBI and the LAPD as organizations. Individuals sometimes forged mutual alliances, but the agencies clashed more often than not. A good deal of the animosity grew from the FBI not having local powers of arrest in California. Unlike in most other states, FBI agents could only arrest on federal charges in California and had to defer to local jurisdictions, usually with hat in hand, to pursue other venues of enforcement. This limitation conflicted with the FBI's omnipotent opinion of itself, and it angered the FBI higher-ups. Coupled with the LAPD's own organizational arrogance, the situation encouraged infighting.

Fey should have started farther down the FBI pecking order with her request, but she hadn't wanted to play games. By going directly to Mackerbee, cooperation was more than likely assured.

She handed over her list of serial numbers and explained what she wanted.

Mackerbee glanced at the list. "What do you expect to find?"

"I'm not sure, but if there is anything, it'll be thirty years old or more."

"Before my time," Mackerbee said.

"Mine too, believe it or not," Fey said with a laugh. "Which means we can't be blamed."

"Don't be so sure," Mackerbee said. "This is the FBI we're talking about. Blame can always be splashed about."

"I suppose you're right," Fey said. "The LAPD has never been short of a scapegoat or two, either."

The mutual agency bashing eased the way for the two individual entities to work together. It was no longer LAPD versus the FBI, but two individuals working together in spite of the monoliths.

Mackerbee raised his eyebrows and looked at the list again. "Do you want to wait for results, or do you want me to call you?"

"I'm not sure how important this is going to be," Fey said. "If it's no imposition, we'll wait." Fey knew if she left, it might be days before Mackerbee got back to her. Other crises would take precedence.

"Okay," Mackerbee said. "I'll get somebody on it immediately. You know where the cafeteria is? I'll find you there."

FORTY-FIVE minutes later, Mackerbee spotted Fey and Monk at a table near the cafeteria entrance. Fey was nursing a second cup of coffee, while Monk finished off a surprisingly good omelette.

"We've got trouble," Fey said, watching Mackerbee approach.

Monk looked up, putting down his fork when he saw the expression on Mackerbee's face.

"You've stepped in a big puddle of crap this time," the FBI supervisor said. His voice had a hard edge to it.

Fey shrugged. "Why should this time be any different?" She silently blessed the instinct that made her book the money as evidence. "Tell me the worst."

"The money was stolen in an armored-car robbery in May of 1969. Two security guards were killed in a shoot-out with a trio of Black Panthers. One of the Panthers was also killed, but the others escaped with the money."

"Were they ever caught?"

"Not for the robbery or the murders of the guards. Even working with the LAPD, we weren't able to do more than identify one of the outstanding suspects. There was nowhere near enough evidence to file a case, let alone get a conviction. The money was never recovered, and the third suspect never identified."

"I take it the suspect you did identify was arrested on other charges."

"You bet," Mackerbee said. "Eldon Dodge is still serving time for the murder of his cousin, Mavis Flynn."

20

"THE COMPOSITE was our lead," Rhonda said, miffed. "We should be following it up."

Hammer accelerated his black van through a yellow traffic signal and entered a freeway on-ramp. The van was a conceit. It was part of Hammer and Nails's overall habit of purposely placing themselves above everyone else around them—part of their professional arrogance, their shtick.

"Let it go," Hammer told his partner. "Alphabet and Brindle won't drop the ball."

"That's beside the point," Rhonda said.

"It *is* the point."

"What do you mean?" Rhonda was sitting sideways in the car with her back half-turned toward the passenger door. She wasn't wearing her seat belt. Neither of them were, never did. It was a bad habit from their patrol days when getting out of the car in a hurry could mean the difference between living or dying.

Hammer took his eyes off the road long enough to smile at Rhonda. Looking forward again, he reached his hand over and rested it on Rhonda's thigh. "Do you agree that together, we are as good as they come?"

"Better," Rhonda said automatically.

"Okay, better," Hammer agreed. "It's why we were able to come up with the composite in the first place. Now it's easy for somebody else to run with the lead. Fey doesn't want to waste us on what somebody else can do. She's freeing us to use our initiative to come up with another direction for the investigation."

Rhonda raised her eyebrows. "Do you really think Fey's mind works that way?"

Hammer shrugged. "Yeah. She's a smart lady. She's using her resources where they'll be most effective. We're the first team. We can finesse or batter away at a situation to achieve a result. Alphabet and Brindle are the follow-up team. They'll take our result and follow it to its logical conclusion. We can do both. Right now, Alphabet and Brindle can't. So, we trailblaze, and they follow up."

Rhonda blew a raspberry. "You are so full of it."

Hammer chuckled. "Come on. What do you want from me?"

"Our superiority complex is going to get us into trouble one day."

"Trouble is my middle name."

"Give it a rest, will you?" Rhonda gave a giggle of exasperation.

Hammer patted her leg. "It's nice to know I can still make you laugh."

Rhonda put her hand over his. "Always," she said.

Hammer winked at her as he powered the van up and over the Sepulveda Pass before picking up the Ventura Freeway east.

The neighborhood where Bianca Flynn had lived with Ferris Jackson was in the upper-middle-class reaches of Toluca Lake. Sandwiched between Studio City and North Hollywood, the area was a haven for aging movie stars and new Hollywood money.

Out of contempt, neither group associated with the other, unless, of course, association could further a deal for either of them.

Hammer slid the van to a stop next to a red curb fifty feet beyond their destination, a two-story brick-and-ivy-fronted residence. A Burbank PD blue-and-white with two uniformed officers inside was parked opposite. Rhonda had called ahead to notify Burbank PD they would be operating in their jurisdiction and requested that a uniformed unit meet them to assist with the warrant service.

Exiting the car, the duo walked across to meet the uniformed officers. Introductions were made and hands shaken. Hammer explained the situation was low-key and asked the officers to cover the back of the residence until entry was gained. Experience with closing barn doors after the horse had fled made detectives take more safeguards than necessary. The unexpected was always anticipated.

As Hammer and Nails walked toward the front of the house, birds could be heard, along with the bark of a dog confined in a yard nearby. There were no other people visible. A green Range Rover cruised down the middle of the street, its windows darkly tinted as to obscure the driver.

"Weird," Rhonda said.

"Like something out of *The Stepford Wives*," Hammer agreed. "Not even a twitching of lace curtains. Far too quiet for normal people."

"How do you want to play this?"

"By ear, as always."

While the uniformed officers took themselves around the side of the house, Rhonda assumed a tactical position to one side of the concrete path leading up to the front door. The positioning was second nature. Standing as she did kept Hammer out of her line of fire.

From the opposite side of the door, Hammer rapped loudly on the hardwood finish. Again, his positioning was second nature.

Even though neither of the detectives felt they were in danger, too many officers had been shot standing casually in front of doors.

Cops never rang doorbells. They always knocked. In the academy, recruits were shown a video of an officer in New York who was blown up ringing the booby-trapped doorbell of a suspect's residence. Although a similar situation had never occurred anywhere in the country again, all cops who saw the video found themselves allergic to doorbells.

Aside from the search warrant resting in the back pocket of his slacks, Hammer had also made arrangements to obtain a register of incoming and outgoing calls from the residence. He and Nails felt it might prove interesting to know whom Ferris Jackson called immediately after they finished the search and left the residence.

When Ferris opened the door, she looked drawn and gaunt. Dark hollows below her eyes gutted the life out of her pale blue irises and blurred the edges of her rounded cheekbones. She was short and compact, with spiked hair and a bizarre choice in clothing. Stripes and dots fought with plaids and geometric patterns, making her look like the victim of an explosion in a thrift store.

"Yes?" she asked.

Hammer introduced himself, displaying his badge in his left hand. He clearly saw the carotid artery on the right side of Ferris Jackson's throat begin to pulse.

"I'm sorry, I can't talk to you now. It's not convenient. You'll have to come back."

She tried to close the door, but the tip of Hammer's cowboy boot was already blocking the transom. The Society of Fuller Brush Men would have been proud. Ferris looked at the boot tip and tried to slam the door on it again.

"Please remove your foot." Her voice was shaky, her eyes darting all around.

"Ms. Jackson," Hammer said calmly. Rhonda moved up next to him on the small porch. "I'm afraid this isn't a matter of convenience. We need to come in and talk with you."

"I'm going out," Ferris said. She tried to close the door again.

Hammer twisted his foot and levered the door open. This was not the greeting they had envisioned. Ferris should have been going out of her way to help them catch her roommate's killer.

Anticipate the unexpected. Roll with it and see where it leads.

"You can leave if you want," Hammer said. He pushed his way through the door, his physical presence forcing Ferris to step back without making contact. "But you may want to stick around while my partner and I search the premises." He was coming on strong, but it was his gut reaction to Ferris's demeanor. His instinct was to pour on the pressure and see if anything burst.

Rhonda followed Hammer through the door, moving past Ferris and into the residence. Her gun was out, held down by her side. Ferris was making her hinky, and she wouldn't be satisfied until the residence had been cleared.

"You can't do this," Ferris said.

Hammer shook his head. "Do you realize how many times a week people say that to us?" He stuffed a copy of the search warrant into Ferris's hand. "I didn't want to do things this way. I try to be nice, do things the easy way, but nobody wants to cooperate anymore. I'd thought you'd greet us with open arms. Your roommate has been murdered. Who's going to find her killer if not us?" Hammer was talking mostly to keep Ferris's attention. When Rhonda let him know the house was clear, Ferris could be secured and they could proceed. Until then, he'd keep flapping his gums.

"What gives you the right to come in here like Nazi storm troopers?"

"That hurts, Ms. Jackson. Going straight to the name-calling. You could at least give us the chance to stomp our jackboots all over your belongings before you go there."

"All clear," Rhonda reported, stepping back into the entry. Hammer could see the two Burbank officers behind her.

"Any sign of the kids?" he asked.

Rhonda shook her head. "A few toys, but no actual rugrats."

Ferris let out a high-pitched laugh. "Is that what you're here for? Are you nothing more than bullyboys for Mark Ritter? Well, you're just shit out of luck. You'll never find those kids. They're never going to go back to that pervert!" Her voice was rising to hysterical levels.

Rhonda took the woman gently by the arm and led her to a couch in an expensively appointed living room. Ferris was looking as if she didn't want to do anything Rhonda suggested, but sat down because her legs wouldn't support her anymore.

"Why don't you tell me about Mark Ritter and Bianca?" Rhonda said in her best bedside manner.

Hammer moved silently into the residence, taking the Burbank cops with him.

"I don't have to tell you anything," Ferris said. "You haven't read me my rights."

"I don't have to read you your rights. You're not under arrest, Ms. Jackson. You are simply detained while we execute the search warrant. There's a big difference."

"Not from where I'm sitting."

"Why so hostile?" Rhonda asked.

"Because cops are only on the side of people who have money. Because cops took my kids away from me and gave them to a man who will beat them like he beat me." She suddenly tore open the front of her striped blouse to reveal an expanse of skin puckered by a six-inch scar. "My ex-husband did this to me with a pizza cutter six years ago, but the judge didn't believe it. My ex-husband's high-priced lawyers told the judge the wound was self-inflicted. The judge believed them. They told the judge I was mentally unstable, an unfit mother, a threat to my kids. The judge believed that as well. I tried to run, but you bastards caught me and took my kids. I haven't seen them since. You're damn right, I hate cops."

Rhonda didn't like the way the story was going, but she saw the inevitability of it. "Who was the judge in the case?"

Ferris spat onto the plush carpet. "The Right Honorable Luther Flynn."

SEARCHING THE house didn't take long. If the mandate had been to find something at any cost, the search could have taken all day or longer. Carpets would have been rolled, floorboards pulled up, medicine cabinets pulled out from walls, closets emptied, attics explored. As it was, the rooms occupied by Bianca Flynn were quite sterile. She was careful. The papers scattered across her desk and filed in the three-drawer metal cabinet were only supportive of her cause and in no way evidence of any criminal behavior. There was no indication of the location of her children, nothing relating to any Underground Railroad operation—no damning evidence of any kind.

Hammer took before-and-after pictures of the search with a Polaroid camera. This was done to document any damage caused during the search. Too often, citizens did damage after a search and tried to sue the city, claiming the damage was done during the search. Pictures also kept cops in check. They couldn't administer street justice by doing more damage than was justified during a search if they knew pictures were being taken along the way.

After her outburst, Ferris sat quietly, refusing to answer Rhonda's questions. When Hammer reported the search was finished, Ferris gave him a smug smile and demanded the names of the involved officers, as she was going to sue. It was another line cops heard several times a week.

"Knock yourself out," Hammer told her. "But you're going to have to get behind everyone else in the city."

Back in the van, Hammer pulled around the corner and parked again. From their location, they could just see the entrance to Ferris's residence.

"Did you put the bug on her car?" Rhonda asked.

"Yeah, when I was searching the garage."

While getting the search warrant signed, Hammer also had the judge authorize the use of an electronic surveillance device.

"What do you think? Are we wasting our time?"

"Hard to say," Hammer told her. "It depends on who she calls and where she goes from here. She's definitely hiding something. When we arrived, she was in a big toot to be gone." He was dialing his portable phone, getting through to their contact in GTE phone security. "I'm betting she blows out of there almost immediately."

"And where she goes . . ." Rhonda said, seeing the garage door of the residence open up and Ferris drive out in an older Mercedes coupe.

"We will follow," Hammer completed the statement.

21

FREDDIE MACKERBEE pressed Fey hard. He was suddenly all FBI. He wanted the story, the whole story, and nothing but the story (so help him God), but Fey wasn't about to give it to him.

She had come to Freddie looking for a quick favor, nothing major, just help clearing up an unsubstantiated investigative lead. She hadn't come to turn an entire murder investigation over to the feds, which was exactly what Mackerbee was demanding.

Behind his pillowy image, the L.A. field office SAC was diamond hard, but Fey was no slouch in the immovable-object-meeting-the-unstoppable-force stakes and wasn't about to roll over and play dead. As the FBI hadn't been able to solve the murder of the two security guards thirty years earlier, they didn't have much standing when it came to appropriating a new lead developed by the LAPD. The Department could handle things themselves, thank you very much. Mackerbee was demanding details. Fey was refusing to come across.

"Maybe later. Let's see where we are on this. We don't have all the details yet. We'll get back to you."

"We're talking about two dead here."

"We're talking about stolen money from a thirty-year-old robbery."

"This isn't about the money. It's about murder of two good men."

"You're damn right, it is, but it's also about the fresh murder of a good woman. That takes precedence at this juncture."

"You haven't heard the last of this."

"Don't be silly."

"Let's see if your chief thinks I'm being silly."

"Threats? Come on, Mackerbee."

It had all been downhill from there. Fey knew she couldn't rely on any further help from Mackerbee. He'd already told her more than he should, certainly more than she'd told him. She also knew Mackerbee's threats to go to her chief were a waste of breath. The chief would crow over a chance to rub the FBI's noses in a pile of their own crap; life would be considered good. The chief would tell her to get on with the investigation and make sure the feds didn't beat her to it.

"Sheeee-it," Monk said through a long breath when he and Fey made it back to their detective sedan.

"In spades," Fey agreed.

Monk had been quiet during the dogfight in the cafeteria. Fey was a big enough canine to take care of herself, and Monk had no desire to come off as a yappy lap pup by comparison.

They sat inside the warm car with the windows down.

"What do you make of it?" he asked, referring to the money being stolen and the link to Eldon Dodge.

Fey shifted in her seat, uncomfortable under the restraints of the seat and shoulder belts. "Beats me. Everything appears connected, but I don't understand how or why. There's an inevitability as the pieces drop into place."

"Are you saying whatever happened thirty years ago involving Eldon Dodge, Luther Flynn, Ellis Kavanaugh, and your father is coming full circle?"

"In a way. But I don't think the thirty-year factor is significant. Whatever is going on now is tied to whatever happened thirty years ago, but it could have unraveled anytime—a year later, ten years later, twenty, whenever. It just needed the right catalyst. I think the consequences have been lying dormant, and something Bianca Flynn did, or found, has brought them to fruition."

"She certainly had something somebody wanted."

"Yes, and it's important. We have to go beyond finding out who was torturing her when she died. Most people, especially people with something to lose, don't do their own dirty work. So, who hired the torturer?"

"This is getting complicated."

"Yeah, ain't it great?"

Monk gave a soft chuckle. "What about Kavanaugh leaving you the money?"

"It's all part of it. He and my father arrested Dodge. Maybe they stole the money from him. Maybe guilt kept Kavanaugh from spending the money. I don't know."

"We can connect Kavanaugh and Bianca Flynn through the underlining of her name in the book you found in his room. Perhaps they even knew each other."

Fey nodded her agreement. "From all accounts, Kavanaugh had turned into an odd duck. Maybe leaving the money to me was his way of making sure the story would all come out."

"A long shot?"

Fey sighed. "Maybe. I don't know. We don't have enough information yet. We'll have to take a closer look at Kavanaugh's death. What made him run out onto the track? Was he plain crazy, or was there something else?"

Fey's beeper vibrated, showing a familiar number on the LED

readout. She used her cell phone and dialed the detective desk at West L.A. It was as if she'd never left.

"Devon Wyatt is here asking for you," Mike Cahill said when Fey was put through to him.

"I guess things are never so bad they can't get worse," Fey said. "Didn't you tell him I work RHD now?"

"He knew already," Cahill said. "I think he's trying to make us jump through hoops."

"Typical. Did he say what he wanted?"

"Nope, just that it was important, and you were going to want to talk to him."

"Like hell I do," Fey said. "If I had a choice, I'd never speak to the maggot again."

Devon Wyatt was a nationally known defense lawyer whom Fey had tangoed with during the JoJo Cullen case. Fey had also been instrumental in convicting Wyatt's son of rape.

For his part, Wyatt had been the force behind tapes of Fey's psychiatric sessions being released to the press, splattering her sordid childhood across the pages of the tabloids.

Wyatt was not known for wasting his own time. If he wanted to see Fey, there was certainly something in it for him—and maybe something in it for her.

"I should tell you to send him downtown," Fey told Cahill, "but we're close to the station. Tell him we'll be there in a few minutes."

"Great." There was a noticeable relief in Cahill's voice. It was typical of Fey's ex–commanding officer to piddle in his pants when dealing with a self-proclaimed VIP such as Wyatt.

Fey turned the phone off and explained the situation to Monk. He started the car and turned left out of the federal building's parking lot onto Sepulveda Boulevard. West L.A. station was less than five minutes away.

"Where are you going?" Fey asked.

Monk took his eyes off the road for long enough to give her a funny look. "The station, of course."

"Don't be silly," Fey said. "I want another cup of coffee first. Head for Starbucks. Wyatt can wait."

FLOATING ON a sea of caffeine, Fey led the way into West L.A. station forty-five minutes later. She hadn't wanted another cup of coffee, but she didn't want Wyatt thinking he could snap his fingers and make everyone jump. He could make Cahill jump, maybe, but not Fey.

Even though she and Monk had only been gone for a day and a half, they were greeted in the squad room as if they'd been away for months. There was a feeling of coming home. RHD was enemy territory, where they couldn't let their guard down. West L.A. was home ground.

"Croaker," Devon Wyatt acknowledged when he saw her enter the squad room lobby.

"Wyatt," Fey said. At least there was no pretense of civility.

Wyatt looked at his watch. "Fifty minutes. I figured you'd make me wait for at least an hour."

"I must be slipping, getting soft in my old age."

Wyatt displayed his whiter-than-white teeth in a smile that would have done a tiger proud. He was a short but dapper man in an expensive dark gray suit with a fine chalk pinstripe. He wore a maroon waistcoat and a darker maroon tie knotted tightly under the collar of a starched white shirt. His pointed shoes were maroon and shone like polished stones.

"What's this about?" Fey asked.

"You owe me a favor."

"I do?" Fey knew it was the truth, as much as she hated it. During the JoJo Cullen case, Fey had been forced to humble herself in front of Wyatt to get something she needed. There had been a method to her madness—a willingness to do anything to solve the case.

Wyatt didn't give a verbal answer. He simply looked at Fey and watched her struggle with her conscience, something he had never experienced for himself.

By the end of the JoJo Cullen case, Fey had triumphed over Wyatt. She had won the game of one-upmanship, but she had been forced to trade Wyatt a future favor in return for the victory, much to her disgust.

"Time to give the devil his due, I guess," she said eventually, and opened the swing door on the side of the counter providing access to the squad room.

Wyatt's smile didn't falter as he stepped into the inner sanctum. "Don't flatter yourself, Croaker. It's not like I'm going to ask you to sleep with me. It won't be that bad."

"Maybe not," Fey said. "But at least if you did, I wouldn't have to be seen in public with you."

Wyatt's laugh was deep, throaty, and genuine. Heads turned in the squad room as he led the way to the interrogation rooms, his confidence giving the impression that he was the detective and Fey the interloper.

Inside the urine-colored interrogation room, Wyatt took the chair closest to the door.

"Oh, no," Fey said. "I'm not that easy. You know your seat is on the other side of the table."

Wyatt changed seats with a superior smile. "The chair closest to the door is the seat of power," he said. "Never let the suspect sit there. Pin him against the wall on the opposite side of the table. Make the suspect feel he can't escape."

"Been taking refresher courses at the academy, have you?" Fey asked innocently.

Monk stepped into the room and took up a position leaning against the wall behind Fey.

Wyatt waved his hands in front of him and shook his head. "I don't want to play games, Fey." His tone had become serious. "I'm in a position to do both of us some good."

"Why don't I believe you?"

"Because you're a cop, and cops don't believe anyone."

Fey dipped her head in agreement. "This is true. What do you want?"

"How is Robbery-Homicide treating you?"

"I'm sure you can guess. If you knew I'd been transferred to RHD, how come you came to West L.A.?"

"I knew you would be at the federal building."

Fey's eyes widened and she raised her eyebrows. "Are you having me followed again?"

"No. You've proven too savvy for that treatment in the past."

"Then how did you know?"

"I have a client who wants to talk to you," Wyatt said, instead of answering.

"This is your favor?"

"Yes. My client is in prison—in San Quentin."

"The Q?"

"Yes. I know doing this will greatly inconvenience you, especially in the middle of a murder investigation."

Fey laughed. "You expect me to go now?"

"Yes."

Fey stood up. "I'm sorry, Wyatt. I know I owe you a favor. Talk to me again when this investigation is over and we'll see."

"My client has found God. He wants to confess and atone for his sins."

"You must be joking. Is he maintaining he's innocent as well?"

"Of the crime for which he was convicted."

"Yeah, him and every other inmate in the Q, and every other state penitentiary. They've all found God, and they're all innocent. Haven't you heard? There are no guilty men in prison."

"I'm serious, Fey."

"So am I. I can't go flying up to San Quentin in the middle of a homicide investigation. It'll have to wait."

"I don't think it should wait."

Fey bowed her head and shook it. "Okay, I'll bite. Why shouldn't it wait?"

Devon Wyatt paused for effect as if he were playing to a jury in a courtroom. "Because my client is Eldon Dodge."

22

WHIP WHITMAN looked at Fey through squinted eyes. "What's your thinking?" he asked. He finished polishing his round-rimmed glasses and fitted them back over his ears. "Is Wyatt trying to run some kind of scam on us?"

Fey parted her hands in front of her in a gesture of exasperation. "It's hard to tell with Wyatt. He must have an agenda."

"He always has an agenda," Monk said.

"Yeah," Fey agreed. "But so do we, and the two don't necessarily have to be in conflict."

Fey and Monk were sitting in Whitman's office at the rear of the RHD squad room. It was a closed-door session. Fey laid everything out for Whitman, including Ellis Kavanaugh's money; the codicil in Kavanaugh's will; the possible connection she had uncovered between Kavanaugh and Bianca; Freddie Mackerbee's reaction when he discovered the money was from a thirty-year-old robbery involving Eldon Dodge; and now Devon Wyatt's forcefully presented request. The only thing she held back was the still unthinkable possibility of somehow being related to Jenna Kavanaugh.

Whitman rubbed a long-fingered hand across his chin. He sighed. "I was warned about you," he said. A slight upturn at the corners of his mouth took the insult out of the words.

"Warned?" Fey asked.

"Yeah. I was told whatever you get involved in is never simple."

Monk gave a short chortle. "You can say that again."

Fey gave him a sharp look. "Thanks, partner."

"Anytime."

"I was also warned about the banter," Whitman said. This time he wasn't as amused. "What do you want to do here?"

"I don't think we have much choice," Fey said, making a decision. "I have to talk to Dodge."

"How are you going to get there?"

Fey checked her watch. "If I contact Air Support Division, maybe they'll fly me to Q in the fixed wing. I could be there and back in, say, eight hours."

Whitman was nodding his head. "All right. This thing smells of wild-goose chasing, but let's take the chance. I can't see too much of a downside."

Fey turned to her partner. "You're going to have to keep everybody pushing while I'm gone."

"No problem."

"Keep Alphabet and Brindle working on the composite. If they get a lead, organize a follow-up. Don't let anyone get hurt rushing into something."

"Yes, Mother," Monk said. "What about Hammer and Nails?"

"They should stay with Ferris Jackson. If they go off on a tangent, it's okay. They know what they're doing." Fey thought for a moment and came to another decision. "There's something else I want you to do. Get over to Hollywood Park and find out what really happened when Ellis Kavanaugh was trampled. There has to be more to the story."

"Leave it with me," Monk said.

Fey took a penetrating look at her second-in-command's strong features etched in ebony-colored skin. His slim body and shiny, shaven scalp gave him a sleek appearance. But over the years, Fey had discovered there was more to Monk than the wrapping. He was steady. True-blue. A rock in any storm. He had always been there for Fey, and he always would be. He wasn't glamorous, but he was the magnetic force holding together the spinning orbits of the other team members.

"One day, partner," Fey said, "we're going to get a case that only goes in one direction at a time."

"Never happen," Monk said. "We're Chubby Checkerized— everything we do, we do with a twist."

"Just make sure it all gets straightened out in the end," Whitman told them.

"I DON'T LIKE handling sloppy seconds," Brindle told her partner. On her toes, she bounced up the few steps leading to the offices of Citadel Productions, the company that owned the crime scene warehouse.

"I'm sorry," Alphabet said, lumbering after her. "My tongue got ahead of my brain."

Brindle paused at the entry, passing on the obvious comeback. Instead, she turned to Alphabet with a frown. "If you ask me, Hammer and Nails get far too much rope." This was the real issue.

Alphabet shrugged his simianlike shoulders. "Maybe. But as long as they keep coming up with the goods, nobody is going to rein them in. You have to admit, they did a hell of a job with the composite. I just wanted a chance to take it further."

"They did do a good job, but it wasn't anything we couldn't have come up with."

Alphabet shrugged.

"I'm serious." Brindle was insistent.

"I know you are," Alphabet said. "But that's pride and ego talking. You may not like Hammer and Nails getting all the kudos, but it doesn't alter the fact they are the go-to team. We've still got a ways to go to match them."

"Following up on their leads is not going to help."

"It will if things pan out under our control."

"They'll still get the credit."

"Then perhaps we better get this cleared up and earn some of our own."

Across the street, the blue roof and architecturally interesting lines of the Pacific Design Center contrasted with the white stucco of the art drecko building the detectives were about to enter.

As a city, West Hollywood was more trendy than cutting edge. The area of Los Angeles Brindle and Alphabet were now visiting, only a few blocks east, could not help being influenced by its faux-arty neighbor. Taste had been replaced by hip, and what was hip this morning was bland by noon.

Brindle straightened Alphabet's tie, wishing she could do something about the way he tied it with the back coming out longer than the front.

"What?" he said, touching the tie himself.

"Nothing," she said, and turned to open the door. If somebody had told her two years ago she would come to enjoy working with a fat, bald Jewish guy who looked like a basset hound and dressed like an unmade bed, she would have laughed hysterically. But times change, and so do people.

Alphabet had never made a pass at her. He liked her, even fancied her. She knew he did. But he always remained a gentleman, as if she were somehow beyond his reach. It was beginning to bug her. She really couldn't see herself in bed with him, could she? Then why had she started feeling incomplete when he wasn't around?

Inside the carved hardwood front door of the main building was an entrance to a hair salon on the left and an open glass door leading to an antiques shop on the right. Straight ahead another wooden door bore the Citadel Productions logo. Alphabet opened it and found a flight of stairs leading to the second floor. Brindle led the way up. Behind her, Alphabet's eyes appreciated the definition of her nylon-encased calf muscles.

When he first started working with Brindle, he felt clumsy around her fragile beauty, but she had proven over time to be anything but fragile. They had kicked butt side by side on several occasions. The sight of her still took his breath away, but at least he could be around her now and not make a fool of himself like a tongue-tied high school kid.

Nice Jewish boys were not supposed to bring exotic black women home to mother—even supposing in his wildest dreams she would come. Alphabet didn't care what his mother thought, but he didn't ever want Brindle to laugh at him, or disappear like a wraith, if he ever let her know how he felt. Better all around to keep everything inside.

At the top of the stairs a plump receptionist in jeans and a sweatshirt sat behind a desk. She guarded the entrance to a corridor of offices on the right, and two larger offices, with front-facing windows, to the left. There were framed movie posters on the walls with obscure titles and lots of close-ups of women screaming.

"Can I help you?" the receptionist asked. She had a throaty voice. Alphabet figured she would sound sexy as hell on the phone.

Brindle displayed her badge. "I'm Detective Jones. This is my partner, Detective Cohen." She nodded toward Alphabet. "We'd like to talk to Mr. Avery." Brindle had found the name of the production company's owner in the original murder book started by the Hollywood homicide detectives.

"I'm Janice Hancock, Mr. Avery's assistant. Is this about what happened at the warehouse? We've already had detectives come and talk to us. We haven't used the place in ages."

Brindle smiled tightly. "This is a follow-up. I'm sure you understand the seriousness of the investigation."

"If you tell me what you want, perhaps we can avoid disturbing Mr. Avery."

Brindle had little patience for receptionists or assistants who always thought they had a right to know what you wanted to talk to their bosses about. She looked pointedly at the movie posters on the wall, her face clearly showing what she thought of them. "I'm sure Mr. Avery can spare a moment from closing his next major motion picture deal to talk with us. We'd prefer to talk directly with him."

Janice Hancock dug her heels in. "He's a very busy man."

Brindle leaned forward. "So am I," she said, ignoring the ambiguity of the statement. Without further comment, she walked past the reception desk and headed for the front offices.

Janice Hancock made to jump up and stop her, but Alphabet's bulk suddenly blocked her way.

"Don't bother yourself," Alphabet said kindly. "There's no stopping her when she gets in one of her moods."

Janice relaxed back into her chair, looking sulky.

Brindle moved between the closed doors of the two front offices. Neither door had a name on the outside, but she didn't hesitate. Opening the door on the right, she saw a slender man in his forties, with a clipped beard, talking on the telephone. To compensate for his receding hairline, he had grown his hair long in back and gathered it together in a short ponytail. Very Hollywood. Very producerlike. This had to be Martin Avery.

Startled by the intrusion, Avery covered the mouthpiece of the phone with the palm of a hand, showing annoyance. He then began to absorb Brindle's beauty. "Casting for *Bitches' Night Out* isn't until two this afternoon," he said. "And where's Janice? You should have checked in with her and left your résumé."

Brindle displayed her badge. Before she could say anything, Avery held up his free hand.

"No, you're not right for the cop," he said. "We need somebody more butch. Perhaps, if you're nice to me, you might have a chance at playing the maid. She dies in the first fifteen minutes, but it's a glorious death. See Janice, she'll give you the lines." He swiveled his chair, continuing to talk on the phone.

Brindle pulled the phone jack out of the wall and spun Avery's chair forward.

This time Avery was angry. "I told you, you're not butch enough for the cop. I'm not impressed by method acting."

"I am Detective Jones, LAPD Robbery-Homicide. I need to ask you some questions about the warehouse your company owns."

"No. No. No." Avery shook his head. He stood up, grabbing Brindle's arm. "The character's name is Cleopatra Smith. Jones has already been used. Now, get out of my office. You actors get more and more brazen every day."

Brindle looked at the hand gripping her arm. Avery ignored the danger sign. Turning Brindle to escort her from the room, he suddenly yelped in pain as Brindle twisted his thumb back, freeing her arm.

With Avery on his toes, Brindle swung him back into his chair. She shoved her face toward Avery's. "Is this butch enough for you?"

Alphabet had stepped into the office. "Easy, girl," he said softly.

When Avery tried to talk, Brindle twisted his thumb harder. Avery's body arched. She put a finger from her free hand to her lips, and Avery fell silent in his pain.

Displaying her badge again, Brindle lessened her pain/compliance hold just enough so Avery could concentrate. "I am a real detective, not some Tinseltown bimbo who can't wait to give you a blow job to get a part in a fourth-rate slasher flick. Do you understand?"

Avery nodded his head.

"My partner and I are investigating the murder of the woman found in your Hollywood warehouse, and we have a few questions we need to ask you. Now, if we're done dancing, perhaps you can answer those questions, and *then* get back to talking to your coke connection."

"How did you know . . ." Avery trailed off, caught in the implications of his own words.

Brindle chuckled. She released Avery's thumb and stepped back. He slumped in his executive leather chair, sweat beading heavily across his forehead. Janice Hancock was standing in the office doorway behind Alphabet. She had a knuckle in her mouth.

"Get out of here!" Avery yelled at her. "I'll deal with this. You're fired."

Brindle stepped forward. Avery snatched his injured thumb and put it behind his back. "Sor . . . sorry, Janice. Forget what I said. How about getting us some coffee?"

Brindle gave Avery a hard look. "If I find out you've fired her, or given her a bad time in any way, I'll be back, and we'll see if you can still make films without two opposable thumbs."

"All right, all right." Avery sighed. He tugged his ponytail. "I'm sorry for the misunderstanding." He struggled to rearrange himself more comfortably in his chair. "What can I do to help?"

"Did your company ever produce a film called *Bad Blood*?" Brindle asked.

"Yeah. Two years ago. It was about a vampire with ulcers who survives by mercy-killing women suffering with AIDS."

"How uplifting," Alphabet said.

"Hey, we made that film for five hundred thousand dollars. It grossed over three million going straight to video in America, and another fifteen million in worldwide release."

"So, it never financially made it into the black?"

Avery laughed. "You obviously understand Hollywood. Citadel Productions lost its shirt on paper."

"How many stuntmen did you employ on the film?"

"Stuntmen?" Avery laughed again. "You must be joking. You don't get stuntmen when you're making a film for five hundred thousand. What you get is people who are about as sharp as Nerf balls who are willing to fall off very tall buildings in unsafe conditions because they think it will make them stars."

"At least you're honest," Alphabet said, and received a funny look from both Brindle and Avery.

"Yeah, well, don't let it get about, will you?"

Janice came back with the coffee. Alphabet slid a folded copy of the composite into Brindle's hand. She shook it open and slid it onto Avery's desk.

"Does this resemble any of your Nerf balls?"

Both Avery and Janice leaned forward. Brindle watched Avery for reaction, while Alphabet watched Janice. There was no verbal or physical communication between the two detectives, but they could both sense their telepathic communication. The feeling between them was almost electric.

Avery's expression didn't change, but Alphabet saw Janice's eyes widen.

Avery pushed the composite away. "No. I don't know him. I just produce the movies. Nerf balls come and go. I never pay attention to them."

"How about you?" Alphabet asked Janice.

Her hesitation answered the question.

Avery turned to look at her. "It's okay," he said. "If you know the guy, tell them. If he's screwing around in one of our old properties, we don't need the grief."

"I'm not sure, but it looks like a guy I dated once."

"Did he work on *Bad Blood*?" Brindle asked.

Janice nodded her head. "I think so. A couple of other titles as well. We probably have a publicity package on him. Let me see if I can find it."

Janice left the room but returned shortly. She was clutching an eight-by-ten glossy. She put it next to the composite. It wasn't a perfect match, but there was a striking resemblance—same blond crew cut, same long nose.

"Do you still see him?" Brindle asked, comparing the photo to the composite.

"No, I don't," Janice said forcefully.

Brindle gave her a sharp glance. "Why not?"

"He was good-looking but weird. He was always talking about bondage and stuff. I also think he was more interested in my ten-year-old daughter than he was in me."

Brindle felt her heart kick up a gear. "What was his name?"

"Ricky Preston. At least it was the name on his publicity stuff. I'm sure it was a stage name, but if he told me his real name, I don't remember it."

"Do you have his address?"

"I just had a pager number for him. We only dated a couple of times. He picked me up. But we'll have his agent's number in our files. It's probably on the back of the publicity still."

Brindle flipped the still over, saw the agent's name and number, and showed it to Alphabet.

"Do we wait for the others or go it alone?" Alphabet asked his partner. He grinned.

"You can wait for the others if you want," Brindle told him with violence in her eyes. "I'm going to go find this asshole and pull his lungs out through his nose."

"Now, that's butch," Avery said. "Are you sure you don't want to be in pictures?"

23

DEVON WYATT wasn't about to travel in a police department single-engine plane, which may or may not get them to their destination without any unscheduled, hard landings. As soon as Fey telephoned him and explained her plans for getting to San Quentin to talk to Eldon Dodge, Wyatt swept them aside and swung into action.

Within thirty minutes, Fey was sitting in the back of a limousine next to Wyatt on the way to the airport, where Wyatt's personal jet awaited them.

In the back of the limo, the two adversaries sat as far apart as possible. Wyatt was oily smooth in his role as host, handing Fey a glass of fresh-squeezed orange juice and producing a tray of recently prepared sushi for a lunchtime repast.

Fey picked a California roll off the sterling-silver serving platter and popped it in her mouth. "You do have a certain style," she told Wyatt begrudgingly after she swallowed. She sipped orange juice from a crystal goblet.

"Do you really despise me so much?" Wyatt asked. He settled back into his corner of the limo and watched Fey as shadows of light played across her countenance through tinted windows.

"Yes," Fey said. She was not telling Wyatt anything he didn't know. To say anything else would have been hypocritical. Fey wasn't concerned about hurting Wyatt's feelings. She knew he didn't have any.

"Why?" Wyatt asked.

"You mean besides your prior attempt to sabotage my career— which doesn't even touch your turning my private psychiatric sessions into tabloid fodder?"

"Besides that." Wyatt gave a shrug and a smirk. "You have broad emotional shoulders. Those things are nothing you can't handle."

"Who died and made you God?"

Wyatt gave another shrug. "Let's not resort to clichéd name-calling. I'm truly interested."

Fey ate another California roll before replying. "Why do you care?"

"You're riding in my limo, eating my food, en route to fly in my private jet—humor me."

"I think you just answered your own question."

Wyatt laughed. "You hate me because I'm rich?"

"No. I despise you for how you became rich."

"But isn't the source of both our incomes the same, the misery of the human condition?"

"Yeah, right," Fey said. "Like my income is in the same bracket as yours." It was her turn to smirk. "I don't despise you because you represent scum. I despise you because you are without morals or scruples. You will lie, cheat, steal, manipulate, blackmail, and defraud to get the scum off, no matter what the cost."

"So, you hate me because I'm good at my job?" Wyatt's false modesty was palpable.

"No. That's my point. You aren't." Fey sat up straighter,

tweaked by her fervor. "Your job is to provide your clients with the best defense possible *within the law,* not the best defense corruption can buy. You don't give a damn about doing your job. All you care about is the temporal, personal power your corruption brings you—fancy limousines, private jets." She waved her hand around. "Right and wrong doesn't occur to you."

"And that is exactly what I despise about you," Wyatt said, suddenly fighting back.

"What do you mean?" Fey was sorry the second the question left her lips.

Wyatt's defense mechanisms were turning on to the attack. "You are so positive about what's right. You judge all cops by your own standards. You think every cop has your integrity, that the police never do anything wrong. You walk through your cases wearing blinders, not seeing that fitting up villains is something that cops do all the time. Everything to you is black-and-white. You bend the rules to fit your own moral imperative because you're so damned convinced you're right."

"I am right."

"You've never made a mistake?"

"Sure, I have—lots of them."

"So, what makes you think *you're* God?"

Fey's feral smile was quick. "Because every time I talk to God, I find I'm talking to myself."

As THE limousine that met them at San Francisco International streaked smoothly along the Golden Gate Bridge, Fey contented herself with the thought that she had stumped Wyatt. Ever since their earlier exchange in the first limo, Wyatt had retreated into his own world and ignored Fey's presence. He worked from a briefcase on his lap, alternately scribbling notes on a yellow legal pad, reading correspondence, talking on a cell phone, and entering data into a laptop computer. If his activity was aimed at impressing Fey, it was failing miserably. She ignored Wyatt in return and tried to order her own thoughts.

Despite her smug answer, Wyatt had hit a nerve with his criticism. In many ways, her time on the job had been sheltered—not from the vagaries and debaucheries of what humans do to one another, but sheltered from making difficult choices between right and wrong.

It had been easy for her to take down Deputy Chief Vaughn Harrison for his part in the death of an LAPD detective a year earlier. But it had been less easy to ignore Harrison's manipulations and corruptions, which led to his demise. Fey's choices boiled down to the traditional lesser of two evils.

She understood the dynamics leading up to the Rodney King incident. She understood what led the officers to strike King with such fury. Those were things that could never be explained to somebody outside the job—and if you were on the job, no explanation was necessary. But for Fey it wasn't the actions of those who struck King that were unfathomable; it was the actions of those officers who stood around and watched.

She often wondered if she would have had the integrity to have made a stand—stopped the incident before it got so out of hand—or would she have stood around doing nothing, not wanting to break ranks, like so many others had done? Not knowing the answer bothered her.

Wyatt was wrong. She didn't think she was God. She didn't know who or what she thought she was. She tried not to think about those types of questions at all. It only made her paranoid.

"Do you know who Saint Quentin was?" Wyatt's question broke into Fey's reverie.

"Some Catholic somebody, I suppose." Fey saw Wyatt had put away his work. He was again sitting with his back to the far corner of the limo sipping from a glass, this one filled with champagne.

"He was a third-century Roman beheaded by pagan Gauls

after they ran heated iron spits through his body from head to foot."

"Charming."

Wyatt smiled. "Legend has it when Quentin's head was mercifully struck off, a white dove issued forth from his severed throat and flew to heaven."

"How appropriate. I'm sure he makes a splendid example for San Quentin's inmates."

"I'm sure he would," Wyatt said. "But unfortunately, he had nothing whatsoever to do with the naming of the prison."

Fey rolled her eyes. "Okay. You got me. I don't know my San Quentin from my Saint Quentin. Are you happy?"

"Partially."

They returned to their own thoughts as the limo drove past the live oaks of Marin County and through hills of blue granite that were still of a quality to justify continued commercial quarrying.

"Okay, I give in," Fey said eventually. "Who was San Quentin?"

Wyatt's smile was broad. A small victory.

"He wasn't actually a saint at all. He was an Indian warrior, a subordinate to the great Chief Marin. In 1824 he led the Licatuit Indians in their last stand against Mexican troops."

"Was he killed?"

"No. He finally surrendered before being driven into the sea at the end of this peninsula now named after him. He was taken to San Francisco, where the fathers at the Mission Delores put him to work as a skipper. He did the same job later for General Vallejo."

"How did he get to be sainted?"

"That's the odd part. He wasn't. When Anglo-Saxons arrived in California, they were under the impression all the inhabitants were zealous Catholics. Hoping to gain their support, they added *San* to the names of all the villages they visited. So Punta de Quentin became San Quentin."

Wyatt finished his travelogue as the limo approached the imposing gates of the prison. An exterior chain-link and barbed-wire enclosure stopped their progress, and Wyatt was forced to begin dealing with the bureaucracy that would gain them entry to see Eldon Dodge.

On the trip, Wyatt had refused to be drawn out on Dodge's reasons for wanting to talk with Fey. He told her it would be up to Dodge to explain. Fey sensed an unease in Wyatt. It was as if he didn't know what Dodge wanted.

"Who's paying you?" Fey asked while waiting for the wheels of entry to turn. "After all this time sitting on death row, Dodge can't have any funds left."

"Icons such as Dodge can always find people foolish enough to support their cause."

"And you're more than willing to take your share?"

Wyatt put on an expression of mock shock. "But of course."

When the limo was allowed entry through the first barrier, another guard directed the stoic driver to a parking location.

Fey got out of the plush ride, stretching her back and legs. The weather was cool, but the temperature did not cause the sudden chill Fey felt starting deep inside of her. The back of her neck tingled, and she smoothed a hand over her hair.

It was her biggest phobia.

More than spiders and snakes. More than being suffocated in a small place, unable to move. More than being raped. More than anything, Fey was afraid of going to prison.

FEY AND Wyatt quickly found themselves being hustled through Reception and Release, where death row inmates were processed when they first arrived at Q. Here inmates were photographed, fingerprinted, and issued their blankets and prison blues. A guard came forward and escorted Fey and Wyatt from R&R to AC, the Adjustment Center, where all death row inmates were held until the Classification Committee determined where on death row they would be placed.

During all of this shuffling and waiting, Fey fought to keep her breathing normal. Her mind betrayed her, however, picking up vibrations of hatred, fear, anger, and evil, all directed specifically at her. She knew this was ridiculous and fanciful, but she was unable to stop her internal trembling. This was not good. She didn't know how much of this she could take.

She was okay in the small holding jails at the various police stations and while visiting court lockups. Even the twin towers at L.A. County Jail didn't phase her too much. But being inside a prison was something that freaked her out.

There were three locations inside San Quentin housing death row's condemned. The first was the AC, where Fey and Wyatt were currently being searched and processed through metal detectors. The AC itself housed inmates classed as Grade B Condemned, mostly prison-gang members with a history of stabbings on the row. Life was monastic and restrictive; an eight-minute shower per day was the only time spent outside a cell.

AC consisted of three floors with thirty to thirty-five cells per floor. The cells themselves were stylishly furnished with a stainless-steel sink, a toilet, a bare lightbulb in the ceiling, and a sheet-metal shelf covered with an inch-thick pad for a bed. One inmate per cell. Cobweb time.

Most inmates managed to get themselves moved to Grade A Condemned in order to be transferred to the vast cavern of East Block. This structure was reminiscent of a huge blimp hangar with gun rails, along which guards patrolled with machine guns and revolvers. Chinks in the concrete of the block floor and walls were more a testament to bad marksmanship than to shoddy workmanship.

There were approximately two hundred and fifty condemned inmates housed in Condemned Row II, on East Block's bay side.

The yard side is home to cons who have had problems in the mainstream population, or have serious mental challenges and require constant monitoring.

Eldon Dodge was housed in North Seg, the original death row, otherwise known as The Shelf. The celebrity status of the thirty-five cells on The Shelf was sacrosanct. North Seg houses the gas chamber, in itself enough to lend an aura of awe to the location. It is a constant reminder. You can't miss it. The gas chamber exhaust stack shoots up right next to The Shelf's exercise yard on the roof. Nothing like a daily reality check.

Fey and Wyatt patiently followed the directions of the guards as they escorted them to a visiting room in North Seg. Fey felt her blood seeming to turn into pure adrenaline.

They waited in the mausoleum-like, metal-walled room for fifteen minutes with nothing to look at but a small window set above head height on the back wall, a metal table bolted to the concrete floor. Four chairs were bolted down around the table, but too far from it to be practical. The only sound was Fey's pulse pounding in her ears.

There was a noise outside the only door. As it swung open, Fey flashed back to the house-of-horror films she had been addicted to as a child. She felt a familiar terror as a tall, muscular man wearing only gray briefs, rubber thongs, and iron shackles filled the entrance space.

He smiled slowly, displaying a mouth full of misshapen teeth.

His voice when he spoke was full and deep.

"I'm Reverend Eldon Dodge. Welcome to hell."

24

SOMEWHERE Ferris Jackson had learned about dry cleaning. Not the "no ticky, no washy" kind of dry cleaning, but dry cleaning procedures used by heroes in bad spy novels to make sure they weren't being tailed.

In keeping with basic dry cleaning techniques, Ferris drove in circles, ran lights, pulled off to the side of the freeway, and on several occasions drove down one on-ramp and up the next. All of this might have helped, except she skipped the chapter where the spy hero thinks about checking for an electronic tracer on the car bumper.

Without the signals from the magnetic bug, Hammer and Nails would have needed to keep Ferris in sight, a guaranteed way to get burned during a surveillance when somebody is checking for a tail. To successfully sight-follow a subject, it took a team of at least six vehicles, all playing leapfrog, or weaving in and out of traffic on parallel routes. Even then, a savvy dry cleaner could possibly pick up the tail.

With the electronic impulses from the tracer on Ferris's bumper bleeping happily away, the duo were able to stay well back and take evasive action whenever Ferris started dry cleaning.

The drawback came when Ferris parked at her destination. Hammer couldn't be sure this wasn't simply another dry cleaning maneuver and almost missed seeing Ferris slip into the colorful shopping arcades of Olvera Street.

"Go! Go!" Hammer said to Rhonda. She already had the van door open and was hopping to the ground. Slamming the door, she also disappeared into the crowd of tourists and local shoppers.

Stretching across the shadows of the imposing art deco train platforms of Union Station, Olvera Street is the oldest thorough-fare in Los Angeles. The area teems with tourists who have come to sample the colorful wares of the Hispanic culture dominating the area.

Dressed in traditional costumes, performers show off their skills at the Mexican hat dance or the calypso to encourage the flow of tourist dollars. Mariachis stroll among the crowds sharing songs from past generations, while street vendors run temporary food stands that would send any God-fearing Health Department inspector into instant shock.

The street is brightly colored, with piñatas, huge papier-mâché flowers, and lanterns hung from crisscrossed wires above head level. Adding to the festival atmosphere are hideous masks of the dead, ornate and gaudy religious paraphernalia, carved effigies of strange animals painted with iridescents, and the beautiful weaves of Mexican blankets.

Behind the desperately bright colors, however, there lurks the squalor and resignation of a community hanging on to its existence by the sharp edge of a knife. This isn't Tijuana or Ensenada, but it isn't far removed for those who live in the broken-down apartments behind the facade. Life is hand-to-mouth, the American dream more a nightmare than a reality.

None of this made any impact on Ferris Jackson. Abandoning

any pretense of dry cleaning, she cut through the vendors' stalls and walked quickly to the stone steps of a church. A small sign proclaimed its name—SANCTUARY OF THE BLACK MADONNA.

The instant before she pulled open the carved doors of the church, Ferris looked behind her and scanned the crowd. Anticipating the action, Rhonda had concealed herself behind an array of Mexican shirts and blouses hung from the top rail of a stall. She watched Ferris furtively enter the church, and then used her rover to contact Hammer and hustle him to her location.

"What do you think?" she asked when he arrived.

"How long has she been in there?"

"Five minutes tops." Rhonda gave her watch a quick check.

"I don't think we have anything to lose at this point," Hammer said. "Lets see who's inside, and what the big rush to get here was about."

The detective duo walked away from the stall, took the short flight of steps to the church entrance two at a time, and entered through the heavy doors.

Inside, it took a moment for their eyes to adjust to the dim light. A huge, winged, black Madonna floated above the flickering candles in front of the altar. The effigy appeared to be reaching out to embrace them in an eerie, contradictory effect, unsettling yet comforting.

Several parishioners were sitting among the pews. Their clothing was made from peasant materials, and their prayers were in the language of their native countries far away. The Madonna above the altar appeared to rivet their attention as rosaries slipped through worn fingers. None of them turned to acknowledge Hammer and Nails's entrance. Ignorance was the blessed path to salvation.

"Anything?" Hammer asked quietly.

"*Nada*," Nails said.

Together they walked down the center aisle, approaching the

rack of candles set before the altar. As they got closer, they could see the craftsmanship of the carved Madonna who lent her name to the church. The wood appeared as hard and shiny as opal, the difference betrayed by the deep grain adding character to the face and lines of the figure. The two black iron rods suspending the figure from the ceiling were almost impossible to see.

"It's beautiful," Rhonda said, staring upward. She suddenly genuflected. She then took a small taper, touching it to the flame of an already burning candle, and transferring the fire to the new wick of another.

Hammer watched as Rhonda closed her eyes for a brief moment, her lips moving silently.

"Catholic upbringings never die," he said when she was done. He wasn't mocking, simply stating.

"Never," Rhonda confirmed.

On the right side of the chapel were two wooden confessional boxes. Neither appeared to be in use.

"If Ferris didn't slide out by another entrance, she must be back there somewhere." Hammer pointed at an unobtrusive door to the side of the altar.

Taking the initiative, Rhonda moved forward. Opening the door, she listened before stepping through. There were voices talking in raised whispers.

"Calm down, Ferris." The first voice was male, attempting to soothe.

"But they searched the house. They probably killed Bianca, too. If we don't do something, we will lose everything." Ferris Jackson was highly agitated.

"Listen to yourself, Ferris. You are not being rational. The police didn't murder Bianca. What would be the point? And there is no need to worry about them searching the house. Bianca would never leave anything lying around that could possibly lead anyone to us. She was much too careful."

"She wasn't so careful she didn't get dead," Ferris said. "Who knows what she revealed before she died."

Rhonda stepped through the door. "If she revealed anything," she said in an unruffled voice, "you've got far more problems to worry about than the police. We certainly didn't torture her for information."

Ferris swore when she saw Rhonda, with Hammer now standing next to her.

"How did you follow me here?"

Neither detective answered her. Instead they concentrated on the man with her.

"Father Romero," Hammer said. He shook hands firmly with the man standing in front of Ferris.

"Señor Hammer," Father Romero said. His smile was small but genuine. "And the lovely Detective Nails." He stepped forward to give Rhonda a hug. "How nice to see you."

"A smooth shifting of gears, Father, but somehow I think our turning up is more awkward than nice for you."

Father Romero waggled his palm from side to side. "Perhaps, but I have always found we have shared a voice of reason in the past. Let us hope this time is no different."

Romero was a short, slender man dressed in black slacks, black shoes, and a black cleric's blouse with the traditional white collar at the throat. His shoulder-length, tar-black hair hung loose around his face. In his fifties, he had angular cheeks that still showed the pockmarked ravages of youthful acne.

An outspoken civil rights activist, Romero was well known within the community. Usually he was a moderate, but he was also a champion of sanctuary for Central and South American political refugees. In such cases, he was known to push politics and the law to the limit.

Hammer and Nails had come into contact with him on several occasions. In two particular incidents, their paths had crossed to mutual satisfaction—once during an Internal Affairs investigation involving a ring of cops shaking down illegal immigrants, and a second time when a refugee seeking sanctuary had committed a double murder as the result of a love triangle. Their relationship remained tenuous, but there was mutual respect on both sides.

"I'm sorry, Father," Ferris said. Her face was red, but whether from anger or shame was hard to tell. "I tried to be sure nobody was following me."

Father Romero turned to Ferris and patted her gently on the back. "Don't berate yourself. I know these two detectives well. There was nothing you could have done. They are like bulldogs. They would have arrived here sooner or later. Perhaps it is best they have come now."

"Father, what is going on?" Rhonda asked.

Romero spread his hands in an odd gesture. "A long and sordid tale, I'm afraid."

"We've got time."

"Yes, but we don't. We are preparing for a dangerous intake. If you delay us much longer, you could put lives at risk."

"Can we help?"

"As detectives or as concerned friends?"

"Does there have to be a difference?"

"I'm afraid so."

Ferris reached out and grasped Romero by the arm. "Don't trust them. They're cops. They will screw us over."

"It's too late, Ferris," Romero said. "Bianca died an ugly death. The railroad may already be compromised. We need help." He looked back at Hammer and Nails. "God has sent us these two. They will not choose following the law over doing what is right."

"Don't be so sure, Father," Hammer said.

Romero considered this statement. "Then we will make a

deal. You give a little, and I'll give you a little. You help us now, and afterward I will arrange for you to talk with Bianca's children. Deal?"

Hammer and Nails exchanged glances. "Deal," they said in unison.

25

ELDON DODGE was very aware of the impression he made standing in the doorway to the visiting room. He was unbowed by the weight of his sixty years, or by the hopelessness of his plight. Nearly naked and wrapped in chains, his black skin glistened with sweat. A small medallion on a thin loop rested between his pectoral muscles. In earlier times, he might have been stepping off a slave ship, bound for the auction block.

If a bolt of lightning had crackled across the room's small window, Fey felt she would have fainted dead away—the horror films of her childhood becoming real. There was no crash of thunder, but looking at Dodge, Fey could only feel embarrassment for what humans do to one another, despite justification.

Dodge broke the short silence. When he spoke, his voice was calm, without even a tinge of anger. "Believe it or not, my civil rights aren't being violated. Even the white boys on The Shelf have to dress up in this jewelry to come to a party." He held his arms as far away from his body as the waist shackles would allow. "Dig this crazy necklace," he said, raising his chin up to draw attention to the shock collar around his neck. "You'd think I was going to rape and pillage all by myself."

He smiled and shuffled into the room. The door closed behind him, but a guard stood watching through the plastic window, a remote transmitter with a red thumb button in his hand, ready to zap Dodge's collar.

"Hello, counselor," he said to Wyatt. "Are all your bills being paid?"

"Very satisfactorily, Reverend."

Fey had stood up when she'd heard the door to the visiting room opening. Dodge was tall, his hair shaved close to his scalp. She could smell a heavy male musk emanating from his body, not unclean as much as unaired. She watched his nostrils flare and knew he was sniffing her. It was disconcerting, as if he were taking some perverted liberty and there was nothing she could do about it.

Dodge widened his eyes, showing large amounts of white. "So, you're Garth Croaker's daughter?"

Fey hated her father, hated to be reminded she was born from his seed. She responded with an attack. "And you're a murderous piece of scum he put in jail to die."

Dodge blinked. "Your father was a corrupt, lying bastard."

Fey nodded. "At least there are some things we agree about, but what's your point? You didn't get your tame lapdog to drag me here to discuss a man we both hate."

"Ah, but I did." Dodge moved forward, making Fey visibly tense. He saw the tightening in her, and appeared to come to a decision. He sat in one of the bolted-down chairs and gestured for Fey to sit across from him.

Mad at herself for flinching, Fey complied with a show of nonchalance.

Wyatt made to sit also, but Dodge stopped him. "Leave us alone," he said. His lack of manners was obvious.

"I don't think that would be wise, Reverend."

Dodge half turned in his chair toward Wyatt. "I don't give a flaming crap what you think. You're being paid very well. Get out."

Wyatt had been caught half sitting and half standing. He was a man used to power and respect off-footed by a man with nothing to lose. Reaching a hand down to the chair seat, Wyatt pushed himself back to a standing position but gave no indication of his anger.

"I think you're making a mistake, Reverend. Croaker is not somebody you can screw around with. She's dangerous."

"I don't intend to screw around with her. I intend to be straightforward with her, but what I have to say is for her ears only."

Wyatt shrugged and walked to the door. It was opened by the guard outside. He turned back to Fey. "Are you all right with this?"

She dipped her head slightly to one side. "Why not? I've come this far. It's beginning to get interesting." She was actually fascinated to see Wyatt put in his place.

Wyatt shrugged and walked out.

When the door closed, Fey brought her eyes back to Dodge. Her heart was pounding beneath her surface cool.

"Please forgive me for playing games," Dodge said. His demeanor had visibly softened. "I have no desire to scare you or irritate you. Nor do I wish to waste your time. I thank you for coming."

Fey sat straight in the hard chair, not relaxing, meeting Dodge's eyes, refusing to give anything away. "Okay."

Dodge sighed. "What do you think whenever you hear a con say he has found God?" he asked.

"It's a very convenient ploy for sympathy. It plays well on a parole board, or when you're trying to get a reprieve from the gas chamber."

"Ah, the gas chamber," Dodge said. He leaned back in the chair, his hands in his lap like two chained spiders. "I've been living in a cell fifty feet away from that sucker for the last twenty-eight years. I'm never going to get any farther away from it, but I'm never going to get any closer either."

"Other men have thought the same and been wrong."

"Ah, but I am political," Dodge said. His voice purposely blackened on the last word, making it *po-litical.*

Fey wondered if Dodge's use of the *ah* exclamation was a natural speech pattern or affected.

"When you are *po-litical* and you die, you become a martyr," Dodge continued. "But when you are *po-litical* and you are left to rot, then you are forgotten and nobody rallies to your cause."

"Somebody must be rallying to yours," Fey said. "Somebody is paying Wyatt."

"Ah, ill-gotten gains invested wisely," Dodge told her with a conspiratorial grin. "I rally to my own cause."

"From the inside?"

"All things are possible on the inside, even finding God."

"And exactly where did you find him? Third cell on the left?"

"Mockery?"

Fey leaned forward. "You said you weren't going to waste my time."

"All right," Dodge said. "I'll make your trip worthwhile, but please let me first answer your question."

Politeness was not something you came across often in cons, at least not toward cops. Fey leaned back again, giving the impression she was willing to listen.

"You asked me where I found God. Perhaps it would be easier to explain when I found God. It was August twenty-first, 1987, at exactly one thirty-eight in the afternoon."

"That's pretty precise," Fey said. "I'm impressed."

Dodge smiled with reminiscence. "No need to be. That was the exact date and time I met Mother Teresa."

Despite herself, Fey found she was interested.

"It was a dog-bitch of a summer day and I was getting ready to push the stone." Dodge saw Fey was missing the slang connection. "Lift weights on the roof," he explained. "We push the stone of this building away like Christ pushing the stone of his tomb away. It don't matter how hot or cold, you don't miss your time in the light."

Fey nodded in understanding.

"I was tying my shoes when one of the guards on the gun rail—you know, the safe end of the target range—calls down and asks how come I ain't going to see Mother Teresa.

"I blew him off, thinking he was making a joke. The guards will do anything to make you break your routine. It's like a game with them. 'When she can bench-press three times her body weight, tell her to come see me,' I said. 'I ain't missing my sun for no nun.' The guard walked away and didn't say no more, which made me think. He'd given in too easily, and when I got to the roof, I could see there weren't the normal amount of muscle pugs around. Screw it, I thought. It's just another head game. I strapped on a weight belt and started pushing the stone."

Fey didn't say anything, not wanting to stop the flow of the narrative. She had no idea where Dodge was going with this story. Certainly she wasn't going to believe a word of it, but there had to be some point.

Dodge sought to keep his eyes locked on Fey's as he continued to talk. "That day, the hour outside seemed to go faster than normal. I was pumped and ripped going back down the stairs, when the same guard as before calls down and tells us not to go back into our cells for lockdown. He says that since we wouldn't go to Mother Teresa, she had come to see us.

"I made my way to the front of the platform, and sure enough, there was this tiny woman looking older than a century, and I felt something click inside me as if somebody had thrown a switch."

Dodge cleared his throat, as if remembering the scene was bringing it alive again. "Here I was, a dead man living only on borrowed time, and this small woman suddenly affected me more strongly than anyone in my life. She smiled at me, her lips moving as she blessed a religious medal. She held it out to me, and I took it, unable to speak." Dodge's hands moved to caress the medallion lying against his chest. "It was like being in the gas chamber when the capsules drop and breathing like there was nothing wrong. I died right then and there, without her saying a word, and was reborn. She then turned to the guard standing next to her, and said in a clear voice, 'What you do to these men, you do to God.' I was chilled."

So was Fey. She didn't want to believe Dodge, couldn't afford to believe him, but instinctively she did. "And since that day?" she prompted in a quiet voice.

Dodge brought out his smile again. "Since that day, I have studied the Scriptures and become a tower of strength in the Lord. I have found life beyond these walls, life beyond death."

Fey had a fleeting image of the dove that flew out of the throat of the beheaded Saint Quentin.

"And you brought me here to tell me this?"

Dodge shook his head. "No, I brought you here so I may atone for my sins. I want you to hear my confession."

"I'm hardly a priest," Fey said. She was flustered. "The only confessions I hear put villains in prison."

"Exactly," Dodge said.

"I'm afraid I don't understand."

"I am a guilty man," Dodge said.

Fey raised her eyebrows. "How long have you been in here? Thirty years, give or take? And you've only just had this revelation?"

"More mockery?"

"It's something I'm good at, especially when it's deserved."

"I said I am a guilty man, but I am not guilty of murdering Mavis Flynn."

"Here we go. I'm supposed to buy off on this crap? You've found God, and you're innocent of the murder that put you on The Shelf?"

"Yes."

Fey snorted. "Pull the other one. It's got bells on." She started to get up.

"Wait, please." Dodge motioned only with his hands, not wanting to give the guard outside an excuse to activate the shock collar around his neck. "Please." He was beseeching.

Fey lowered herself back into the chair. Her claustrophobic feelings had receded, but she was still unsettled by Dodge's demeanor. There had to be more to his story, some stronger reason for him to get Wyatt to request her presence.

"Thank you," Dodge said. "Please bear with me a little longer. I have killed men. I have robbed with impunity, stolen hundreds of thousands of dollars. I have done many things for a cause I no longer believe in. But I did not kill Mavis Flynn."

"Then who did?"

Dodge paused for effect before answering.

"Your father."

26

HAMMER AND NAILS were not exactly sure what they were letting themselves in for, but they were used to flying blind. If pinned down, they would probably say they enjoyed it. Whatever Father Romero had in mind, they were up for it. They would deal with the consequences, moral and otherwise, later.

Their shared arrogance was their biggest strength and their biggest weakness. It made them so very good at what they did, yet blinded them to realizing the world did not revolve around their viewpoint, that answers right for them might not be right for others. If they were ever to fall, it would be far and hard.

Ferris was still not happy with Father Romero's decision to involve the two detectives. Her wounds were obviously raw. She had idolized Bianca Flynn and wanted nothing more than to carry on in her heroine's stead. She knew she did not have the education, poise, or intellect to run the West Coast arm of the underground with the confidence and assurance that Bianca had done. Ferris's insecurities left her angry and confused, unable to decide if Bianca would have agreed with Father Romero or fought him furiously. In the end, being swept along by events was easier than thinking for herself.

Father Romero led Hammer and Rhonda farther back into the church, with Ferris reluctantly bringing up the rear.

"Please," he said, stopping outside what appeared to be a solid panel in the back wall. "I need your promise you will not use what I am about to show you against us."

"You have it," Hammer said with a glance at Nails.

"Don't do it, Father," Ferris said in token objection.

Father Romero smiled at the woman he knew was running on the ragged edge of her emotions. "We have no choice, child. Put your trust in God to provide."

Ferris was silent. God had never helped her before, certainly not when it came to her personal drama.

Father Romero slid aside the wall panel without any show of flair. This was a passageway he frequently used, and there was nothing in his attitude to indicate it was anything special.

"Do you remember when the Sanctury of the Black Madonna was the center of controversy over giving sanctuary to political refugees considered illegal aliens by the government?" Father Romero asked.

"It was how we first met," Hammer said.

Father Romero nodded. "Yes. There were many searches until we were able to establish a special dispensation for sacred ground. If the refugees could get to the church, they were safe."

"Like reaching embassy soil in a foreign country," Rhonda said. She was new on the job during the peak of the sanctuary movement, but she remembered it well. She followed Father Romero as he stepped through the opening revealed by the sliding panel.

"The problem, of course," Father Romero continued, "was getting the refugees to the church and supporting them once they were inside."

"You frustrated a lot of politicians," Hammer said, smiling. He always admired a good wool-over-the-eyes trick.

Father Romero turned to smile at them. "It was obvious nobody remembered the role this area played in the history of Los Angeles." They were standing in a narrow passageway dimly lighted by bare electric bulbs supported by exposed wiring.

Hammer shook his head. "I'm not sure I follow."

"Well, you can't always lead," Father Romero said lightly. "And if you don't follow, you're likely to get lost."

Rhonda snickered. It wasn't often somebody got away with a quip at Hammer's expense.

"What I meant was—"

"I know what you meant," Father Romero said, leading the way down the passage. "What *I* meant was that before Olvera Street became known for its tribute to Hispanic pageantry, this area was home to Los Angeles's first Chinatown. Above us is the site of the infamous Chinese Massacre in 1871, as well as the location where Latin, Indian, and black jail prisoners were sold as day laborers. Turn-of-the-century Los Angeles was a place of crooked cops, protection rackets, illegal immigration, and rampant criminality. The opium and gambling dens of Chinatown had to be protected not only from police raids, but also from the vengeance of competing tongs."

"The catacombs," Hammer said, realizing where the priest's colloquy was leading.

"Exactly." Beyond Father Romero, the dank passage expanded into a large room with bunk beds lining the walls. There were tables and old armchairs scattered around, and freestanding wardrobes against the rough walls. Beyond the room were the entrances to three other passageways. "The catacombs had been abandoned for years, dilapidated and crumbling. About seven years ago there was a civic movement to restore parts of the tunnels along with several historical buildings that were contained in them."

"I've heard about it," Rhonda said. "They called the area El Pueblo de Los Angeles and turned it into a historical monument celebrating the birth of L.A."

"That's right." Father Romero nodded. "It gave us a scare at the time, because we had already restored many of the catacombs for our own use, connecting them to the church. They worked wonderfully as hidden pipelines during the time when sanctuary for the refugees was needed—and they still work wonderfully in making the Underground Railroad for abused children and women truly underground." The priest walked unerringly to one of the three exit passages and led his entourage into its depths.

"You must be careful," he said, taking out a flashlight. The jerry-rigged electric lighting had ended in the large room. "The tunnels renovated for the tourists are completely safe. We only renovated the passages we needed to run the operation, and then only to the point where they are usable. There are still many tunnels on the verge of collapse. Some are even poisoned with unstable pockets of methane gas from old landfills."

"Far from perfect conditions," Hammer said. Tunnels had never been his favorite place to hang out. He was glad to feel Rhonda's reassuring hand on his shoulder.

"You work with what God gives you."

"Where are we headed?" Rhonda asked.

Both detectives had missed Alphabet and Brindle's briefing on the Underground Railroad. However, they had gone over the information when reporting back with the composite.

They knew they were on track again, as they had been when looking for clues at the crime scene. They didn't reveal the extent of their knowledge to Father Romero; there was always more to learn by listening to different sources.

"What experience have you had with sexually or physically abused children?" Romero answered Rhonda's question with another.

"We've seen more than enough over the years," Rhonda said.

"Then you'll know courts don't always make the right decisions." This came from Ferris, who was bringing up the rear. "There are a lot of places in this country where money speaks louder than the rights of children. Places where women are considered hysterical simpletons if they dare accuse their husbands of molestation or abuse. There are court cases where young children have been returned to their abusive fathers even after fully documented evidence from doctors and psychologists has proved they were being raped and abused. There's even a case where a video was shown of a father forcing his eight-year-old daughter to have sex with him, and yet he was still given unsupervised visitation rights because, even after the child's tearful testimony, the video was declared not to be in focus enough to prove that it was indeed the child's father on the screen."

Hammer sighed. "We're aware the law is far from perfect and has little to do with justice."

Rhonda directed another question to Father Romero, hoping to get Ferris off her hobbyhorse. "How large is this underground movement?"

"Right now, there are about six hundred families involved nationwide, with more coming every day," Father Romero told her. The passageway ended at a locked grate. Romero took a ring of keys from his pocket, unlocked the grate, and led the way into a disused offshoot of the L.A. River. "All those involved are running from obsessive, abusive, and dangerous spouses who have the whole weight of the law behind them, including the FBI and federal task forces. Mostly it's mothers and their children, but there are also fathers who need the underground. We have several cases where, after a divorce in which the mother gets custody, the mother's new boyfriend has abused the child or children. When all legal venues have been exhausted, and these bastards still get to enjoy the same sickening and abusive habits, then the fathers have nowhere to turn but the underground."

Hammer spoke up. "How in hell do you determine these people you're supposedly helping are telling the truth? Maybe they're the abusers. Maybe they're just overprotective, obsessive mothers with a psychotic fixation against their ex-husbands."

Romero shrugged. "It's not easy to get into the underground." He led them up the bank to where a brown sedan was parked in a little-used cul-de-sac. "The underground has a whole slew of volunteer lawyers and mental-health professionals who screen everyone who contacts us for help. The screening is demanding. They examine all the documentation in the cases, and then interview and evaluate the victims and the parents who are on the run with them. Once the evidence has been reviewed, they advise us if someone is right for the underground. Believe me, we know how to test these people. If molesting parents try to run a scam on us, they don't get past first base, and we turn them in to the proper authorities."

"It sounds like a civilian-run version of the Federal Witness Protection Program," Rhonda said, unknowingly echoing Alphabet's comparison when explaining the setup to Fey.

"You're close. But it's not an easy life. Those who enter have to be prepared to withstand great hardship. And we have to be very careful not to allow inductees to have access to information that would endanger the program if they were ever caught."

"You mean you've had people turn on you?"

"Twice since I've been involved with the program, we've had inductees back out and give up the names of the people who helped them. The cases have been fought in court, and we've come out okay, but we learned our lessons the hard way. We now know that even the people we're trying to help can hurt us, so we have to take even more precautions."

"Is it worth it?"

"Once you've spent time with the children, heard their stories and seen the looks on their faces, or examined the medical and court reports of their ordeals, there is never a doubt that all the effort is worth it."

"But what you're doing is illegal."

"Perhaps, but that doesn't make it wrong. You said yourself the law has little to do with justice."

"I take it we're about to be involved in a pickup?"

Romero nodded as they all stood beside the car. "A dangerous one. The husband in this case has employed a private security specialist named MacAlister to get his daughter back."

"MacAlister," Hammer and Nails said in unison.

"You know him?"

"If he's involved in this, you have major problems. He's an ex-cop who has joined the dark side. Works for some of the highest-priced criminal defense attorneys. He specializes in witness intimidation and blackmail."

"He was a heavy-handed, rotten bastard as a cop," Rhonda said. "And he's far worse since he's been taken off the legal leash."

A thought struck Hammer. "Isn't he on permanent retainer to Devon Wyatt?"

"He certainly is," Father Romero answered before Rhonda had the chance. "Bianca often went up against Wyatt in court. MacAlister was always there—a malevolent force."

"I wonder if Fey knows?" Rhonda said, speculating.

Having been involved when Wyatt defended JoJo Cullen, they knew Fey hated the flashy lawyer, but they didn't yet know she was currently with him in San Quentin.

"I doubt it," Hammer said. "We'll have to get the information to her."

Another thought struck Rhonda. "What do you think of MacAlister as the torturer?"

"He doesn't fit the composite," Hammer said.

"But he could be involved."

"It's definitely his style," Hammer agreed. "If there were two people involved, it would have made the kidnapping and transporting of Bianca easier."

"The waters are getting deep."

Hammer took the car keys from Father Romero. "If you're up against MacAlister, you really do need us."

Romero looked at Ferris. His smile was serene. "As I told you, the Lord always provides."

27

FEY FELT SHE had been holding her breath forever. She knew Dodge wasn't lying. No matter how much evidence there was against him at trial. No matter how guilty he was of other murders and mayhem. No matter how ludicrous the supposition. There was an inevitability about his statement regarding her father.

"Bullshit," she said, despite what her gut was telling her. "You killed Mavis Flynn, and my father arrested you for it. You're using Bianca Flynn's death to mess with my head. What is this, some freaky little revenge plan you've cooked up with your crooked shyster to get your case reheard? Who do you think you are? Geronimo Pratt?"

Dodge didn't respond to the bait. He sat quietly, watching Fey squirm in her chair, waiting for her to move beyond token denial.

"Well?" she asked eventually.

"I know what your father was. You know what he was. I know you do. I've heard your psychiatric tapes from the JoJo Cullen case."

"Damn Devon Wyatt to hell," Fey said. "There will come a time he will pay for what he did to me."

"Playing God?"

"You're the second person to accuse me of that today. But if it's what it takes, I'm going to do it. When he exposed my private life, Wyatt took everything from me."

"No, he didn't."

"You don't know what you're talking about."

"Of course I do. I thought your father took everything from me when he killed Mavis and set me up to take the fall, but I was wrong."

"Wrong about my father killing Mavis Flynn, that's for sure."

Dodge ignored the protest. "I was wrong because I am still here. I am still who I am—as you are—day in and day out. I have my soul, as do you. They can take my freedom, your dignity, my manhood, your private past, but they can not take our inner core. We continue on, even though it would be far easier for you to put a gun in your mouth, or for me to tie mattress strips around my neck and hang from the top bar of my cell. I lie on my bunk every day staring at that top bar. You touch your gun every day and think about kissing the tip of the barrel. We aren't very different."

"Screw you," Fey said. She let silence fill the void between them for several long beats. Finally she relented. "Tell me about it," she said.

Dodge's shoulders pulled back and raised up as if he were about to float from the chair. "Let's start with the first lie. I was an angry young black man, but I was never a true Black Panther. The movement was strong. Huey Newton and Bobby Seale had set us on fire. When Cleaver published *Soul on Ice*, we started a movement in L.A. because it was the cool thing to do. I became a Panther, not because I was *po-litical*, that came later, but because it was a good way to pull chicks."

Fey had to laugh.

Dodge grinned at her. "I got to tell you, wearing leather trench coats and black berets during summer in L.A. was not an easy cross to bear."

"Get on with it," Fey said, but without harshness. Dodge's voice and story were verging on hypnotic. He was taking Fey out of the cold interview room, away from the physical and emotional chains they both wore.

"The Panther rhetoric eventually rubbed off on me. I became *po-litical*. It would have been hard not to become *po-litical*. Black men in America were being killed, beaten, and incarcerated at a genocidal rate."

"Spare me the one-sided history lesson," Fey said. "I'm not impressed. I've worked side by side with black cops all my career. Some of them were also *po-litical*, but they didn't rob and murder in retaliation."

Eldon shrugged. "To each his own. In my case, the movement became my reason for existence. Mavis called me in May of 1969. We had always been close as family. She was a straight— worked at a bank—but she also supported the struggle, and we sometimes used her as a go-between. She called me with information she'd found out about an extralarge shipment of money leaving the bank in an armored car."

"I'm ahead of you here," Fey said. Remembering what Freddie Mackerbee had told her about the armored-car robbery, she quickly made the connection to where Eldon's story was leading. "She must have given you the inside information you used for the armored-car robbery in which the two security guards were killed."

Eldon looked surprised. "How do you know about the robbery?"

"A little birdie told me. The money was never recovered. One of the Panthers was killed. Two got away. You and somebody else. The other guy was never identified. You were arrested, but there wasn't enough evidence to charge you. It didn't matter in the long run because shortly thereafter you were arrested again and convicted of killing Mavis Flynn."

"Shit," Eldon said. "You make it all sound so clean and simple." He was becoming agitated. "You weren't there when the gloves came off in the interrogation room. They couldn't prove I was a killer, but they did everything short of killing me while trying to prove it. If it wasn't for Devon Wyatt, they probably would have done."

"My heart bleeds. You *were* a killer. How did Wyatt get involved?"

Eldon sighed in exasperation. "Money—how else?"

"Money from the armored-car robbery?"

Eldon shrugged. "There was a lot of it."

"So who was the third Panther?"

"There was no third Panther. The other player was a brother, but he wasn't *po-litical*. He came with the package from Mavis."

"Do you know who he was?"

Eldon shrugged. "You can't figure it out?"

Something dark moved in the back of Fey's mind, a shark swimming through a dark sea. It wasn't clear, but she pressed on. "Luther Flynn?"

Eldon's expression didn't twitch.

Fey nodded her head. "So what happened with Mavis?"

"After most of the fuss over the robbery had calmed down, Mavis came to stay with me, claiming Luther was diddling with her kids. He was a bad-ass muther. Mavis wanted a divorce. She was scared witless of Luther, but she was even more scared for Bianca and Cecily. She ran with the kids."

"Why didn't she go to the police?"

Eldon sneered. "She tried, but Luther already held sway within the black community. He was an up-and-comer. Liberal whites were kissing his black ass big time. He had the courts in his pocket. Luther told the cops Mavis was angry with him for having an affair and was trying to get even by coaching the children to make allegations of sexual abuse against him. Nobody in those days really wanted to deal with the subject of incest. It was easier to say Mavis was a hysterical mother."

"If he was such a golden boy, why would Luther risk participating in an armed robbery with you?"

"I never said it was Luther."

"Now, you get real."

Eldon shrugged. "Money is power," he said cryptically.

"Wasn't he worried you'd tell the cops about him?"

"Luther knew I'd never tell on principle. Anyway, I couldn't without implicating myself."

"And you expect me to believe you're willing to talk now because you've come to Jesus."

Eldon was silent, fingering the medallion at his throat.

"Okay." It was Fey's turn to shrug. "So, what happened next?"

"Luther knew how bad the man wanted me for something, anything. He got court orders giving him custody of his children, and then told the cops I was harboring his wife and concealing his kids from him."

"And were you?"

"Hell, yes." Eldon was indignant. "I heard what little Bianca had to say. There was no doubt in my mind Luther was molesting her, but there was no way any white cop or judge was going to take my word."

"What happened when the cops came to get the kids?"

"We were all asleep. The kids were in the front room. Mavis and me were sleeping in a bed in the back room."

"Like that, was it?" Fey asked.

Eldon shrugged. "Woman gots to pay her way." The implications of the statement didn't appear to register with him.

Fey shook her head. First cousins wasn't incest, but it was close.

"Mavis lived in fear Luther would come with his own thugs, but he was smarter than that. When the door was kicked in, it was your father and his partner, Kavanaugh, leading the charge."

"And you tried to shoot your way out using Mavis as a shield. Only problem was, you missed and shot Mavis in the back of the head."

"Bullshit!" Eldon bounced to his feet. Suddenly remembering where he was, he put a hand to the stun collar around his neck and immediately sat back down. His voice was filled with anger and frustration. "I loved Mavis. We'd grown up together. I would never have done anything to hurt her. I never fired a shot."

"Bullshit."

"I didn't. I swear it." Eldon's hands moved again to the medallion on his chest. "There were suddenly cops everywhere, but your father and Kavanaugh had been there thirty seconds earlier. I had a gun, but I couldn't get to it. Your father grabbed it and shot at me, but I was rolling away from him and diving out a window. He missed me but hit Mavis, who had stood up screaming."

"You want me to believe he was there to assassinate you?"

"I can't change the truth. The other cops grabbed me. He didn't get a second chance. Blaming me for shooting Mavis got him off the hook. Not only did he not get questioned about the shooting, but I got sent to The Shelf because she was killed with my gun."

"If he was trying to assassinate you, why did he use your gun?"

"I think he was improvising. If I was shot with my own gun, it would have been cleaner for him. It would have been called suicide. No *po-litical* repercussions."

"What does it matter if I believe this cock-and-bull story or not? What's the point? It's old news."

"I want you to prove what really happened that night."

Fey laughed. "Why should I? It's already been proved."

"Because if you do, I will admit to being involved in the robbery of the armored car that resulted in the death of the two guards."

"So what?"

Eldon put the palms of his hands together and pointed them toward Fey. "Please understand, I want to atone for my sins, but I also want redemption for those I did not commit."

"I still don't see why I should bother. You're already on death row, the same place you'd end up if you were convicted of killing the guards."

"Exactly. You have nothing to lose."

"Yeah, but even if I could do it, why make the effort for a static result?"

"Because I know why Bianca Flynn was being tortured."

This took Fey by surprise. "No way."

"You prove I didn't kill Mavis Flynn, and I'll tell you how to prove who was behind the torture."

"No way," Fey said again. "Not from prison. You can't."

"I can."

"You're bluffing. This is all bullshit. I owed Devon Wyatt a favor. I came and listened. Now I'm out of here." She stood up.

Eldon stayed seated. He made no move to stop Fey, but he did speak. "Before you leave the facility," he said, "check my visitor's list. Then decide if I'm bluffing."

28

"HAVE THEY turned up yet?" Devon Wyatt asked from the other end of a cell phone. He was still waiting for Fey to finish her conference with Eldon Dodge.

"The woman and the child are here. The priest won't be far behind."

"Don't screw this up, MacAlister. This deal is worth too much." Wyatt had his back turned on the guard who was watching Eldon Dodge through the small door window. There was nobody else in the corridor.

"I don't screw up," MacAlister said. "The client will get the delivery."

"Don't take this lightly. If we're not careful, the cops are going to be all over us. I don't like taking chances. Whatever the hell happened with Bianca has already stirred up more shit than we need."

"Not my fault somebody chose an amateur to do a pro's job.

When the daughter of a prominent judge gets murdered, the cops are going to take an interest."

"I don't like this. There's something going on we don't know about or have control over."

"You think somebody else was after the locations of the families in the underground?"

"I don't know what other information would have been worth killing Bianca for."

"Do you think they got it?"

"The word I get from our source inside the coroner's office is that Croaker and her crew don't think the torturer was successful. I happen to agree."

"How's it going with the Frog Lady?"

Wyatt's voice carried his shrug down the line. "All I can do is delay her. How much it slows her down is anybody's guess. She's a dangerous opponent, and there is still the rest of her crew to reckon with."

"Then pull out of the game," MacAlister said.

"Too much money involved."

MacAlister laughed. "I knew there was something I liked about you, Wyatt. You're a greedy bastard."

"And you're not? You think I don't know you're double-dipping on this case?" Wyatt's voice was tinged with agitation. "Take notice. I don't care what happens with the mother and child, or your deal with the father, just make sure the damn priest knows what will happen to his precious pipeline if he tries to deny us the delivery."

"You take care of tying up Croaker. I'll take care of the priest. He ain't never met a nightmare like me," MacAlister said. He turned the phone off with the flick of a wide thumb.

At six foot six inches tall, packed with close to two hundred and eighty pounds of muscle and bone with a face like a bucket of elbows, MacAlister was more than just a big man. He wore size sixteen shoes and had hands so large they made phone books tremble with fear.

He wore a black T-shirt stretched taut across his chest, down over his flat stomach, and tucked into a tapered waist. Huge biceps bulged from the short sleeves. His lower half was encased in tight black jeans, which clung to the muscles of his legs. Specially ordered black high-tops covered his large feet.

MacAlister liked his clothing second-skin tight. It gave him a feeling of barely contained power capable of exploding at any given second, tearing the clothing to shreds. As a kid, his favorite comic book character was the Incredible Hulk. The steroids and growth hormones he'd taken since high school now helped him emulate his childhood hero. Unfortunately, their side effects also sent him into regular bouts of dark depression.

When he'd been a cop, he'd used his bulk to intimidate and terrify. He was a certified five-star bastard. Everybody knew it, including MacAlister. It was his vanity—he loved being hated, reveled in it. He was a blunt instrument. Whatever didn't get out of his way got smashed. If someone tried to smash back, they soon regretted the decision. MacAlister didn't like to lose, and he never did in the long run.

With unnatural gentleness, he placed the car phone on the console of his black Aerostar van. With his left hand, he caressed the pistol stock of the sawed-off shotgun resting across his lap. The double barrels were cut down to eighteen inches and contained high-density, hand-loaded shot. The kick from firing both barrels would almost tear the arm off a normal man. MacAlister, however, was far from normal.

He had waited a long time for a score this big. He made a good living picking up stubborn bail jumpers. But tracking kids who had been snatched by one parent or another had become a profitable sideline. He enjoyed it most when the women took the kids because they were nearly always ready to offer him anything not to take their kids back. He enjoyed their favors and then took their kids anyway.

He didn't give a damn about the kids. What their parents did to them could never be half as bad as what the bastard who'd sired him had done. MacAlister's attitude was to let the little jerks learn to fend for themselves. He'd had to do it, and he'd turned out all right, hadn't he?

He'd left the Department when dangling suspects by their ankles over a bridge to gain confessions became no longer acceptable. Worrying about civil rights took all the fun out of things. Devon Wyatt, however, had provided an acceptable outlet for MacAlister's talents.

It never occurred to MacAlister that he was joining the other side. There was only one side—his. The association with Wyatt was profitable and entertaining. Wyatt would do anything as long as the chance of being caught wasn't too high. This time, however, MacAlister sensed Wyatt was being extracareful. It only added to the excitement.

When MacAlister heard the rumors on the street about an underground organization protecting abused kids, he'd passed the information along to Wyatt, and the lawyer did the rest. There was a lot of money to be made by reclaiming the kids. It tickled MacAlister that he was actually on the legal side of the scam.

The setup was even better than the days when he'd been hired to kidnap spoiled rich kids back from wacky religious cults. Of course, he missed the fun of the deprogrammings, but you couldn't have everything.

Now, things were getting even more interesting. Up to now, it had suited Wyatt's agenda to leave the underground intact. Any contracts he sent MacAlister for missing kids were cleared up with ruthless efficiency before they got to the underground. However, Wyatt had now been hired to use the underground as a way to assure a very special delivery for a client. Enlisting MacAlister into the scheme was only natural.

For MacAlister, finding a situation to lead him to the underground was not difficult. The Hudson case was perfect. It was even easy to get Hudson to hire him, so MacAlister could pick up a fee on both ends. One from Hudson for the return of his kid, and one from Wyatt's client for assuring the delivery of another product.

All MacAlister had needed to do was find Judy Hudson and her daughter, pathetically easy for a man of his experience, make sure she got nudged in the direction of the underground, and then sit back and wait. A simple scenario, thought MacAlister, calmly watching the motel where Judy Hudson and her daughter were housed.

He'd followed the woman for two weeks, gently guiding her until she'd finally made contact with the right segment of the underground. Using illicit technical skills developed over the years, MacAlister tapped the phone lines of the hotels and motels where Judy and her daughter, Stella, stayed. He'd listened to the conversations she had with the underground and the plans being laid. He knew Father Romero was coming for the pickup tonight.

No problem, MacAlister thought. He'd dump the woman, assure the priest's cooperation by putting the fear of the devil into him, then take the kid back to Daddy and pick up his fee on both ends.

In the gathering dusk, a brown Ford passed in front of the hotel. MacAlister saw the profile of a man in the driver's seat and another silhouette, possibly a woman, on the passenger side.

No problem, MacAlister thought again. He hefted the shotgun in his lap and waited for the Ford's next pass. Sometimes life was almost too good.

INSIDE THE motel, Judy Hudson stared through the lobby window into the beginnings of dusk. She felt she was a sitting target, lighted up and on display, but she would have felt even more vulnerable outside. For what seemed like the millionth time, she looked out the window and glanced up and down the street. There was still no sign of the brown sedan she had been told to expect.

Sitting beside her mother, Stella happily flipped the pages of an oversize picture book. The young girl's long blonde hair had been sacrificed in favor of a little boy's haircut with a precise part down the right side. Blue jeans, Keds, and a boy's plaid flannel shirt completed the disguise. Stella thought the game was neat. She even liked her mom calling her Josh. Make-believe was a lot more fun with Mommy than it was with Daddy. For one thing, it never hurt with Mommy.

If someone had a photo of Judy Hudson in his hand, he wouldn't have recognized her either. Her own blonde hair had been dyed black, the curls straightened and falling across her forehead in lank strands. Her cheeks had hollowed from loss of weight, and a pair of large clear glasses could not hide the heavy purple stress bags beneath her eyes. A faded fabric coat hung from her shoulders, buttoned across a small pillow, making her look pregnant.

Unlike her daughter, Judy hated the make-believe, but she knew her husband well and she refused to underestimate the risk she was running. If playing dress-up could give her any edge, she'd continue to do it till Max Hudson dropped dead.

She stared through the motel's lobby window again and was finally rewarded with a glimpse of a brown sedan. Approaching the motel, it slowed, and the appropriate turn indicator flashed on. Judy prayed the car was the right one. She prayed the waiting was over. She prayed the nightmare would end.

"Mommy, are you okay?"

Judy opened her eyes and bent down beside her daughter, hugging her. "I'm just a little tired."

"Are we waiting for Daddy?" the child asked, and then added with a child's bluntness, "I don't want to see Daddy."

Judy hugged her daughter again. "Don't worry, darling, you

won't have to see Daddy again." Standing up, she looked out the window.

From across the street, she saw the door of a parked van open and a huge man step out. Over his right arm, concealing his hand, was a folded raincoat. Judy's mind clicked on to the words of an old song claiming it never rained in California. She took a closer look at the man and realized she'd seen him before. Twice, actually, since she'd been on the run, but it hadn't registered.

As Judy watched the man, the brown sedan pulled into the motel entrance and came to a stop in front of the lobby. The man from the van was now blocked from her sight, but Judy knew what he was doing, and she knew what she had to do.

As FATHER Romero brought the car to a halt in front of the motel lobby, he could see a pregnant woman and a little boy peering through the window at him.

"That's her," Ferris said from the passenger seat.

Father Romero looked slightly confused. "I thought we were looking for a woman and a little girl. Nobody said she was pregnant."

"Standard disguise techniques," Ferris said. "You know the drill, Father."

Romero shrugged and opened the driver's door.

The woman suddenly moved away from the window and burst through the lobby door. Her obvious agitation alarmed Father Romero.

"We've got a problem," Ferris said. She pushed open the passenger door and got out.

Judy Hudson was pointing across the street and yelling something.

Father Romero and Ferris turned to look. They saw a huge man running toward them. His left hand was tossing aside a raincoat. Underneath the raincoat was an ugly, sawed-off shotgun pointing directly at them.

29

MACALISTER BROUGHT the sawed-off shotgun into a hip-firing position, his finger tightening on the trigger. He figured he'd give the priest a blast across the bows, maybe even pepper the front end of the brown sedan. The whole scene would be noisy and messy, but MacAlister wanted to make sure his point got across. Before his quarry could even begin to deal with the shock, MacAlister knew he could be reloaded and ready to rain more terror down on the small group. Damn, he loved his job.

Blinkered by the focus on his mission, MacAlister presented an unlikely yet vulnerable target. As he dashed menacingly forward, he barely registered the black muscle-van roaring toward him.

Rhonda timed her actions perfectly, opening the van's passenger door at the precise moment MacAlister's brain was sending twitch messages to his trigger finger. The door caught MacAlister flush on the meat of his right shoulder, slamming him sideways through the air and down to the ground, the sawed-off flying free from his hand.

The illegally altered gun spun three times before stabbing muzzle first into the street asphalt. The force of the contact discharged the shotgun round in the chamber, blowing the gun twenty feet back into the air again. Chips of asphalt peppered everywhere, kicked up with explosive force by the muzzle blast. They splattered MacAlister's torso and stung Father Romero's ankles like angry bees.

It had been Hammersmith's idea to retrieve his black van before leaving the area of the church. He and Rhonda would then be able to shadow Father Romero and Ferris in the brown sedan during the pickup procedure. Everybody recognized the staked-goat scenario, but nobody mentioned it. The way things were turning out, the precaution had been worthwhile.

As MacAlister was bouncing off the Tarmac, Hammer screeched the van to a halt in the middle of the street. Jumping to the ground with his gun drawn, he yelled, "Move! Move!" while waving at Father Romero and Ferris, who were standing shell-shocked beside the brown sedan.

Rhonda followed Hammer through the van's driver's side. Her own shoulder hurt from being hit by the passenger door rebounding off MacAlister. The door had a dent in it, and jammed shut when it ricocheted closed after putting MacAlister into orbit. As she jogged after Hammer, she switched her nine-millimeter to her left hand and let her right arm dangle.

Ferris recovered faster than either Father Romero or Judy Hudson. Perhaps it was because of the traumas she had undergone in her personal life. Perhaps she was just better at responding in a crisis. Whatever the reason, she knew to leave MacAlister to Hammer and Nails and take care of her own responsibility.

Slapping the roof of the sedan with the palm of her hand and yelling to get Father Romero's attention, she grabbed Judy Hudson and shoved her into the priest's arms. The pillow under Judy's jacket plopped out.

Ferris ran into the lobby of the motel and scooped Stella Hudson into her arms. The child was in hysterics but immediately calmed as if Ferris were emitting some universal mother code.

Moving at speed, Ferris was back at the sedan while Father Romero was still stashing Judy in the backseat. Not pausing to pass Stella to her mother, Ferris carried the child with her into the front passenger area. She had the key turned in the ignition before the priest was back in the driver's seat.

Seeming to finally kick himself into gear, Father Romero punched the accelerator and swung the vehicle out of the motel driveway.

Cars on the street were either screeching their brakes or pounding on their horns as they approached Hammer's middle-of-the-street abandoned van and the three-figure confrontation on the asphalt.

Hammer had drawn down on MacAlister, but the big man ignored his commands to stay put. MacAlister had been a cop. He knew Hammer wasn't going to shoot him, couldn't since MacAlister now appeared unarmed. He pushed himself to his feet and began a stumbling run away from the scene.

Hammer paused long enough to jam his gun into his hip holster before giving pursuit. Behind him, Rhonda collected the sawed-off from its final resting place in the gutter before joining the chase. It was amazing how quickly something like the sawed-off could disappear, giving someone like MacAlister the opportunity to say, "Gun? What gun? I never had any gun."

Hammer was not as buffed as MacAlister, but he was younger and faster. He also hadn't been hit by the door of a speeding van. As he caught up with his target, he reached out and slapped the big man's right heel. This minor action caused MacAlister to trip over his own leg and tumble to the ground.

Hammer launched himself onto MacAlister's back, trying to get a pain/compliance hold on MacAlister's right arm. The intention was fine, but MacAlister was by nature a dirty street fighter and used his bulk to roll away from Hammersmith's grasp and deliver a vicious head butt. Hammer slipped off MacAlister, who delivered a hefty kick to Hammer's ribs as he regained his feet.

Rhonda wasn't far behind the action. It was all she could do to hold the sawed-off in her weakened right hand, the arm still hanging like a partially paralyzed log. She swung her left hand in an arcing loop and clouted MacAlister over the ear with the flat of her nine-millimeter. He howled in pain and staggered away from his attempt to put the boot to Hammer.

Rhonda followed through, delivering a side kick to MacAlister's thigh that made little if any impression. She'd been aiming for his knee, but racing adrenaline threw off her aim.

She tried another kick, but MacAlister was ready for her. He parried the kick and lashed out with the flat of his hand upside her head.

Rhonda's ears rang and her vision blurred. She slipped to a knee. MacAlister was moving away again, running through traffic down the main street.

"You okay?" Hammer asked. He was up, dragging Rhonda back to her feet.

She nodded her head, wincing. She was going to have a hell of a headache later. "Yeah." She started running forward to give chase. "Let's get the bastard," she said.

In the distance there were sirens headed toward them.

Hammersmith was soon closing the distance with MacAlister again.

"Give it up, man," he said through ragged breaths. "We know who you are. There's no getting away."

MacAlister's answer was to whirl around, swinging his arm wide, hoping to catch Hammersmith with the blunt end of his fist.

Hammersmith reacted quickly enough to duck under the attack. He pushed forward with his legs, driving his shoulder into MacAlister's ribs. MacAlister grunted in pain and slammed his joined fists down on Hammersmith's back.

Still churning his legs, Hammersmith pushed MacAlister into the side of a parked car. MacAlister reached his arms around Hammer's waist, lifted him off the ground, and threw him aside. Hammer went sprawling into the oncoming traffic, skinning hands and knees. An oncoming Toyota truck squealed metal to metal brakes and steered wide in panic.

The momentum of his action swung MacAlister around. Rhonda had holstered her gun, but still held the shotgun in her weak hand. Seeing MacAlister's broad back turned toward her, she leapt on it, locking her legs around his waist and sliding the short barrels of the shotgun across MacAlister's Adam's apple. She pulled back on both ends of the gun with all her might.

MacAlister flailed around, reaching back to claw at Rhonda's face, which she buried in the big man's shoulder.

"I'll kill you!" he screamed.

Hammer was back on his feet. He used his grazed fists to pummel away at MacAlister's exposed abdominals.

Rhonda could feel her grip weakening. Her right arm was almost useless, and she knew she couldn't hold on to the shotgun much longer. Taking a chance, she let it clatter to the ground.

Moving with precision and speed, she wrapped her right arm around the front of MacAlister's neck and slapped the left side of his head with her left palm, driving the point of his chin into the crook of her right elbow.

With her right arm around MacAlister's neck, she grabbed her left shoulder with her right hand to secure it in place. She then brought her left arm up and over behind MacAlister's head and grabbed her own right shoulder. This movement effectively locked MacAlister into a hold: Rhonda's bent right arm was pressing tightly against his carotid artery. There was no way to break the hold.

MacAlister was in deep trouble. He flailed desperately around and then fell to the ground with Rhonda underneath him. She hung on with reckless abandon, knowing if she quit, MacAlister would kick their butts.

Within a few real-world seconds, as opposed to the elongated hours it took in the hypergenerated universe of physical confrontation, Rhonda's hold cut the flow of blood to MacAlister's brain. He began to *do the chicken*, flopping around before his bladder opened and urine soaked his pants.

"Enough!" Hammer called out. His words barely penetrated Rhonda's intense concentration. He was pulling at her arms. "He's out! He's out!" Hammer repeated over and over.

Rhonda came back to reality and released her hold. Rolling MacAlister onto his back, Hammer used two pairs of linked handcuffs to secure MacAlister's arms behind him.

"You okay?"

Rhonda nodded. She didn't have breath for more than her own one-word query. "You?"

"Yeah," Hammer said. He sat down on the curb next to where Rhonda was proned out. MacAlister lay next to them, unconscious but breathing.

A squad car rocked to a stop in front of them, its lights flashing and siren wailing. Two others weren't far behind.

"Next time," Rhonda gasped, "let's do something easier."

"What?" Hammer asked, playing straight man.

"Like running with the bulls in Pamplona, wrestling alligators, chasing King Kong up the side of the Empire State Building, anything."

"Oh, you mean kid's stuff."

30

DETECTIVES BORN under lucky stars are few and far between. Those who are, such as Hammer and Nails, always seem to be in the right place at the right time with the ball bouncing their way. They catch burglars stepping out of broken windows. Suspects they are searching for jump into the backseat of their police cars as they drive down the street. Their clues closet is constantly replenished. They sneeze and suspects confess. They walk in on robberies in progress and disarm the villain before he's aware of their presence. If a gun is pointed at them, it jams. If it doesn't jam, it misfires. If it doesn't misfire, the shot goes wild. And if the shot doesn't go wild, it never hits anything vital. Their luck never runs out or runs cold. They are blessed, and they have no understanding of the great majority of detectives who aren't.

Other detectives, especially those who have worked hard to get to the top of their profession, understand how large a part luck plays in police work. They admire the lucky star detectives, but often resent them because they are immune to the axiom "Shit happens."

To most detectives, shit happens, and it happens most often when they are working hard, trying to bull their way through an investigation. When they are pushing the edge of the envelope, gambling their lottery numbers will pop up, Lady Luck simply goes back to watching over her favored few, leaving those depending on her to the whims of that other favored axiom, "Whatever can go wrong will go wrong."

Alphabet and Brindle were forcing their hand. Ricky Preston, the wanna-be stuntman who'd starred in Citadel Productions' *Bad Blood*, was being elusive. They went from the offices of Citadel Productions to the address for Preston's agent listed on the back of his publicity photo.

The office was in a five-story gray brick building on the fringes of Beverly Hills. The agency was a stripped-down operation, with a secretary whose bust size was probably larger than her IQ.

Fitz Culver, the agent, wasn't much better. It was as if all of Hollywood was striving to fit a standard stereotype: secretaries chewed gum and had big breasts in tight sweaters; agents wore ill-fitting suits and grew ponytails to compensate for the bald spots on top. Creativity didn't seem to be a requirement.

Culver admitted to representing Ricky Preston, real name Rico Prestavanovich, but stated he could only contact Preston using the same pager number given to Janice Hancock, the Citadel assistant.

Brindle called the office and caught Monk on his way out to Hollywood Park. Monk entered Preston's real name in the computer and ran it every which way.

"I've got a driver's license with an address on Crenshaw." He provided Brindle with the numbers. "His record shows several arrests for ADW and battery. One conviction. He did a year in county back in 1990. He also has a conviction for lewd acts with a child in ninety-two. He must have copped a plea because he only did three years in San Quentin before being paroled. He got off parole in ninety-seven." Monk continued to give the highlights of the information regurgitated by his computer inquiries. "Preston is a registered sex offender, but he hasn't been in for his annual renewal since his parole was terminated."

"Any cars registered to him?"

Monk rustled through the printouts. "He's got a Toyota Celica registered to the same address on Crenshaw. It hasn't been registered since ninety-seven either." He gave Brindle the license plate number. After looking up the VIN of the car in a book published by the National Auto Theft Bureau, he was able to give the car's color as green.

"Can you get a felony stop put on the vehicle?"

"Sure, no problem."

"Does he have any warrants?"

"Nothing I can see. But he's good to go on the failure to register as a sex offender. That should give you something to squeeze."

"Have to find him before we can squeeze him."

The address on Crenshaw was a dead end. It was a halfway house for parolees, providing a stable residence and a stay under the thumb of their parole agent. The house manager confirmed Preston split the day after his parole was terminated. There was no forwarding address.

"Even prison time hadn't knocked the stars out of that one's eyes," the manager commented to Brindle. He had seen hundreds of men come and go from under his roof, but somehow he never lost hope for them.

"What do you mean?"

"Ricky wanted to be in movies. A stuntman. He was always working out, always dreaming about his big break. I tried to help him get a real job, but dreaming was easier."

"What about his conviction for child molest?"

The house manager shrugged. "I run a straight house. No drugs, no alcohol, and no sex on the premises. I found Ricky with a couple of kiddie porn magazines once. Threatened to throw him out and tell his PO, but he swore he'd fly right. Everybody deserves a chance, so I gave him one."

"Any more problems?"

The manager shook his head. "Nope. He put in his time and split as soon as Parole detached the leash."

"Any ideas where he is now?"

"This is reality, baby. He could be anywhere. But wherever he is, he's probably trying to find a way to get himself back to the big house."

Contacting Preston's old parole officer didn't get them any further. Irma Watkins kept tabs on Preston while he was in her charge. He didn't cause any problems, so she ignored him. She had more than enough problem cases to concentrate on. Once Preston's parole ran, Irma closed the books and didn't think about him again. She had no idea where he was, what he was doing, or where anybody who might be interested could find him. He didn't exist for her anymore.

That left the pager number.

Not wanting to page Preston and tip him off, Alphabet and Brindle had to find an alternative way to track him down. A contact in the phone company provided Alphabet with the name of the firm to whom Ricky's pager number was assigned. The pager business, however, insisted on a search warrant before releasing its subscriber records.

Getting the warrant only took an hour and a half, but the results were frustrating. Ricky Preston's billing address led to a private mailbox business in Canoga Park, a run-down suburb in the northern end of the San Fernando Valley. The cops called the area Congo Park as it was a jungle of Hispanic heroin junkies and crack houses.

The business was a small square in a dingy strip mall anchored by a corner liquor store on the west end and a coin-operated Laundromat on the other. In between were a neighborhood bar catering to Mexican laborers, an insurance office, and a Ninety-Nine Cents outlet.

The Mail It Plus store boasted a dirty reception area with a service counter and two walls full of locked metal boxes registered to private parties. The owner appeared Middle Eastern and was behind the counter dealing with a stack of UPS packages and FedEx orders.

He recognized Alphabet and Brindle as cops and, although he spoke five languages fluently, had an immediate brain fart and forgot how to speak English.

Alphabet came at him in Spanish. The owner's brain fart expanded. He only remembered a little Spanish.

The situation reminded Brindle of the politically incorrect police joke about why Mexicans were like cue balls—the harder you hit them, the more English you got out of them. Even though the owner was Middle Eastern and not Mexican, Brindle was willing to bet the same principle applied. Brindle, however, had a more civilized solution, surprising everybody by speaking in labored but passable Farsi.

Before he was forced to acknowledge the use of his own language, the phone conveniently rang, distracting the store owner's attention.

"Where did you learn to speak camel jockey?" Alphabet asked, impressed.

"You don't want to know," she said, giving Alphabet a dirty look for using a racist term. Such insensitivities were the quickest way to get a complaint lodged against you.

"Sure I do."

Brindle shrugged, trying to make light of her explanation. "I worked undercover narcotics out of the academy. I was sleeping with the enemy. It was his language, so I learned it."

Alphabet felt a rush of irrational jealousy. "You're not supposed to sleep with your targets. It's entrapment." His vision of Brindle sleeping with an Iranian drug dealer made him feel sick.

Brindle shrugged. "You're not supposed to do dope with them either, but you do what you have to do to make the case."

Alphabet didn't have time to respond, as the store owner hung up the phone and began jabbering with Brindle again.

It turned out speaking Farsi didn't help much. The owner began shouting about his rights in America and insisted on a warrant before providing further information on the box renter.

Brindle tried explaining he didn't have the right to insist on a warrant. Like hotel and motel registries, post office–box rental records are not protected from police scrutiny. But it was to no avail.

Alphabet took Brindle aside to urge her to threaten to bring in drug-sniffing dogs to go through all the packages and letters in the store, but Brindle prevailed. The store was in a rough area, and the owner would be inviting major trouble if the word got out that he had cooperated with the police.

The detectives could have forcibly checked the store records, but it was quicker and safer to get another warrant. Being legally correct was no longer enough to avoid complaints or civil actions.

The second warrant took two hours to write and get signed. The judge who signed the first warrant was tied up in court, so another had to be found. Finally, however, with the signed warrant in hand, the two detectives returned to Mail It Plus.

When they pulled into the parking lot, a green, rusted Toyota Celica, the muffler held up by baling wire, was parked in a spot close to the storefront. Lady Luck was trying to smile, but neither detective noticed.

"I know we started out in hot pursuit this morning, but it's lukewarm pursuit now," Alphabet grumbled, parking their detective sedan, with its cheap black-wall tires and roof-planted antenna farm, in front of the Mail It Plus store's glass-front door. It had to be a police car. It couldn't be anything else.

"More like stone-cold pursuit at this point," Brindle agreed. She levered herself out of the car and followed Alphabet up to the store. They were both tired, their initial enthusiasm for the chase waning as the long day proceeded.

They had not told the manager what specific box they were interested in, so they were not worried that the manager would alert Preston. It was always amazing how many people tried to give the bad guys the edge. After all, the police only harassed innocent citizens; the newspapers said so.

"Let's get this done," Alphabet said, reaching for the door.

Lady Luck felt ignored so she disappeared from the scene.

Before Alphabet's hand could grab the door handle, the door opened, jamming the handle into Alphabet's outstretched arm with jarring impact. Swearing, he recoiled with pain running up his shoulder. He grabbed at his fingers. They felt broken.

Concerned, Brindle turned toward her partner, only to be knocked down by the body that flew out of the doorway. She rolled as she hit the ground, but a solid kick caught her in the stomach and lifted her off the curb. She scraped her hands and arms pushing herself off the ground.

"Shit! It's him!" Alphabet yelled.

31

BRINDLE STRUGGLED to a knee as she fumbled for her gun. When it wouldn't come clear, she realized she was trying to pull it free without opening the holster snap. Cursing, she took her eyes off the fleeing back of Ricky Preston and looked down to see what she was doing.

The overdose of adrenaline coursing through her body was giving her the shakes. With both hands, she unsnapped the holster and slid out the nine-millimeter Smith & Wesson.

"Shoot the asshole," Alphabet was yelling. He was reaching across his body, pulling at his own gun with his off hand, his normal shooting hand still useless.

"What good will shooting his asshole do? There's already a hole there." Brindle felt a hysterical giggle trying to pop out of her throat.

With her gun out, she started to limp after Preston. He was well ahead of her, entering his car. He turned the ignition and backed out of the parking spot at speed, crashing into the car behind him.

Brindle was at the side of the Toyota, but her mind had drawn a blank on the first rule of police work: No good deed goes unpunished.

Preston was a fleeing felon, a murder suspect.

Even though she could have legally shot Preston, Brindle couldn't shoot somebody who wasn't shooting back. Instead, she swung the butt of her gun, smashing the driver's window in a shower of safety glass.

She pointed her gun in a two-handed grip, legs slightly spread, weight forward. "Freeze!" she yelled, her voice husky. The corny line sounded stupid even to her own ears. It was bad movie verbiage, but it was what cops said.

Preston didn't even flinch. He jammed the car into gear and accelerated forward, fishtailing the rear end as he turned into the parking lot lane. The rear tires of the car almost ran over Brindle's toes, forcing her to sprawl to the ground again.

This time, she rolled onto her right side, bent her left knee to lock her foot behind her right knee, extended her gun in a two-handed, modified Weaver grip, and cranked off two rounds. She saw one bullet blow chips of metal and rust off the Toyota's trunk, and the other tear the rear license plate from its holder. Neither shot was fatal to the car, and it pulled out into the boulevard traffic like a crazed squirrel.

There was a screech of tires behind her, and Brindle rolled to the side against a parked car.

"Get in!" Alphabet yelled, reaching across to shove open the passenger-side door of the detective sedan.

Completely disheveled, Brindle hauled herself into the car, allowing Alphabet's acceleration to slam the door closed behind her.

"It is Preston, isn't it?" Brindle was trying hard to catch her breath and stop the shakes.

"Who the hell else do you think it is? We were stupid, stupid, stupid!" Alphabet slammed his hand down on the top of the steering wheel in emphasis. "We parked right in front of the damn mailbox store."

"How were we supposed to know he'd be in there picking up his junk mail?"

"That's not the point. We should have anticipated the chance he might have been inside." Alphabet pulled into traffic, cutting off several cars, and took off after the Toyota two blocks ahead.

Getting focused, Brindle flipped down and activated the car's red light from its position above the rearview mirror. Alphabet activated the siren.

Brindle pushed the rover radio into the unit's console and adjusted the frequency before keying the radio mike. She couldn't remember the team's new Robbery-Homicide unit designation, so she reverted to their old West Los Angeles handle. "Eight-W-seventy-eight, we are in pursuit in a brown dual-purpose vehicle eastbound on Sherman Way from Winnetka Boulevard." She paused for the RTO to acknowledge.

"Eight-W-seventy-eight, roger. All units on all frequencies stand by, eight-W-seventy-eight is in pursuit in a brown dual-purpose vehicle, eastbound on Sherman Way from Winnetka Boulevard." The radio telephone operator's voice was calm and assured. She went through this procedure several times a shift.

Brindle keyed the mike again. "Eight-W-seventy-eight, we are in pursuit of a possible murder suspect driving a green, mideighties Toyota, no rear plate. It's being driven by a male white, blond, blue, six-one, one-ninety, unknown if he is armed at this time."

"Eight-W-seventy-eight, roger." The RTO went on to broadcast the pursuit to all the other units on the frequency.

Patrol units across the West Valley area turned up their car radios and began heading to intercept and assist in the pursuit. The police helicopter peeled away from where it had been hovering over a shopping center, looking for car thieves.

A traffic reporter sitting in the observer seat in a cruising news copter spotted the sudden, decisive movement of the police air unit. With adept fingers, he flipped his copter's radio to the local police frequency and picked up the pursuit. The pilot was already turning to follow the police air unit.

The Toyota was almost a full block ahead of Alphabet and Brindle. Preston knew how to mash the accelerator to the floor, but compared with Alphabet, he knew nothing about driving. Where Preston swerved wildly to pass slower cars or avoid obstacles, Alphabet was smooth and easy.

Alphabet had his initial panic under control and was settling into a pursuit rhythm. Feeling was coming back to his gun hand, and his brain had kicked into action.

For her part, Brindle had the shakes under control and was competently broadcasting the pursuit as the cars flashed down Sherman Way. Juggling the radio mike and her gun, Brindle performed a combat reload, exchanging the partially used clip in the butt of her nine-millimeter with a full clip from the pouch on her belt.

Preston took a wide turn through a yellow light from Sherman Way to southbound Tampa. Two black-and-white patrol units joined the pursuit behind the detective sedan, and all three blew the red light, sirens at full tilt, just as southbound traffic was entering the intersection.

"Stupid muther is going to get us all killed," Alphabet said.

Both Brindle and Alphabet knew they should have pulled their plain car out of the pursuit and let the marked patrol units take over, but neither verbalized the option. There were manual procedures that sounded great on paper, but in the real world things rarely work the way the pencil jockeys with no hands-on experience expect them to happen.

Overhead in the news copter, cameras were rolling, sending images of the pursuit directly back to the station. Television viewers all over Los Angeles were hearing sonorous tones enunciating,

"We are interrupting our regular broadcast to bring you a special report." As the pursuit continued, other TV and radio station helicopters crowded the sky to tag along.

Preston had the Toyota weaving in and out of the thickening early afternoon traffic. Twice he took to the sidewalk to bypass stopped traffic. On the second occasion the chassis of the small car crashed against the curb, popping the last rusted joints on the exhaust system and dropping the muffler down to drag along the ground, sparks flying from the friction.

Alphabet was right behind the quarry now. The Toyota was a gutless wonder, so Alphabet was not worried about losing Preston to a speed contest. The detective sedan had power to spare.

The pursuit had become more a matter of time than anything else. How long could Preston run before he ran out of gas, made a mistake and crashed, or simply gave up?

Preston was now on Ventura Boulevard heading east. Traffic was becoming heavier and he was having much more trouble simply keeping moving through red lights and roadwork.

As they approached the intersection of Ventura and Sepulveda, Brindle pointed out the window. "He's slowing," she said. "Get ready to bail out if he makes a run for it."

Alphabet stayed behind Preston as the Toyota took the turn onto Sepulveda and stopped in the middle of the road across from a gas station.

Brindle turned off the car siren. She briefly told the RTO the situation and then switched the radio over to PA. Using the microphone, she gave instructions over the car's loudspeaker.

"Turn off your engine."

Alphabet had his car door open and was crouched behind it with his gun out. Brindle was out on her side in the same manner. The patrol units assumed flanking positions.

"Turn off your engine," Brindle ordered again. "Throw the keys out of the window. It's over."

Preston still sat in his car, its hood pointing at the gas station, police cars arranged behind it, helicopters circling like vultures above.

"Turn off—"

That was as far as Brindle got before Preston accelerated.

"Shit," Brindle said, the word coming clearly over the open speaker.

The Toyota bounced over the curb. Sparks from the dragging muffler pinwheeled into the air like those of a Fourth of July sparkler. With deliberation, Preston drove the Toyota forward at speed, to crash into the closest set of gas pumps. Before the gas pump's shear-off valves kicked in, enough gasoline spurted free to cover the Toyota. Sparks from the dragging muffler instantly found the fuel to ignite the car into a fireball.

The Toyota's gas tank had ruptured in the crash, and a second explosion tore the vehicle apart with Preston inside it.

32

"FOR HELL'S sake. What's been going on around here?" Fey asked in exasperation. It was day three at RHD. "I leave you people alone for five minutes and the damn unit splashes itself all over the national news."

It was early morning and Fey's crew were the only detectives in the office.

The explosion of Preston's Toyota had been a perfect example of the "If it bleeds, it leads" mentality of the media. A suicide filled with flames and explosions at the end of a car chase with the cameras rolling was a news editor's wet dream. The scene had been repeated over and over in living rooms across the country.

"We tried to call you," Alphabet said.

"Bah!" Fey shook her head as much at herself as at Alphabet's pathetic salve. Her phone battery had been dead and she'd forgotten to charge it before leaving for San Quentin.

"We left messages on your machine at home," Brindle tried to explain.

That didn't even rate an outburst. Fey had been so tired when she finally arrived home the night before, she had plopped straight into bed without even showering, let alone checking her phone messages. How was she supposed to know the world was falling apart?

It had been morning before she turned on the television while she was getting ready for work. Nothing better had come in overnight, and the scenes of the gas station explosion were still the big story. Fey's throat had constricted. She couldn't swallow, and she'd felt light-headed. This was not good.

She didn't bother calling anyone. She just got in the car and headed downtown.

She pointed a finger at Hammer and Nails. "Shotgun battles at high noon in the middle of the city streets." The finger swung back to Alphabet and Brindle. "Chasing suspects until they decide to commit suicide by damn near blowing up half a block." The extended digit continued its journey until it singled Monk out. "And where were you while all this was going on?"

Hammer and Nails were not about to correct Fey, telling her the shootout had been closer to late evening than high noon. Conversely, Brindle and Alphabet were not going to argue that Ricky Preston's explosion had been limited to his vehicle and nothing more. The gas pumps shear-off valves had worked well, ensuring the whole station didn't blow up. Everyone was glad to have the buck passed to Monk, no matter how unfair.

"I was at Hollywood Park checking up on Jack Kavanaugh's fatal accident," Monk said, calmly sitting at the end of the long squad room table.

"You shoot anybody while you were there? Blow up any stables?"

"Nope."

"I thought I asked you to keep this bunch out of trouble?"

Monk spread his hands on the desk in front of him and didn't say anything further. He knew Fey well enough not to comment.

"You can't make an omelette without breaking eggs," Alphabet ventured.

Fey looked ready to explode until she realized how unreasonable she was being.

"Okay," she said more calmly. She ran a hand through her hair and blew a deep breath out in a whoosh. "Were any of you hurt? You all scared the crap out of me." She took another deep breath and attempted a smile.

Tentatively, her crew smiled back at her.

"All right, all right. I'm sorry," she said. "I'm feeling guilty because I wasn't around. Let's break out the coffee and see if we can figure out where we all stand."

The crew had been up most of the night dealing with the aftermath of their confrontations. The department's Officer Involved Shooting Team had been kept busy. In Fey's absence, which she would no doubt be hearing about, Whip Whitman had stepped in and kept things moving.

The chief had put in an appearance—GOD coming down off his cloud, Hammer had remarked—but he'd not seemed overly displeased. Low-key arrests might not catch as much heat from the media as shoot-outs and explosions, but then, he hadn't ever expected Fey and company to be low-key. As long as the shooting scenarios were in policy, it was Press Relations' job to handle spin control.

Sleeping late would have been a luxury all of the team would have enjoyed, but it clearly wasn't a choice. Their actions of the day before had opened new leads that had to be followed up.

Leaving Penny with Rhonda's mother was a good, if temporary option for Hammer and Nails. They realized, however, it was not a long-term solution. If both of them were going to keep working, another plan needed to be found for Penny's care.

The baby's special needs also complicated matters. Rhonda was still struggling with guilt and worry. She realized how dangerous their confrontation had been with MacAlister, and her mind was still considering the repercussions of what would happen if both she and Hammer were killed.

As for Alphabet and Brindle, the death of Preston had hit them hard. It was difficult not to think of themselves as the catalyst, even if the result had been unintentional.

At the long desk in RHD, Fey noticed the pair were sitting closer together than normal, as if drawing strength from each other. At least Fey hoped that's all it was.

As other RHD detectives began arriving, full of questions and advice, Fey moved the crew into Whitman's office for privacy. Everyone had coffee and was eager to share thoughts.

Fey took the lead, briefing them on her trip to San Quentin and her conversation with Eldon Dodge.

"He's implicating Judge Luther Flynn?" Hammer asked.

"I know," Fey told him. "It's an improbable story, but if we can corroborate it in any way, it may give us a direction."

Fiddling with his coffee mug, Hammer shook his head. "It could all be a wild-goose chase."

"Maybe," Fey agreed. "But it seems a bit elaborate."

"What's Devon Wyatt's stake in all of this?" Monk asked.

"I'm not sure," Fey told him. "He must have an angle, but I'm damned if I can figure it out at the moment."

"We may have something there," Hammer said.

"How so?" Fey asked.

"When we booked MacAlister, he immediately started yelling for his lawyer. Guess who?"

"Wyatt."

"The one and only," Hammer agreed. "You're aware of MacAlister's history?"

"I've never run into him, but I know he's an ex-cop who retired in lieu of facing corruption charges."

"He's a major bad-ass," Hammer told her. "He does mostly

strong-arm work for high-priced defense attorneys. He specializes in witness intimidation and getting dirt on the officers involved in a case. He's on a permanent retainer to Devon Wyatt."

"I don't see how it fits," Fey said, "but it can't be coincidence."

"The type of torture isn't his style," Rhonda said. "He would have been far more professional. However, we think he might have helped Ricky Preston grab Bianca Flynn. It would have been a lot easier with two, and MacAlister's van is more functional for a kidnapping than Preston's Toyota."

"Where's the van now?"

"We impounded it. Scientific Investigation Division is giving it the bumper-to-bumper treatment. We have a friend down there who owes us a couple of favors, so we should see results pretty quick."

"What's MacAlister's current status?" Fey asked.

"He's being given a little freeway therapy," Rhonda said. "He was allowed to make his phone call, but since then he's been on the road."

Freeway therapy meant after MacAlister was booked, he'd been transported to another jail within the system, left there for a short period of time, and then shuffled on to another location. All of the shuffling could be justified in various insincere ways: The defendant needed to be booked into a jail where he could be seen by a doctor; the jail where the defendant was booked had become overcrowded and the defendant needed to be moved; the defendant was judged a suicide risk and had been moved to a more secure location for his safety. There were any number of ways to move a defendant and lose him within the system so his lawyer couldn't bail him out.

"Are you going to take a whack at interrogating him?" Fey asked.

"That's the plan," Hammer told her. "He's a tough nut, so I don't hold out much hope of cracking him. Our best bet is probably to set a surveillance team on him after he bails, but if we didn't go through these motions first, he'd get suspicious."

"Good thought," Fey said. "I'll talk to Whitman about borrowing a team of Swoop Dogs."

The department's Special Investigations Section, known as Swoop Dogs, had been termed an assassination squad by the media. Their main job was to follow known hard-core criminals until they committed a serious crime. When the crime went down, SIS swooped in. A target criminal and his cohorts were given one chance to surrender before the bullets started to fly. In most cases, the criminals didn't give up, and in some cases the criminals started shooting before SIS even had a chance to offer surrender. It was a controversial unit, filled with officers who put their lives on the line every day and loved it.

"Is Father Romero going to come through with his agreement to let you speak to Bianca's kids?" Fey asked.

Hammer nodded. He'd explained earlier about the deal they had cut to get to the kids. "His word is good."

"You're going to have to see the kids in person, so you know who you're talking to. If you do so, then we have an obligation to return those kids to their father," Fey said. "We'd be legally liable if you let Romero disappear them again."

"Agreed," said Rhonda. "But there is another option. We've talked to a DA specializing in child custody cases, and to the Department of Children's Services. Romero has agreed to put the kids in protective custody with DCS. The DA is going to reopen the abuse case and not let the father have custody until it can all be heard in court."

"I know you two," Monk said, speaking up for the first time. "What happens if down the line Mark Ritter gets the kids back?"

"I don't even want to go there right now," Fey said, holding up a halting hand. "We have too much else on our plate." She pointed at Hammer and Nails. "So, you're going to follow up on MacAlister and Bianca's kids, right?"

"Yep," Hammer said.

"What about you two?" Fey asked, turning to Alphabet and Brindle. "How sure are you it was Ricky Preston in the Toyota? And if it was him, how sure are we that he's the guy we're looking for?"

Brindle shrugged. "The body remains were too charred to get a positive ID from the coroner until dental records can be checked. But the car was registered to Preston, and the guy driving it was a dead ringer for the publicity pictures we have, right down to the crew cut and dark glasses. Anyway, why else would he run?"

"We had the publicity shot put in a photo lineup and showed it to the clerk from the Dollar Hardware Emporium," Alphabet said. "She immediately picked Preston out as the guy who bought the staple gun, hand saw, and table vise."

Fey nodded. "Okay. It's good enough for now. What about his pad?"

Alphabet placed his hand on Brindle's shoulder, and Fey noticed she didn't move away. "We went back to the post office–box store and served the warrant," Alphabet said. "That got us a good address on Preston, and we've secured it with two uniforms outside. We'll get a warrant this morning and see what's inside."

Fey looked at Monk, who was patiently waiting his turn. "Sorry I jumped on you," Fey said, specifically seeking forgiveness from her second-in-command. "You know how I am."

Monk's lips contorted in a wry twitch. "That I do," he said. "No problem."

"How about the racetrack? Did you get anything solid?"

"A couple of things," Monk said. "I talked to the track security guy, Frank Bannon. Kavanaugh was persona non grata at the track. There were days when he was okay, but there were other days when he would start raving and causing a commotion. Bannon chased him off a dozen times, but Kavanaugh kept coming back. On the day Kavanaugh was killed, Bannon chased him into the men's room, but Kavanaugh beaned him with a toilet seat." The group tittered. Other people's misfortunes fed their dark humor. Monk continued with a smile. "Clearly, Bannon hadn't expected to be attacked. Kavanaugh got away and somehow got onto the track."

"Anybody else see him or talk to him?"

"I'm getting there," Monk said. "Don't rush me." He checked a small notebook he'd opened in one hand. "I interviewed a Mr. Horace Naylor. He's a regular bettor at the track and has a fetish for loud plaid jackets."

"Can we skip the fashion commentary?" Fey couldn't help herself. There was always a curve in any investigation. Once you began to slingshot around it, the investigation picked up speed and you had to be there with it or it could pass you by. Experience was telling Fey this was happening now, and she felt the need to kick into high gear.

Monk waved a hand. "Kavanaugh had a collision with Mr. Naylor prior to being chased by Bannon. Naylor stated Kavanaugh was babbling about a railroad and trains, and some kind of game. Naylor took it as a sign. He bet on a horse named Chattanooga and won a bundle."

"It figures," Fey said.

"I also interviewed Don Pritchard, the paramedic who treated Kavanaugh after he'd been trampled. Pritchard claims Kavanaugh said a few words before he kicked his ashes, but they didn't make any sense—something about training a game well."

"Training? Not train?"

"I questioned Pritchard further, and he isn't sure. Kavanaugh could have said *train* as opposed to *training*. Pritchard said it didn't make sense to him either way."

"What about the words *a game*? Any ideas?"

Monk shrugged. "Pritchard said the words were something about 'a game well.' Did Kavanaugh play any games?"

Fey shrugged back. She felt she was on the verge of something but she didn't know what. "He said something to Naylor about a railroad, and we know there's a connection between Bianca Flynn and Jack Kavanaugh." She and Monk quickly filled the others in on the books and underlining found at Kavanaugh's apartment, and about the FBI's reaction to the money Kavanaugh left to Fey. "By railroad," Fey summed up, "Kavanaugh could have meant Bianca's Underground Railroad."

"But he spoke about a train. That doesn't make sense in the context of the underground," Nails said.

Fey turned back to Monk. "Give me Pritchard's interpretation of Kavanaugh's last words again."

"Training a game well."

"Hmmm." Fey was thoughtful, and then her eyes sparked. "Wait a minute. Let's leave the training or train part out of it for the moment. What are we left with?"

"A game well?" Monk shrugged.

"Not a game well," Fey said. "A Gamewell."

Monk and the others looked confused.

"What's the difference?" Monk asked.

"Not three words," Fey said. "Two words. One of them capitalized. A Gamewell. A brand name."

"The old call box system," Monk said with a flash of insight. "The boxes were called Gamewells." He was excited, but had no idea why.

"I found a brass call box key under Kavanaugh's pillow in his apartment. It had been taken out of his shadow box."

"Okay," Monk said. "But where does that get us?"

"I'm not sure yet, but we're damn well going to find out."

33

TO BE BURIED in the bowels of Parker Center, the police head-quarters building, was to be cast aside and forgotten. To be buried off-site at the department's Piper-Tech facility was to be exiled to Siberia.

Piper-Tech was a four-story collection of concrete warehouses and garages built on an abandoned acre of waste ground between connecting freeways. The gleaming architecture of the sheriff's department's Twin Towers jail facility and the new transit author-ity building were close in distance, but universes apart in aesthet-ics. The only saving grace for Piper-Tech was the recent relocation to the site of the department's Scientific Investigation Division, SID. This heralded a makeover for the location, or at least for the sections containing the SID labs. There were still other parts of the facility that felt the full blast of Siberian winds.

Fey steered past the police garages on the ground level and found a place to park on the next floor near a cluster of abandoned generators. Using a 999-key, Monk led the way into the building and thumbed the elevator down button. The building was colder than the coroner's offices.

"When they call these guys the Cold Squad, they aren't kidding," he said. Noises behind the elevator door sounded like the torment of lost souls.

"Any organization hates to admit its failures, so they get hidden away," Fey said. "A homicide doesn't make it down here until the clues closet is bare. When the Mole, Doc Freeze, and Kid Cool get a case, it's an ice cube."

The elevator doors groaned open and the two detectives stepped inside.

"How many cases have they solved?" Monk asked, pushing the bottom button.

Fey thought for a moment. "They average one or two a year, which isn't bad considering what they have to work with."

The elevator came to a jarring halt, the doors only opening partway. Fey and Monk turned sideways to slip out, and found themselves in a hallway crowded with overflowing file boxes.

A voice reached them from behind the stacks. "Don't touch anything or you'll start an avalanche. Just follow the yellow brick road."

Looking down, Fey could see a path of yellow bricks painted on the concrete floor. She and Monk followed the path through the maze of stacked files until they reached a large, tidy clearing dominated by three desks and several computer terminals.

A heavyset, balding man with thick glasses walked forward to shake hands. A leaner, younger counterpart looked up from one of the computers with a grin, but kept his fingers tapping.

"Not exactly the Emerald City," the heavyset man said as he shook hands with Fey and Monk, "but it's home."

"Nice to see you, Mole," Fey said.

"Before you ask," Mole jumped in, "we haven't solved the

Black Dahlia murder or Hoffa's disappearance yet. We can't even figure out how my wife got pregnant again when I'm never at home."

"I'm sorry to hear that. We came here hoping for good news."

"Good news? In this place? Everything here is old news—and all of it bad." Mole waved a hand at the surrounding stacks. "You'd never believe the department is planning on going paperless within the next few years."

Monk nodded at the detective using the computer. "How's it going, Kid? Long time no see."

"Long time no see anybody around here—except Mole and Doc Freeze, of course." Detective Mark Anderson, aka Kid Cool, and Monk had been classmates at the academy fifteen years earlier.

Kid Cool's mother, a single parent with five children, had been murdered twenty-five years earlier. The case was never solved. Ten years later, Kid had become an LAPD officer with every intent of finding his mother's killer. He'd become a detective in record time, worked area homicide units, and then apprenticed himself to Mole and Dr. Freeze as the youngest member of the Cold Squad. His mother's murder was still unsolved, but Kid Cool worked away at it with the same unperturbed determination he used to worry along all of the cases in the Cold Squad's files.

"Where's Doc Freeze?" Fey asked.

"She's on a bagel and designer-coffee run," Mole explained. "We may be heathens down here, but we still have needs." The elevator started its tortured whining again. "Ah, that should be her."

Fey and Monk waited until a short, unremarkable blonde woman bustled in and placed spreads of cream cheese next to a large bag with a Western Bagels logo on the side. She handed cups of foamy coffee to Mole and Kid Cool. There were several backups still in the transport tray.

"Sure you won't have some?" she asked Fey and Monk, slicing through a pumpernickel bagel and smearing it with cream cheese and strawberry jam. "There's plenty."

"No thanks," Fey said. "We had our limit earlier."

"Any more caffeine this morning and we'll begin to vibrate," Monk agreed.

"That might not be a bad thing," Doc Freeze said in a saucy tone. Her two compatriots laughed.

Fey and Monk forced themselves not to look at each other. These three had possibly been underground a little too long.

"Okay," Mole said, spitting crumbs. "What can the Cold Squad do for you?"

"How about a little research?" Fey asked.

"Our specialty," Mole said. "What do you have in mind?"

"In 1969, there was an armored-car robbery in which two security guards and one suspect were killed. At the time, a Black Panther named Eldon Dodge was believed to be one of two suspects who got away."

"I remember looking this case over," Mole said. "Didn't the FBI run most of the investigation?"

"They did," Fey agreed. "But we would have taken the preliminary reports. No charges were brought against Dodge and the money was never recovered. Dodge was later involved in a shootout with detectives resulting in the death of his cousin, Mavis Flynn. Dodge is on death row now, doing time for her murder."

"You don't have enough to do without opening up closed cases?" Mole asked.

"We have plenty to do," Fey assured him, "but this stuff could all tie in. The murder of Mavis Flynn might be officially closed, but the armored-car robbery is still unsolved. I want to see what we have, if anything, on both the armored-car robbery and the murder. Maybe something in there can give us a break."

"Mavis Flynn?" Doc Freeze asked. "She wouldn't be connected to Judge Luther Flynn?"

Fey gave her a tight smile. "She was his estranged wife at the time of her murder."

"Sounds as if you're kicking the lid off a major can of worms."

"My specialty," Fey said.

"We'll see what we can track down in the files," Mole told her. "You need this yesterday, of course?"

"Of course." Fey smiled. "When has anybody ever asked for something and told you no rush?"

"You really think something from thirty years ago is going to have a bearing on a current case?" Kid Cool asked.

"I don't know," Fey said, "but there's a twist you may appreciate." Most people knew about Kid Cool's obsession. "My father arrested Eldon Dodge for the murder. If Dodge didn't kill Mavis Flynn, then my father did."

Kid Cool gave a low whistle. "Heavy."

"The past is always with us," Doc Freeze said, unknowingly echoing the quote that had run through Fey's sleepless night.

"Who said that?" Fey asked.

"I did," Doc Freeze told her. "What did you think, somebody was throwing their voice?"

"Too weird for me," Monk told Fey when they were in the car heading back into the heart of the city.

"Those three definitely walk with a different set of ducks," Fey agreed. "Still, we'll take any help we can get."

"Where to now?" Monk asked.

"City Hall East. I want to check in with Mapping and Surveying to see if they have a list of the Gamewell call box locations."

"There won't be many left in their original locations. Most of them have been ripped off as collector's items."

"Yeah, but I have a gut feeling I can't ignore."

"In that case, lead on."

A harried clerk spoke to them in the Mapping and Surveying

office when Fey asked if there were any maps of the Gamewell system available.

"I doubt it." The clerk moved away without further response. What exactly she was busy with, Fey had no idea. How rushed could things get at Mapping and Surveying?

"Do you think you could check?" Fey asked.

"Check what?"

"To see if you have a map of the Gamewell system." Fey's frustration with bureaucracy was rising to the surface.

"I told you," the clerk said. "We don't have any."

"You said you *doubted* you had any. If it wouldn't be here, then where would it be?"

"I don't know." The clerk moved away again.

"Is there a supervisor here?"

"He's out," the clerk said unhelpfully. She had her head down, busy scribbling in a logbook.

"Monk," Fey said. She moved her head with a jerk.

Monk responded by boosting himself up onto the office counter, swiveling on his butt to swing his legs over, and hopping down on the other side.

"Hey!" the clerk said.

Along the wall behind the counter were a number of cardboard boxes holding rolled maps and blueprints. Monk started pulling them out and unrolling them on the counter.

"What are you doing?" The clerk's agitation was obvious. She flattened her hands on the maps, but Monk unrolled another on top of her hands. "You can't do this."

"What's going on?" A slim man in a white short-sleeved shirt and a Father's Day tie came out of a back room.

"We're looking for a map," Fey said sweetly.

"What?" The man looked confused.

Fey flashed her badge. "Are you the supervisor here?"

"Yes."

"I'm Detective Croaker with Robbery-Homicide. Your counter clerk was unable to help us with our inquiry, so we decided we'd better help ourselves."

A disgruntled expression moved into place on the supervisor's face. The clerk quickly busied herself rolling up maps from the counter.

"Janice has a problem with authority figures," the supervisor said.

"Really?" Fey said. "I never would have guessed."

Janice disappeared into the back of the office clutching the maps to her flat chest.

The supervisor watched her go with a scowl before giving his attention back to Fey. "I'm Brett Hardy. What is it you need?"

"A city map of the old Gamewell call box system."

"I haven't seen one of those in fifteen years."

"Does that mean they don't exist?"

"No. But it does mean you might have a problem."

"How so?"

"El Niño dumped a lot of rain a couple of winters ago. The city drains overflowed and the old mapping offices became a reservoir. Much of our historical stuff was damaged and thrown out before the other files were dried out and moved here."

"Great." Fey was glum.

"Can I make a suggestion?" Hardy asked.

"We could use one about now."

"Why don't you try the LAPD Historical Society?"

THE LAPD Historical Society was housed in a large trailer parked behind the new Seventy-seventh Street station. The trailer acted as a mobile museum and was driven to numerous public functions.

Fey had called ahead to rouse Roger Lund, the retired sergeant who ran the society. He'd agreed to meet them and see if he could help. When they arrived, Fey and Monk found Lund elbow deep in a file drawer under a display of LAPD badges.

"Howdy," Lund said. "I think I may have what you want." He was a stocky man with leathery skin from years as a motor officer. He hauled a series of folded papers out of the file and spread them on the floor of the trailer, where he was sitting. "Aha!" He plucked a trifolded paper out of the collection and stood up with it. "This is it."

Fey and Monk followed Lund to a low table, where he spread out the map.

"The department's system grew to two hundred and eight Gamewells across the city," Lund explained.

"Two hundred and eight," Fey said, realizing how long it would take to check all those locations. She looked at the map, which was faded with age.

"Problem is," Lund continued, "I'm not sure how accurate this map is. When the Gamewells were serviced, they were some-times moved to more convenient locations and the maps were never updated." He pointed to the chart on the low desk. "There are only a hundred and eighty boxes shown on this map. Where the other twenty-eight were located is anybody's guess."

Fey looked at Monk.

"I know," he said. "Why can't anything be easy?"

"It might help if I knew what you were looking for," Lund said.

"Yeah, it would," Fey told him. "We wish *we* knew."

"Any particular area where your box may be located?" Lund asked.

"That's a thought," Fey said. "The box, if it even exists, would most probably have been in what was then called University Divi-sion." It had been the area where her father and Jack Kavanaugh worked.

"Okay," Lund said. With a red marker, he circled the area on the map. "That cuts it down to, let's see . . ." He started counting. "Possibly thirty-two boxes. They were packed in pretty tight. In those days University was a hot division."

"It's a start," Fey said.

"Tell me . . ." Lund rubbed his chin. "Are you planning on trying to track down these boxes?"

"If they still exist. Why?"

"Well, we don't have a Gamewell box in the collection. Historically, it would be nice to have one. I run the Explorer Scout post out of the station here. I could mobilize the kids to help you check. If we find several boxes, we could auction off the extra."

"Sounds like a win-win situation to me," Fey said. "When can you start?"

34

MacAlister stared at Hammer and yawned widely. He didn't bother to cover his mouth. Halitosis and stale sweat wafted from him in waves.

"Where's the bimbo?" he asked. "She's a lot easier on the eyes than you are. What's she like in the sack, anyway? I bet she just lies there."

Hammer shrugged. "She's probably not a patch on the farm animals you screw."

MacAlister laughed. "Okay, so you're not going to let me rile you. How about stopping this freeway therapy crap and let me get out of here?"

Hammersmith and Rhonda had agreed that approaching MacAlister one-on-one might get more out of him than a concerted effort. It could make him cocky.

"Let you out?" Hammer questioned. "I thought a million-dollar bail enhancement would be more appropriate."

"Why bother? Wyatt will get it knocked down in a heartbeat. You've got nothing."

Hammer curled his fingers back and checked the tips. "Wasn't it 1988 when you arrested Cyril Rathbone for the murder of his wife? You had nothing, until Rathbone waived his rights and confessed. Unfortunately, the tape in the interrogation room wasn't working. Still, confessions were your specialty. Your sterling reputation as a Los Angeles Police detective would easily sway the jury—despite Rathbone swearing blind he'd never waived his rights or confessed."

MacAlister's face had clouded over, his shoulders hunching forward.

Leaning easily against the bars of MacAlister's locked cell door, Hammer continued in an even tone. "If it wasn't for me and the bimbo coming up with a confession from the real suspect, the next-door neighbor, Rathbone would have gone down clean."

"Where is this little fairy tale leading?"

Hammer pursed and relaxed his lips. "Payback? A million-dollar bail enhancement shouldn't be too difficult to get. The assault with a deadly weapon charges may not be enough, but since you've waived your rights and confessed to being involved in the kidnapping of Bianca Flynn . . ." Hammer let the sentence hang.

"Bullshit," MacAlister said, his eyes wary. "You can't be serious."

"Serious as a heart attack." Hammer had run down this path with MacAlister on instinct. It was interesting to see the big man's physical reactions. A pulse was clearly visible over the carotid artery in the neck, and there was a slight sheen of sweat on his forehead.

"Don't bluff a bluffer," MacAlister said. "You'd never lie to get me put away. You don't have the balls for it."

"I might not, but the bimbo does. What was it we got you for in the end when we were working IA? Photographs of you playing bagman for a city councilman?"

"Shit," MacAlister drawled. "You got lucky. I'm making more money now than I ever did on the job, corruption included." MacAlister gave a rude chuckle and flatulated loudly. "You might be having a wet dream about putting me in jail, but it ain't going to happen. By the time Wyatt is done taking you and the bimbo apart, there won't be anything left."

"Others have tried."

MacAlister yawned again. "You're boring me. Why don't you go home and take care of that spaz you call a daughter."

Hammer iced over. When he smiled, it was more rictus grin than living expression. His voice changed to a whisper. "Okay. You talked me into it," he said, pushing away from the bars. "See you on the streets."

BRINDLE and Alphabet were waiting at Devonshire Station in the north end of the San Fernando Valley when Fey and Monk arrived.

"Any problems getting the warrant?" Fey asked.

Alphabet shook his head. "Routine. Judge Wallace didn't even bother to read it."

"We'll have to remember him next time we want to get something shaky signed."

Two uniformed officers joined the detectives in the squad room for the warrant service briefing. Everything was expected to be straightforward, but standard procedures had been established for a purpose. Alphabet handed out a form showing an outline of the location to be searched, a list of everyone's positions during the initial entry, the agreed-upon radio frequency, a description of the objects of the search, and the location of the nearest hospital, in case something went drastically wrong.

Preston's rented condo was in a small, run-down complex

near the 118 freeway, which ran across the top end of the Valley. Noise from the speeding cars filtered down on the dust-swept, sun-broiled buildings.

A black-and-white unit was already on the scene, securing the location. The two officers were happy to have their nightlong vigil terminated. Thinking ahead, Alphabet had stopped for coffee and fat pills at the local Winchell's. The offering was gratefully received by the bored officers.

"Do we have a key to the place?" Fey asked.

Alphabet produced a ring of keys in a baggie. "These were recovered from Preston's car after the fire department put the flames out. I don't know if any of them will still work."

"It's worth a try," Fey said.

At the front door, Alphabet's struggles with the keys produced eventual success. He and Brindle entered first with one of the uniformed officers. The other officer and Monk covered the sides of the condo, with Fey hanging back and observing. Using a disposable camera, Fey took pictures of the entry.

The interior of the condo was decorated in early trailer trash. Hung on a wall, over a television positioned on a plastic milk crate, was a velvet painting of a Polynesian woman with suspiciously Caucasian features and huge, exposed breasts.

"Tacky," Fey said, observing the painting.

"Hip," corrected Brindle. "Tacky is in style."

The rest of the living room was dominated by a thrift-store couch, a drugstore sound system, a scattering of CDs, a battered coffee table, exercise equipment, and the debris of marijuana and alcohol usage. There was a stack of videotapes piled on the floor next to a VCR.

"Lifestyles of the young and stupid," Fey said.

"That's a bit harsh, isn't it?" Monk asked. He turned, holding several publicity head shots of Preston picked up from a Formica kitchen table. "After all, he was one break away from stardom."

"Him and every other eighteen-to-twenty-five-year-old in this city."

The warrant stated the search was for evidence tying Preston to the torture of Bianca Flynn. What that might be was anybody's guess.

While Brindle and Alphabet worked the living room and the kitchen, Fey and Monk moved through to the largest of the two bedrooms. The room smelled of stale sweat and unwashed clothing.

Grayish sheets were twisted down the middle of the bed. Monk turned the mattress over, disturbing a family of silverfish.

"Someday I'll find something worthwhile under a mattress," he said.

"You have to go through the motions," Fey told him.

The wall behind the bed was a homage to Preston's so-called career. Photo stills from the Citadel films in which Preston had been employed as a "stuntman" were pasted haphazardly, along with underground-magazine reviews of the miles-off-Broadway plays in which Preston had bit parts.

"Anything?" Alphabet asked, sticking his head in the doorway.

"Not yet," Fey told him. "You?"

"Cold pizza and moldy cheese."

"No diamonds hiding in the ice cubes?"

"To be honest, I didn't check."

"Tsk, tsk."

Alphabet grinned. "We'll start on the bathroom and the other bedroom," he said before withdrawing.

Fey was going through the drawers of a battered dresser. The top drawers held T-shirts, undershorts, and socks. Bills and receipts, the paperwork of life, were crammed into the lower drawers. She was sifting through them for anything of interest, when Monk finished with the closet and returned to the bed.

The mattress was still leaning against the closed drapes of the room's window, where he and Fey had placed it. With his hands covered by plastic gloves, he felt the top of the box spring for irregularities. Before finishing, he grasped the edge of the bed frame and turned the box spring over. "Better finish going through the motions," he said, and then grunted, causing Fey to look over.

"What?"

Monk reached into the frame and pulled a large manila envelope free. He held it up. "More publicity shots, maybe?"

"Who knows?" Fey said.

Monk was opening the metal clip on the envelope, when Alphabet's voice called Fey. Following the sound across the hallway to the second bedroom, she stopped abruptly at the door. Brindle and Alphabet stood in the middle of the room, turning around to stare at the walls. Fey followed their eyes and felt instantly sick.

The collage of career shots behind Preston's bed was nothing compared with this display. Images of child pornography were pasted everywhere. The pictures were not just pornographic, but sadistic.

A mattress with a red comforter over it sat in the middle of the room. A thirty-five-millimeter camera was on the floor next to a video camera on a tripod.

Fey retreated from the overwhelming room and leaned her shoulder back against a hallway wall.

Monk came out of the bedroom holding several oddly cropped photos he'd taken from the envelope he'd found. "Look at these."

Fey took them, wanting anything to replace the images she'd seen in Preston's other bedroom, but the cropped photos Monk gave her were even worse. Worse, because they showed Preston himself engaged in carnal acts with two different children, a boy of about eight and a girl of around five. There were other adults in the photos, but careful cropping had removed their faces.

Fey threw the photos on the floor in anger. "How can anyone do that!" She was more than disgusted. "It—it pisses me off! I'm glad the bastard blew himself up. I hope he's roasting in hell!"

THE TEAM met back at base. The SID criminalists and photographers had been turned loose at Ricky Preston's condo. Fey didn't know what they could accomplish, but she couldn't walk away without doing anything.

Hammer had put his scavenging skills to good use. Canvassing Parker Center, he'd uncovered a small conference room tucked away in the corner of the eighth floor.

Robbery-Homicide was already crowded, and the addition of Fey's unit had not helped. The team's desks were down in the office, but Hammer's find was the perfect place for them to use as a retreat. Fey immediately dubbed the location the Bat Cave.

"Using this place is not going to ingratiate us with the troops below," Brindle observed.

"Tough," Fey said. "They either accept us or they don't—on our terms, not theirs." She was in a foul mood.

"I'm not complaining," Brindle said. "I'm glad to be out of the microscope."

"Did you get anything from MacAlister?" Fey asked Hammer.

Everyone was seated around the battered conference table. Hammer had brought in an old-fashioned coffee machine rescued from Noah's Ark. It was bubbling noisily.

"Nothing but aggravation," Hammer replied. "Bail was posted an hour ago. He's on the street with an SIS unit following him."

"They'll have to be good," Fey said. "MacAlister is street savvy."

Hammer shrugged. "Don't worry about MacAlister. I'll take care of him when the time comes."

Fey didn't like the tone in Hammer's voice, but didn't pursue it. "How about Bianca's kids?" she asked.

"I took care of that end," Rhonda reported. "Neither one of them will disclose anything. In my opinion, they're scared stiff. The situation has traumatized them. The Department of Children's Services is caring for them on paper only. For stability and continuity, DCS ran an emergency approval and are letting the kids stay where they are."

"You found somebody with common sense in a city agency?" Fey was mock aghast.

"I'm very persuasive," Rhonda explained. "How about you guys? What did you come up with at Preston's pad?"

Alphabet gave a quick briefing. He finished by saying, "We found these on the wall in the second bedroom," and dropped six Polaroid photos in the middle of the conference table.

Hammer and Nails looked at them together. "Bianca Flynn," Rhonda said, recognizing the crime scene.

"Took them for his own enjoyment during the torture session," Alphabet said.

The photos were ugly and harsh.

Hammer tapped the snapshots with a finger. "I thought we agreed this was not a sexually motivated crime."

"I don't think it was," Fey said. "I think the motive was to get information. But Preston was a sick puppy—he couldn't help enjoying his work. If Bianca had lived long enough, Preston may have progressed to sexual attacks, but sex wasn't the focus of the crime."

"Do you think Bianca's dying panicked Preston?" Rhonda asked. She was sifting through the Polaroids again.

"Possibly," Fey told her. "Especially as it doesn't appear Preston got the information he needed from Bianca."

"Any ideas what information he wanted?" Hammer asked.

"Yeah," Fey said, handing the photos from the manila envelope to Hammer. "Monk also found these. There was a note attached—a blackmail threat. Preston was ordered to find where

Bianca hid the originals. If he didn't, the partials would be given to the police."

Hammer shuffled through the cropped prints with Rhonda looking over his shoulder. Rhonda blanched.

"What is it?" Fey asked, seeing her reaction.

"The kids in the photos," Rhonda said. "They're Mark Junior and Sarah—Bianca's children."

35

"WHAT GAME do you think they're playing?" Devon Wyatt asked MacAlister.

The big man was slumped over a chair in the corner of Wyatt's Beverly Hills office. He had showered and shaved since Wyatt had bonded him out, but the smell of incarceration still clung to the hairs inside his nose. "Who cares? They've got nothing. They know nothing."

"You're not that stupid, are you?"

"Listen, asshole. I eat jerks like Hammer and Nails for breakfast and fart them out by lunch."

"Is that why instead of handling the Hudson pickup and terrorizing the priest, you end up in jail on ADW charges?"

MacAlister's voice rose sharply. "There was a felony warrant out for the mother. I was simply preparing to use whatever force was necessary to effect a citizen's arrest. We'll beat the rap in court."

"*I'll* beat the rap in court," Wyatt said harshly. "You'll sit there like a good little boy, consulting with a female defense associate to show how harmless you are."

MacAlister grinned. "Just make sure she has big tits."

Wyatt made a face. "You disgust me, MacAlister."

"Sure. That's what you say now. What about when you want somebody to do your dirty work? I tell you what—why don't we file a personnel complaint against Hammer and the bimbo for letting a felony warrant suspect go?"

"They didn't."

"What do you mean?"

"Exactly what I said. They have coerced the DA into cooperating with them. Judy Hudson and her daughter are currently in court protective custody pending a hearing on their case in California—a state notoriously sympathetic to mothers. Max Hudson is not going to be very happy with you. The last thing he wanted was headlines."

"Screw him." MacAlister was disgruntled. Sooner or later, he would find a way to make Hammer and Nails pay. Hammer had reacted to the crack about his spaz daughter. Maybe there was something he could do in that arena.

Wyatt sighed. He wouldn't admit it out loud, but dealing with MacAlister scared him a little. The man was unstable. "I didn't get you out of jail to argue. Just go and find the priest and do the job that you were hired for."

FATHER ROMERO sat in the cool darkness of the confessional. So many sins, so few true repenters. It was the burden of all priests, their own sins making them as vulnerable as the people who came to them for forgiveness.

The afternoon rush to confess was over. Father Romero checked to see the church was empty, then returned to sit in the confessional. The small space soothed and comforted him. Perhaps there would be a late penitent, somebody who needed forgiveness for true transgressions.

As if cued by the priest's longing, the air in the tiny booth swam sluggishly through the dividing screen as a dark shape moved into the attached cubicle. There was the noise of the shape settling onto the hard bench seat.

"Forgive me, Father, for I have sinned." The voice was harsh, repressed. "It has been ten years since my last confession."

"A long time, my son. What has brought you back to the fold?"

"A grievous sin."

"Your Father in heaven will forgive you if you are truly repentant."

"Will your God forgive a sin not yet committed?"

"My God is your God. He will forgive the thought of sin as easily as the sin itself. Through his strength, he will help you to resist the sin."

A thick arm suddenly burst through the thin wooden screen separating the confessional booths. Splinters flew, and the hand on the end of the arm snapped closed around Father Romero's throat like a striking serpent.

"But I don't want to resist, Father! I enjoy sin all the more because it is a sin."

Father Romero had both his hands clasped about the iron wrist of his attacker. He couldn't speak. No air could creep past the fingers locked on his throat. He found himself thrust back against the thin wall of the confessional box, gasping for breath as the hand released its grip and withdrew.

Before Father Romero could move, the curtain on his side of the confessional was torn aside and MacAlister's hand was again at his throat. MacAlister picked the priest up by the neck and shook him like a terrier with a rat. He chuckled deep in his throat. "Where's your God now, Father? Are you praying for him to smite me down?" MacAlister shook the priest again. "He doesn't appear to be answering you—unless the answer is no."

"What do you want?" Father Romero asked agonizingly, his voice rasping like flesh over a cheese grater.

"I want you to show me how your little underground operation here works. I want to know all the ins and outs—and if you don't tell me, I'm going to tear you apart."

"I am not afraid to die."

MacAlister still held the priest at arm's length with no visible effort. "I'm glad to hear it. But remember, with you or without you, I will get what I want. So, you decide if dying is worth it, or if it's better to live to be a worm another day." MacAlister tightened his grip.

"All right," Father Romero croaked, his eyes rolling up in his head.

MacAlister released his stranglehold, and the priest fell to the floor like a shot duck.

"Glad you could see it my way, Father, because the train and its contents belong to me, and there is nothing you or anybody else can do about it."

OUTSIDE the church, a three-car, six-member SIS team had MacAlister's van—freshly recovered from the police impound lot and carrying a tiny tracking device—under surveillance. Two other members of the team had taken up positions outside the church doors.

Using a state-of-the-art video camera equipped with a super-sensitive directional microphone and a night-vision lens to pierce the gloom of the church, the two officers at the door recorded the action inside. That they did not intervene when MacAlister physically assaulted Father Romero was part of the controversy surrounding the mandate of the unit.

By allowing Father Romero to be roughed up, the results

could lead to uncovering more serious criminal activity. Arresting MacAlister for simple battery would accomplish nothing — a misdemeanor charge, which might not even be filed by the city attorney due to lack of any real injuries.

By letting MacAlister proceed, letting whatever larger crime he was planning come to fruition, it could mean a long prison term for MacAlister and those controlling him.

Hammer had arranged for SIS's Predator team to cover MacAlister. Lieutenant Gene Budrow, the leader of the unit, had long waited for a chance to repay Hammer for getting him out of a fix in a major internal investigation. Helping to nail a douche bucket like MacAlister would be partial payment. Other RHD entities might resent the intrusion of Fey's team, but whatever information SIS came up with, Budrow would see it got straight back to Hammersmith.

Rightfully or wrongfully, Special Investigative Services did not arrest suspects for minor crimes. MacAlister could slap people around all he wanted. He could shoplift, spit on the sidewalk, steal cars, or let his dog crap in the park. SIS specialized in violent crimes involving life or death — rape, robbery, murder. When the time of reckoning came, if MacAlister chose to fight rather than surrender, he'd just be another unmourned six on SIS's record: six feet under in a six-foot box.

36

FEY TRIED TO examine her feelings about Bianca's children being with Ricky Preston in the pornographic photos. There was an odd quality of displacement. Because of her own sexual abuse by her father, Fey knew what Sarah and Mark were going through in the photos. She could see in their eyes the sense of detachment abused children develop to close themselves off from the horror of the situation. She was intimate with that detachment. Once learned, it was never forgotten.

She shuffled through the cropped photographs. The black-mail note with them was a Xerox copy of a computer-printed file, second generation with no prints or other helpful markings. The photographs had obviously been cropped to hide the identity of the other participating parties. Still, there was an extra arm showing in one picture, an extra hand in another, enough to show other adults involved. The skin pigment of the arm was black. The pigment of the hand was white. Child abuse was the great equalizer, cutting through all socioeconomic and ethnic strata.

Fey stared at the photos, trying to connect to the background, to find something to give her a clue as to when or where they were snapped. The photos were taken from an elevated position. The bed itself was nondescript, and the floor and walls were fuzzy. The bed was fitted with a brass headboard, but there was nothing to distinguish it from a million others.

When Fey put the photos down, the only solid conclusion she could make was that the photos were not posed. Preston and the children did not know they were being photographed. The camera was stationary, maybe hidden in the corner of the ceiling. If this was true, it begged the question of who placed the camera there and why.

Hammer hung up the phone and broke into Fey's reverie. "That was Gene Budrow from SIS. His people followed MacAlister to the Sanctuary of the Black Madonna, where they taped him slapping Father Romero around. MacAlister was talking some crap about a train, before Romero reluctantly led him into the back of the church. SIS couldn't follow at that point, but clearly MacAlister was forcing Romero to take him down into the catacombs."

"MacAlister was saying something about a train?" Fey asked.

"Yeah. The tape is on its way to us. Budrow's people waited for MacAlister, but he never reappeared—probably went out through the tunnels with Father Romero, like we did."

"Too bad," Fey said. "Maybe they can pick him up again later." She thought for a moment. "Before he died, Jack Kavanaugh said something about a train."

"Right. Either trains or training, and a game well. Naylor, the bettor who Kavanaugh bumped against, also said Kavanaugh mentioned trains and railroads."

"Yeah. We're working on the assumption that the words *game well* are really one word referring to the old telephone system. The railroad could be a reference to Bianca's Underground Railroad. But if he also mentioned a train, and now MacAlister is talking about a train . . ."

"And that would mean?"

"I have no idea."

"Big help."

"Well, unless *you* have an idea, you'd better grab Rhonda and go talk to your priest friend. I don't think he's been totally up front with you."

As Hammer headed for the door, Brindle asked, "What do you want us to do?"

Fey reached out a hand and touched the pictures of Ricky Preston again. "Something here isn't clear. I want you to take Ricky Preston's life apart brick by brick. He's connected to Bianca's children, and I want to know how."

"We're on it," Alphabet said.

When the others left, Fey called the Cold Squad.

"Were the reports we sent over any help?" Freeze asked as soon as Fey identified herself.

"What reports? I was calling to see if you'd come up with anything."

"Kid Cool hand-carried a whole stack of stuff to RHD for you."

Fey felt her face turning red. "Do you know who he gave it to?"

"Sorry, I don't, and he's not here right now to ask."

"Doesn't matter," Fey said. "The stuff you sent, was it copies or originals?"

"Copies. I've still got the originals here. They haven't been refiled."

"Great," Fey said. "If you could run them through the copy machine again, Monk will come right over and pick them up."

"Sure, but what happened to the stuff Kid Cool brought over?"

"I don't think everyone at RHD has got the cooperation gene," Fey said. "If assholes could fly, Robbery-Homicide Division would be an international airport."

AWARE her messages were not finding their way through the RHD gauntlet, Fey phoned Zelman Tucker.

"Don't tell me, let me guess," she said when Tucker said hello. "You've been leaving messages all over the place for me and I haven't called you back."

"You must be psycho—I mean psychic," Tucker came back at her, recognizing the voice. "I've been trying your mobile for ages."

"The battery is dead."

"They can be recharged."

"Really? What will they think of next? Time to do the recharging?"

"How about a spare battery?"

"I'm too cheap."

"You're honest, anyway."

"I take it you have something for me on Luther Flynn?"

"You could say so. It's stuff like this that makes me sorry I retired from the tabloids. This guy has dirt written all over him. It would make an award-winning piece on *American Inquirer*."

"Now there's an oxymoron. An award-winning episode of *American Inquirer*. That's almost as good as *jumbo shrimp* or *military intelligence*."

"Do you want the information, or do you want to keep taking potshots at my venerable past?"

"Like shooting cows with a sniper scope."

"How would you like me to put my dirt-digging skills to work on you?"

"I bow to your greater threat. What do you have on Flynn?"

"I get the book exclusive when this has played out, right?"

"Don't tease me. Just give."

There was the sound of papers being shuffled at Tucker's end of the line. "On the surface, Luther Flynn appears to be the perfect candidate for the California Supreme Court. He's been short-listed for the current open position, but from what I can gather he's been tainted."

"By what?"

"Nothing public yet, but there are rumors he gets his kicks with little kids."

"Old news. Bianca Flynn made those allegations against him years ago. Flynn got a restraining order stopping her from making the statements in public a few years back."

"His daughter's allegations aren't the problem."

"Whoa, you mean there are new allegations? A criminal case?"

"Nothing that substantial. There's word he has all the wrong connections. His e-mail address turned up on a couple of child pornography lists on the Internet during an unrelated FBI investigation."

"He can't be that stupid."

"You'd be surprised. Most people have no idea about the information trail they leave behind when they visit regular legitimate Internet sites, let alone the pornography sites."

"Surely it isn't enough to stop him from getting to the California Supreme Court?"

"Not by itself, but there is now an independent-counsel investigation to explore the background of judges who have heard recent child pornography and pedophile cases. When Flynn's name turned up unexpectedly during the unrelated Internet investigation, he became part of the current inquiry."

"Any idea what brought about the new investigation?"

"Irony."

"I don't understand."

Tucker gave a short snort. "The new probe is based on information gathered by Bianca Flynn."

"As you say—irony."

"There may have been a restraining order stopping her from making allegations against her father, but it didn't stop her gathering information pertaining to known judges who are tainted when it comes to hearing child sexual abuse hearings in their jurisdictions—judges who defense lawyers know will use every technicality to block child pornography and pedophile cases from proceeding. If cases do get heard, and a conviction is handed down, then there is a very soft sentence waiting at the end of it all. And there are the judges in family court who give children back to accused abusers. Bianca Flynn cast a wide net."

"Are you saying these judges are compromising themselves over sympathy for child molesters? That's insane."

"Not if the judges are molesters themselves. Not if evidence of their predilections is in the wrong hands. From what I've been able to gather, Bianca's report caused quite a reaction in the Justice Department. There are four California judges who are going to be investigated, with Luther Flynn at the top of the list."

Fey's mind spun. "Does Flynn know about this?"

There was a pause at Tucker's end of the line. "I'd say so. He's got to know there's a reason for holding up the decision on the vacant California Supreme Court seat. I'd say he's scrambling to get himself out of town before he finds himself indicted."

Fey thought for a moment. "Those Internet lists you talked about—"

"The ones Luther Flynn's name turned up on?"

"Yeah. Can you check two other names and see if they turn up on the same or related lists?"

"Sure. Who do you want me to check?"

"Ricky Preston and Mark Ritter."

"Preston is the guy who blew himself up all over the news yesterday?"

"Yeah, and Ritter is Bianca Flynn's estranged husband."

"Oh, baby," Tucker said. "The way you think scares me sometimes."

"Then we're even. I'm scared to ask how you found out all this information."

"A reporter is only as good as his sources."

"You should have been a cop working with informants."

"You have to be kidding. Me, a cop? I'd be so crooked I'd have to sleep in a corner."

"You're still amazing."

"Then hang on, Frog Lady, because the best is yet to come."

"There's more?"

"I caught a rumor going around about a bunch of kids from South America being brought stateside to be sold into sexual slavery. Flynn's name is connected with the rumor."

"In what capacity?"

"It's not clear."

"Speculate."

"I think he's planning a get-out score. You know, grab a large chunk of change and retire to Thailand, where the fruit is sweet and so are the boys."

"Not on my watch."

"Then you better find a way to take him down."

37

WHEN MONK returned with the Cold Squad files, he found pizzas and salads laid out on the conference table with a selection of canned sodas.

"I ordered in," Fey said.

Monk pushed the stack of files into Fey's arms and used a napkin to snitch a slice topped with mushrooms and pineapple.

"You're a mind reader," he said. "I'm starved."

"I might as well glue this pizza right to my thighs," Fey said, setting the files down and taking another slice for herself. "It's going to end up there eventually."

"With your time on the job," Monk told her, "your genes should be immune to carbohydrates by now."

"My genes may be, but my jeans aren't." Fey wiped her fingers and turned her attention to the files. "Did you look through any of these?" she asked, quickly leafing through the pile.

"No," Monk said through a mouthful of pizza dough. "I wanted to get out of there before I was transmogrified into a geek. Ten more minutes in the Cold Squad's dungeon, and Doc Freeze might have started to look good."

"Don't worry, you're not her type—too much upstairs."

"Brains can be sexy."

"Yeah, right. Then why do big boobs win out every time?"

Fey located the original crime report for the armored-car robbery and pulled it clear, unprepared for the instant shock it gave her. The cramped printing was instantly recognizable as her father's. His presence was a cold, malevolent ghost suddenly surrounding her.

There was more to bother her. Garth Croaker had been working dicks in University Division at the time of the robbery. He shouldn't have been taking the original crime report. That job should have been handed down to a uniformed patrol officer.

Scanning the report, Fey could see that no effort had been put into it. The basic information was there but nothing else. The suspect information was generic, listing the two unidentified suspects as male blacks, no further.

As Fey deciphered the cramped report, she felt a hollow ache deep in her chest. She didn't want to think about her father. She had buried him literally and figuratively. Just looking at his writing brought back her despair and his depravity. She could feel her father's rough hands touching her, poking and prodding in all her secret places. She could feel the punches, hear the vituperation—"You're a bad girl. A very bad girl. You'll have to be punished." She closed her eyes and saw hands undoing a belt buckle, a special detective belt buckle formed to make the numbers 187, the penal code section for homicide.

She felt a hand on her shoulder and jumped in her seat.

"Whoa!" It was only Monk. He'd pulled his hand back, but tentatively replaced it. "You okay?"

She gave him a tight smile. "Yeah. Fine." More than anyone on the team, Monk seemed to recognize her demons.

"Sure," Monk told her cynically.

Fey brandished the reports. "My father's printing," she tried to explain. "He wrote this report, even though there are two other officers' names at the bottom."

Monk studied the report, giving Fey time to regain her composure. "You see this?" he asked after a few seconds. He put the report on the table in front of her. "Look at the date of occurrence and date reported."

Fey looked where Monk was pointing. "Okay," she said. "They're the same—as they should be. What's the deal?"

"Now look when the report was run off by Records."

Down at the bottom of the report was a box to be initialed and dated by a civilian clerical worker when the original report was copied and distributed to the various file locations.

Fey looked at the box. "That can't be right."

"No. It can't. But it is."

The date in the box initialed by the civilian records clerk was three months after the date of occurrence filled in by Fey's father at the top of the report.

"Shit," Fey said. "He fixed the report. Changed it from the original. Why?"

"The sixty-four-thousand-dollar question."

"Even that game show wasn't rigged as much as this report. My father must have pulled all the copies of the original report and then sent this bastardized version through to replace them."

Monk picked up the reports from the shoot-out in which Mavis Flynn was killed. "These are dated two days before your father sent through the replacement report on the armored-car robbery."

"Odder and odder," Fey said, taking the shoot-out reports and perusing them. Here, too, she could read between the lines of cop jargon to see her father covering himself with phraseology.

Fey had done her own share of butt-covering in reports, her own share of screwing suspects with a pencil—not lying, but writing a report on the slant. She'd certainly been around long enough to recognize it in reports written by others.

"Who else would have a copy of the original robbery report?" she asked, thinking.

"Your father knew what he was doing. It wasn't nearly as complicated then as it is now. He must have replaced all of the reports in our system."

Fey snapped her fingers. "In *our* system, maybe." She picked up the phone and dialed a number from memory.

"Freddie Mackerbee," she said when the phone was answered at the other end. She paused, waiting to be put through.

"Uh-oh," Monk said, seeing trouble coming.

The head FBI agent's secretary picked up the line.

"This is Detective Fey Croaker with the LAPD calling for Agent Mackerbee," Fey stated, and was put on hold again.

Freddie Mackerbee's voice came on the line. "Fey? You must have some set of balls calling here."

"Calm down, Freddie. I need some help."

"The FBI doesn't practice therapy."

"Ooh, ouch," Fey said flatly. "Now that you've got that out of your system, how about a little interagency cooperation?"

"You must be joking."

"I'm not. I need a copy of the original LAPD report on the armored-car robbery."

"Check your own archives."

"Freddie, I know you have the damn file sitting in the middle of your desk so you can keep your anger with me fueled. Just fax me a copy of the report."

"Why?"

"Freddie, have I ever left your butt hanging out to dry? Who covered you in glory in the JoJo Cullen case?"

"Don't even try tugging on my heartstrings."

"Don't do it for me Freddie, do it for Ash." Fey made the statement in a callous fashion, but the effect was still electric.

"You are a real bitch," Mackerbee said.

"One hundred percent," Fey agreed. "You ready for my fax number?" Fey rattled it off without waiting for an answer. "I'll be sitting by the machine twiddling my thumbs," she said, made a kissing noise into the phone, and hung up. She looked at Monk.

"He gonna send it?" Monk asked.

"He'll send it."

Thirty minutes later, the fax machine Hammer had installed in the office spat out the appropriate paperwork. Fey had to laugh when she saw the cover sheet. Mackerbee had photocopied an image of his hand with the middle finger extended.

Taking the still-warm sheets to the table, Fay placed the faxed report next to the one written by Garth Croaker. The one sent by Mackerbee was clearly written by another hand with far more detailed information, especially in the boxes reserved for the description of the two suspects who fled the scene.

One specific characteristic leaped out at Fey. In the description box for physical oddities, there was the notation *scar running from left corner of the mouth to under the chin.*

"Something?" Monk asked, sensing Fey's reaction.

"Only confirmation that there is a God," she said.

The chief sighed. He rubbed his eyes. "Let me rephrase my question. How can you prove it?"

Fey's smile was grim. "Then you accept my assumptions?"

The chief looked at Whip Whitman, who was studiously studying the carpet shag.

Fey leaned away from the pictures and sat back in her chair again. "My father was not only a child molester, wife beater, and all-around asshole, he was apparently also as corrupt as hell. What a surprise." She paused to shift in her seat before continuing. "My father wasn't your standard pedophile. He didn't pick on other kids, just my brother and me. It wasn't about sex; it was about control. He was a control freak, and this whole investigation stinks of the kind of control he delighted in." She took the abbreviated armored-car robbery report from the Cold Squad, and the true report faxed over by the FBI, and let them settle on top of the pictures.

"Three months after the armored-car robbery, my father runs around collecting all copies of the original robbery report distributed through the LAPD system. He then stiffs in a counterfeit, leaving out any salient details that may identify a suspect.

"Most of the grunt work had been done in the case by that time. Eldon Dodge had been put through the interrogation ringer without cracking. The witness who gave the original suspect description disappeared. The investigation was at a standstill. My father couldn't do anything about the FBI report, but as the LAPD's robbery liaison, he and his partner, Jack Kavanaugh, could stymie any investigation there. The FBI didn't have many agents on the ground in L.A. in those days, and relied heavily on LAPD liaisons as shoe leather."

"I'm familiar with departmental history," the chief said, but without displaying any impatience.

Fey continued. "The true, original report describes the third suspect as a male, black, with a scar running under his chin from

38

"You're going after a highly respected judge based on the word of a tabloid scribbler and a thirty-year-old report missing from the LAPD's files?" Gordon O. Drummond asked. Whip Whitman had heard Fey's tale and figured he had to kick it upstairs to the chief.

Fey tossed the cropped photos from Ricky Preston's residence on GOD's desk. They scattered like pornographic playing cards. She pointed a forefinger at the black arm in one photo. "That's Luther Flynn's arm," she said. Her emphasis couldn't have been more positive. She moved her finger to indicate the white hand seen in another photo. "And I'll bet the house that hand belongs to Mark Ritter."

Drummond shook his head, his eyebrows rippling like fornicating ferrets. "Fey, you are making a jump across a gulf of logic like I've never seen before. How do you know?"

Fey's fingers moved to dance across the faces of Sarah and Mark Junior. "I've been there. I know."

the left side of his mouth." She had highlighted the pertinent part. "You only get one guess as to who has a scar in the same location, the result of being slashed with a bottle as a teenager."

The chief grunted. "Luther Flynn does, but I bet you could easily find a hundred more in the city."

"With connections to this case?"

The chief's eyebrows bobbed and weaved as he frowned.

Fey took that as a cue to continue. "When I talked to him, Eldon Dodge fingered Luther Flynn as the third suspect in the robbery, which makes sense since Mavis Flynn provided the inside information."

Drummond steepled his fingers and touched the tips to his lower lip. "If you believe that part of Dodge's story, does that mean you also think your father killed Mavis Flynn and framed Dodge?"

Fey sighed heavily. "There's no corroboration yet, but my gut tells me it's true. I'm working under the assumption that between the armored-car robbery and the murder of Mavis Flynn, my father found a way to feather his nest with stolen hundred-dollar bills. I've thought about this a lot. Shortly after the murder of Mavis Flynn, my father moved us to a much larger house in a nicer part of town. He always drank the best booze, and he had a gambling habit—thought he could control the bookies and all. That kind of money didn't come on a dick's salary."

"What about the money Jack Kavanaugh left you?" Whip Whitman asked, entering the conversation now that the bomb had been dropped.

"I think it was his share of the booty. He was my father's partner. Whatever payoff they got from Luther Flynn for taking out Mavis, they would have split. If I'm calling this right, when he made the deal, my father manipulated Kavanaugh just like he manipulated everyone else. Kavanaugh must have gone along, but he stuffed the money away and never did anything with it."

"Guilt?" Drummond asked.

"Probably," Fey said. "I think he left that money to me because he wanted me to find out where it came from. Dodge told me to check out his visitor records before I left. Jack Kavanaugh had been to see him three times in the past six months. I think guilt was eating him up. He was losing ground mentally. Some days were better than others, but he was on a downhill slide. Leaving me the money was a backup plan, a not very well thought out guarantee I'd follow up and find out the truth."

"Why a backup plan?" Drummond's eyebrows had settled down as he took in all Fey was saying.

"I'm not sure. But I think he had something else going, possibly directly with Bianca Flynn. If he knew time was running out on his mental faculties, maybe he decided to take a run at Luther Flynn to atone for the actions my father had forced him to take years before."

"It's still weak," Drummond said.

"Perhaps," Fey agreed. "But is there another scenario to fit the facts?"

"Facts are your problem," Drummond said. "You don't have many. You have the Polaroid photos Ricky Preston took during the torture. Those are more than enough to close out the murder investigation."

"I can't do that," Fey said bluntly. "Ricky Preston may have been the bullet, but somebody else pulled the trigger. If we walk away, so does the true murderer."

"There are other cases—"

Fey didn't let Drummond finish. "Screw the other cases. You didn't bring me to RHD to do a half-assed job. If you expect me to back off, then you'd better return the whole lot of us to West L.A."

Drummond smiled. "Does this mean our honeymoon period is officially over?"

"If you're going to try and pull a wham-bam-thank-you-ma'am screwing over, I'd say so."

The intercom line on the chief's phone blinked red. Drummond punched the button for the speakerphone. "Yes?"

The voice of the chief's secretary entered the room electronically. "There's a Zelman Tucker on line two. He said Detective Lawson told him to call through to Lieutenant Croaker on your line."

Drummond looked at Fey. She nodded. "This could be a couple more of those facts you think are so scarce."

"Put him through," Drummond told his secretary. Leaving the speakerphone on, he punched line two.

Fey stood up to get closer to the phone. "Tucker?"

"Yeah. Hey, am I on a speakerphone?"

Fey was astounded by how sharp Tucker could be. One word and he knew something was different. "Speakerphone. The chief is here along with Whip Whitman."

"You're traveling in high company these days, Frog Lady."

Fey winced at the nickname. "The altitude is so thin I'm getting nosebleeds. Give me something to stop the hemorrhaging."

They could hear Tucker chuckling. "Okay. You ready for this? I ran Ricky Preston's real name, Rico Prestavanovich, through my systems. Not only does he turn up on the membership list of MBLA, the Man Boy Love Association, but he also turns up on both of the child porno lists traced to Luther Flynn. Is that enough to staunch the flow?"

"For now, Tucker, for now. I owe you."

"As always," Tucker said, and broke the connection.

Fey looked at Drummond. "Are you going to let me run with this, or do we have to go two out of three falls?"

A flash of anger crossed Drummond's face. He wasn't used to being challenged. "Your father isn't the only control freak in your family."

The gibe cut Fey far more than Drummond realized. She hated any comparison between herself and her father.

Fey tried to keep her tone even through gritted teeth. "Maybe not, but I had to learn control in order to survive."

That stopped Drummond. "Okay," he said. "I give in."

Fey gathered up the photos and reports. As she turned to leave, Drummond's voice stopped her.

"One more thing, Fey."

She turned back to face the chief. "Yeah?"

"Make sure you nail the bastard."

39

Driving from the shadows of Parker Center's covered parking into the late-afternoon sun, Fey knew she had won a major battle.

Drummond had told her to nail Judge Luther Flynn. The cliché about being given enough rope to hang yourself flitted through Fey's mind. Drummond was right. So far the investigation had yielded little proof of Flynn's involvement in any wrongdoing. His name on a pair of Internet child pornography lists might be enough to launch an investigation into his fitness to be a judge, but his name on a hundred lists wouldn't get him into court on charges of child molestation and conspiracy to torture.

The black arm in the photographs of Ricky Preston and Bianca's children was just that—a black arm, nothing more. No matter how convinced Fey was that the arm belonged to Flynn, her feelings wouldn't get the man into court without proof.

The rest of the day was filled with frustrations. Whip Whitman offered no wise counsel. He'd ducked out to supervise another team working a multiple-victim drive-by shooting.

Hammer and Nails had called in. The Sanctuary of the Black Madonna was locked up tight, and Father Romero had done a disappearing act. They had tried to find their way into the catacombs, but were unable to negotiate the rat warren of tunnels.

They switched their attentions to Ferris Jackson, but she was also among the missing, and the house she'd shared with Bianca Flynn was locked. They would keep pounding the asphalt, but there was nothing happening immediately.

Brindle and Alphabet were digging into Ricky Preston's background, but so far they had found nothing to help them identify the location in the photographs or to tie Preston directly to Luther Flynn or to the Ritter children's father.

Monk, with the help of Roger Lund's Explorer Scouts, had located two of the old Gamewell call boxes and rescued them for the historical society. One contained a half-pint bottle with an inch of bourbon and a pickled spider in the bottom, but neither harbored anything to do with Jack Kavanaugh or Garth Croaker.

The investigative momentum was waning, which could be dangerous to any inquiry. Cases could rapidly become lost causes when the breaks stopped coming. Fey knew she had to do something to reinvigorate her forces.

Without conscious thought, she found herself in Santa Monica near Brink Kavanaugh's studio. She didn't know what she could gain from talking to Kavanaugh again, but she was being drawn to him.

Kavanaugh looked haggard when he opened the door. He was stripped to his shorts again, his massive shoulders and chest muscles covered in granite dust, his hair wild. Red-rimmed eyes took in Fey with a look verging on madness.

"You!" he almost spat.

"Last time I checked," Fey said. Despite the increase in her heart rate, her voice remained calm. Brink Kavanaugh had the power to take her breath away if she wasn't careful.

"You! You! Arrrgh!" Kavanaugh gritted his teeth and turned to stomp back into the studio, leaving the door open.

His inarticulateness didn't throw Fey, as she suddenly knew exactly what Kavanaugh was upset about. "I was right, wasn't I?" she pressed, stepping through the doorway. "There were three figures in the rock."

Kavanaugh's response was unequivocal. "Arrrgh!"

Fey followed the bearlike figure to where the afternoon sun flooded the massive piece of stone with shadows and curves.

"I almost lost it," Brink said, facing the rock, his back to Fey. The sunlight gleamed around him in a halo effect. He stood straight, his legs together, holding his hands out from his sides, a mallet in one, a heavy chisel in the other. From Fey's position behind him, he looked crucified.

"How?" Fey's voice had gone soft, almost to a whisper.

Brink dropped his arms suddenly and whirled to face her. "Through anger, of course."

"Anger?"

"Yes. I've worked with rock since I was a child. A stone like this sings to me." He gestured behind him with a sinewy, hair-covered arm. "Yet you waltz in here not knowing a rock from a stone from a pebble and tell me you see three figures." He paused.

"And I was right?"

"Right? Yes, damn you! You were right, but I didn't want you to be. I had to be right. It was my stone. I told you I saw two figures— lovers embracing for the last time. What infernal crap!"

"So you tried to force the rock . . . tried to force it to be two figures."

"Of course. A huge, egotistical mistake. I was barely able to stop myself from destroying the rock on purpose—striking a fissure and demolishing it to rubble. And it was your fault."

"How could it be my fault? You asked me what I saw. I told you. Three figures."

"Damn it! If you hadn't said three in your ignorance, I would not have lost the vision of two!"

"Ignorance! You were the one who couldn't see what the rock truly held."

"But why three figures? Why not four, or five?"

Fey shrugged, words slipping out before she thought about them. "Because, for me, there are always three figures."

That stopped Brink short. "What? Father, Son, and Holy Ghost? You don't strike me as religious."

"What's God got to do with anything? I'm talking about the past, the present, and the future—three figures that are always with us . . . me."

Brink smiled gently. "A philosopher as well as an art critic."

Fey shook her head. "No. Just a survivor."

Brink reached out and took Fey's hand, leading her into the sandbox surrounding the rock. His touch was rough, fingers scarred by years of sculpting.

Other cuts in the stone had been made since Fey had first seen the rock. There were definitely three separate shapes emerging. Brink took her hands and placed them flat on the granite. It was not cold, but chilled, like a cadaver.

From behind her, he placed his own hands over hers. "Close your eyes," he said. Fey hesitated for a second. "Close your eyes," Brink said again, his mouth close to her ear. "Run your hands over the rock. Feel what is living inside."

She closed her eyes. Brink began to move her hands. She felt his body pressed against her back, the contours of his muscles hard, the thinness of her own clothing the only thing separating their skin. She smelled the musk of him.

"Feel the rock," he said. "Make the rock your entire world."

His body was locked into hers. As he moved her hands with

his, he also moved her body with his body. With her eyes closed it was as if she were weightless, gliding in a human harness. She felt the gritty surface of the rock beneath her palms, the leathery touch of Brink's hands brushing against her knuckles. For a second she felt herself falling into the rock, taking strength from it, finding . . . renewal. The force of it scared her, and she pulled away, turning into Brink's embrace.

He didn't hold her. He stepped back in fact, giving her room.

"You felt the power, didn't you?"

She paused, orienting herself again. "I felt something. I don't know what. A trick of the mind, perhaps."

"Perhaps," Brink said, his eyes knowing.

"Is this the way you seduce all your women?" Fey asked bluntly.

Brink didn't take offense. "Don't bring your defenses up. I am not a threat. This was not about sex. It was about you and the rock. To answer your question, though—no, I do not seduce women like this. Never. Good enough?"

Fey leaned back against the rock. It put a smidgen more breathing room between herself and Brink. "Do you really believe your sister Jenna and I could possibly be half sisters?"

"You look remarkably alike."

"That's not what I asked."

"Do you want to know if I think your father could have been screwing my mother?"

"Yes."

"I went to see my mother after you visited. I knew there was no way my father would have been having an affair with your mother, so I asked my mother if she'd been having an affair with your father. She told me your father had controlled her as he'd done my father. He screwed her and got away with it because he knew he could."

"Rape?"

"Not in a court of law, but still the same to hear my mother tell it."

"And Jenna?"

"The timing is right."

Fey swallowed. She didn't know if she wanted an answer to her next question. "Did she say if you could be my half brother?"

Brink's lips twisted into a wry smile. "Are you worried that when we make love it will be incest?"

"*When* we make love? Not *if*?"

"Has there ever been a doubt in your mind?"

"It depends on what your mother said."

"We could have blood tests to be sure."

Fey pushed herself forward, away from the rock, forcing Brink to capture her in his arms. "To hell with it," she said.

40

"Well, that was interesting," Fey said, shaking back her hair and gasping for breath.

Brink chuckled. "Never made love in a sandbox before?"

"I haven't even been in a sandbox since I was five," Fey said. "It's more fun as an adult, but the end result hasn't changed much. You still get sand everywhere." She pushed herself to her feet and picked up her clothes from outside the sandbox surrounding the huge hunk of granite. "Last one in the shower makes the coffee," she said, heading for the stairs.

"Fey," Brink called after her.

She stopped at the bottom of the stairs, turning to face him with no embarrassment, not bothering to cover her nakedness. She was in better shape than she had been a few years earlier, but she was still closer to fifty than forty. Brink either accepted her the way she was or he didn't. She'd just screwed the man's brains out. False modesty wouldn't change anything.

"I never planned this," he said.

"I know," she said. "I did."

A laugh rumbled out of Brink and he stepped forward to take her in his arms. He kissed her hard, his tongue probing. The sheer bulk of his body felt massive around her. Making love to him had been like making love to the rock itself. He was all hard angles and harder flat surfaces.

I hate men with so much hair on their bodies they could be mistaken for bears in the dark, she thought as she kissed him back. How has he managed to get to me so quickly?

She broke the kiss but not the embrace. "I hate hairy men," she said, voicing part of her thought.

"I'm not shaving my back," Brink said.

"In that case, I'll learn to live with it, but I won't always be this easy."

"Not the most appropriate choice of words under the circumstances," Brink said, making it Fey's turn to laugh. He led her up the stairs to the shower.

Later, as Fey was drying her hair with a towel and a borrowed blow-dryer, Brink made strong coffee. He held up a bottle of whiskey, and Fey nodded her assent. He poured a large dollop into two mugs of steaming brew.

With so many changes in her life over the past few days, Fey was surprised at how calm she felt. Her world was in turmoil, yet here in Brink's loft, wearing one of Brink's oversize plaid shirts, she felt great. She tried to check herself, not wanting to read anything into the situation, but as relaxed as she was, it was difficult to maintain perspective.

With the noise of the hair dryer blocking out any chance of conversation, Fey mentally chastised herself. The more she tried to put her feelings down to postcoital contentment, the more she realized her satisfaction went beyond the joys of having an overdue itch scratched. She knew she was setting herself up for the possibility of a big fall, but there was something pushing her to believe Brink was also infatuated with her.

She turned off the hair dryer and was running a brush through her hair when Brink approached and handed her a mug of coffee. He kissed her lightly on the back of the neck, and then moved away.

"How involved was my father in whatever it is you're investigating?" he asked. He was barefoot, but was now wearing jeans with a gray polo shirt.

Fey took the offered mug and followed Brink to where two matching handmade rocking chairs were placed in a sun spot. The chairs sat on a colorful woven rug with a low table between them.

Fey sipped her coffee before speaking. "I think your father was trying to do the right thing thirty years too late. How much do you remember about his time on the job?"

Brink added another splash of whiskey to his coffee and held the bottle out to Fey. She shook her head and covered her mug with a palm. Brink placed the bottle next to his chair.

"I remember Dad was never around when Jenna and I were kids," he said. "He and your father would always be off on some investigation that was always too big to talk about. By the time Mom took us and left him, he was no more than a token male in our lives. Since Jenna and I have grown older, we've stayed in touch, but we've always taken care of him, not the other way around."

"Did he ever talk about an armored-car robbery investigation or a shoot-out in which a woman was killed?"

"Not that I remember," Brink said. He placed his mug down on the low table. "What's this all about?"

Making a snap decision, Fey launched into an abbreviated explanation. "Thirty years ago, our fathers were working University Division. They caught the squeal on an armored-car robbery in which two guards were killed. One of the robbers, a Black Panther, was also killed, but two others got away with several hundred thousand dollars."

Brink whistled. "A lot of jingle then or now."

"You bet," Fey agreed. "The incident kept the newspaper headline writers busy for a few days, especially after the FBI took primary responsibility for the case. Our fathers stayed on as the LAPD liaisons. In those days, the Department did a lot of the Bureau's footwork."

"Not standard procedure today?"

"Far from it," Fey confirmed. "The antagonism between LAPD and the Bureau is now legendary. Individuals get along, but the organizations are constantly playing Brutus and Caesar."

"Interesting image."

Fey rocked the wide, low-set chair back and forth, finding its stark construction surprisingly comfortable and the motion soothing. "One of the main suspects in the case was another Black Panther named Eldon Dodge. He was cousin to Mavis Flynn, who worked at the bank where the robbery took place and was probably the source of the inside information."

"Is this Mavis Flynn any relation to Judge Luther Flynn?"

"You know Luther Flynn?"

"His name has been all over the newspapers lately, what with one daughter being murdered and the other being on the police commission. I do more than chew up rocks, you know. I can read."

Fey held out her hands. "Pardon me. It can sometimes get claustrophobic as a detective. You begin to think nobody else knows what's going on except for your immediate associates."

"So, Mavis is related to Luther?"

"*Was* related—she was murdered about three months after the robbery. She was married to Luther, but she'd taken her two daughters to stay with Eldon when one of the daughters claimed Luther was molesting her."

"And how did our fathers get involved in all this?"

"I think their investigation led them from Eldon to Luther, but Luther had a proposition for them. I think he paid them off with the money from the robbery to turn a blind eye to his involvement and to take Eldon Dodge out of the picture."

"Are you saying Luther paid them to put a hit on Dodge?" Brink had retrieved the coffeepot and refilled the mugs. This time, Fey also took a refill from the whiskey bottle.

"I think that's the way it was originally planned. More than the money from the robbery, Luther Flynn wanted his daughters back. He made child concealment charges against Mavis, giving our fathers an excuse to kick in the door where she was living with Eldon. Eldon was the intended target of the hit, but the way things played out, it was Mavis whom my father killed, using Eldon's gun. He turned the whole situation around, with the backing testimony of your father, to pin Mavis's murder on Dodge."

Brink was looking shell-shocked. "And you think your father—our fathers—turned two little girls back to a man who was molesting them? Why would they do such a thing?"

"You mean besides money?"

"Of course, besides money. How could they?"

"I don't know if it mattered what your father thought. I'm sure it was my father pulling the strings and making the decision. Child molestation wasn't of any concern to my father. Hell, he was doing it himself on a regular basis."

Her statement reverberated in the void between Brink and Fey. The look in Brink's eyes was telling.

"Not you, too?" she said softly.

Brink didn't take the opening. "Where is Dodge now?" he asked, taking a long pull on his spiked coffee.

"On death row."

"For thirty years?"

"Yup. Stinks, doesn't it?"

Brink poured more whiskey in his mug. "And you think the money my father left you was part of the payoff from Flynn?"

"The serial numbers on the bills identify it as money from the armored-car robbery. I maintain that in any male partnership there is a wolf and a sheep, a leader and a follower. My father was always a wolf, constantly looking for someone like your father—a sheep— to follow him around as a witness to his vilest deeds. It seems your father deteriorated piece by piece after going along with my father. Eventually, he was in so deep there was no way out."

"You believe he left the money to you, knowing it would show up dirty and lead you to find out what had happened all those years ago? Why didn't he just call you, or send you a letter?"

Fey stopped the rocking chair, and ran her fingers through her hair. "I think the money was simply a backup plan—something he'd left in place in case what he was actually doing didn't work out."

"And what was he actually doing?"

"In his apartment there were a number of reference books and magazines dealing with the sexual abuse of children. Bianca Flynn's name was highlighted. She worked as a child advocate, and I think your father finally got up the nerve to approach her and tell her his story."

"And then she and he cooked up some scam to take Luther Flynn down?"

"Yes. Luther was the albatross around both their necks. Your father was running from somebody that day at the racetrack, somebody who scared him more than the racetrack security personnel. I'd say he was chased onto the track."

"By Flynn?"

"No, but somebody connected to him in some way."

"You're kidding, right?"

Fey shrugged. "I'm not sure what I'm going to be able to prove, but that's the way I see this playing out."

"How can you prove any of this? Everything is either speculation or it happened thirty years ago. Both my father and Bianca Flynn are dead, so they can't help you."

"Maybe they can."

"How?"

"I'm sure your father left more behind than the money. We have some pictures of Bianca Flynn's kids being molested. I'd say the location of the negatives and copies of those pictures were what Bianca Flynn was being tortured to reveal. If your father was working with Bianca, he might have helped her obtain the photos, or even have hidden them for her."

"But where?"

"Ah, now you're asking the difficult questions. Remember, under your father's pillow, I found his old brass call box key. The system of call boxes used by the department was abandoned fifteen or more years ago. The boxes were either destroyed or stolen. One or two may remain around the city, but they're difficult to find. Your father didn't take the key from his shadow box without a reason. He had to have had a use for it. In the old days, coppers used Gamewell boxes for secreting all kinds of things. It's possible, in his mental confusion, that your father might have resorted to something with which he was familiar. Do you have any ideas where he might have hidden something, or if he knew where a surviving call box was located?"

Brink blew air through pursed lips. "Hell, I don't know. My father never did anything in a straightforward manner when there was a more difficult way to do it."

"Did he have a safety-deposit box at a bank?"

"He couldn't afford one. Anyway, he hated bureaucracy."

"Did he have a favorite drinking hole?"

"Yeah, a place called Code Four."

"I know it. An old-time cop bar. The name is cop talk for 'everything's under control.'" Fey stood up to retrieve a briefcase-size, black canvas bag in which she kept her gun and all the other necessities of her life. Back at the chair, she opened it and pulled out a copy of the Gamewell map from the historical society.

"The Code Four is on the edge of what was the University Division boundary. There are three spots marked nearby where call boxes used to be. The bar has always been a cop hangout. It would make sense that there were several Gamewell boxes in the area when the system was operational."

"Do you think they're still there?"

"I don't know. My partner and a bunch of Explorer Scouts have been checking the locations without success." Fey looked at her watch. "They've probably checked these, but I say it's worth going back to try again."

"You want company?"

Fey didn't hesitate. "Sure. Why not?"

41

FEY'S INITIAL enthusiasm began to lessen after she and Brink checked all three Gamewell locations near the Code Four. The area was depressing—an urban ghetto abandoned even by the predators. A few small stores still operated to provide the needs of the elderly who clung to the once upscale area by the tips of arthritic fingers.

It was dark, the only light provided by a single streetlamp and the neon of the letters C, O, F, and R in the sign over the Code Four bar.

"It's a bust then?" Brink asked.

"Looks that way."

"How about a drink?" Brink indicated the Code Four with a twitch of his head.

"You do take a girl to the nicest places," Fey said.

Brink held the front door open for Fey. "Ever been here before?"

"Once or twice," she told him. "It's been a cop institution for years, but after University Division was absorbed into other areas, only the dinosaurs remembered it from its heyday. I never worked this specific area, so it never became a personal hangout. Anyway, it's depressing. A home for cops who have nothing else going for them."

Inside, the bar was murky, worn leather booths hidden in shadows, scuffed floorboards covered with a scattering of sawdust and cigarette butts. The bar was a long stretch of scarred hardwood. There were several drinkers gathered at the far end watching ESPN, and several of the booths sported couples whose looks wouldn't hold up in the light.

Brink rested a boot on the tarnished brass foot rail running along the bar's length. He ordered a beer for himself and a vodka-and-seven for Fey.

The bartender took a long look at Fey. "You haven't been in here for a while."

Fey was surprised. "More than a while," she said. "More like fifteen years."

"It's Croaker, right?" the bartender asked. He looked close to seventy with a battered pug's face—nose like a mountain of lumpy mashed potatoes, and stringy hair doing little to hide ears pulped by a thousand heavy punches.

"Right." Now she was amazed.

"Bomber Harris," the bartender introduced himself. He held out a plate-size hand.

"How can you possibly remember my name?" Fey asked, reaching out to take the proffered hand.

"What's the name of the first guy you arrested?"

Fey didn't even have to think. "It was a woman. A shoplifter. Maggie Swanson."

"You ever see her again?"

"No."

"But if she walked in the door behind you, would you recognize her?"

"Probably."

"I rest my case."

Fey raised her glass in a toast.

"It also helps that you've been in the news some. It's hard to forget a face the *Eye Witless* twinkies keep shoving in front of you," Bomber said, giving away a little of his secret.

Fey returned Bomber's laugh with a smile, never at ease with the notoriety publicity had brought her.

"Years ago," Bomber continued, unaware of Fey's discomfort, "I poured drinks for your father. Is he still on this side of the grass?" He automatically refreshed Fey's drink. Code Four was a drinker's bar.

"No," Fey said, in a tone forbidding more questions. "He died shortly after he retired."

"Sorry to hear that," Bomber said. "He was a good cop."

Fey was sure everyone was a good cop in Bomber's eyes. Especially if they paid their tab.

"You might also have known my father," Brink said. "Jack Kavanaugh? He worked with Garth Croaker."

Bomber swiveled his eyes toward Fey's companion. His attitude changed subtly, becoming wary. "No. Can't say as I did."

Fey reached out a hand and plucked at Bomber's sleeve. "Never lie to a cop, Bomber."

The bartender returned his glance to Fey. "*He's* not a cop."

Cops know cops. Bomber had walked a beat after giving up the ring. He'd then worked across the bar from cops for more than threescore years. He'd know a cop blindfolded, in a black dungeon, while unconscious.

"Bomber, we know Jack Kavanaugh used to drink here," Fey said. "Recently."

"Did he?" Bomber wouldn't meet Fey's eyes. He wiped the

bar in front of him. "I have to take care of other customers," he said and moved away.

Brink looked at Fey. "What was that about?"

"I don't know. It's almost like he was scared."

"Of what?"

Fey finished her drink, twisting the glass around on its napkin. "The question might not be of *what*, but of *who*." She turned. "Let's go back to the car. I need a flashlight."

Having retrieved the needed item from her glove box, Fey led Brink on another walking tour of the spots where the three local Gamewells had supposedly been located. The weight of the gun in her shoulder rig was reassuring. She'd put the rig on and taken the gun out of her bag when she realized how much ground they were going to be covering on foot.

The first two locations still produced nothing like a call box. The third and last location was almost next to the Code Four. There was a telephone pole at the curb where the box should have been located, but no box.

Fey used the flashlight to examine the pole closely at the height where the box should have been. "There are no mounting holes," she said to Brink, who was following behind her like a faithful bloodhound.

"Maybe the pole has been replaced. You said the call box system went out of service fifteen years or more ago."

"Possibly," Fey said. She shone the flashlight at the area around the pole. "A lot of things can change in fifteen years."

Shining her light in a wider arc, the beam caught the dull pattern of chain-link fencing behind the Code Four. Fey walked up to the fence. On the other side, rails of disused train tracks rusted quietly. There were large clumps of bushes at intervals along the track, one clump directly behind the bar.

"What have you found?" Brink asked.

"I'm not sure yet," Fey told him. "Help me see if there is a cut in the fence."

Fey moved left and Brink went right. After less than fifty paces, Brink called out. Fey moved to join him. He showed her a rend in the chain-link.

"Come on," Fey said, and pushed through. "Look." She pointed with the flashlight beam to an ancient telephone pole near the tracks. The pole was broken off ten feet from the ground.

"Fifteen years ago the phone lines must have run along the rail lines. The poles were likely moved to the curb when the lines were upgraded or something."

"Probably made them easier to service after the tracks were no longer in use," Brink said, catching some of Fey's excitement.

Fey walked rapidly back toward the rear of the Code Four. There was the stump of another pole, this one about four feet high. She walked along, past a clump of bushes grown high and wild, to another pole sheared off at ground level. This pole was twice the distance from the second one. Looking back, she could see the clump of bushes she'd passed was almost exactly halfway between this pole and the last.

Jogging back to the clump of bushes, Fey made her way around the circumference of the plant. Almost immediately, she found an entry into the heart of the leaves.

"Yes!" she said, blood coursing through her veins when she saw the splinter-ridden pole in the middle of the bush.

Brink was on Fey's heels. "Is there a box?"

"Absolutely," Fey said. She reached out to touch the blue shell, running her fingers over the Gamewell logo on the front, the wide opening of the keyhole. From her pocket, she took out her own brass Gamewell key, retrieved earlier from her uniform belt as a talisman.

She inserted the key into the box without ceremony, giving it a hard twist. The key turned, and Fey pulled the door open. Inside, a black Bakelite phone receiver still hung on a rusting hook, but there was nothing else.

"Shit," she said. "Come on. Back to the bar." She pushed

Brink ahead of her as they left the clump of bushes and jogged to the hole in the fence.

"Is that the box my father was using?" Brink was slightly breathless.

"Probably. But I think Bomber beat us to it. It's why he clammed up when you mentioned your father. There isn't much he doesn't know about what goes on in or around the Code Four. If your father was using that call box, Bomber is too sharp not to know about it."

When they reentered the Code Four, there was another man behind the bar. Fey thought she recognized him as one of the drinkers from down at the far end.

"Where's Bomber?" she asked.

"Went home. He wasn't feeling well."

"Shit," Fey said with feeling.

"What can I get you?" the new bartender asked.

"A bullet so I can shoot myself."

42

THE NOISE level in the unit's office the next morning was reaching pandemonium levels with everyone trying to talk at once.

"Okay! Cool it!" Fey called out. "We're not getting anywhere. Since I'm the boss, I go first."

This proclamation received the small chuckle it was due, but it had a calming effect.

After leaving the Code Four the night before, Fey ran a check on Bomber Harris—true name Bennie Harris—and had a patrol unit meet her at his residence. She made Brink wait in the car while she checked the location with the uniformed officers. Nobody answered the door, and a spot of illegal entry confirmed Bomber was not there.

Fey pulled Harris's vehicle info out of the DMV computer and put a want on the car, and issued a detainer for Harris. She blamed herself for playing the situation wrong in the Code Four. Clearly, Bomber had been hiding something, but she had not followed fast enough.

Afterward, she had dropped Brink at his warehouse loft and, despite his gentle hints about coming in for a nightcap, drove herself home to take care of her horses and cats. She lay in bed for the few hours left to her, going over the case, looking for anything they had missed. She drifted off to sleep forty-five minutes before the alarm jarred her awake.

Crying over her missed opportunity with Bomber wouldn't do any good, so she shared the screwup with her troops. Her self-deprecating manner earned their sympathy when she knew she deserved their scorn. If any one of them had made the same mistake, she would have chewed them a new orifice.

"You're sure something was in the Gamewell?" Alphabet asked.

"I can't be positive, but between finding the key under Kavanaugh's pillow, the Gamewell being hidden behind his favorite drinking hole, and a bartender who starts acting like a hinked-up suspect, I'd say the odds were favorable."

"What do you think was in the Gamewell?" Rhonda asked.

"I want to believe it was the negatives and more prints of the shots we found in Preston's bedroom," Fey said.

"What else could it be?" Alphabet asked.

"Who knows at this point," Fey told him. "What about you guys? Did you come up with anything?"

Alphabet grinned. "It took a while, but we found a solid connection between Preston and Mark Ritter."

"Okay," Fey said. "Spit it out. We're all waiting."

Brindle took her cue from Alphabet's glance and produced a sheaf of paperwork from a briefcase. "We decided to pull the transcripts from the Court Clerk's Office for all of Preston's arrests. The reports from his battery and ADW cases produced nothing—"

"But?" Fey asked, pushing for the point.

"But," Brindle teased, "his arrest for lewd acts with a child, the one for which he received his three-year sentence, was very interesting."

Alphabet took over the telling. "Preston had been working as a janitor in day-care centers and after-school programs. He was arrested when several kids made allegations of molest. The original allegations were focused on Preston supplying kids to outside sources as well as for his own needs. The kids were all under six and the prosecution had a difficult time establishing them as court qualified. The fifteen counts boiled down to two provable instances. All of the allegations regarding supplying the children to outside sources were dropped. Preston still should have hit the bucket for eight to ten years, but the judge lowballed with five, and he was out in three."

"Don't tell me. Let me guess," Fey said. "The judge was Luther Flynn?"

"Even better," Brindle said.

"Better?"

"Better," Alphabet said. "The judge was Luther Flynn, and the defense attorney was Mark Ritter."

"It always fascinates me how perverts seem to find one another," Brindle said. "If we're right, and Preston, Ritter, and Flynn were all molesting Sarah and Mark Junior, then this court case is a direct link."

Fey had seen similar links before in ritual-abuse cases. "Recognition of their shared kinks must have occurred in some fashion — birds of a feather."

"Maybe Ritter and Flynn were already in cahoots," Alphabet said. "It's possible Flynn and Ritter, or somebody else within their circle, were the outside sources Preston was supposedly supplying. After he was released, Preston probably hooked up with Flynn and Ritter again, looking for a reward for keeping his mouth shut."

"Sarah and Mark Junior?" Fey added to the theory.

Alphabet shrugged. "It's a possibility."

"More like speculation," Fey said, "but it does fit. Further digging might turn up a stronger connection. Get on to the Sexually

Exploited Child Unit and see if they can do some interviews on kids from the places where Preston worked."

"That's going to take major effort. SECU is going to kick and scream."

Fey dropped the transcripts on the table. "I don't give a damn if they throw a *seven* right there in the office. It's their job, and I want these bastards. If Scarborough gives you any problems, you tell him to take it up with me."

"Consider it done."

"Okay, who else?" Fey looked expectantly around the table.

Hammer half raised his hand. "I'm disgusted to say, we're drawing a blank. We talked to the Ritter kids again, but they're either too scared to disclose, or they've blocked out the memories. We don't think we can press them any harder without doing damage. It's going to have to be left up to the shrinks, which means time."

"Time we don't have," Fey said. "But I agree with you. The kids are the major victims, and we have to work in their best interest. How about Ferris Jackson or Father Romero?"

"Also a blank. They've disappeared," Hammer said.

"Ditto MacAlister," Rhonda chipped in. "Everyone has gone to ground. The tracking devices on both MacAlister's and Ferris's vehicles are either out of range or have dropped off and aren't functioning. We've got feelers out everywhere, but so far no joy."

"Okay, keep on it. I also want you to liaise with Transit Division. Zelman Tucker claims there's a rumor connected to a shipment of children from South America to be sold into sexual slavery. Tucker thinks Luther Flynn is running it as a get-out score. Between Jack Kavanaugh's ramblings about trains, and the catacombs of Father Romero's church being so close to Union Station, I have a hunch those kids may be brought in by train. Check the schedules, and see if anything sets off alarm bells."

Rhonda nodded as Hammer scribbled something on a notepad.

"Monk?" Fey turned her attention to her second-in-command. "You've been awful quiet. What's up your sleeve?"

"You know me too well," Monk said. "But I don't know how significant this is."

"What?"

"I've been breaking down the reports and follow-ups regarding the murder of Mavis Flynn. I made a matrix of all the names involved and their connections. There was one brief reference on an SID report of a request made to a Peit Muller, but there was no further mention of what or why."

"And you don't like it when things trail off to nowhere," Fey said.

"Exactly. I found out Muller was a criminalist working for the Sheriff's Department's forensics unit as a ballistics expert. He specialized in shooting scene reconstructions."

"Is he still alive?"

"He's alive," Monk said. "I've got an address for his daughter's residence, where his retirement checks are sent."

"Okay, let's see where it leads." Fey stood up. "What are we waiting for, people? It's time to wrap this up. Ferris Jackson, Father Romero, MacAlister, Bomber Harris—they can't all have disappeared. Find 'em and break 'em."

43

THE WINDING road known as old Topanga Canyon detoured off Pacific Coast Highway and led through a mix of old hippie hideaways, hidden celebrity retreats, and houses where old California families had lived for generations. It was not unusual to see a mansion worth ten million dollars next to a weather-beaten, ramshackle barn worth eight million dollars only because of the land it was on.

At the far end of the road, real estate prices dropped back to typical high-dollar California prices, four hundred thousand to the high six hundred thousands, but it was still the land that held the value, not the structures.

As Monk slowed the detective sedan to check for obscured street numbers, Fey closed the files she was sifting through.

"You're right," she told her partner. "There's only the one reference to Peit Muller. No follow-up information. No indication he even followed through on the request."

Monk drove slowly past two more houses. "We know your father screwed with the reports. He could also have destroyed any report made by Muller if it didn't fit with the scenario he was creating."

"But even if there was a report," Fey said, "there's no guarantee it will prove anything."

"No," Monk agreed. "But if there was a report, and it was worth destroying, it might help lead us to solid ground where Eldon Dodge is concerned."

"I don't know why we're bothering."

"We're bothering because it's the right thing to do. We aren't happy with loose ends. You taught me from the start not to ignore loose ends."

"There are always loose ends."

"Don't be argumentative. There's a world of difference between a loose end you've tracked as far as it will go, and a loose end you ignore for the sake of convenience."

"Dodge belongs in jail. We're not going to be doing anyone any favors by finding evidence that might set him free," Fey said, unwilling to be fed her own medicine.

"You don't think he's telling the truth about admitting to being involved in the robbery where the two guards were killed?"

"If you were cleared of a murder you didn't commit, would you immediately confess to two you did?"

"Can't say as I would."

"I've never known a con yet who was sincere about finding God." Fey pointed a finger toward a sign on the east side of the street. "There it is."

The numbers 778 were prominently displayed on a sign advertising Old Topanga Kennels over the silhouette of a large, muscular dog. Below the silhouette were the words, *Home of World Champion Portuguese Water Dogs, Member PWDCA,* and a listing of several AKC-registered dams and sires in residence. A smaller sign next to the first stated *Muller Dalmatians* with a painted picture of the instantly recognizable breed.

"What the hell is a Portuguese water dog?" Monk asked. He could see several of the curly-haired dogs trotting along with the car's progress behind a low chain-link fence. "Looks like a giant poodle with an attitude."

Fey laughed. "And you call yourself an animal lover."

"I hate dogs."

"Come on."

"No, really. Messy, stinky, slobbery, constantly following you around and sticking their heads in your crotch."

Fey laughed. "This is a side of you I don't know. Dogs are lovely animals, and PWDs are about as fun loving as they come."

"PWDs?"

"Portuguese water dogs. They are not overgrown poodles. Not even close."

"Miniature bears then," Monk said. He'd pulled into the driveway and felt the six or seven dogs who had gathered were assessing his meal potential even though their tails were wagging.

"PWDs are an unusual working breed. They're damn near half fish. Love the water. They worked on fishing boats in Portugal as a well-kept secret for centuries."

"They should have stayed a secret," Monk said, watching as Fey approached the low fence, holding her palm out for the dogs to smell.

"No picking up strays while we're here," Monk told her.

"Ah, come on," Fey complained. "Two horses and two cats — I need a dog to balance things out."

A tall woman wearing Levi's and a man's denim shirt came from an outbuilding and saw the two detectives.

"Can I help you?" she asked. There was a very slight trace of an accent in her voice.

"Lovely dogs," Fey said.

"Ay, that they are," the woman said, walking among the brood, who all crowded around her. She shared out pats and bumps. "But a lot of work just the same."

"See, told you," Monk said in a low voice. He was close enough to Fey to receive a sharp jab from her elbow.

"I'm Lieutenant Croaker, and this is my partner, Detective Lawson," Fey said to the woman. "Are you Joanna Muller?"

"Joanna Tripp, actually," the woman said. "Muller is my maiden name. What's this about?"

"We understand your father lives with you," Fey said. "He retired from a civilian position with the Sheriff's Department?"

"That's right. But that was a number of years ago."

"If it's okay," Fey said, "we'd like to talk to him about an old case he worked on."

The woman looked uncertain.

"Is there something wrong?" Fey asked.

"Dad's not well," Joanna said. "In fact, he's dying."

Fey put a suitable expression on her face. "I'm sorry."

"It's all right. It's been a long time coming. Lung cancer. Smoked too much, too long."

Neither Fey nor Monk knew how to respond.

The woman seemed to make up her mind about something. "Well, come inside. I'll see if he's up to talking to you. I don't expect you can do any more damage than what he's done to himself."

The kennel grounds were in good condition. The grass was trimmed, and the outbuildings appeared clean and well maintained. The house they entered, with several dogs trailing behind them, reflected the same level of care and grooming. There was nothing fancy or expensive in the furnishings, but everything was squared away and free of grime.

The conditions prompted Fey to comment, "Everything is so well taken care of. How do you manage it with all the dogs?"

Joanna laughed. "It's not easy. My husband and my brother work their tails off with me. However, we're expecting two litters within the week. The kennels will become a madhouse overnight. Come back then and see if you think everything is shipshape."

Joanna walked them in through the kitchen and down a hallway to a large family room with an attached enclosed patio.

"Dad likes the sun," Joanna said. She motioned to a hospital bed set up on the patio. "It reminds him of South Africa."

"You're South African? I thought I detected an accent."

Joanna shook her head. "California born and raised. The accent comes from hanging around the family. Mum and Dad immigrated before I was born. My brother took out his citizenship papers a few years back, but Dad never did. It's why he stayed a civilian working for the police force. You had to be a citizen to become an officer."

Joanna led them on to the porch, which was filled with light and gave a beautiful view of the trees along the back of the kennel property.

The man on the bed had a sheet pulled up to his chest. His arms held the sheet down on either side. He was sleeping, his face gaunt. An oxygen tube rested in his nostrils.

Laying a gentle hand on her father's arm, Joanna spoke softly. "Dad?"

The man's eyes opened.

"You have visitors," Joanna told him.

Peit Muller turned his head slowly, pale blue eyes seeming to fight to focus on his guests. "Hello," he said. His voice was low but strong. "Do I know you?"

"I'm Lieutenant Croaker," Fey said, stepping closer to the bed. "This is my partner, Detective Monk Lawson. We're with the LAPD. Robbery-Homicide."

Peit Muller gave Fey a long look. "Croaker, you say? Any relation to Garth Croaker?"

"He was my father. I'm surprised you remember him."

Peit snorted. "How could I ever forget him? He was a fucking bastard." He spat on the floor, as if it were a grave.

"Dad!" Joanna said, shocked.

"It's okay," Fey said. "He's right." She brought her attention back to the old man. "I'm more interested in why he feels that way." It put a lump in her throat, learning how many people her father had screwed over, how many people hated him. For years she had thought she was the only one and had felt guilty for those feelings.

Peit Muller was silent, lying back on the bed.

"Do your feelings about my father have anything to do with a report you were asked to compile on a shooting scene thirty years ago?"

Muller's eyes popped open. His breathing quickened.

Joanna stood up from where she had been sitting on a low stool next to the bed. "You're agitating him. You'll have to go." The concern in her voice was very real.

Muller reached out and touched his daughter's arm. "No. Let them stay. I've carried this weight a long time. It is good I should get rid of the effin' thing before I die."

"Dad." Joanna now gripped her father's hand.

"Help me sit up," Peit said, his voice seeming to gain strength.

Joanna quickly set to arranging pillows, and Peit, his body frail with cancer, maneuvered to prop himself onto them with his daughter's gentle guidance.

"Do you know what my forensics specialty was?" Peit asked when he was settled.

"I believe it was something to do with the reconstruction of crime scenes," Fey told him.

"Specifically, ballistics reconstruction," Peit said. "You must remember this was in the days before officer-involved-shooting teams were commonplace. I was a pioneer in my field. I would respond to shooting scenes and use the physical evidence of bullet holes, expended shells, and anything else available to re-create the shooting scenario. Your father wasn't very pleased to see me turn up at the Mavis Flynn murder scene."

"No offense," Fey said, "but this was thirty years ago. You must have worked hundreds of other cases since. How do you so clearly remember dealing with my father in this investigation?"

Peit was silent for a few moments, then he looked at his daughter and gripped her hand. "Because he threatened to molest Joanna if I made my findings official."

44

DEVON WYATT opened the door to his law office at exactly nine o'clock. Since the door was unlocked, he expected to see his secretary at her desk. When he saw she was not there, he cursed, hoping she had only stepped out for a moment and had not left the office unlocked overnight.

Even the prestigious Beverly Hills address was not a guarantee against office creepers. Three months earlier, Wyatt's office had reported twenty thousand dollars in computer equipment stolen. The fact Wyatt hadn't lost the equipment and was only soaking his insurance company, taking advantage of the other recent burglaries in the building, didn't make him any less of a potential victim.

Wyatt did have a safeguard. If he was ever really burglarized, he could turn MacAlister loose with every assurance of the equipment being returned and the perpetrators punished. There was something to be said for not having to play by the rules. Fear, pain, and intimidation worked far better.

Wyatt checked the phone system on his secretary's desk and saw it was still switched over to the answering service. He cursed again and switched it to ring straight through to the office. As he did, the office door swung open and a harried-looking young woman stumbled in.

"I'm sorry I'm late, Mr. Wyatt. Traffic was terrible and I stopped to pick up coffee and bagels." She held up a cardboard tray with two disposable cups and a pastry bag balanced in cut-outs.

Wyatt gave her a sharp look, which he immediately tried to modify. She was relatively new and he hadn't gotten her into bed yet. He took in the overlarge breasts and the well-shaped legs beneath the short skirt. Chasing her out in a fit of temper might be what she deserved, but it wasn't what Wyatt believed *he* deserved. Having her legs in the air with him between them was what he deserved, and he wouldn't get there if he frightened her away.

"It's all right, Paige." Wyatt managed to keep most of the aggravation out of his voice. "But the door was unlocked when I arrived. You must remember to lock it when you leave."

Paige was so flustered she almost dropped the coffee tray as she tried to set it down while also balancing a large purse and an armload of notebooks. "But, Mr. Wyatt," she said, "you were still here when I left last night."

Wyatt felt like screaming, but then realized Paige was right. He'd been doing paperwork while waiting to hear from MacAlister, and he had let the secretary go home.

He smiled and took a container of coffee, trying to remember locking the door. Surely he had, but he couldn't remember.

He walked through to his inner office, set his coffee down, and picked up the phone. The door softly closed behind him. He hesitated and then replaced the phone receiver.

Tuning slowly, Wyatt saw Arch Hammersmith casually leaning against the closed door. Rhonda Lawless was draped elegantly across a nearby armchair.

"Why am I not surprised?" Wyatt asked. "Breaking and entering has always been one of your specialties."

"Ah, but you are surprised," Hammer said. "Your carotid artery is pulsing so hard in your neck, I can see it from here. Always a sign of guilt."

"Anyway," Rhonda said, "we didn't have to break in. The front door was open."

"Bullshit," Wyatt said. He could feel sweat suddenly on his forehead. There was something preternaturally calm about the pair.

"Language," Hammer cautioned.

"What do you want?" Wyatt leaned against his desk. He'd butted heads with Hammer and Nails in the past. It had not been an exhilarating experience. They had the rare ability to make Wyatt feel unsure of himself. Like the best interrogators, they always appeared to know far more than they did.

"Actually," Hammer said, sitting in the chair behind Wyatt's desk, "we have a proposition for you. Something mutually beneficial."

Hammer's maneuvering forced Wyatt to turn to look at him, leaving his back exposed to Rhonda. Wyatt could feel the sweat running from his underarms. This was ridiculous. He'd warned MacAlister about these two, but he hadn't reckoned he would end up as the subject of their attentions.

"I'm listening," Wyatt said. He slid off the desk and moved to another chair in his spacious office where he had both of the detectives in sight.

"We're going to take down MacAlister and Luther Flynn, and we want you to help us do it," Hammer said. He swiveled in Wyatt's chair and put his feet up on the desk.

Wyatt forced a laugh. "What does Judge Flynn have to do with MacAlister?" He stood up. "You must be mad."

"Settle down," Rhonda told him. "If you notice, Hammer didn't say we *want* to take down MacAlister and Flynn. He said we're *going* to take down MacAlister and Flynn. With you or without you doesn't matter much to us. It could be less messy with you."

"And if you help us," Hammer added, "it means you don't go down with them."

Wyatt was recovering his composure. "Your amateur intimidation act doesn't cut squat with me. You have nothing on MacAlister, Flynn, or myself. Now get out before you embarrass yourselves further."

Hammer took his feet slowly off the desk and brought Wyatt's chair to an upright position. He looked over at Rhonda. "Amateur intimidation act?"

Rhonda shrugged. "Guess we're going to have to turn up the intensity."

As she spoke, Hammer launched himself over the wide polished desk, scattering pen sets, paperweights, coffee cup, and blotter. Wyatt was still concentrated on Rhonda when Hammer's shoulder struck the middle of his body and sent him flying backward into the chair behind him.

The chair went over backward. Wyatt followed it, arse over teakettle, smacking his head on the wall and sprawling on the floor.

Hammer had Wyatt by the tie before he stopped moving. He smacked Wyatt's head into the wall again and slapped him across the scalp, sending Wyatt's hairpiece spinning off like a hairy flying saucer.

"Listen, you bag of shit," Hammer said through gritted teeth. "We've played games with you for years, but playtime is officially over."

"I'll break you assholes," Wyatt said.

Using his grip on the tie, Hammer slammed Wyatt's head into

the wall again. "No, you won't. You might try, but if you even got close, I'd kill you without thinking about it. You know me, Wyatt. You know I'd do it. MacAlister might be your big-time bullyboy, but he isn't even close to me."

Wyatt tried to call out for Paige, but Hammer's knee was suddenly digging into his chest. He couldn't talk, couldn't breathe.

"This doesn't have to be this way," Hammer said. "I know you love money. It's lawyers like you who give the remaining one percent a bad name. But I'll give you the benefit of the doubt that you don't really know what you're into here."

Hammer held his free hand out behind his back, and Rhonda stepped forward to hand him copies of the prints found under Ricky Preston's bed.

Hammer shoved the graphic images in front of Wyatt's face. "Look at these!" His voice was low, but insistent—on the edge of control. "This is what child molest is all about. This is what your buddies are into. Is this what you do? Screw little children? Or do you just let others get on with it? Either way, it amounts to the same thing."

"I don't make moral judgments," Wyatt said when Hammer eased the pressure on his chest.

"Of course you do," Hammer said. "Every time you turn a blind eye to what your clients have done, every time you bend the rules to let a bad guy go free."

"And you don't bend the rules?" Wyatt was half exasperated.

"Bend them? Hell, we break them every chance we get. But the difference is, we have a moral compass. Your only concern is where the next retainer check is coming from."

"You're even worse than your boss." Wyatt grunted out the words. "I thought her God complex was bad, but it's nothing compared to you two."

"It has nothing to do with a God complex," Hammer said. "It has to do with right and wrong. Those aren't difficult concepts."

Hammer pushed the prints against Wyatt's nose. "And this is wrong. Do you have a problem with that?"

Wyatt seemed to make an attempt to focus on the prints. "No," he said finally. "I don't have a problem with that."

Hammer took his knee off Wyatt's chest. "Let me throw something extra in to sweeten the pot," Hammer said. "Something to make joining forces with us more palatable."

Wyatt pushed himself onto his elbows, trying to catch his breath.

"After we take down MacAlister and Flynn, we're quitting," Hammer said. "This is our last case. We're getting out."

"What?" Wyatt was shocked.

"Congratulations. You're the first person we've told," Rhonda said, feeling better than she had in a long time. She and Hammer had gone out to dinner the previous evening and decided to make a number of changes in their lives.

Hammer began to stand up, hauling Wyatt to his feet by the tie. Rhonda stepped forward to help him.

Wyatt grunted, having to hold on to Hammer for a second to steady himself. "Why?" he asked. "I thought you two white knights were in for the duration."

Hammer shrugged. "Our priorities have changed. We have a daughter who needs special care. Rhonda is going to stay home with her, and I'm going to take a position with a private security firm."

"I don't see you in a uniform shaking doors."

"Har, har," Hammer said. "Ethan Kelso at Thistle One is expanding. He's offered me my own branch—industrial espionage work."

"Why are you telling me?"

"We wanted to see the look on your face," Hammer said.

"Croaker doesn't know yet?"

"Doesn't even suspect," Rhonda told him.

Wyatt took his tie out of Hammer's hand and straightened his clothing. "She's going to go crazy."

"Yeah, we want to see her face, too," Hammer said.

Wyatt retrieved his hairpiece. He shook it out.

"Leave it," Rhonda told him. "It always looked like a dead pigeon. You're better off without it."

Wyatt looked at her and then chucked the offending mass into the trash can beside his desk.

"How do you know I'm even connected to Luther Flynn?" Wyatt moved to the chair behind his desk and flopped into it.

"It took a while for us to figure the connection," Hammer said. "But when we began considering all the smoke you've been blowing with Eldon Dodge, it became clear."

Wyatt pushed the button on the intercom box, shoved aside when Hammer vaulted over the desk. "Paige, bring me a glass of water." He released the button and looked back at Hammer. "I still don't get it."

"Let me spell it out for you. For thirty years, Dodge has kept his mouth shut about Luther Flynn's involvement in the armored-car robbery in which the two guards were killed."

Wyatt's eyes widened.

"That's right," Hammer said. "We've got that little piece of information cornered. Somebody was supporting Dodge all these years. When we found the connection between Dodge and Flynn, it was logical to assume Flynn has been paying the tab for Dodge's silence."

Rhonda picked up the thread. "Now Flynn is in deep trouble with the feds. Bianca was running an investigation that's threatening to topple her father's personal empire. He needs a big score to get out. When Bianca was killed, and the heat was put on, Flynn needed something to distract us. Eldon Dodge was perfect."

Paige came in and placed a glass of water on Wyatt's desk. If she was shocked by the presence of Hammer and Nails, or by the state of the office and her boss, she hid her surprise. "Is there any-thing else, Mr. Wyatt?"

Wyatt sighed. "Not right now, Paige."

When she left, he drank the glass of water straight down.

"Bianca Flynn's death isn't down to Luther," Wyatt said. "He never would have used an amateur to get information from her when he had MacAlister at his disposal."

Hammer shrugged. "Maybe he didn't want to be that beholden to you. We've got Flynn and his son-in-law Ritter con-nected to Ricky Preston. It's not hard to see Flynn trying to cut corners by using Preston to get to Bianca."

"It doesn't track," Wyatt insisted after thinking about it.

"Details," Hammer told him. "Something to clean up later."

"Why are you so intent on taking down MacAlister? How about I give you Flynn and MacAlister walks. He's a valuable tool."

"Find another," Hammer said. "It's personal. He goes down and Flynn goes down. If you don't help us, then we stay around long enough to make sure you go down, too." Hammer tossed the prints onto Wyatt's desk. "You've got a lot to answer for. We start rattling skeletons in your closet and the orange jumpsuits you'll be wearing won't have the Armani label in the collar."

Wyatt looked at the pair. Cooperating went against all his instincts except for his instinct for self-preservation.

He watched as Hammer and Nails exchanged one of their patented nonverbal-communication glances. He hated it when they did that.

"We know about the get-out score," Rhonda said, her atten-tion focused on Wyatt again. They didn't know all about it yet, but Wyatt wasn't to know that. There were times to bluff.

Wyatt fought not to react. "What are you talking about?"

Hammer moved forward and Wyatt half pushed himself back from his desk as if expecting another attack. Hammer leaned over the desktop.

"Flynn is planning on selling a shipment of Latin children as sex toys to big-money pedophiles. He's bringing them in on a train and is going to use the catacombs under the Sanctuary of the Black Madonna as a staging area before delivery." Hammer wasn't exactly winging it. He and Rhonda had checked train schedules and analyzed logical probabilities prior to visiting Wyatt. "If you don't help us stop him, we'll bury you so deep even the worms won't find you."

"Okay," Wyatt said, holding up his hands. "I give up." It was time to save what he could. "If it will get the pair of you out of my life, it'll be worth it."

45

FEY WAS WORRIED she was taxing Peit Muller too much, but she needed the information he had to give, and there was nobody else who could provide it. She realized there was a dubious morality in possibly hastening a man's death in order to solve a case. The moral thing to do would have been to walk away. Was a crime clearance, even a murder clearance, worth a few days, or even a few hours of a man's life? Most detectives would say no, but they would mean yes. For cops, the job always loomed bigger than the individual. Self-sacrifice was nothing new in the wasteland of cops' personal relationships. And if they demanded selflessness from themselves, they also demanded it from others.

Muller was not complaining. If anything, he appeared to be getting stronger as the interview progressed and had sent his daughter to fetch a large steamer trunk from his bedroom. Monk helped carry it from Muller's bedroom to the patio.

"A man's life is his work," Muller said, as Fey opened the lid. The trunk was filled with reports, folders, measuring tools, draft-

ing implements, and a bundle of long straws. Everything was preserved in immaculate condition, reflecting the tidy nature of the house and kennels—a family trait handed down from generation to generation.

"The reports are filed by month and year," Muller said. "What you're looking for should be easy enough to find. It was one of my earlier cases and will be somewhere near the bottom of the trunk."

Monk and Fey began carefully removing the contents of the trunk. Together, they made neat stacks on the floor under Muller's watchful eyes.

"You kept copies of all your reports?" Fey asked.

"Not everything," Muller said. "Just the reports in which ballistics reconstruction was the focus. I told you I was a pioneer in my field. I always meant to write the definitive book after I retired. I finished three-quarters of it before my condition got worse. We always think we have more time than we do."

Fey knew a lot about that subject. Her relationship with Ash had taught her about time, and the lack of it.

Monk uncovered the report for which they were searching. The name Mavis Flynn and the date were printed in large block letters across a white label stuck to the front of a maroon cover.

"If this was an LAPD case," Fey asked, "why were you called in?"

"I had a friend working as an LAPD criminalist. He was familiar with my work and would bring me in on anything interesting."

"And he called you out on the Mavis Flynn case?"

"Yes. I'd had several good court successes already, and district attorneys liked the work I was doing. As you know, it's always best to back up eyewitness testimony with physical evidence. But, you must understand," Muller said, "I went to the scene believing I would be preparing a report showing Eldon Dodge responsible for killing his cousin."

"But that's not what you found?"

Monk handed the slim report to Muller. The frail man flipped through several pages until he came to a foldout graph.

"Come here," Muller said, and both Fey and Monk moved closer to the bedside.

With a long finger, Muller pointed at the graph. It was filled with lines and trajectories. "I started working with the description of the shooting provided by your father and his partner. It was pretty straightforward, but after I started to reconcile the position of the body with the bullet entry and exit wounds, things were not quite so clear."

"What do you mean?"

"The angles weren't right. Mavis Flynn was a tall woman. As tall as your father, but not as tall as Eldon Dodge. If Dodge had shot her, the exit wound would have been lower than the entrance wound."

"And it wasn't?"

"No. If anything, the exit wound was on a slight up angle."

Fey tapped the graph. "But what does that really prove? Anything could have been happening in the struggle leading to the shooting."

"True," Muller said. "But it was enough to start me looking further. I was approaching the investigation with the mind-set of a scientist. I didn't give a thought to what would happen if I disproved your father's story. I was neutral, simply trying to gather facts."

Monk posed the next question. "Did you find anything significant?"

For a moment, Muller struggled for breath. Joanna came over to check on him, but he pushed her gently aside. "I did," he said. "There was both an entry and an exit wound in the victim's head. That meant the bullet itself had to be somewhere." He paused, his breathing shallow. "I found the bullet in the wall beside the window through which Eldon Dodge fled. . . ."

Fey picked up the significance. "Meaning Dodge didn't fire

the bullet. If he had, it would have lodged somewhere behind my father. Not in front of him."

"Exactly," Muller said. He appeared to run out of steam, lying back on his pillows, the report sliding from his grasp to the floor.

Fey could imagine the scene, thirty years earlier, when Muller would have tried to point out the discrepancies in the shooting scenario. Her father must have gone nuts, especially when he found Muller was only there to do research. Garth Croaker's survival and manipulation skills must have resulted in his threat to molest Muller's daughter if Muller made his findings public.

Fey placed a hand on top of Muller's arm. "I'm sorry," she said.

Muller's eyes popped open. For a moment they were a clear and sparkling blue, seeming to poke directly into Fey's psyche. "No. It is I who am sorry. I know who you are now. I remember hearing about your background when you were involved in the JoJo Cullen case. If I had taken a stand, perhaps your father wouldn't have done the things he did to you."

"He was already doing them," Fey said. "You have no guilt. You had to do what you thought best to keep Joanna safe."

A tear rolled from Muller's left eye and ran down his sunken cheek. "But that man Dodge—he went to jail."

"Death row," Fey said. "I know. I went to visit him recently."

"He was innocent."

"Of murdering Mavis Flynn, perhaps, but not of other murders."

"That doesn't make what I did right."

"No," Fey said. "But it doesn't condemn you either." She picked up the report. "May I have this?"

"Will it make a difference?" Muller asked.

"It's the truth," Fey told him gently. "The truth always makes a difference."

46

THE CALL FROM the patrol watch commander caught up with Alphabet and Brindle while they were in the offices of the Sexually Exploited Child Unit. Detective Leon Scarborough was turning an interesting shade of purple while Brindle was explaining what Fey expected of the unit. The beep of Alphabet's pager defused the moment, and the fighters went to neutral corners while Alphabet dialed the number on the readout.

He spoke briefly before hanging up and smiling at Brindle.

"Something?" she asked.

"Yeah. Earlier today I called VPU and added my pager number to the detainer warrants for Father Romero and Ferris Jackson." Aside from other duties, the Vehicle Processing Unit did all the data entry on stolen/recovered vehicles and warrants attached to license plates. "I don't trust everyone at RHD to pass our messages along, and if something broke, I wanted to be sure we were contacted."

"And?" Brindle asked impatiently.

"Ferris Jackson has just been stopped by a North Hollywood motorcop for running a red light. He ran the plate and the hold popped up."

"Great! Where is she?"

"She's still in the field with the motor officer. Apparently, she's spitting mad and making life miserable for everyone. I've asked for her to be taken to North Hollywood Station and for her car to be impounded."

"Anyone with her?"

"No. She was on a solo run and in a hurry. Said she was coming to see us."

"Yeah, right, and the Clippers will win more games than they lose next season."

"You never know."

"Why didn't she just call us?"

"Broken dialing finger, maybe. I don't know. Do you want to stand around here arguing about it, or do you want to go and ask her for yourself?"

"Shall we call Fey?"

Alphabet shook his head. "We can't go running to Mother every time we get a chance to hit a home run. This is ours. We'll call her when we have something substantial."

Brindle walked across the room to where Scarborough was sitting at his desk, still fuming.

She tried a smile on him, but it didn't appear to make a dent. "I know we're asking for a lot," she told him. "I know you have a ton of other cases, but any effort to help track down other victims associated with Ricky Preston would go a long way to nailing this case."

"You're talking a wild-goose chase here," Scarborough said. "We've got enough victims without looking for more."

"That's not the point," Brindle said. "Will you help us or not?"

"You people at RHD think your shit doesn't stink. You figure all you have to do to get additional manpower is snap your fingers. We can't even get enough personnel to handle the cases assigned to us, let alone to do the job properly."

Brindle threw up her hands. "Okay. Forget it. It's a tough life." She grabbed the file on Ricky Preston from the desktop. "We've got another lead to roll on, and then we'll do this ourselves."

"You wouldn't know where to start," Scarborough sneered.

"I know where not to start," Brindle fired back. "Maybe you need something to remind you what your job is all about."

The shot hit Scarborough where it hurt. The tall detective sighed, letting his fury go. "All right, give me the information. Let me see what we can do."

"No way," Brindle said. "This has got to be done right, not some halfhearted effort from a burned-out has-been."

"Screw you," Scarborough said. He reached out and tore the file from Brindle's grip. "If there are any other victims out there, we'll find them."

Brindle slid a smile back on her face. "I'm sure you will." She turned to follow Alphabet out the door.

In the deserted hallway outside the office, Alphabet ran his hand lightly down her back between her shoulder blades. "You are hell on wheels, aren't you?"

She turned her face toward him and put an arm around his waist. "You should see me in bed," she said, and then pushed him gently away as somebody else entered the corridor.

ON THE drive to North Hollywood Station, Alphabet kept up a nonstop verbal barrage of chatter about nothing in particular. It was as if he had to have words coming out of his mouth to block any chance that he might say what was truly on his mind.

Brindle didn't know why she had made the comment in the corridor, or why she had pulled him close with her arm around his waist. Nor did she know if she was sorry she had taken those actions. It was all very confusing. She was getting used to having Alphabet around, getting used to depending on him.

As he slid the police car into the parking lot for North Hollywood Area Station, Alphabet was still chattering. When he fumbled with the emergency brake and had trouble undoing his seat belt, Brindle leaned over and placed a finger on his lips. The expression on his face was of a basset hound caught peeing in the corner of the living room. Brindle laughed. "It's okay," she said. "Let's get this damn case done and over with and then we'll handle what's going on with us. Deal?"

Alphabet grunted. "Deal," he said, visibly fighting to change the expression on his face and get his mind back to business.

Entering the station, they checked with the watch commander, who told them Ferris was being detained in an interrogation room.

"Anybody get her a cup of coffee or let her smoke a cigarette?"

The watch commander shook her head. "Coffee costs a quarter, and there's no smoking in the station."

Alphabet shook his head wearily. "Anybody ask her if she needed to use the bathroom?"

"Didn't have a female officer available," the watch commander said without blinking.

Alphabet looked around. He could see at least three other uniformed female officers at the front desk and in the records section. It never ceased to amaze him how cops thought they had to be hard-nosed every second of the day. Ferris Jackson wasn't even a suspect, but she was guilty by association. There was a detainer out for her, so she must be guilty of something and didn't need to be treated like a human being.

The Department had made great strides in recent years in the areas of human relations and sensitivity, but it still couldn't break the them-against-us mentality, which pervaded police forces from

312 • PAUL BISHOP

the first day of their existence. As far as cops were concerned, there were two teams in the world, law enforcement versus everyone else. Every day the Super Bowl crown was up for grabs across urban sprawl and through rural farmlands. You never gave an inch, not even when giving an inch could gain you a mile.

Treating a person with respect costs nothing. Make sure their minor creature comforts were addressed, and maybe they would cooperate. But treat them like pariahs, deprive them for the sake of depriving them, and you guaranteed hostility.

Cops never learn this lesson. They only saw the small picture. Knowing the vagaries of the justice system, which many times did result in criminals walking away unscathed, cops delivered as many little miseries as they could. Vigilante justice at its most pathetic.

Alphabet opened the door to the first interrogation room and found Ferris Jackson huddled and hostile inside.

She took the fingernail she was biting from her mouth. "Who are you?" Her voice was hard, closed. Sitting on the hard bench across one wall, her legs were wrapped almost twice around each other, her arms hugging her scrawny chest, eyes blazing.

"I'm Detective Cohen," Alphabet said. He didn't offer to shake hands. "This is my partner, Detective Jones."

Brindle inclined her head and followed Alphabet into the room. They both sat down on the bench across the opposite wall and left the door to the room open.

"Where are the other two?" Ferris demanded. "I thought they would be here."

"Hammersmith and Lawless?"

"Whatever," Ferris said. "The two who followed me to Father Romero's church."

"They're the varsity team," Brindle said. "You don't rate them anymore. You're going to have to settle for us."

"What does that mean?"

"It means you could be in a lot of trouble."

"Am I under arrest?"

"Not at the moment."

"Then I can leave?"

"No."

"Then I *am* under arrest."

Alphabet inserted himself into the pissing contest by holding up his hand. "You are not under arrest, but you are detained. If you force the issue, we will arrest you as a hostile material witness."

When Ferris didn't respond, Alphabet continued. "I'm sorry you had to be brought to the station in this manner. Whether you believe it or not, we are trying to do the right thing. We are trying to make sure whoever was involved in the murder of Bianca Flynn does not get away with it."

"That will only last until you find out somebody with clout is involved." Ferris's voice was almost a whine. "Then you'll back off."

"If that's what you think," Alphabet said, "then you don't know us, or our boss, very well. We know you and Father Romero are in over your heads. We know Luther Flynn is involved. We know Mark Ritter is involved. However, we're going to need your help to take them down."

Ferris's legs untwisted slightly, the arms gripping her chest loosening some. "I know you won't believe this," she said, "but when I was stopped by that asshole on the motorcycle, I really was coming to see you." Her arm swept out. "Well, not you specifically. The other two. Hammer and Nails."

"Why?" Brindle asked.

"Because Father Romero has disappeared and I'm so damn scared."

47

"WHERE TO now, boss?" Monk asked as he backed the car out of Muller's driveway.

Fey had been thinking briefly about their next steps as they had said their good-byes to Muller, his daughter, and their dogs. Fey found out she couldn't even get a puppy if she wanted one. All of the expected litter were sold.

Plugging the portable rover into the car's built-in radio unit, Fey said, "I figure it's time we stopped pussyfooting around and went directly to the source."

"You talking about confronting Flynn?"

Fey settled herself into the car seat and put on her seat belt. "Luther Flynn is at the center of everything we've uncovered. It's time we put him on notice. Maybe it will force his hand, or shake something loose."

"Aren't we going to be fighting outside our weight?"

"What? You think just because Flynn is a judge he's exempt from the law, or from being questioned?"

Monk swung the car onto the road and accelerated. "No, but I'm not sure we have anything substantial to back us up if he starts to push back."

"Since when did you become an old lady?"

Monk gave a radiant smile. "It's my job," he said. "If I play the little old lady, it keeps you grounded. You still drag me into things, but you take a second look at the lay of the land before you do."

"Wiseass," Fey said. She punched Monk hard in the arm, a curiously old-fashioned yet affectionate gesture. "Does that mean you're up for taking on Flynn?"

"It means," Monk said, "I've been wondering why we haven't busted his chops before now."

Fey borrowed Monk's cellular, cursing because she still had not reactivated her own, and called the desk at Detective Head-quarters Division. A roster of all judges and their home residences were kept on hand, and a male detective who sounded as if he hadn't reached puberty yet provided an address for Flynn.

"We're in luck," Fey said, ringing off.

"That will make a change," Monk said.

"Flynn lives in Pacific Palisades, off Sunset near Will Rogers State Park." She gave numbers and named a street.

"Home ground," Monk said, as the location was within the West Los Angeles area.

"Yeah," Fey agreed. "Let's hope that gives us the advantage."

Fifteen minutes later, Monk pulled up to a large, gated resi-dence. He pushed the button on the intercom box.

"Yes?" a tinny female voice responded.

"West Air Patrol," Monk said. Not seeing any closed-circuit cameras, and gambling that the detective car couldn't be seen from the house, Monk invoked the name of the security company whose sign was planted next to the gate. "Your alarm has been activated, and we need to check the grounds."

"Everything is okay," the tinny voice replied.

"I'm sure it is," Monk said, "but we have to check. It's standard procedure."

There was no response from the intercom, but after a few seconds the electronically controlled front gate began to swing open. Monk drove through.

Following the circular driveway, he stopped the car by the front door.

Monk's cellular rang, and he fished it out of his jacket and handed it across to Fey. She flipped it open and pressed the receive button.

"Hello."

"Fey, it's Hammer," the voice on the line said. "How come you're answering Monk's phone?"

"Probably for the same reason you're calling his number. My phone is still down. What's happening?"

"Too much to go into over the phone. Can we meet?"

"We're pulling into Luther Flynn's residence in Pacific Palisades."

"Ooooh, bad idea," Hammer said.

Fey looked out her window and saw the daughter, Cecily Flynn-Rogers, step out of the front door and give them a questioning look. "Too late to tell me now. We've been seen."

"Shit," Hammer said. "Play for time. We're fifteen minutes away." The line went dead.

"Trouble?" Monk asked.

"You expected something different?" Fey opened her door and stepped out to talk to Cecily.

"You're not West Air Patrol," she said accusingly.

"Is Judge Flynn at home?" Fey asked, ignoring Cecily's observation.

"No, he's not. What is this about?"

"Routine follow-up," Fey said.

"But Chief Drummond told me the man who died in the car crash was responsible for my sister's death."

"He was," Fey told her. "But there are still a few loose ends. Can we come in?"

"Why did you say you were from West Air Patrol?"

"Why are you being so uncooperative?" Fey answered Cecily's question with another. "Ricky Preston may have been the person who tortured your sister, but somebody was pulling his strings. We need to find out who."

"Ridiculous," Cecily said. "Who would do such a thing?"

Fey took a good look at Cecily. The woman's hostility from the start of the investigation bothered her. The reconciliation act she'd put on in her office with her father present had been transparent. This was the real woman. Her reactions to dealing with the police were not normal, even for somebody with an agenda. Something was wrong.

Luther had not called in favors to get Cecily appointed to the police commission because she loved cops. If anything, she had a mad-on for everyone in law enforcement.

"We both know who was pulling Preston's strings," Fey said bluntly, going for shock value. The front steps of the residence were not exactly the place for a confrontation, but you went with what you were given.

"You're out of your mind," Cecily said. She started back into the house. "I'm going to call Chief Drummond."

Even though she reacted quickly, Fey couldn't get to the door before Cecily slammed it shut and threw the lock. "What's going on?" Monk yelled as he moved past the front of the car.

"Damned if I know," Fey said. "This was the last thing I expected." At the front door she knocked and twisted the handle. "Cecily," she called out. There was no response. Fey cupped a hand and tried looking through a frosted-glass side panel.

"Quick, Monk, get around back," she said. "I can't see a damn thing, but she may be trying to do something stupid." Fey banged on the door with the fleshy part of her fist.

Monk began jogging toward a tangential driveway, which he

assumed led back to the residence garage. As he did, the electronic gate, which had swung closed after he and Fey had entered, suddenly activated and began to swing open. There was the sound of a car engine, and he was forced to jump out of the way as Cecily raced past in a black Mercedes.

"Shit," Fey said, seeing Monk hit the ground. She cleared her gun from its shoulder holster, but knew she'd never be justified in shooting at the fleeing vehicle. Still, she had to do something, Shooting Review Board questions be damned.

The electronic gate was half open when Fey took a two-handed grip on her gun, set her feet shoulder-width apart, and fired one round. She qualified with her weapon every month, and the constant practice paid off. The electronic box controlling the gate exploded in a small ball of fire.

When the gate stopped opening at the halfway point, Cecily slammed on the Mercedes's brakes, but she was too late to stop the front of the car skidding forward and plowing into the edge of the wrought iron. The car slew sideways, smashing its passenger side into the slump-stone wall surrounding the residence, and knocking a decorative carriage lamp from its perch. The lamp toppled and hit the car roof with a thud, the globe exploding in shards of milky glass, electrical wires streaming out behind it.

Stunned by the action, neither Fey nor Monk moved. The sound of the driver's door creaking open refocused their attention. Fey had her gun up, but saw no immediate threat.

Cecily wiggled out of the car. Unsteady on her feet, her balance made more precarious by her high heels, she staggered past the front of the car and squeezed through the gap between the radiator and the badly damaged gate. She made an attempt at what would have been running if her movements had not been so erratic.

Monk picked himself up from the gravel drive and brushed himself off. He looked up at Fey. "What is going on?"

"Hell if I know. And if you're waiting for me to chase her, you should remember who's wearing the lieutenant's bars."

Monk shook his head before starting after Cecily at a slow trot. He could have walked at a good pace and still had no worries about her outdistancing him. "What are we stopping her for again?" he asked, as he moved away.

"Suspicion."

"Suspicion? Suspicion of what?"

"Let's start with being totally unqualified to be a police commissioner, move on to contempt of cop, throw in no gloves in her glove compartment, no air in her spare, and how about leaving the scene of an accident. We'll work something out from there."

She heard Monk chuckling as he worked his way past the crash site and disappeared after Cecily.

48

EVENTS BECAME kaleidoscopic after Fey called for reinforcements. Using the radio again, she requested a traffic unit to do a report on the collision between the Mercedes, the gate, and the wall. City liability was involved since Fey had caused the accident by shooting the gate's electronic opener.

She also put out a call for the Officer Involved Shooting Team. She wasn't about to let them stop her investigation while they conducted their own, but she needed to give them a heads-up and let them get started.

Monk brought Cecily back in handcuffs, slung over his shoulder like a recalcitrant child. As he turned into the driveway, several patrol units pulled up. They had their lights flashing, but their sirens were silent.

Cecily was yelling almost incoherently about Luther leaving her behind, white spittle flicking off as she screamed. Kicking with her legs and wiggling around, she forced Monk to hobble

her before placing her in the back of a police car with a definite lack of delicacy.

Hammer and Nails pulled up in their black van and got out. "What did you do to upset her?" Hammer asked Fey.

"Not us," Fey told him. "Her father."

"What did he do?"

"Left her, apparently," Monk said. "At least that's what she's screaming about. Don't know what it all means yet."

"We may know where Luther Flynn is," Hammer said.

"Not actually where he is at the moment," Rhonda said. "But, if everything plays right, we know where he's going to be in about six hours."

"And MacAlister is going to be with him," Hammer added.

"I want to hear all about it," Fey said. "But as long as we have time, we need to do other things first." She gestured toward the black van with her chin. She knew it was rigged like a mobile command post inside. "How quickly can you bang out a search warrant for the judge's house?"

"Fifteen minutes," Hammer told her. "I have everything on a computer template. All we need to do is plug in the information. I've got a remote fax in the van and we can get telephonic approval."

"Okay, do it."

Hammer nodded at Rhonda and they scooted away.

"See if you can get Winchell Groom on the phone," Fey called after them. "Ask him to make a house call." Groom was a top deputy district attorney with whom the team had worked closely in the past. He wasn't afraid of hot issues, but he liked to be called in as soon as possible.

"Why don't we go right in?" Monk asked. He was trying to straighten his suit after his tussle with Cecily. "Call it exigent circumstances—the need to check on the judge's well-being based on his daughter's irrational behavior."

"Now who wants to jump the gun?" Fey asked, amused. "We don't give a damn about the judge's well-being. We need to get in the house to find out if it's where the photos of Sarah and Mark Junior were taken."

"And we don't want to be second-guessed in court," Monk completed the lesson.

Fey agreed. "Fifteen minutes now could save the whole prosecution later."

While they were waiting, Monk's cell phone rang. It was Alphabet this time, bringing Fey up to date on the circumstances surrounding Ferris Jackson.

"Once we were able to get her to unwind, she spilled her guts."

"You'll have to keep it bubbling," Fey said. "Don't tell me what she said yet. This phone is cellular, not digital. It isn't secure." The media's penchant for cellular eavesdropping was well known. "Where are you now?" Fey asked.

"North Hollywood Station."

"Is Ferris with you?"

"Clinging like a leech."

"Okay," Fey said, "take her down to Parker Center. We're going to serve a warrant at Luther Flynn's residence, and then we'll be on our way there with Cecily Flynn-Rogers."

"A warrant? Are we being left out of the loop?"

"It's a long story, and no, you're not. If you've got Ferris, you're a major part of the loop. Hammer and Nails are with us. They've got something cooking as well. Let's rendezvous in"—she checked her watch—"say, two hours. And be prepared for a long haul. We're on this thing till it wraps."

"No problem," Alphabet said. "Riding the dragon is becoming our specialty. See you in a couple." He rang off.

The warrant proved painless to obtain, and they entered the house through the unlocked rear door. It took five minutes to discover a bedroom on the second floor containing the brass head-

board matching the photographs. From there it was easy to find the pinhole in the corner where the camera must have been placed. Hammer crawled into the attic and found a bonanza of high-tech video-transmitting equipment secured on the rafters above where the pinhole was located.

"Whoever set this stuff up," Hammer said, "could sit back at a distance, maybe in a van a couple of blocks away, and watch the room in real time. When the action started, whoever was watching could run a video and take stills off it later."

There were several other items of minor interest. Flynn's toiletries were missing. There was an empty space in his closet where luggage could have been stored. Dresser drawers showed a lack of underwear and socks. No passport or other personal identification for Luther Flynn was found. Cecily was right. The judge had left without her.

Poking through the ashes in the fireplace, Rhonda turned up the curled edges of a number of glossy prints. The searchers thought they knew what the prints had originally depicted. Rhonda gathered the ashes together. Perhaps there was something the technical wizards could do to reconstruct something.

The team didn't have time to tear the house apart for further evidence, so they called in reinforcements from SID. Fey gave orders when the Scientific Investigation Division crew arrived and left the project in their capable hands.

The Officer Involved Shooting Team turned up just as the unit was preparing to leave. Winchell Groom, the deputy DA, hadn't put in an appearance yet, so he would have to wait. So would the OIS team.

Fey gave two detectives the *Reader's Digest* version of her actions, promising chapter and verse later. Proper procedure be damned at this point. The case was cracking wide open, and Fey wasn't going to let anything stand in her way.

49

FEY CALLED GOD on Monk's cell phone. She implied the call was to update the chief, but in reality there was information she needed before interviewing Cecily.

Something had been bothering her since the beginning of the case. Cecily had been a strange appointment to the police commission. The appointment must have been repayment of some political debt, or perhaps a payment for a future consideration. The questions were who and why.

Chief Drummond told Fey the appointment had been spearheaded by Anthony Barrington, the police commission president. Barrington was a powerful force within city government. He had enough dirt on enough people to get his way on many issues, personnel appointments being one of them.

As to why Barrington would appoint such an unpopular commissioner, the answer was easy: he was a partner in Luther Flynn's law firm. He also played golf with Flynn on a regular basis, and often went with him on fishing vacations.

Drummond said Cecily had screwed up several cases as a lawyer for a civil law firm. Luther was looking for a prestigious but safe place to keep her out of trouble. Barrington had obliged, perhaps thinking he could control Cecily and do a favor for his old buddy.

Interesting, Fey thought. If Flynn was deep into child sexual abuse, there was a damn good chance Barrington was as well. If he wasn't, it was doubtful Flynn would have maintained such strong ties with him. *Fishing vacations, my ass. Trolling for kids was probably more likely.*

Alphabet and Brindle had waited for Fey in the Parker Center parking garage. Their eyes were sparkling, riding the dragon.

"Where's Ferris?" Fey asked.

"We took her to a safe house used by the Underground Railroad," Brindle replied. "Ferris knows the people and feels protected."

Walking around the back of the detective car, Monk asked, "Any chance the place has been compromised?"

Alphabet shrugged. "Ferris tells us MacAlister has been making a living snatching kids back from the underground, but the underground has been changing strategies to deal with him. This location is new."

Hammer and Nails joined the group after parking their van.

"Why would MacAlister want Ferris?" Fey asked.

It was Brindle's turn to answer. "MacAlister doesn't know we're aware he has Father Romero. Ferris is a loose end. MacAlister wouldn't want her raising a stink. With her loose, he's operating at a higher risk of exposure."

Fey nodded. "All right, I know everybody has information," she said, "but let's take this somewhere less public. Hammer and Nails tell us we're running on a time schedule, so keep everything brief."

The six detectives shared an elevator with four other Parker Center employees. In the confined space, it was as if the team emitted an electrical shield, repelling the other riders quickly out at their various floors.

In the conference room, Monk started a fresh pot of coffee, while Fey and Hammer settled for the dregs from the previous pot.

"Tell us about Ferris," Fey said to Alphabet. She settled in her chair, and the other detectives followed her example.

Alphabet took a breath and started in. "Bianca and Father Romero worked closely together in organizing the West Coast lines of the Underground Railroad. Ferris stepped up her involvement after Bianca's death. Father Romero needed her help. Bianca had expanded her activities in many areas. We know she was a child advocate, a major player in the underground, and was moving against lawyers and judges, including her own father, whom she thought were involved in child molestation."

Brindle took a fresh mug of coffee from Monk, and took over the narrative. "Bianca also took her fight to international battlefields. With Father Romero's help, she twice arranged for a trainload of orphans to be brought into California illegally from Central and South America. They stretched the resources of the underground to find homes for the orphans across the country. When she was murdered, Bianca was in the middle of arranging a third shipment of orphans."

"A real do-gooder," Fey said. "The kind who doesn't think breaking the law is wrong as long as your reasons are pure."

"Sounds a lot like a number of detectives we know," Monk said, bringing in a different perspective.

"Irony?" Fey asked.

Monk took a sudden interest in the rim of his coffee mug. "What about the pictures from Preston's pad?" he asked to change the subject. "Did Ferris know anything about them?"

Brindle set her mug down on the large circular conference table. "Ferris told us Jack Kavanaugh turned up without any notice at her house looking for Bianca about a month ago. He and Bianca were together for a long time. She got the impression Bianca didn't know Kavanaugh, but when he left, she appeared very excited.

"A week or so later, Kavanaugh paid another visit. This time, he gave Bianca an envelope. From what Ferris described, the envelope contained a set of the photos found at Preston's."

"Bianca must have gone insane," Fey said.

"She did. Ferris claims she exploded, but it was half in anger and half in righteous justification. All the years she'd been accused of lying about what her father had done to her, and now she had proof he was doing the same thing to her children. It was what she had needed all along."

"Why didn't she go straight to the police?"

"Ferris says it was because she wanted it all. Wanted to take down not only her father, but the other judges and lawyers she felt were involved in the court scams. She put her children into the underground to protect them while she prepared to drop her bomb. When the federal hearings started, she planned to use the photos to give herself credibility."

"So, it was Flynn and Ritter in the photos?" Fey asked.

"There's the catch," Alphabet told her. "It was definitely Flynn's arm we saw in the pictures, but Ferris said she didn't recognize the man to whom the white hand belonged."

"It wasn't Ritter?" Monk asked.

"Definitely not."

Monk raised his eyebrows. "Any ideas who?"

Fey had a couple, but she was keeping them to herself. When nobody else answered, she looked around the table. "You can stop squirming," she said to Hammer, smiling. "What have you got?"

"We can confirm Alphabet and Brindle's information. We had a long talk with Devon Wyatt, and he's decided to come over to the side of the white hats."

"No way," Fey said. "He must have an angle. Are you sure?"

"Let's just say he won't be wearing that ratty hairpiece anymore."

"What does that mean?" Monk asked.

"It means," Rhonda said, "Wyatt told us Luther Flynn found out about the orphan shipment and is planning to hijack it with MacAlister's help."

"Okay, we're impressed," Fey said, when Hammer paused for effect. "Tell us more."

"As far as anyone is concerned, the children in the shipment don't exist," Hammer continued. "They're orphans from Third World countries, coming into America illegally. There is nobody who will, or can, complain when they go missing. They're a perfect target for sexual predators."

Rhonda took up the narrative. "To Flynn, the orphans are a commodity. Somehow, he found out about the photos in Bianca's possession. He knew she was holding back on exposing him until the federal hearings. He used the lag time to prepare his get-out score. The orphan shipment was perfect for somebody with his connections in the pedophile community. There are thousands of perverts willing to pay major money for a live sex toy."

Fey used her hands to dry-wash her face. She looked pale. "Every time I think I've heard it all, there's another sicko waiting to surprise me. Wyatt gave you all this?"

"And more," Hammer told her. "When Bianca died, Flynn still couldn't take a chance on the photos turning up. He had to continue with his plan. He also couldn't risk us stumbling across the answers too soon."

"So he went to Wyatt and got him to distract me with Eldon Dodge," Fey said, seeing where Hammer was leading.

"Through Wyatt, Flynn also hooked up with MacAlister. He couldn't run the hijacking alone. He could set up the buyers, but he needed muscle to intimidate Father Romero and help take possession of the orphans."

"I'm surprised he's giving himself this exposure," Fey said.

"He didn't have any choice," Rhonda explained. "Flynn is desperate. He knows he'll go to jail if the pictures get out. Wyatt limited his own exposure by insisting Flynn have hands-on involvement. That way, Flynn couldn't flake out and leave Wyatt and MacAlister holding the bag."

"So, Wyatt is flaking out and leaving Flynn holding the bag," Fey said.

"And MacAlister."

"Wyatt is giving up MacAlister?"

"It's all part of the deal," Hammer told her.

"You made a deal with that snake?"

"He walks away clean."

"He would anyway," Fey said. "There's no evidence to implicate him at the moment. There has to be more to your deal."

"There is," Hammer said. "But it's unimportant right now."

"I don't think I want to know," Fey said.

"Trust us," Hammer said. "We're in the catbird seat on this. We've checked train schedules against the information Wyatt gave us. The orphan shipment is coming into Union Station at twenty-two hundred hours. The kids are going to be in an enclosed freight car supposedly filled with clothing from manufacturers in Mexico. It's a regular shipment and will be attached as part of the normal San Diego to Los Angeles run."

"What about Customs?" Fey asked.

"Paperwork only. Father Romero handled it through his old sanctuary contacts in Mexico."

"That's got to be a rough trip," Alphabet said. "Loaded in a freight car like cattle."

"Anything for a better life," Fey said. "If they only knew what the supposed better life was going to be like." She changed threads. "I take it Flynn and MacAlister are going to be using Father Romero's catacombs to siphon the kids out of Union Station and into the church?"

"It's what Wyatt tells us," Rhonda said. "The church will be used as a holding station until the kids are distributed to the buyers."

"But we'll be there waiting for them instead," Hammer said.

"You bet," Fey agreed. "But before then, I think we can get more answers."

50

THE PATROL officers who transported Cecily to Parker Center stuck her in a cell in the bowels of the jail. By the time Fey reached her, the woman had moved from hysterical to merely distraught. Tears streamed down her face.

Fey guided her out of the cell and into an interrogation room. She provided a box of tissues and waited while Cecily blew her nose and tried to get control of herself.

The room was small. A filthy metal table sat in the middle, with a hard-backed chair on either side. The walls were covered with white acoustical tile; the floor was cracked linoleum. The odors of thousands of sweaty, nervous suspects hung like vague ghosts in the air.

"It's over, isn't it?" Cecily asked.

"It would appear so," Fey said, not at all sure it was. She wasn't even positive what Cecily was talking about.

The hidden microphone in the room was hot. Fey had to read

Cecily her rights before asking any questions, but it was perfectly legal to let a suspect ramble without prompting.

Monk was sitting in the tape room listening on headphones. They had decided it was best to let Fey handle Cecily by herself. They didn't want to crowd her.

"I know about you," Cecily said.

"You do?" Fey asked.

"Your father loved you, like my daddy loved me." Cecily's voice was an octave higher than normal.

"I don't know what you're talking about," Fey said, her pulse racing.

"Sure you do," Cecily insisted. "It was all over the papers a couple of years ago."

Fey again silently cursed Devon Wyatt for blasting her psychiatric tapes throughout the media during the JoJo Cullen case. He would never be a white hat in her book, no matter how much help he gave them on this case.

"My father sexually molested me," Fey said. "I don't call that love."

"Don't you?" Cecily's expression was of a child trying to be coy. "That was always Bianca's problem. She said she didn't want Daddy touching her. But I did. I liked it. Daddy loved me. Bianca became jealous when Daddy stopped touching her and would only touch me. I was special, you see? Bianca hated that I was special."

"Cecily, why are you telling me this?"

"Because he told me I would always be his special girl, and now he's left me and I'm not special anymore."

Fey shook her head. Cecily was regressing. This wasn't the catty bitch she'd dealt with earlier in the investigation.

"Are you going to read me my rights?" Cecily asked.

Here we go, Fey thought. This is where she clams up.

"Don't worry, I'll waive them," Cecily said, surprising Fey.

"All right," Fey said. "You have the right to remain silent," she began reciting from memory. "If you give up the right to remain silent, anything you say can and will be used against you in a court of law. You have the right to an attorney, and to have an attorney present during questioning. If you can not afford an attorney, one will be provided for you without charge before questioning. Do you understand these rights I've explained to you?"

"Of course I do."

"Do you want to give up your right to remain silent?"

"Yes."

"Do you want to give up your right to an attorney?"

"I am an attorney."

"Is that a yes?"

"Yes."

The two women looked at each other. "What do you want to know?" Cecily asked.

Fey thought for a moment. It was like discovering a genie in a bottle and being given a free wish. "I want to know about the photos with Ricky Preston and your father in them."

Cecily's expression clouded over and Fey thought she'd lost her.

"That was typical Bianca. She was jealous of her own children. She couldn't stand it that her father loved his grandchildren and me more than he loved her."

This is coming out of left field, Fey thought. Talk about a rubber room candidate. "How did you find out about the photos?" she asked.

"Bianca showed them to me." Cecily was playing with her hair, winding it around a finger. "She thought she was so smart. There had been a break-in at Daddy's house. A few little things were taken—jewelry and loose money. We thought it had been kids, but it was Bianca."

"Bianca broke into her father's house?"

Cecily laughed. "Not a chance. She had it done. She told me it was that man, Jack Kavanaugh. He broke in and planted some special camera before taking the stuff to make it look like a burglary. The camera was very high-tech. Bianca paid for it, of course."

"Of course," Fey said, keeping the conversation going. She thought about Kavanaugh. The man was a dichotomy—deteriorating mentally in some areas, yet able to hold it together through obsession in others. Trying desperately to right the past, while making a mess of the future.

"I was so angry when Bianca showed me those photos."

"With your father?"

"No. I was his special girl. I was angry with Bianca and that man, Kavanaugh. They both came to see me. Bianca thought if she showed me the pictures I would help her get Daddy in trouble. I didn't let them know I was angry. I had to help Daddy. I told them I'd help. They just didn't understand that Daddy and the others just wanted to love Sarah and Mark Junior."

Fey felt close to fainting. She couldn't get enough air. "Who else was in the pictures?" she asked.

"You don't know?"

"I've just seen the cropped set you gave to Preston."

"Daddy was in the pictures."

"I know. Who else?"

"Tony and Ricky."

Fey was confused for a second and then connected Tony to Anthony—the police commission president. "Tony Barrington?"

"Of course. I went to Tony after Bianca left. I didn't know what else to do. I didn't want to upset Daddy. Tony called Ricky Preston. Ricky told me if I'd pay him, he'd take care of Kavanaugh and get the originals from Bianca."

"You turned a sadistic killer loose on your own sister?" Fey was losing it.

"No," Cecily insisted. "What happened to Bianca was her own fault. Ricky said he was only following Kavanaugh at the racecourse. He only wanted to talk to him, make sure there were no other copies. Kavanaugh ran out onto the track all by himself."

Fey realized Kavanaugh had known what Ricky Preston looked like. He must have spotted him following him at the track and spooked himself into taking the action that cost him his life.

"What about Bianca? Did she shoot staples into her own breasts and thighs?" She desperately wanted to say something that would shock Cecily back into the normal world.

"All she had to do was tell Ricky where the original photos were. Everything would have been fine, if she had cooperated."

Delusion city, Fey thought. There was no normal world for Cecily any longer. Maybe there hadn't been for a long while. Long-term sexual molestation changed the rules of normality.

"If you're Daddy's special girl, why are you telling me all this?" Fey asked.

"Because Daddy left me," Cecily said. She was still playing with her hair. "He told me if I always did what he said, he would never leave me."

Fey couldn't take any more. She stood up. Calmly she said, "You're going to jail for a long, long time, Cecily."

"Why?" Cecily said with a frown. "I just did what Daddy told me."

51

"THERE'S A GUY at the desk to see you, Fey," Frank Hale told her as she breezed in through the rear entrance to the RHD offices. The large room was experiencing an afternoon lull of activity. Except for Hale, there were only three other detectives in the squad bay. Two were on the phone, while the third looked as if he was about to nod off from too many carbohydrates at lunch.

"He'll have to take a number," Fey said, referring to her visitor. "I've got several more pressing issues at the moment." She had turned Cecily over to Monk. He'd arrange to have her booked. Reports would have to wait. "Have you seen Whip?" she asked Hale.

"Back in his office," he said, gesturing with a thumb. "But I think you should talk to the guy out front first. He appears very anxious, like he's about to go postal or something if he doesn't get to see you."

"Who is he?" Fey asked, moving past Hale and forcing him to walk with her toward Whitman's office.

"Said his name was Bomber Harris." Hale read the name off a note he'd been writing to leave for Fey.

She stopped in her tracks. "Bomber?"

"Yeah."

"Hot damn," Fey said. "My lotto numbers just hit." She reversed direction.

"Fey," Hale called after her.

There was something in his voice that made her stop to take notice. "Yeah?"

"We're not all like Rappaport," he said. "Most of us at RHD are damn good detectives. We wouldn't be here if we weren't. You don't have to prove yourself to us, and neither does your team. Don't force us to prove ourselves to you."

Fey tightened her lips, but inclined her head in acknowledgment of the olive branch. "Are the rest of these testosterone cowboys on your side?" She encompassed the room with a wave of her hand.

Hale chuckled. "Except for a couple like Rappaport, but we hate them as much as you do. Anyway, you don't appear to have any problem handling his kind."

"It gets boring."

"You're breaking my heart."

"Okay." Fey flipped her fingers. "One big happy family from here on."

"I'll believe it when I see it," Hale said, but Fey was already moving away.

As she entered the reception area, she could see Bomber Harris vibrating in one corner. He was standing with one foot on top of the other as if trying to keep his anxiety contained.

"You're here," he almost shouted when he saw Fey. He thrust out a half-moon sports bag, which he'd been holding behind his back. "Take this!"

Fey looked at the bag, but made no move to do as requested. "What's in it?" she asked.

Bomber looked around as if expecting to be attacked. Frank Hale had drifted unobtrusively into the reception area, to back Fey up if there was a problem. Bomber gave him a pointed look before saying, "You know what's inside."

"Tell me."

Bomber plunked the bag down on the counter separating the reception area from the squad room. "It's the stuff Kavanaugh put in the Gamewell box." He backed away, leaving the bag where he'd plopped it.

"What's the matter, Bomber?" Fey asked. "What are you so nervous about?"

"I'm not nervous," Bomber said, making a visible effort to pull himself together. "I'm ashamed."

"Ashamed?"

"Do you want me to spell it out?"

"Up to you," Fey said. "But I think you need to get it off your chest."

Bomber looked at Hale again. Fey followed his glance. "It's okay," she said. "He's with me."

Bomber took a step back toward the counter. "I've known Jack Kavanaugh a long time. He often ran a tab, but he always paid up. Lately, he'd been acting odd. I knew he was losing it some days, but this was different. I saw him coming out of the bushes one day when I was putting the trash out. It didn't make sense. Later I went and checked. I saw the Gamewell. We all used to use them in the old days." He paused, licking his lips.

"What did you do?" Fey prompted.

Bomber shrugged. "Nothing then. It was Kavanaugh's business. He wasn't hurting me. I figured I'd leave him to it."

"But when you heard he was dead?"

Bomber twitched his head. "Yeah, well . . ."

"You checked out the Gamewell to see what was inside."

"Anybody would have."

"I agree," Fey said. "But most people would have turned in what they found. Most cops, anyway."

Bomber didn't say anything.

Fey unzipped the bag. "What happened, Bomber? Did you think you could make a score?" She rummaged around inside the bag and pulled out photos matching the set recovered from under Preston's bed. These had not been censored by Cecily's scissors. They showed Ricky Preston, Mark Junior, and Sarah, along with the complete images of Luther Flynn and Anthony Barrington.

"Bingo," Hale said softly, looking over Fey's shoulder.

"How could you, Bomber? All those years you were a cop. All the years you've worked with cops."

"I didn't," Bomber said. "I thought about it, but I didn't."

Fey took several other items out of the bag. Several pieces of jewelry, a handful of loose monetary bills. She was willing to bet they were the items taken from Luther Flynn's home when Kavanaugh made the break-in look like a burglary after he had installed the surveillance camera.

There were also several notebooks. Fey flipped through them. They were filled with scribbled writing, detailing in rambling prose what Kavanaugh had been trying to accomplish. A written confession if ever there was one. She didn't know if any of it would be admissible in court, but it was sure to fill in a few holes.

"Why did you disappear on me?" Fey asked Bomber.

He looked down at his feet. "I'd never make a good criminal," he said. "I have too much of a conscience. I couldn't let what was going on in those photos continue. I thought I could, but I can't."

"It's okay," Fey said. "You've done the right thing. We'll just say you brought this stuff in as soon as you found it. Nobody has to know any different."

"I will," said Bomber.

"We all have to live with our misjudgments," Fey told him. "Just be glad you were able to rectify yours."

Bomber nodded his head and left without another word.

Hale was still looking at the pictures. "I know a couple of these people," he said.

"Not socially, I hope," Fey said.

"Screw you," Hale replied without heat. "Don't you ever let up?"

"Not while I'm on this side of the grass."

Hale tapped the photographs. "Is this what you wanted to see Whip about?"

"These and a couple of murders I'm trying to clear up. You and your crew want in?"

Hale realized Fey was making her own peace offering.

"In a heartbeat," he told her. "What do you want us to do?"

52

SOPHIA UNGARTE looked at the cheap watch pinned to the waist of her worn madras skirt.

Nine-fifty.

They should be pulling into Union Station in ten more minutes, and then they could get free of the hellhole the freight car had become.

Fifty children and five adults in the enclosed space, with no toilet facilities and no windows, had turned the freight car into an oven of oppression almost before the train had pulled away from the station where they had been smuggled on board.

Now, after the five-hour trip, they would be lucky to find nobody suffocated when they were finally let out.

She looked at the children around her. Most were between the ages of five and eight. There were a few older and a few younger, but they all shared the haunted look of small wild animals. It was a look that came from not knowing where your next

meal was coming from, or if the shadow you just saw was a predator waiting to strike.

Life had to be better in Los Angeles. It couldn't be any worse
than in the rotting jungles of Nicaragua, or El Salvador, or
Guatemala, or any of the other countries where the orphans had
been gathered.

The lives they left behind were scarred by death squads who
murdered parents before the terrorized eyes of their children, and
were filled with the despair of pestilence, famine, brutality, and
depravity. Sophia figured any life would be better than the ones
these children were leaving. She had no idea what a monster by
the name of Luther Flynn had in mind.

Sophia felt the sudden change in the speed of the train and
realized they must be slowing down for the scheduled stop at
Union Station.

She checked her watch again.

Nine fifty-five.

53

THE DOORS TO the Sanctuary of the Black Madonna were locked tight. No passing sinner with a yen to repent was going to find the sanctuary for which the small church was so well known.

"What do you think?" Fey asked Monk.

They were standing on the opposite side of the street a block away. They could see Hammer walking back down the church steps after his abortive attempt to open the front doors.

Lurking behind them, Winchell Groom gently cleared his throat. He was tall and rapier thin. With a long index finger, he adjusted the round wire-rimmed glasses he wore to fill out the sharp features of his face. In the past, he had kept his skull shaved, but recently he had allowed a thin covering of kinky black hair to grow out. Fey thought it looked weird, and wished she knew him well enough to tell him.

In the darkness, Monk cupped his fingers around his watch and illuminated the face: 10:00 P.M. "I'd say they should all be waiting at Union Station by now."

Fey brought a rover up to her lips and pressed the transmit button. "Raven One to Raven Four. You have anything on your end?" The RHD units had secured a private frequency for the operation.

Frank Hale's voice came softly back over the handheld radio. "Raven Four. A large van just pulled into the parking lot. MacAlister is driving. I don't see Flynn, but there is a guy with a dog collar in the passenger seat. It must be Romero."

"Has the train arrived?"

"Negative. It's running ten minutes late."

"Have you seen Flynn?"

"Wait for it—" There was a pause. "He's getting out of the side door of the van now—nervous as hell. His head is bobbing like a bird looking for predators."

"Okay," Fey told Hale. "You have all three players. We're going to enter the church. Let us know when they head for the catacombs."

The rover in Fey's hand beeped in acknowledgment. Hale's crew was staked around Union Station as point guards. This was Fey's crew's operation. The bust belonged to them, but they were happy for the extra help.

Fey tapped Groom on the arm. "You've reviewed the warrant to get in the church?"

"It's a go," the deputy district attorney told her.

Fey keyed her rover again. "Raven One to Raven Three."

Alphabet's voice came back almost immediately. "Raven Three."

"Is the Department of Children's Services Emergency Team here yet?"

"Raven Three, roger. They're standing by at the command post."

Fey was glad the thought had come to her a few hours earlier, regarding what they were going to do if they took a trainload of children into custody. The team had been so focused on Flynn and MacAlister, they had almost forgotten about the children.

To get DCS motivated in a hurry usually needed an act of Congress. *Efficient, adaptable, fast,* and *helpful* were not words showing up regularly in dictionaries belonging to social service organizations.

Surprisingly, Alphabet and Brindle had beaten Hammer and Nails to a solution. They had a contact at DCS who owed them a big favor. Fey was convinced the entire law-enforcement and judicial superstructures depended on favors. If you weren't busy calling in your markers, you were busy paying them off. However, she wasn't going to argue with success.

Alphabet and Brindle's contact came through, putting together a task force and organizing a strategy to place the expected shipment of orphans in group homes until their fate could be decided. It wasn't a perfect solution for the children, but it was far better than what they were fleeing, and infinitely better than falling into Luther Flynn's hands.

Fey acknowledged Alphabet's report. The command post was a small Mexican restaurant on a side street two blocks east of the church. It had been commandeered to stage the operation. The owners were part of the PACT organization, Police and Community Together, and were more than pleased to be of assistance.

Fey spoke into her radio again. "Raven One to Raven Two and Raven Three, effect entry."

Hammer's voice confirmed quickly, and was instantly followed by Alphabet's confirmation.

Fey looked at Monk and Groom. "Deep breath, boys. Here we go."

54

LUTHER FLYNN knew he was getting old. In his youth he would have handled a situation such as this with supreme cool. He vividly remembered the day he and Eldon Dodge had hit the armored car—must have been thirty years ago. It was the first major criminal action for both of them.

Eldon had been so full of Black Power and doing everything for the cause. Even then, despite his immaturity, Luther believed it was all crap. The reason you put yourself on the line was money. Money meant personal power. Black Power was only a facade. You put yourself on the line for the big M and the jangle it gave your spine when the shotguns were blasting and the gunpowder stuffed your nostrils and caught in the back of your throat. When he thought about it, Luther could still conjure up traces of that taste and smell.

The jangle could last for days. It was doubly intensified when there were white cops looking to put your black ass in jail. Damn right. Luther knew about white cops. What he hadn't known at the time, he learned fast. They wanted the same thing as everybody else: Money. The big M was the great equalizer. It didn't matter if you were black or white. If you had money, you had power. You were somebody.

It had cost Luther almost all of the proceeds from the robbery to pay off Garth Croaker and his partner, Kavanaugh. Croaker, however, had given value for money.

When Mavis split with Bianca and Cecily, Luther hadn't hesitated to sacrifice her and Eldon. Garth Croaker had proved to be a willing and formidable tool.

When Luther heard Mavis had been killed, but Eldon was still alive, he had been terrified everything had gone wrong. He sat almost paralyzed, sweating, jumping at every knock at his door, every ring of his phone.

Gradually, though, he had seen the beauty of the situation. Eldon was *po-litical*. He wouldn't be talking to no jumped-up white crackers. Mavis being dead solved myriad problems. The kids were returned to him, to do with as he pleased despite Bianca's accusations. He fixed that little bitch all right. He didn't mess with her anymore, but he took gratification in rubbing her nose in his pleasuring of her sister. It drove Bianca crazy, because Cecily enjoyed the attention, responded as a woman should. Luther had loved the power, the control.

And Luther learned even more from the experience. He realized how easily he could have ended up trading places with Eldon. He quickly came to see the path of crime he was running could only lead to disaster. He had observed Garth Croaker. Here was a man more depraved and crooked than Flynn had ever imagined himself becoming, and yet Croaker would never be going to jail. Aside from being white, he was protected by the badge, protected by the system.

He also knew he'd found a kindred spirit. Garth Croaker

hadn't even thought twice when he returned Bianca and Cecily to their father. His only response had been a leering look and a reminder to leave no evidence. Garth Croaker had taken Flynn's money, but had given him something far more precious—an education. From then on, Luther trod the straight-and-narrow corkscrew of influence and corruption.

For years he had been very shifty. He had power, influence, and money. His depravities had eventually grown beyond his control, his corruption becoming absolute. But he was determined to beat the executioner again. Selling the shipment of orphans would give him everything he needed to relocate and live out an old age filled with leisure and young children. In Thailand, they understood the needs of the rich.

Though he hated to admit it even to himself, Luther was scared. Too much easy living had made him soft. His corruptions had become too open. His backers had deserted him. He was furious when Devon Wyatt had insisted on Flynn's personal participation in the operation. In earlier years, he could have crushed Wyatt without even thinking about it. But that was then, and this was now. Now, Wyatt had the power, and Luther had to acquiesce to get what he wanted.

He didn't want to be standing in the parking lot of Union Station with MacAlister, a man he knew was a maniac. But he had no choice. He tried to focus on his goal, but his knees still felt weak, and he couldn't shake the foreboding filling his mind.

"Little jumpy there, Judge?" MacAlister asked. The sneer was clear in his voice.

"Shut up," Luther said. He didn't like the way his voice sounded. From behind the raised courtroom dais, cloaked in the importance of his black robes, his voice was sonorous. Out here on the street, it was nothing more than a squawk in the dark.

MacAlister chuckled as he opened the passenger door of the van. "Come on, Padre," he said to Father Romero. "Out you get."

Father Romero stepped down, and MacAlister slammed the

door behind him. Looking around, Father Romero could see there were two dozen cars in the parking lot. Presumably they belonged to employees, or to people waiting for the ten o'clock Amtrak from San Diego to arrive.

The Mule Run, as rail employees referred to this particular journey, was not a commuter flier. It was a slower train running only occasionally from the Mexico border to San Francisco. It carried its share of passengers, but its main function was the transportation of freight. When there was enough freight built up to justify the outing, a trip was scheduled. The train stopped at every station, dropping off or picking up parcels, larger freight, passengers, extra cars, and anything else paid for in advance.

Many nonperishable goods from Mexico and other Central American countries made entry into America attached to the slow-moving, rail-bound caravan. Father Romero had used it often to smuggle political prisoners across the border as part of the sanctuary movement. When Bianca Flynn had proposed rescuing orphans from across the border, Father Romero realized the Mule Run was the perfect vehicle.

Twice, they had successfully smuggled over twenty orphans into the country and dispersed them to American homes through the underground. It was a minuscule number compared with the risks involved and the total number in need.

This did not overly concern Father Romero. He lived by a credo where he believed one man's efforts could make a difference. The effort might not make any difference in the total amount of children suffering in Third World countries, but it made all the difference in the world to the orphans who had actually made the journey to a new world.

This latest shipment was to be bringing fifty young orphans to a brighter future. Except now, that future looked bleak. MacAlister's brutalization had made Father Romero more determined to salvage the situation.

He had gone this far with MacAlister because of his faith in

Hammer and Nails. He cursed himself for not confiding in them from the beginning, but he could not change what was past. Now, he clung to the belief they would never let MacAlister beat them.

In the parking lot, he searched for any sign of a police presence. He saw nothing, and began moving his lips in silent prayer. His faith in the Lord was strong. His faith in Hammer and Nails was solid. And his faith in the switchblade that hung on a lanyard down his back was absolute.

Father Romero was a practical man. Years of missionary work in South America had left him prepared to handle all contingencies. He had never been easy with the commandment "Thou shall not kill." Father Romero's God was a God of vengeance, and he was but a tool of that vengeance. He might die in the service of the Lord, but so would the Lord's enemies.

"Where does this train of yours pull in, Padre?" MacAlister asked.

"Platform eight," Father Romero replied. "It is close to the largest of the catacomb entrances. We'll take the children off the train and move them quickly to the entrance. Make sure you follow me."

MacAlister took a fistful of Father Romero's black shirt, popping loose the right side of the white collar tab at his throat. "And you make sure you do as you're told, or I'll kill you and every last one of those poxy, illiterate, homeless bastard orphans, which are so precious to you."

Traffic around the mammoth art deco edifice of Union Station was too light to mask the rumbling of the rails and the sound of tortured brakes as a long train lumbered into the station.

Flynn put a hand on MacAlister's shoulder. "Enough," he said. "The train is here."

55

THE CHURCH doors had yielded to the application of what was affectionately referred to as an Arkansas toothpick—a four-foot-long, three-inch-diameter steel spike with a point on one end and a claw at the other. Alphabet needed only a single blow to bury the spike deeply in the seam where the heavy wooden entrance doors met. Using his considerable bulk as leverage, he pried at the doors until the lock snapped with a resounding crack.

Hammer led the charge through the door with Rhonda close behind. Monk and Fey followed, with Brindle and Alphabet behind them.

Winchell Groom had returned to the command post, where he would wait with Whip Whitman and another team of RHD detectives. Even though he liked to be involved in all phases, Groom was not a point man. His job would come in court.

The smart thing would have been to throw a visible police

presence around Union Station and search the train for the refugees when it pulled in. But in doing so, they would possibly lose Flynn and would certainly lose MacAlister. Even if they could catch up with Flynn later, the evidence against him would only put him away for a handful of years. Fey wanted the whole pie—molest, kidnapping, conspiracy, murder. Good-bye and throw away the key.

The rear of the church was dimly lit. Near the altar, the only light came from a wrought-iron rack of candles guttering in the breeze from the now open door. Hovering above the altar was the sculpture of the black Madonna, arms outstretched to embrace and enfold. Fey fleetingly wondered what Brink Kavanaugh would make of the effect. He'd probably argue there should have been three arms instead of two.

The fittings of the small church were poor, suitable to the people to whom Father Romero ministered. He ran the church with volunteers. As she followed Hammer and Nails past the worn wooden pews, Fey acknowledged the dedication and sacrifice Father Romero applied to keep the church open.

"Over here," Hammer called, indicating the path he and Rhonda had taken when following Ferris Jackson. It took him several minutes to find how the wooden panel hiding the entrance to the catacombs swung aside. While he fiddled, everyone stood quietly but anxiously. There was nothing to be gained by pushing Hammer. He was the team's gadget man. He would find the trick before anyone else.

Still, waiting was not easy, and Alphabet was getting ready to strike with the Arkansas toothpick again when there was a distinct click, and Hammer swung the panel aside.

The unit followed Hammer down the dank corridor. The jerry-rigged electric lights gave off a ghastly glow like something out of a Gothic horror show. Fey fancied she could hear an invisible audience yelling, "Don't go into the cellar!"

As they entered the catacombs' central holding room, the team fanned out. The rows of bunk beds lining the walls looked as if they would have offered refugees scant comfort. "How long did people stay here when Romero was running the sanctuary program?" Fey asked.

"Some for days, others months," Rhonda replied. "It all depended on how much fuss surrounded the individual."

Fey looked around. "It's more primitive than prison."

Hammer ran his hand along the back of a sagging armchair. "Maybe, but it's no more primitive than where the sanctuary refugees came from, and nobody here was trying to kill you."

"Where do these other tunnels lead?" Monk asked.

Hammer pointed. "We took the middle tunnel when Father Romero led us to the far side of Union Station. I don't know where the others go."

"You think Father Romero will be bringing the orphans back down the middle passage?"

Hammer shrugged. "It would be my best guess."

"What did Wyatt tell you about the plan to distribute the orphans?" Fey asked.

"They were to be held here overnight. Tomorrow, Flynn was to bus the group to his buyers in Vegas."

"Who are the buyers?"

"Wyatt didn't know."

"Bullshit."

"Maybe, but he claimed Flynn was very secretive about that end of the operation. Wyatt planned to have MacAlister follow the bus and find out everything he could. You know Wyatt. He'd store the information until he could use it."

"We'd better get ready," Alphabet said. He was riding the dragon big time, eyes ablaze, blood pumping. "They could be coming through anytime."

"Hale will let us know," Fey said.

"What if our rovers don't work underground?" Alphabet pointed out.

Fey gave him a look, but brought the radio up to her lips. "Raven One to Raven Four." Silence was her only reply.

She tried again. "Raven One to Raven Four." Static crackled quietly on the airwaves. "Crap!" Fey rolled her eyes. "Hammer and Nails, you take the passage on the right. Alphabet and Brindle on the left. Monk and I will pull back toward the church. Everyone stay out of sight until they are all in the holding area, then try to take MacAlister first. We don't want hostages."

56

FATHER ROMERO opened the door to the freight car, but was forced back by the stench. There was the sound of soft crying and a woman's soothing voice. "It's okay," Father Romero called out softly in Spanish. "You are here."

The freight car was lined with stacks of clothing, the center hollowed out for its special cargo. Located at the back of the train, followed only by the empty caboose, it was far away from the bright lights of the platform. The door Father Romero had opened was also on the off platform side, providing even more concealment.

Sophia Ungarte poked her head around the door and smiled at Father Romero's reassuring presence.

"Hurry," Father Romero told her, reaching up to help her exit.

Quickly, she turned and began lifting children down onto the darkened siding. There were five other women with her. MacAlister's eyes brightened when he saw them. He wasn't into kids, but women were another thing altogether. There could be a larger bonus than he had anticipated from this operation. After he was done with them, he would turn them over to a pimp. There was always a way to make a profit.

Holding the hands of two children, Father Romero led a double-file line of the ragtag refugees along the track and over a dirt embankment.

"This way, this way," he urged in Spanish. The children were tired and filthy, but their short lives had trained them well in the realities of stealth and survival. They were quiet and docile.

Flynn took the hands of several children, helping them stumble through the darkness. He still thrilled to the touch of the young, and he would treat them and love them as his own.

At the rear, MacAlister helped the last of the women out of the foul-smelling freight car and slid the door closed using both hands. Brushing them on his jeans, he turned to follow the retreating figures.

Up front, Father Romero's mind was racing. He had believed Hammer and Nails would have been here by now and taken charge of the situation. Perhaps they were not as good as he judged. Once in the catacombs, he would have no choice but to take matters into his own hands. He would not let these children suffer any more than they had already.

Reaching up to his neck, Father Romero loosened his collar and pulled on the lanyard there. The switchblade resting in the small of his back was pulled up until he was able to grasp it and transfer it to his pocket. He steeled himself internally for the assault ahead.

The children never questioned Father Romero's directions. For most, it was a trip to be endured. When Father Romero led them into the catacombs through the wash floodgate, it neither surprised nor delighted them. They were too tired from the journey, too numb from what life had handed them to see it as part of a grand adventure.

From the flood tunnel, Father Romero led them down and then pulled them up to the higher ground of the catacombs. The darkness was broken only by the light of the lantern Father Romero picked up at the entrance, and the flashlights brought by Flynn and MacAlister.

Father Romero's heart was pounding as he followed the intersecting tunnels with an unerring sense of direction. Before long, he entered the holding room. The electric lights were welcoming, and he set the lantern on the floor before stepping to the side and allowing the children to filter through.

Following the children, Sophia Ungarte and the other women immediately began to take charge. Flynn entered the underground cavity, looking about him in amazement.

Pressed against the wall, Father Romero held his breath, waiting. The switchblade was in his hand, held down by his leg. He snicked it open. Flynn turned to face him, not recognizing the intense expression on the priest's face as a danger sign.

"You've done well, Father," Flynn said.

As he spoke, MacAlister stepped into the cavernous room. Father Romero took his chance and stabbed out at MacAlister with the knife.

The instincts of a lifetime took hold in MacAlister. He turned to the side, raising a leg to take the point of the knife in his thigh. With the other hand he pulled out a gun and smacked Father Romero on the side of the head. He brought the gun around to shoot. He didn't need the damn priest anymore.

"No!" Hammer yelled, coming out of the tunnel on the right side of the room. He had his gun up, but was aware of the kids around him and the women, who had suddenly started to scream.

MacAlister whirled, almost toppling on his injured leg. He brought his gun around, but as he fired, Father Romero threw his body forward and knocked MacAlister back into the main passage. The bullet buried itself in the roof, bringing down a trickle of dirt.

Fey was out of the entrance tunnel, Monk behind her, jumping on Luther Flynn and forcing him to the ground. Alphabet and Brindle came out of the other tunnel, but were blocked by too many small bodies in the confined space.

Hammer, followed by Nails, literally ran over Father Romero's body to chase after MacAlister. Entering the main tunnel, they flattened themselves against the wall, but MacAlister was gone. Hearing his running footsteps, they started after him.

The electric lights quickly ran out, but Hammer had come prepared. Reaching into his pocket, he brought out the three-inch tube of a plastic earthquake light. He twisted and snapped the contents inside the clear tube, and suddenly the tunnel was filled with an eerie phosphorescence.

A bullet winged back at them and both Hammer and Nails dove to the floor.

"Give it up, MacAlister!" Hammer yelled. He had his hand over the earthquake light, plunging the tunnel into darkness. MacAlister still had his flashlight, and they could see the dull glow around the next turn.

"Hammer?" It wasn't MacAlister's voice, but that of Frank Hale, who with his partner had followed the procession into the catacombs.

"Sit tight, Frank. He's on his way back to you."

When a minute passed with no more sound from MacAlister, Hammer came up into a crouch and moved forward. He was holding the earthquake light in his left hand, and his gun in his right.

"Shit," he said, when he saw a branch tunnel leading off. He listened, but he couldn't hear over the pounding of his own heart. Rhonda was right behind him.

"You got anything, Frank?" he called out to Hale.

"Negative," Hale said, suddenly appearing in the tunnel. He was followed by his partner, Dave Manchester.

"Did you pass any other branches?" Hammer asked.

"Not since I called out to you."

"Then he must have disappeared down here."

The quartet of detectives was silent, each knowing the dangers of going down the tunnel.

"I hate tunnels," Hammer said. "You three wait here."

"No, I'll go," Hale said.

"Not a chance," Hammer told him. "MacAlister belongs to me."

He reached out and touched Rhonda's hand, but didn't say anything before starting into the offshoot.

This tunnel started out the same size as the main tunnel but rapidly became smaller. Before long, Hammer was walking crouched over, knowing he was nothing more than a target.

There was no glow from MacAlister's flashlight. No sound. If he was down there waiting for Hammer, he was stopped in the dark.

Hammer passed three other offshoots. Not knowing where they led, he bypassed them and kept going. The tunnel he was following abruptly ended in a Y intersection, splitting into two tunnels.

Hammer crawled on his stomach to the first and looked down it. Nothing but black. As he was about to uncover the earthquake light for a better look, he heard a slight noise from the next tunnel.

He crawled carefully over. His nose twitched. What was that vague smell? The rotting corpse of a dead rat, perhaps?

Holding the earthquake light concealed in his fist, Hammer suddenly flung it through the tunnel entrance. As it illuminated

MacAlister waiting on one knee with his gun extended, Hammer realized what the smell was.

"No!" he yelled, diving back the way he had come.

MacAlister fired, the flame from the gun igniting the methane gas surrounding him and blowing it down the tunnel in a fireball.

57

SITTING IN the large booth at the Blue Cat was like coming home. Brink Kavanaugh had his muscular bulk wedged in next to Fey. They were surrounded on both sides by the rest of the unit.

"And you're serious about this?" Fey asked.

"As a heart attack," Hammer said. He had broken the news about the plans he and Rhonda had to leave the job. The hair on the right side of his scalp was badly singed, and there were several raw patches on his face from the cave-in of tunnel dirt and rocks that had descended on him when MacAlister blew himself up in the gas-filled offshoot.

"You almost gave us a heart attack," Monk said. "I still can't believe how lucky we were the whole damn underground didn't collapse. It seemed to take us forever to get to you."

The cavern room where the children were had suffered only a minor shower of dirt and a heavy dust cloud. The children, and the women who came with them on the train, were later turned over to DCS, whose job it was to find accommodations and provide for their other needs.

Farther down the tunnels, Rhonda, Frank Hale, and Dave Manchester had been buried under a layer of soft earth. Hammer had been buried deeper, but the tunnel he was in had not collapsed completely, and he was eventually able to dig his way out. He wasn't going to tell anyone, not even Rhonda, about the panic he had felt at being buried alive. The thought of never seeing Rhonda or Penny again had terrified him. Now, more than ever, he knew that he and Rhonda were making the right decision to move on.

"I can't believe you're quitting," Brindle said. She had always resented Hammer and Nails' superiority, but the thought of not having them as part of the team left a vacuum in her stomach. She wanted to believe she and Alphabet were ready to step up and play varsity, but the thought also scared her.

"We'll miss you," Fey said. She reached out and touched both of them.

"It's the right thing to do," Hammer said.

"We can't care for Penny properly and still do our job right," Rhonda said. "She needs us more."

Zelman Tucker, wearing a yellow-and-black-striped jacket over red pants, socks, and shoes, suddenly appeared, like a magician. He was bearing a round of drinks on a tray.

"Tucker," Fey said.

"You guys are amazing. I've already sold my editor on writing this story up for my next book."

"Why is it he makes more money, yet we take more risks?" Alphabet complained. What he wasn't complaining about was Brindle's hand on his thigh under the table.

"We all have our calling," Tucker said, and slid a pacifying beer toward Alphabet.

"Is that what you believe?" Alphabet said, but he smiled and took the beer. Brindle's hand moved a little farther up his thigh. Life was too rosy at the moment to be difficult.

"How is the FBI responding to Flynn's confession?" Tucker directed his question and an Irish coffee toward Fey.

"Devon Wyatt is trying to cut Flynn a deal by having him turn state's evidence in the federal probe Bianca initiated. Freddie Mackerbee and the FBI are delighted. A feather in his cap. All is forgiven between us. Wyatt is also defending Cecily Flynn-Rogers. None of this is going to go away in a hurry."

"Are they really going to give Luther a deal?" Tucker asked.

"Maybe, if he gives up the names of the Vegas buyers. It's beyond our control," Fey said. She gave a cynical shrug. "We're supposed to move on to the next case and forget."

After digging Hammer and the others out of the rubble, it had taken the rest of the night and most of the next day to get things sorted out. The press should have been all over them, but Whip Whitman and Drummond ran strong interference, so they could get on with the mountains of paperwork.

Whip Whitman looked good on television, his chances of being promoted to commander growing stronger with each interview. Winchell Groom was also smiling. He wasn't afraid of Devon Wyatt. If anything, the deputy DA relished the challenge.

Chief Drummond even managed to ride the tail end of the dragon when he put in a personal appearance at the scene when Fey arrested Anthony Barrington. With Cecily also locked down, the police commission would soon be advertising for people to fill several openings.

"What are you going to do about Eldon Dodge?" Tucker asked. To a certain extent, Tucker had become a fixture within the group, but there were times when he still pushed his luck.

Fey raised her glass and swallowed the whipped cream before answering. "I've turned Peit Muller's ballistics-reconstruction report over to Wyatt along with the original reports from the armored-car robbery. What Wyatt does with them is up to him. Whatever happens regarding the murder of Mavis Flynn won't matter much. Freddie Mackerbee has enough information to go after both Flynn and Dodge for the murder of the armored-car guards. Thirty years is a long time, but there's no statute of limitations on murder."

For his part, Brink Kavanaugh was virtually goggle-eyed, amazed by what the detectives took in their stride as everyday occurrences. This was too much real life for the artist in him. There were many facets of Fey's personality he had yet to explore. He only hoped she gave him the chance to do so.

"My concern is Sarah and Mark Junior," Rhonda said. "We have nothing to tie Mark Ritter into the abuse except for his connections to Flynn."

"Nothing is ever clean," Fey said. "The best we can do is work with Ferris Jackson and her underground contacts to fight the case in court. It's going to be a difficult battle to stop him from regaining custody."

"The children can always disappear again," Hammer said.

"Don't even joke about it," Fey said. "I don't want to end up investigating you."

"Never," Hammer said. He and Rhonda knew, as Fey knew, that Mark Ritter wasn't getting his children back. Everybody draws lines in the sand. "There has to be evidence somewhere. We'll find it."

"Not if you're not on the job," Fey said.

"I will be after a fashion," Hammer said. "When Ethan Kelso offered me a partnership in Thistle One, I made a stipulation that we do all work for the underground pro bono."

"How altruistic of you."

Hammer smiled, holding Rhonda's hand. "As Tucker said, we all have our calling."

"The baloney is sure getting deep in here." The low voice of

Booker, the Blue Cat's bartender, insinuated itself into the conversation. "I'm going to have to put my fishing waders on to deliver drinks if this keeps up."

"No congratulations for a job well done?" Fey asked.

"Nothing more than expected," Booker said. "You want the you-are-special plates every time you solve a murder?"

"It would be nice. If it doesn't happen here, it's not going to happen anywhere."

"How about a round of drinks on the house instead?" Booker asked, lifting a tray of freshly filled glasses.

Fey glanced at Brink, then took her new drink and raised it toward Hammer and Nails. Everyone was silent. Waiting.

Deep inside, Fey knew she had accomplished something she would not have dreamed possible. She had righted one of her father's wrongs. Maybe now she could bury his memory forever.

"To new beginnings," she said eventually, with a catch in her voice.

About the Author

Paul Bishop is a twenty-three-year veteran of the Los Angeles Police Department. He has worked many varied assignments, including a three-year tour with a federal antiterrorism task force, and has more than ten years' experience in the investigation of sex crimes. He currently supervises the LAPD's Sex Crimes and Major Assault Crimes units in the West Los Angeles area, where he has twice been honored as Detective of the Year.

Bishop is the author of eight novels, including the four titles in his Fey Croaker series: *Kill Me Again, Twice Dead, Tequila Mockingbird,* and *Chalk Whispers.* He has also written scripts for episodic television and numerous short stories.